Bad to the Bone

Also by Gwen Madoc

Daughter of Shame
By Lies Betrayed

GWEN MADOC

Bad to the Bone

Hodder & Stoughton

A CIP catalogue record for this title
is available from the British Library

ISBN 0 340 82348 8

Typeset in Plantin by Hewer Text Ltd, Edinburgh
Printed and bound in Great Britain by
Mackays of Chatham plc, Chatham, Kent

Hodder and Stoughton
A division of Hodder Headline
338 Euston Road
London NW1 3BH

To my agent Judith Murdoch in grateful acknowledgement of her faith in me, and the tremendous encouragement and guidance she has provided over the years. Also to my editor, Sara Hulse, whose friendly, cheerful and helpful voice at the other end of the telephone always brightens my day. Thank you, Sara, for your enthusiasm.

1

Swansea, November 1899

'I've dreaded this day for many a year,' Luther Templar said gravely. 'Dreaded the moment when some man would ask for my stepdaughter's hand in marriage.' He shook his head, his expression sombre. 'Mansel, as an honourable man, and in all good conscience, I can't allow Kathryn to marry you.'

'What?' Mansel Jenkins leaped to his feet, towering head and shoulders above Luther. 'Why the devil not?' he roared. 'You insult me. What do you mean by it?'

'It's no reflection on *you*, my dear fellow,' Luther said hastily, mindful of the bodily power of the man facing him. 'Kathryn can never marry any man.'

Luther stood before the fireplace in his study, watching his young companion's angry face, and was aware of the irony of the situation.

Mansel Jenkins, handsome, well bred and of wealthy family, was a most eligible suitor for any man's daughter; it would have been a very desirable marriage, indeed, but it didn't suit his plans. Kathryn would marry no man while he could prevent it; at least, no man he couldn't control or manipulate.

'It's regrettable the matter's gone so far,' Luther went on seriously. 'Had I known earlier I could've saved you much pain.'

'But the wedding's to be in June,' Mansel said raggedly. 'Damn it!' Anger again flared in his eyes, and he looked dangerous. 'I can see no reason for your refusal. I demand an explanation.'

Luther shook his head again, feeling certain he had the measure of the other man, yet instinct warned him to tread carefully. 'There is, I regret to admit, a grave impediment to marriage for Kathryn,' he said, and then hesitated as though reluctant to say more. It had the desired effect.

'I demand to know why you refuse me,' Mansel burst out furiously. 'I'm not used to being treated in this cavalier manner.'

Luther watched him, seeing his face suffused with blood, and was pleased with the reaction. Grievously angry and offended, Mansel was off balance, and Luther intended to keep him that way.

'What I've to tell you about Kathryn mustn't be repeated beyond these four walls,' he said earnestly. 'Do I have your oath that you'll never reveal her secret?'

'Secret?' Mansel looked startled. 'I don't understand . . .'

Luther's tone hardened. 'Do you solemnly swear it, on your honour, on your very life?'

Mansel paused, staring at him, then sat down heavily. 'You have my word,' he answered in a low tone. 'But for God's sake, tell me what's wrong.'

His expression suitably serious, Luther strode to the desk and took the chair behind it, deliberately taking his time. His next words must be chosen with care, for he was about to take a risk, albeit a calculated one. Mansel wasn't a clever man, yet he was no fool either, and what he had to tell him would shock him to the core . . . if he believed it.

'You may have heard of hereditary insanity?' he said at last.

Mansel shook his head, and Luther was reassured. Everything depended on the young man's ignorance of such matters.

'Medical science is at last understanding more about it. It's a terrible madness passed down from mother to child, and quite incurable, of course,' he explained somberly. 'This terrible disease is in the blood of Kathryn's family, and has been for generations.' He paused, letting that sink in. 'This is why she can never marry and bear children.'

'What?' Mansel blustered, half rising from his chair only to slump down again. He appeared stunned for a moment, and then exploded. 'Stuff and nonsense! Kate's as sane as I am.'

'Yes, she is, at the moment,' Luther agreed. 'But it's just a matter of time. Should she bear a child it's inevitable she'll pass on this dreadful scourge.' He shook his head sadly. 'The line must end with her.'

'Oh, my God!'

Luther sighed in sympathy. 'So you see, Mansel, I couldn't agree to this marriage without warning you of the terrible future you face. It would've been criminal to do so.'

Mansel stood up abruptly and strode about the room, and Luther eyed him warily. It would be better if the doctor wasn't brought into it, but Luther held that trump card in reserve should Mansel prove less credulous than he believed him to be.

'I know this must be a great shock,' Luther said after a moment.

'Shock?' The young man swung round, his expression agitated yet stubborn. 'That's putting it mildly. I can't believe it.' He strode to the desk and crashed down a fist. 'I don't believe it!'

Appearing unmoved by the other man's passion, Luther sat

back in his chair, making a steeple of his hands as though praying. 'My reaction was the same after I married Kathryn's mother, Alice,' he said soberly. 'No one warned me beforehand. Only her death eight years ago ended the nightmare. Suicide.' Luther whispered the word.

With a sharp intake of breath, Mansel took a step back, looking disconcerted for a moment. He ran his fingers through his hair. 'I must look into this matter,' he said shakily. 'Seek medical advice. There must be something we can do for her.'

'No!' Luther thundered, thrusting back his chair to stand up. 'You've already given your solemn oath that you'll not repeat what I've just told you.'

Mansel looked shattered. 'But I can't leave it like this,' he insisted. 'I love Kate and I want to marry her. If there's the least chance that you're wrong—'

'Very well!' Luther interrupted sharply. 'You want medical corroboration. You'll have it.'

He strode to a door in the corner of the room and held it ajar, speaking to someone on the other side.

'Kindly come in, Doctor, if you please.'

A tall man wearing pinstripe trousers and a dark morning coat came into the room, and stood by, fumbling uncertainly with pince-nez.

'You may already know the Vaughans' medical practitioner, Dr Penfold,' Luther said by way of introduction. 'Doctor, this is Mr Mansel Jenkins.'

The two men nodded at each other, obviously not total strangers.

'We're slightly acquainted,' Dr Penfold said. 'Members of the same gentlemen's club in Wind Street, I believe.'

Luther resumed his seat behind the desk, well pleased. That

made things easier. Mansel wouldn't dispute the word of a man of his own class.

'Doctor, you've already heard the subject of our conversation,' he went on, then paused, noting a sharp glance from Mansel. Luther realised he'd made a slip. Now the young man knew the doctor's presence was no coincidence. He hastened to explain it away. 'Yes, Mansel, I asked the doctor to be present,' he admitted. 'I *did* have an intimation of your errand here today, and I surmised his expert opinion would be needed.'

Mansel stepped forward, looking anxious. 'Is it true, Doctor? Is Kate insane?'

'Ahem!' Dr Penfold removed his pince-nez, tapped his thumb with the lens for a moment as if deep in thought, and then clipped them back on his nose. 'I'm afraid there is no doubt, my dear sir,' he said.

'And Kate's mother killed herself?' Mansel asked incredulously. 'But there was no talk of it at the time. Kate has said nothing to me.'

Dr Penfold flushed and looked confused.

'She doesn't know,' Luther interjected quickly. 'It was hushed up for the sake of Alice's children, and the business, of course. Such a scandal would've done irreparable damage. Vaughan & Templar, High-Class Emporium, has an unblemished reputation going back three generations. The illness has been a well-kept secret all these years.'

'Is there no hope, Doctor?' Mansel asked desperately. 'In a matter of weeks we'll enter the twentieth century. Medical science has already taken some strides forward. Can nothing be done?'

Dr Penfold shook his head. 'Sadly, no. It's a matter of the blood, you see. Bad blood will out. Lunacy can strike at any time, any age. Miss Vaughan may have twenty good years ahead of her, or she may turn raving mad tomorrow—'

Luther gave a sharp cough and stood up quickly. 'I think that's all we need say on the matter, Doctor,' he interrupted forcefully. This fool of a doctor was about to spoil everything with his loquacious tongue. 'Perhaps you'd be kind enough to leave us now.'

'Oh, very well.' Dr Penfold glanced briefly at each man, then retreated the way he'd come.

When he and Mansel were alone again, Luther sat down. 'There you have it, Mansel,' he said, putting his hands on the desk. 'The corroboration of science. What will you do now?'

'I must see Kate,' Mansel said wretchedly. 'She knows I'm here. She'll be in her sitting-room upstairs, waiting to know the outcome of this interview. I can't keep the truth from her.'

Luther felt a quiver of alarm. 'What good would it do to see her under the circumstances?'

'I think it only right I explain why we can't marry,' Mansel said tersely. 'Good God, man! She's only eighteen, yet is already condemned to spinsterhood.'

Luther stood up hastily, and hurried around the desk. He couldn't allow them to talk together now. 'That's very unwise,' he said quickly. 'It would be cruel and distressing for her beyond words. Better to go now without seeing her. Leave her some dignity. She'll have precious little when the time comes.'

Mansel sat down heavily and buried his face in his hands. 'Oh, God! I can't believe this tragedy has happened to us. We were so happy and carefree yesterday. Kate's so beautiful, so full of life and energy. I'd rather she were dead . . .'

'Tut-tut! Mansel, my dear fellow,' Luther exclaimed. 'That's hardly proper talk. Whatever happens to Kathryn,

6

she'll want for nothing. She's a wealthy young woman . . . or will be in time.'

Mansel looked up sharply. 'What about Evan? Is Kathryn's brother affected, too?'

'Yes.' Luther nodded. 'It was my sad duty to apprise him of the facts last month when he intimated he was considering matrimony. He didn't take it well. Don't approach him on the matter, Mansel, I beg you. He wishes it kept secret during his lifetime.'

Mansel stood up, and Luther saw he was a changed man from the young hopeful who had arrived earlier. The fight had gone out of him.

'I'll have the groom bring your horse and gig around to the front entrance,' Luther said, eager for him to be gone.

'I ride today,' Mansel said dispiritedly.

A heavily built sombre-looking man answered Luther's ring.

'Chivers, tell Trott to bring Mr Jenkins's horse around, and see him out, will you?'

The butler closed the door behind him silently, and Luther turned to Mansel.

'What are your plans?'

'We're at war with the Boers,' Mansel said grimly. 'I promised Kate I wouldn't volunteer for the coming campaigns in South Africa. Now I see no other future for myself.'

'Perhaps that's a most wise decision,' Luther agreed, feeling the tension leave him. He'd feel safer with Mansel Jenkins out of the country for the next few months.

Luther permitted himself a triumphant smile as the study door closed on the young man's drooping shoulders. Within minutes Mansel would ride out of Kathryn's life for ever.

Luther sat back in his chair, relaxed and pleased. He was

free to advance his own plans for his stepdaughter's future, her considerable fortune, and, in particular, her inherited shares in the family business. *His* business by rights if there was any justice in this world. He'd worked and schemed to build it up, and it would be his, at any cost, no matter who must be sacrificed.

Her heart thumping with excitement, Kathryn Vaughan jumped up as her friend came into the snug little sitting-room at the top of the staircase and she grasped Cecille's hands with enthusiasm.

'Cecille, I've wonderful news,' she exclaimed, her voice rising. 'I'm to be married! What do you think of that?'

'Married!' Cecille squealed with astonishment. 'You cunning little minx! You never told me.'

'I couldn't until Mansel proposed, could I?' Kate chuckled happily.

'You must tell me everything; every single detail,' Cecille commanded imperiously, sitting on the sofa. 'Did he go down on bended knee?' She put both hands to her breast dramatically. 'Oh, you *are* a lucky little puss, Kate. Mansel Jenkins is so handsome and manly.'

Kate sighed. 'Yes, he is. He's wonderful.'

'Are you very much in love?' Cecille asked, then sailed on without waiting for the answer. 'I'll be in love one day,' she declared. 'Someone wonderful will come along, rich and handsome.'

'Mansel's with my stepfather now, asking his permission,' Kate said, determined to keep the limelight. 'I'll be a bride by the end of June. Mansel's built a house for us in Sketty village. It's beautiful. We can see the sea from our bedroom window.'

'Your bedroom!' Cecille giggled. 'Risqué talk!'

Kate shook her head at Cecille's silliness, and rose from the sofa to take quick steps to the sitting-room door.

'Mansel's a long time,' she said, though she wasn't worried. Mansel was an excellent catch. Luther would be pleased at the wealthy connection. 'Of course, they've a lot to talk about.'

She thought of the considerable sum she'd inherit from her father's estate on her marriage, held in trust for her, and also a twenty-five per cent share in the family business. She was unclear what that meant exactly, except that, were she a man, it would entitle her to a seat on the board of directors of Vaughan & Templar.

She planned to make everything over to Mansel after the wedding, so he'd probably sit on the board in her place.

Kate opened the door a little wider. Luther's study was directly below her sitting-room, and she wanted to hear when Mansel came out into the hall. He had promised he'd come straight to her. She could hardly wait to see him bounding up the staircase.

'What about your trousseau?' Cecille squealed, springing up and down on the sofa. 'You must make plans, Kate. Oh, what excitement. I do envy you.'

'I intend to take a trip to London in the New Year,' Kate said. 'Perhaps you'll come with me, Cecille, if your parents allow it. I'll ask Mrs Trobert to accompany us.'

'London!' Cecille gave a shriek of joy. 'Oh, Kate, how thrilling.'

Kate's quick ears heard the study door open below and a low rumble of men's voices as they parted company. Her heart leaping in delicious anticipation, she rushed out on to the gallery and leaned over the banister to look down into the glass-domed hall below.

'Is he coming up?' Cecille was at her elbow, stretching her neck to see.

'He will be,' Kate said confidently. 'When he does you must make yourself scarce, Cecille.'

'But why?' Cecille was petulant. 'I want to see what happens.'

'Because,' Kate said impatiently, 'you'll be in the way, you silly goose.'

Mansel appeared suddenly below, marching very quickly across the hall towards the open front door, while Chivers stood by ready to hand him his hat and riding crop.

Puzzled by his hurried departure when he'd promised he'd come straight to her, Kate called out. 'Mansel, dearest, have you forgotten your future bride?'

He didn't turn at her call and his urgent stride was interrupted for only a split second before he plunged on, grabbing at his hat and crop.

Thoroughly alarmed, Kate dashed to the head of the staircase. 'Mansel, what's wrong?'

He turned to stare up at her, and Kate was shocked at his expression, his features drawn and white.

'You're upset.' She took a few steps down. 'What's happened?'

'Kate, I can't,' he cried out in anguished tones. 'I can't marry you!'

'Mansel!'

He turned and fled. As he passed through the open front door, Kate rushed down the stairs, calling his name repeatedly, but he wouldn't turn back to her.

'Come back, Kate,' Cecille cried in a shocked voice from the top of the stairs. 'You're making an exhibition of yourself.'

Kate ignored her and raced across the hall to follow in Mansel's footsteps. As though deliberately, Chivers closed the door on his retreating figure.

Kate angrily tugged the doorknob from the butler's grasp and, wrenching the door open, rushed out into the darkening November afternoon, oblivious to the chill winds. Mansel was just mounting his horse, and Kate ran towards him.

'Mansel! For God's sake, speak to me. Tell me what's happened. What has Luther said to turn you away from me?'

Mansel didn't turn and look at her and her anguished cry was swept away on the wind. Instead, he spurred his horse forward and cantered down the tree-lined carriageway to the road. Kate ran after the horse, feeling cold sleet beat at her shoulders through the silk of her afternoon dress.

'Mansel, don't leave me like this, I beg you,' she cried out desperately. 'Mansel! Mansel, you said you loved me.'

The moaning of the wind in the trees was the only answer. Feeling as though she were in some nightmare, Kate stood numbed and motionless, watching the horse and rider until they reached the turn in the carriageway and disappeared from sight.

For all his declarations of undying love, Mansel had abandoned her. All hope of escape from Luther's domination was gone.

'You can come out now, Penfold,' Luther called when the door closed on Mansel Jenkins.

Dr Penfold emerged from the other room, seated himself in the chair Mansel had vacated, and reached for a cigarette from the open box on the desk.

'So the young fool's gone off to war,' he remarked derisively.

Luther watched the doctor through lowered eyelids. It took a fool to know a fool, he mused, and then leaned back in his chair, pleased with the turn of events. War had come at an opportune time for his schemes.

'Undoubtedly,' he said pithily. 'Mansel Jenkins will cut a dashing figure astride a fiery charger, racing to his death at the hands of the Dutch.' He chose a cigarette himself and lit up. 'But he'll not be a successful officer, I'll wager. He has little real intelligence.' He sighed. 'It was almost too easy to convince him.'

'Nevertheless,' Penfold said gravely, 'I took a serious risk in misleading him so badly. You realise, Templar, I could be struck off for that alone.'

Luther looked down his nose at his companion, not bothering to hide his disdain. 'Not for that alone, Penfold,' he sneered. 'You're forgetting your vile appetites in private life. Then there's the little matter of covering up my wife's suicide.'

'You can hardly make *that* public, Templar,' Penfold retorted, his voice trembling. 'You're as guilty as I am.' He gave an angry snort. 'Even more so. There was no insanity in Alice Vaughan, and she wouldn't have taken her own life if it hadn't been for your heartless treatment of her.' He paused. 'In fact, I'm not convinced she did kill herself.' He eyed Luther slyly. 'I suspect foul play.'

'Be silent, damn you!' Luther thundered, his face reddening. 'Alice was weak and a fool.'

'Not so weak!' Penfold snapped. 'She prevented you taking full control of the business. You'll fare no better with Kathryn, for all your devious schemes.'

Luther's expression hardened as he drew on the cigarette. 'You may be right,' he said thoughtfully. 'Kathryn's made of far tougher metal altogether.' His lips thinned. 'She defies me at every turn. But I'll vanquish her.'

'Yes, the girl has spirit,' the doctor agreed. 'I suppose you'll use that against her to have her committed if she proves difficult?'

'If necessary,' Luther replied shortly. He stubbed out the cigarette viciously. He'd already waited too long and had worked too hard to be denied his just reward much longer.

'I won't help you there,' Dr Penfold declared stoutly. 'That's too much to ask.'

'You'll do as I tell you, Doctor,' Luther snarled. 'Or face condemnation and prison. And you won't like prison, Penfold, I promise you.'

The doctor rose to his feet. 'I won't sit still for such threats or insults,' he quavered. 'You've no right to speak to me like that.'

'Rights?' Luther was scornful. 'What about the rights of those wretched boys you've callously corrupted to feed your own despicable desires?'

With an oath the doctor turned towards the door.

'Don't attempt to thwart me, Doctor,' Luther warned in ringing tones. 'Remember, I've the power to make you do exactly as I please, or face complete ruin.'

Dr Penfold stood for a moment, unmoving, his face white.

'You can go now.' Luther waved a dismissive hand at him. 'Oh, and by the way,' he added with a sneer, 'keep your filthy paws off the boot boy as you leave.'

'By thunder, Templar!' Dr Penfold exploded. 'That's an abominable thing to say to a gentleman.'

'What hypocrisy, Penfold,' Luther jeered. 'You are the abomination. Now get out of my sight.'

'Miss Kate, come inside.' Chivers placed a cloak around her shivering shoulders.

Obediently, Kate turned and walked slowly back. She could hardly believe what had happened. Inexplicably, Luther had ruined her chance of happiness; he'd turned Mansel against her. But why? Her stepfather was such a grasping man. It was inconceivable that he'd spurn the most eligible suitor in Swansea.

As Kate entered the warmth of the hall she threw off the cloak angrily. Luther would answer for this. She'd confront him immediately.

Cecille was at the bottom of the staircase staring at her in consternation. 'Kate, that was the most outrageous conduct for a young woman of fine birth. You behaved worse than a scullery maid,' she burst out. 'A lady never runs after a gentleman, especially one to whom she is betrothed.' She gave a nervous giggle. 'I say, are you jilted, Kate?'

'Oh, do be quiet, Cecille!'

'No need to be cross, Kate.' Cecille pouted prettily. 'Girls are jilted all the time. My cousin, Ceinwen, on my mother's side, has been jilted three times, but she always manages to catch another suitor.'

'Go home, Cecille,' Kate snapped angrily. 'Can't you see you're in the way.'

She turned to the butler who was hovering nearby. 'Chivers, have Miss Cecille's groom bring her trap around,' she told him haughtily. 'She's leaving now.'

'But, Kate . . .' Cecille squeaked. 'I want to stay.'

'Goodbye, Cecille!'

Kate walked determinedly towards the study, but was intercepted by Chivers who barred her way at the door.

'I'm sorry, Miss Kate,' he said, in the sibilant tones that Kate found so repellent. 'The master's in conference, and can't be disturbed.'

'How dare you block my way!' Kate burst out. 'Stand aside immediately, and know your place. In conference or not, I intend to speak with my stepfather this instant.'

The matter was resolved when the door was jerked open

and Dr Penfold came out. He looked upset as he swept past Kate, and she saw his hands were shaking as he reached for his hat, cane and gloves.

Kate marched into the study and, slamming the door shut behind her, stood before Luther's desk, hands on hips.

'Luther, what's happened? Why has Mansel gone?'

'Come in, Kathryn,' Luther said with sarcasm, not looking up. 'Don't stand on ceremony.'

'What damnable thing have you done now?'

He raised his head then, his lean, rather fine-boned face wearing the pained expression of one most grossly misunderstood. 'Kathryn, I deplore such coarse language in a young woman of your breeding.'

'Never mind my language or my breeding,' Kate said angrily. 'What've you said to upset Mansel so badly?'

Luther stood up and came around the desk towards her. 'My dear child—'

'I'm not a child, and certainly not *your* child, Luther,' she snapped. 'He came to ask your permission for our marriage. Obviously, you have refused it, and I demand to know why.'

'Demand!' Luther's tone hardened and his expression turned stony. 'I'm your legal guardian, Kathryn, and also the head of this household, while you are merely an under-age girl.' His lip curled in scorn. 'You can demand nothing.'

'I won't be treated like this,' Kate stormed in fury. 'In God's name, what do you have against Mansel? He's the most eligible man in Swansea; in Glamorgan, for that matter. What are your grounds for refusal?'

'Blasphemy and gutter language won't shock or influence me,' Luther said. 'But you'll watch your tongue, or this interview's over.'

Luther moved to stand before the fireplace, his ascetic finely chiselled features mask-like. In his frock-coat of fine alpaca, his figure was commanding, but Kate wasn't impressed, and watched him with undisguised dislike and contempt. Years of experience had taught her that his implacable will couldn't be defeated.

'All I want is the truth,' she said dispiritedly.

To her astonishment the stiffness of his shoulders loosened, and he held out a hand, indicating a chair. 'Sit down, Kathryn, please,' he said in an even tone. 'I've something very painful to tell you.'

Kate sat, wondering at his change in attitude.

'How much do you remember of your mother's death?' he began.

She stared, startled and disconcerted at the question, unable to answer for a few moments. Mother's sudden passing eight years ago had been a terrible blow, leaving her a lonely and frightened child. It had seemed like the end of her family, especially as her brother drifted further and further away. There was no one to stand between her and Luther's cold authority.

'I remember the pain of loneliness,' she said at last.

A look of impatience flitted across his features briefly, but she saw he tried to quell it.

'I mean the cause of her death,' he said tersely.

Kate shook her head. 'I've never been told.'

'Precisely,' he snapped.

He sat on the corner of the desk, his expression almost friendly. This informality was unprecedented in her presence and she was immediately suspicious.

'You were kept in ignorance for your own good, yours and Evan's,' he said. 'The sad fact is . . . Alice took her own life.'

'No!'

Kate jumped to her feet and Luther rose, too.

'Now, hear me out,' he said quickly. 'This is as terrible for me as it is for you, Kathryn. I've lived with the knowledge for years. Your mother took poison deliberately.'

'That's a lie!'

'I only wish it were,' he said. 'She stored up the sleeping powders Penfold prescribed for her, and took them all at once.'

Kate couldn't prevent a sob escaping her. 'But why?'

'Insanity, Kathryn,' Luther said gravely. 'Hereditary insanity. It's in the blood of your family, I'm afraid, passed down from parent to child.'

Kathryn shook her head. 'I can't believe it,' she gasped. 'You're not making sense, Luther. There's no insanity in my family. Why are you saying these awful things?'

'Because it's the truth,' he answered heavily. 'This insanity was in Alice and it is in you. We have to face the fact that you can never marry; never bear children.'

Kate stared at him, horror-stricken. She searched his face for some telltale sign that he was lying, but his features were immobile, cast in stone.

'I've Dr Penfold's expert assurance this is so,' he went on soberly. 'And this is what I had to tell Mansel. It was my bounden duty, my Christian duty, to make him aware of the terrible future he faced in marrying into this family.'

Kate was silent for a moment, her mind churning.

'No!' she cried out at last. 'It can't be! I don't believe it.' She stared at him defiantly. 'If it were true Evan would know, and he'd have told me before now.' She glared at her stepfather. 'This is some monstrous trick, Luther. What're you trying to do to me? What have I ever done to you?'

Kate turned to flee the room, but Luther caught her arm.

17

'Do you trust Dr Penfold?' he asked sharply.

Kate hesitated. The doctor had tended the medical needs of the Vaughan family for many years. She remembered him visiting when she was a child. Surely she could trust the doctor. 'Of course I do.'

'Well, then,' Luther said evenly. 'I had to call him in to explain matters to Mansel.' He gave a deep resigned sigh. 'It may be distressing for you, but if you wish I'll ask him to see you, to go through the matter thoroughly.' He paused, gazing at her keenly. 'Personally, I'd rather live in ignorance of what's to befall me. Madness, Kathryn, madness and degradation.'

Kate stared into his unrelenting face, and felt a terrible weight descend on her shoulders and with it despair. Luther put his hand under her elbow in a paternal manner, and she flinched at the unexpected gesture.

'This is distressful for both of us,' he went on. 'Although we've never been close in the past, Kathryn, I only want your happiness. Unfortunately, fate's taken a hand in your life.'

Kate lifted her head high. 'I can't accept this, Luther,' she said tensely. 'I'll speak to my brother.' She jerked her arm from his grasp. 'I'll also see Mansel immediately. We *will* marry, despite you.'

With one last challenging look at him, she fled the room.

2

———◆◆◆———

Kate rushed to her bedroom and fell sobbing on to the bed. Tears gushed and she gave herself over to them, not knowing whether she cried with renewed grief for her mother, Mansel's departure or in anger at Luther.

The room was considerably darker when she finally composed herself. A stealthy footfall in the passage outside her door made her sit up with a jerk. Chivers was on the snoop again. He was always spying on them. With his silent tread and hissing speech, he reminded her of a reptile. He was Luther's creature, all right, reporting everything he saw or heard, and Kate didn't trust him an inch.

But this wasn't the time to worry about that. She must decide what to do next. Now she understood Mansel's sudden departure, even if she couldn't forgive him. Although, to be fair to him, she told herself, it must have been a terrible shock. She'd see him and put things right.

Kate's lips tightened in anger. Luther was guilty of the utmost wickedness, and she was determined to expose him for the liar he was.

She was just slipping out of her afternoon dress to put on a warm skirt, planning to slip down the back stairs, go to the stables and persuade their groom to take her to Sketty, when the dressing gong sounded.

To her dismay she realised it was too late to see Mansel now.

His family might be entertaining dinner guests and her sudden unexpected appearance would cause embarrassment, not to mention gossip.

She ought to speak with Evan first, common sense told her. He'd been twelve going on thirteen when their mother died, and would know the truth.

She was startled by a light tap at her door, and Watkins, their young footman, came respectfully into the room.

'Light the gas, I will, with your permission, Miss Kate,' he said. 'And stoke up the fire.'

Kate sat tight-lipped on the bed while he did the necessary chores.

'Is my brother in his room?' she asked.

'Mr Vaughan hasn't been home all day, Miss Kate,' Watkins replied. 'He sent word to Mrs Trobert that he won't be dining here this evening.'

Kate was disappointed and put out, but tried not to show it.

'That'll be all, Watkins,' she said sharply.

He gave a little cough. 'Shall I send Ethel to help you dress, Miss Kate?'

'No. I won't be going down to dinner.'

'Very good, Miss Kate,' he said and left.

Kate paced the room in anger. She couldn't bear to sit eating alone with her stepfather after what had happened, and she had no appetite, anyway. It made her blood boil to think Luther had taken everything that had belonged to her father: his home, his business and even his wife. There he'd sit this evening in solitary splendour surrounded by every luxury the Vaughans had acquired over generations, and not one member of the family to share them.

That notion gave her pause for thought. She didn't relish

dining alone with Luther, yet wouldn't give him the satisfaction of thinking he'd won some obscure battle.

Ethel arrived in answer to her summons.

'Help me dress for dinner, please, quickly,' Kate said.

'The master suggests you might wear the green velvet this evening, Miss Kate,' Ethel said innocently.

Kate's mouth gaped, then she clenched her teeth firmly. 'Fetch me the blue silk, Ethel,' she said.

Luther was coming out of the drawing-room, crossing the hall to the dining-room as Kate descended the stairs. He glanced at her blue gown with raised brows. 'The green would've served better,' he remarked. 'The colour has a calming effect on inflamed senses.'

Kate bristled with indignation. 'There's nothing wrong with my senses,' she blurted, unable to hold her tongue, and would have said more, but his expression cautioned her not to provoke him further.

They sat at opposite ends of the dining table. Kate kept her lips firmly closed and her gaze guarded. Chivers put plates of food in front of her, and they were taken away again untouched. She knew anything that passed her lips this evening would taste like sawdust.

She watched Luther covertly, the ever-present Chivers hovering not far from his elbow. He lifted a finger and Chivers produced another bottle of fine wine, taken from her late father's extensive cellar. Luther seemed in a lighter mood, different from his usual weighty seriousness.

'You're not eating, Kathryn,' he commented.

Kate looked down her nose at her stepfather, but remained silent.

'The Beef Wellington is really very good. The pastry just

melts,' he went on, then turned to Chivers. 'My compliments to Mrs Trobert.'

'Very good, sir.'

Luther glanced at Kate again. 'Your plates being returned with the food undisturbed will offend her,' he went on with a narrow smile. 'She's such an excellent cook. We wouldn't want to lose her, would we?'

Kate was stung into a response. 'Mrs Trobert's been with the Vaughans all her working life, since she was a scullery maid,' she snapped. 'She's loyal to *my* family.'

She bitterly resented the levity of his tone when her world was crashing around her: the man she loved turned against her, her very future uncertain.

'I'm sure,' Luther said offhandedly. He paused a moment. 'I thought you'd have invited your friend Cecille to dinner this evening. Empty-minded creature, of course, but attractive for all that. She'd have entertained me with her vapid chatter and cheered you up considerably.'

'Cheered me!' Kate exploded, throwing her napkin on to the table. 'You talk very lightly of my situation this evening, Luther, when earlier you offered only doom and gloom, condemned me to spinsterhood and childlessness.'

An angry frown marked his face, and he glanced sharply towards the silent Watkins standing statue-like as though guarding the food-laden chiffonier.

'Kathryn! Have some decorum, if you please,' he said in an undertone.

'Oh, don't concern yourself with the servants overhearing our secrets,' Kate burst out, her voice crackling with scorn. 'Chivers keeps them well informed. Don't you, Chivers?'

There was a soft hissing sigh of disapproval from the butler, and Luther looked furious.

'That's enough!'

'It certainly is.' Kate stood up, pushing her chair back. 'I'll speak to Evan as soon as he returns. We'll see what *he* has to say about the awful things you've said about my mother.'

With a swish of blue silk, Kate moved towards the door. Watkins sprang forward to open it for her. With one last disdainful glance at her stepfather, she stalked from the dining-room.

Kate stayed in her sitting-room at the top of the stairs until she heard Evan's hurried tread go past the door. She flew along the gallery after him, following him to his rooms in the east wing, and found him warming his hands at his fire.

'Evan, I must speak with you,' Kate burst out. 'Something terrible's happened.'

'Can't it wait until morning?' he asked impatiently. 'I've no time now. I'm about to confront Luther.'

Kate was startled, wondering if he had heard already. 'Confront him? What about?'

'He hesitated, biting his lip, then gave a weak smile. 'Money,' he said. 'What else?'

Kate studied him. Slight of build and of medium height, he was so like their father in looks and ways. He was no match for Luther's deviousness, and Kate's heart ached for him.

'Are you in debt again, Evan?' she asked gravely. 'He'll only humiliate you. He takes pleasure in it.'

'It's not a debt,' he assured her. 'Quite the reverse.'

'It's business, then?'

She was even more concerned. Evan was no more an astute businessman than their father had been, and she was certain Luther Templar had duped and tricked their father before his

23

death. As far as she was concerned, her stepfather was a plunderer, a pirate.

'You're too young to understand financial matters,' Evan said sharply. 'I want only my just rights. Now, if you'll excuse me, Kate, I'll go downstairs.'

Kate was stung by his dismissal. 'What I've got to tell you is much more important than your silly business, Evan, whatever it is,' she exclaimed tartly. 'Luther's refused my hand in marriage to Mansel Jenkins.'

'What?' Evan looked astounded. 'Refused one of the wealthiest families in Swansea? What's he thinking of?'

Kate put a hand to her throat, remembering Luther's terrible pronouncement on her. 'That's not all. He says Mother killed herself. Have you ever heard anything so despicable?' Kate couldn't prevent a sob escaping. 'You must know the truth, Evan. Face him, show him up for the liar he is.'

Evan stared at her for a moment, his complexion turning deathly pale, then he turned to face the fireplace as though he couldn't look her in the eye. Kate darted forward to grasp his arm, and pulled him around to face her.

'Evan? Say it isn't so.'

'It's true, Kate,' he whispered miserably. 'I saw and heard everything that went on in this house that terrible night. Dr Penfold was called. She'd taken some kind of poison. Luther instructed the doctor to cover it up so there'd be no family scandal.'

'Oh, my God!' Kate fell back a few steps. 'It's true then. I am done for, doomed and condemned.'

'Don't be melodramatic, Kate,' Evan said impatiently. 'It can't affect us now. It was years ago, forgotten. It'll never come to light.'

Kate pressed fingers to her lips in an effort to hold back sobs of sheer terror. 'Luther says Mother was insane and that the insanity is in me, too. I can never marry or have children. That's why he stopped my marriage to Mansel. His Christian duty, he said.'

Evan stared stonily.

'Hereditary insanity, Luther calls it,' she whispered. 'Don't you see, Evan,' she went on quickly. 'It affects you, too. If I can't marry, then neither can you.'

He looked stunned for a moment, then anger flashed across his face. 'This is too much! He goes too far,' he barked and marched to the door. 'I'll have this out with him now.'

'But if it's true about Mother,' Kate called after him, 'what can we do?'

Evan disappeared without answering.

Furious, Evan didn't bother to knock but marched straight in to the study. Luther was sitting at the desk, and even though it was getting quite late, he had the housekeeping account books spread in front of him. Watching every penny, like a miser, Evan thought.

Luther looked up at Evan's entrance, a vaunting smile curving his mouth, but his gaze remained cold. 'Ah, Evan, come to your senses, I take it?' he began. 'Are you ready to comply with my wishes?'

'I've made a decision,' Evan retorted sharply. 'But before we discuss it, I'd like to know what the hell you're doing to Kate.'

Luther sat back, chin elevated in his usual haughty manner. 'I don't know what you mean.'

'You sent Mansel Jenkins packing,' Evan exclaimed disbelievingly. 'He and Kate are perfect together, and apart from that, their union would make a very worthy and profitable connection.'

Anger flashed briefly across Luther's face. 'It's none of your business,' he snapped. 'Kathryn is *my* responsibility. I'll do what's best for her.'

'Best?' Evan repeated with scepticism. 'You spoiled her best match, and to do it in such a way. Hereditary insanity, my foot! What're you really up to, Luther?'

Luther sprang to his feet, looking furious. 'How dare you, sir! I'll not have my actions questioned by a whippersnapper like you. You're hardly in a position to know what's right and proper, judging by the disastrous marriage you've made.'

Evan felt an angry pulse beat strongly in his throat, but withheld a rash outburst. Concerned though he was for Kate, he had delicate negotiations to go through with his stepfather and mustn't lose his temper.

'My marriage is my affair,' Evan retorted in a choked voice. 'I don't wish to discuss it.'

'Huh! I'm not surprised. One of the firm's shop-girls; a trollop from the Valleys.'

'That's not so!' Evan burst out. 'My wife, Eirwen, may be unsophisticated, but she's also guileless.'

Luther gave a scornful laugh. 'She knew enough to set her sights on you, and catch you. What possessed you to marry her, man?' Luther asked, exasperated. 'She could've been bought off with a few sovereigns.'

'I did what was right,' Evan declared, unable to stop the telltale catch in his voice.

'And now you regret it,' Luther said sardonically. 'And bitterly, too, I suspect.'

He moved to a sideboard where a whisky decanter stood, and poured some into a glass, splashing in some soda water. He made a motion, offering a glass to Evan, who shook his head, unwilling to drink with a man he so despised.

26

Luther took a sip. 'How you found an opportunity to get her into the family way stumps me,' he said. 'With the shop not closing until nine thirty weeknights; ten thirty on Saturdays; the girls tucked up in their dormitories immediately after, and with the formidable Mrs Croaker standing guard over them.'

Evan felt his neck swell with rage. 'I won't stand here listening to this coarse talk,' he blustered.

'There's always half-day, of course,' Luther went on as though Evan hadn't spoken. 'But even then the girls must be back by six or risk the sack.'

Evan felt his anger would choke him. There was an amused and knowing glint in Luther's eye which told him his step-father knew all about the rented rooms Evan kept in Salubrious Passage, and that he'd taken Eirwen there every Thursday afternoon. Kate was right. His stepfather had spies everywhere.

Luther drained his glass, then went to the desk to sit, fingering some legal-looking documents that lay on the blotting pad.

'Of course,' he went on when Evan didn't respond, 'your wife can never come into polite society. She must be kept out of sight, otherwise your peers will ostracise you, and the scandal of such a low marriage could damage the reputation of the business.'

'Damn the business!' Evan shouted. 'That's all you think about. You'd even sacrifice Kate for the sake of it.'

Luther looked angry. 'Have a care, Evan,' he warned. 'Your livelihood depends on the very business you appear to disdain.'

'No, it doesn't,' Evan retorted. 'I have my inheritance, a considerable fortune. It's due to me now that I'm married, and I demand it immediately.'

'You can demand nothing,' Luther snapped, stony-faced. 'As executor of your father's estate, I can withhold your inheritance if I feel your marriage isn't a suitable one, which it isn't.'

'You can't do that. It's not lawful.'

'I assure you it is, Evan,' Luther said. 'You're forgetting the special clause I persuaded your father to add to his will. If you or Kate make unsuitable marriages I've the power, as executor, to withhold your inheritance until you're thirty. This is to protect the estate against fortune-hunters.'

Evan was stunned, but Luther wasn't finished.

'Furthermore,' he went on in a hard tone, 'I could sack you as a department manager very easily. Then you'd have no income at all.'

'But . . .' Evan stammered, panic beginning to affect his breathing. 'I've already contracted to buy property. The completion is due this week.'

'Ah, yes.' Luther nodded. 'You plan to install your wife and child in a house outside town. Very wise. The village of Fforestfach is very suitably out of the way. I've had the property inspected, by the way.'

'You had no right!'

'Two acres of land, yet the house is in poor repair. Hardly a residence fit for a gentleman. I presume you don't intend to live there yourself?'

'You presume too much,' Evan snapped, though filled with consternation that Luther read his intentions so well.

The prospect of living out of town didn't appeal as it once had, but Luther was right. Damn him! Eirwen would be an embarrassment in his own social circle, and already her uninformed company was proving irksome to him. The only consolation of this marriage was his beautiful baby son.

28

Luther waved a dismissive hand. 'I'm not concerned with your piffling mistakes,' he said. 'But I warn you, I won't suffer interference in my plans.'

'I don't know what you mean.'

'Kathryn's future,' Luther said. 'You'll leave it to me.'

'But—'

'You'll get your inheritance . . . eventually,' Luther assured him. 'But not yet. First, you'll make over your shares to me immediately, tonight. I have the papers drawn up ready. Just sign them.'

'I won't sign away my inheritance to you,' Evan stormed. 'This is dirty blackmail!'

Luther's lips tightened. 'You try my patience, Evan. You've no choice, man. Now, sign!'

'But I need money now to complete the purchase,' Evan blurted desperately. 'Renovations must start straight away. We can't stay in those cramped rooms in Salubrious Passage much longer. My son's health may be at stake.'

'I'll personally lend you sufficient funds to cover the purchase and renovations,' Luther said evenly, a sly gleam in his eyes. 'You'll be in *my* debt, Evan, dance to *my* tune. When Kathryn's shares are in my possession, you'll get your inheritance. Until then' – his smile was sneering – 'you belong to me.'

Evan still hesitated, yet knew he had no choice.

Luther's jaw tightened at the delay, and his glare was malevolent. 'I've put up with ageing dolts on the board for years; men with no vision, just like your father,' he said bitterly. As though in sudden pique, he crashed his fist down on the table. 'I *must* have more power in the boardroom.'

'Power. That's what you live for, isn't it,' Evan said scathingly. 'That's the only reason you married my mother. And look where it drove her.'

'Silence!' Luther thundered. 'Your mother was insane.'

'Oh, don't try that with me, Luther,' Evan said through gritted teeth. 'You've got some kind of hold over Dr Penfold, I'll be bound. He covered up Mother's suicide on your instructions, and now you're both bamboozling Kate with this insanity twaddle.'

'I'm warning you, Evan,' Luther fumed. 'You're driving me to ruin you.'

Evan checked himself, realising he was pushing too hard. Luther had power over how he lived the next decade of his life. He had a baby son to consider; a new Vaughan to carry on the dynasty. He couldn't let his son be deprived of his birthright. Yet his heart ached for Kate's dilemma.

'But it's cruel beyond words to force Kate to live like a nun,' he said.

'I couldn't allow her to marry Mansel Jenkins,' Luther said firmly. 'Yet the postponement clause wouldn't be valid there, since Mansel is obviously an ideal suitor. Hence the hereditary insanity ploy. And it worked.'

Evan was appalled. 'It's . . . barbaric!'

Luther's jaw set like granite, and his eyes glittered. 'Mansel would've taken Kathryn's quarter share in the business and a seat on the board. He's not very astute, but his father is. I've crossed swords with Jenkins senior before. He'd like nothing better than to get a foot in the door of Vaughan & Templar.'

'Jenkins is a builder, not a merchant,' Evan pointed out impatiently.

'Don't you believe it,' Luther said. 'Jenkins senior has a finger in too many pies in Swansea.' He paused, and Evan was aware of the intensity of his stepfather's shrewd gaze.

'Meanwhile,' he went on in a hard voice, 'if you want to own that property outright and get out of debt, you'll back me up in convincing Kathryn she's tainted with insanity.'

'I won't betray my sister,' Evan cried out. 'You can't demand it of me.'

'I can and I do, Evan,' Luther thundered. 'You must choose between Kathryn and your newborn child. Defy me in this, and I swear I'll cast you into penury, you and your baby son.'

'But Kate is so young and lovely,' Evan pleaded wretchedly. 'She has such a lot of love to give a husband and children. It's such a waste.'

'You young fool!' Luther snapped. 'Kathryn will marry eventually, but to a man of *my* choosing.'

'A man you can control, you mean,' Evan muttered.

Luther smiled coldly. 'Ah, how well you know me, Evan.'

3

Kate was leaning over the banister waiting for Evan to come out of the study. When the door opened below she rushed to the head of the staircase and watched her brother cross the hall. He climbed the stairs slowly, almost reluctantly, head bent, gaze downcast. She was reminded of Mansel's hurried departure and her heart sank with foreboding. She didn't trust herself to speak until her brother was with her.

'Evan, what did he say? Did you call him a liar to his face?'

He lifted his head, but his gaze wouldn't meet hers. 'Kate.' He shook his head. 'I don't know what to say, except that I'm sorry, so very sorry.'

'What?' She stared at him, aghast. 'You *believe* him?'

He gazed at a point above her head. 'Dr Penfold has confirmed it,' he murmured. 'We can't argue against medical science.'

Kate grasped his arm. He was far too composed and she wondered if he were in shock. 'You're sorry for *me*,' she said quickly. 'But what about you? Do you calmly accept you can never have children on Luther's say-so?' She shook her head vehemently. 'I won't. We must take this further, consult another physician.'

'No!' He hesitated, looking agitated for a moment. 'Dr Penfold's already done so,' he went on in a subdued tone. 'There's no doubt.'

Kate was angry. 'How can there be no doubt when he hasn't even examined us?' She straightened her back, jaw set in determination. 'I can't let this rest. I'll find Aunt Agnes Vaughan.'

Evan looked startled. 'But don't you remember?' he said hurriedly. 'Luther's forbidden contact with her. He said she is a troublemaker within the family.'

Kate's lips thinned. Young as she'd been then, she remembered how Agnes Vaughan, her father's older sibling, had been forced out of Old Grove House when Luther married Alice Vaughan. It could only mean one thing: Luther feared her. Aunt Agnes saw and understood too much.

Evan looked directly into her eyes for the first time since he'd come upstairs. 'Kate, trust me. Do nothing at this time. Involving Aunt Agnes would be a mistake. We don't want to make Luther angry—'

Kate snapped her fingers. 'I don't give a fig for Luther, and neither should you,' she cried fervently. 'I *will* marry the man I love. I'll find Aunt Agnes. She'll tell Mansel the truth . . .'

In a passage, just off the gallery, a floorboard creaked, and Kate grasped Evan's arm in alarm.

'We are being overheard,' she whispered urgently. 'Luther has spies everywhere.'

'Oh, stuff and nonsense,' Evan exclaimed in a low voice, but suddenly he looked worried too.

'We'll talk tomorrow, Evan,' she whispered back. 'Luther may want to see the Vaughan dynasty ended, but I'll not go down without a fight.'

Since she had been a small child Kate always took breakfast in the kitchen with Mrs Trobert. It was a practice frowned upon by her stepfather, but Kate persisted.

Mrs Trobert's round cheery face beamed at her. 'Morning. You're extra early, Miss Kate.'

'Morning, Mrs Trobert,' Kate answered. 'Yes, I've a lot to do today.' She glanced around, making sure they were alone, wary of the butler. 'Where's Chivers?' she asked cautiously.

Mrs Trobert brought the big brown earthenware teapot from the hob and put it on the table. 'Helping the master dress, Miss Kate,' she said. 'Did you want him for something?'

'No. I want to talk to you in private, Mrs Trobert. No one's to know.'

'Of course, Miss Kate.'

'Where's my Aunt Agnes Vaughan, Mrs Trobert?'

The housekeeper's fingers twitched and milk spilled from the jug over the pristine tablecloth.

'Oh, dear me! What a mess,' she exclaimed, her voice rising. She grabbed a tea towel and mopped at the spill.

'Mrs Trobert?'

'What makes you think I know where she is, Miss Kate?' the housekeeper asked defensively. 'The master left strict instruction years ago—'

'You're still in touch with my aunt, aren't you?' Kate said firmly. 'Despite what Luther Templar says.'

Mrs Trobert looked agitated. 'It's more than my job's worth if the master found out,' she said. 'And Chivers is just waiting for the chance to get rid of me to make a place for one of his many female cronies – and that's a polite word for it!'

'It's urgent that I find my aunt,' Kate insisted.

Mrs Trobert sat down at the table. 'She rents rooms in a house in upper Craddock Street in town.'

'Give me the exact address,' Kate said. 'I must see her today.'

'Oh, I don't know, Miss Kate. If the master—'

'Mrs Trobert,' Kate interrupted, deciding to be frank. 'You must've heard how my stepfather ruined my marriage chances with Mr Mansel Jenkins.' Kate couldn't hold back a sob. 'Perhaps with any man. You *must* tell me where my aunt is. My whole future depends on it.'

'Oh, Miss Kate, don't take on so,' Mrs Trobert said kindly, then she told Kate the number of a house in Craddock Street. 'It didn't come from me, mind,' the housekeeper went on. 'I'm too old to find another position. Besides, the master would blacklist me. He's done it before.'

After breakfast, Kate dressed quickly in outdoor garments, and went to the stables to speak with their groom. Trott was busy vigorously brushing down one of the horses, but didn't pause in his task as she entered and spoke to him.

'Trott, I need the trap, immediately. Take me into town.'

He carried on grooming, not looking at her. 'Can't be done, Miss Kate.'

'What do you mean?' Kate demanded, annoyed at his offhand manner.

He stopped grooming and turned to her. Kate stared into his weather-beaten face. She'd known him all her life, but now there was defiance, even insolence in his gaze.

'Master's orders,' he replied shortly. 'Master says you're not allowed to use the trap or carriage or horse without his strict permission, and then only with an escort.'

'But I'd have an escort in the trap: you.'

Trott shuffled his feet as though suddenly embarrassed. 'You're not allowed out alone, Miss Kate. It's for your own good, the master says, in case – mischief befalls you.'

'What?'

'Orders is orders, Miss Kate, and I wants to keep my job.'

Unwilling to demean herself arguing with a groom, Kate

stalked away in fury, back to her room to rage against Luther in private, and think what to do next.

The town was perhaps only two or three miles distant, yet she dared not attempt to walk it. Sketty Road was difficult, the surface marked by potholes and rutted by the passage of many wheels. At this time of year the ground would probably be frozen, too.

The horse omnibus passed by twice a day, bringing people into town from the many villages westward. Kate fumed that she had no money of her own for the fare. She could ask Mrs Trobert for a loan, but that might put the housekeeper's job at risk. No, this was her battle and she must fight it alone, if necessary.

Kate almost allowed herself to burst into tears with frustration, but held herself in check. Evan must help her, and she hurried to his rooms.

He had just finished dressing, wearing pinstripe trousers and a black tailcoat over a black waistcoat, the correct mode of dress for a department manager at Vaughan & Templar. He glanced around from viewing himself in the long oval mirror, and wasn't pleased to see her.

'Kate, I've no time,' he said sharply, turning from her. 'I haven't had breakfast yet, and Luther doesn't like tardiness in managers. It sets a bad example for the shop-girls.'

'How can the shop-girls be late for work when they live on the premises?' Kate asked tartly.

'That's beside the point.'

'Take me into Swansea this morning and bring me back,' Kate demanded imperiously. 'Luther won't let me use the trap. He's trying to make me a prisoner.'

'Don't be absurd, Kate,' Evan snapped. 'He's concerned for your welfare.'

'You don't really believe that!' she burst out. 'He wants everyone to think I'm insane. Trott was positively insolent this morning.'

'Kate, you're obsessed,' Evan said impatiently. 'It'll do no good.' He paused, avoiding her gaze. 'You must resign yourself to the inevitable, as I must.'

But he didn't look the least resigned, Kate thought, and was stabbed through with grief at the thought that her own brother had washed his hands of her.

'Are you against me, too?' she said, a catch in her voice.

'Of course not! Now look here, Kate,' Evan said irritably. 'I can't afford to annoy Luther—'

'Annoy him!' Kate was astonished at his manner. 'You speak as though what he's done to me is some trifling matter. He's ruined my life, Evan. Nothing will ever be the same.'

With an exasperated glance, he pushed past her to move to the door. 'Excuse me, Kate, but I'm already late.'

Kate remained in her sitting-room, fuming and frustrated until mid morning, when an unexpected visitor was announced. Cecille flounced into the small sitting-room as soon as Ethel spoke her name.

'Cecille!' Kate leaped to her feet, excited. Here was the answer. 'How good of you to call on me.'

Cecille sniffed and tossed her ginger head, sending the feathers in her hat shivering.

'Oh, I wondered if you still wished to know me after yesterday,' she said archly.

'I'm so sorry,' Kate apologised humbly, reaching forward and drawing Cecille to the sofa before the fire. 'I'd just been jilted, if you remember,' she went on sarcastically. 'I wasn't in the best of moods.'

The corners of Cecille's pert mouth lifted. 'Very well,' she said. 'I accept your apology.' She whipped off her hat. 'Now, tell me exactly what's happened since yesterday. Has your errant beau come crawling back on his stomach begging forgiveness?'

Kate held on to her smile, but it was a strain. 'No,' she said. 'I'm afraid it's not that simple.'

'You're too tender with him, Kate. Men mustn't be allowed to believe they can have things all their own way in matters of love,' Cecille remarked, with all the worldly wisdom of her seventeen years.

Irritated at her friend's silliness, Kate held back a sharp retort, remembering that she wanted a favour.

'Cecille,' she began. 'I wonder – could we take a drive in your trap into town this very minute? There's a lady I want to visit.'

'Why not take your own?' Cecille looked surprised.

'Our horses are with the blacksmith being shod,' Kate lied serenely. 'Would it be too much trouble for you?'

The trap was sent for immediately, and Kate hurried out, almost afraid that someone would prevent her leaving the house. They were safely rolling down the carriageway to the road before she instructed the Villiers' groom on their destination.

'Craddock Street?' Cecille wrinkled her nose. 'Not a very fashionable part of town,' she remarked. 'Who's this person you're visiting? A dressmaker?'

'Actually, she's my aunt,' Kate admitted. 'My father's sister. There's been an estrangement, you understand. I feel it's time to make amends.'

As they neared Craddock Street in the centre of town, Kate asked the groom to rein up outside a chemist's shop on the corner, opposite the Albert Hall Theatre. She had no wish for the Villiers' trap to be seen outside her aunt's lodgings. Reports might get back to Luther and he'd put two and two together.

'You can wait here in the trap if you'd rather,' Kate suggested casually to her friend. There were things she needed to say to her aunt, things she didn't want bandied about, and Cecille was a notorious gossip.

'Oh, no,' Cecille said, quickly stepping down from the trap. 'You're being very mysterious, Kate. I intend to get to the bottom of it.' She paused, looking startled. 'You're not meeting Mansel Jenkins secretly, are you?'

Without answering, Kate turned the corner and hurried up Craddock Street. The number Mrs Trobert had given her proved to be a house three doors up from the chemist, and looked clean and respectable. Her hand trembled as she lifted the large iron knocker, wondering what sort of reception her aunt would give her. She half expected to be ordered out, yet that would be unfair. She'd had no hand in turning Aunt Agnes out to fend for herself.

A middle-aged woman in a white apron answered the door. She looked at Kate and Cecille enquiringly, her glance running swiftly over their fashionable clothing.

'Yes?'

'I'm looking for Miss Agnes Vaughan. I'm her niece,' Kate said. 'Is she at home?'

The woman paused, biting her lip, looking from one to the other. 'You'd best come inside a minute.'

She led the way down a passage smelling strongly of carbolic soap and bleach, which didn't quite hide the older smell of boiled cabbage. Cecille wrinkled her nose again, and gave Kate a sharp nudge with her elbow. Kate ignored her.

The woman opened the door of a back room and ushered them in. She stood before them, hands lapped together over the front of her skirt.

'Miss Vaughan's not here,' the woman said.

Kate felt a stab of acute disappointment and annoyance, too. This might mean another contrived journey.

'When will she be back?'

'No, you don't understand,' the woman said. 'Miss Vaughan has disappeared.'

'What?'

'Miss Vaughan always likes . . . liked to visit the new Swansea Market of a Tuesday morning, ever since it opened three years ago,' the woman went on. 'Week in week out, she'd go, come rain or shine. Well, a month back she goes out as usual and she never comes back. Weird, it was.'

Kate was appalled. 'But didn't you report her disappearance to the authorities?'

The woman wiped an index finger under her nose in a defensive gesture. 'Well, I would've done since she was owing a week's rent, but then that man came here and paid the rent up to date, and gave me a pound extra for my trouble.'

'What man?' Kate questioned sharply.

The woman shrugged her shoulders. 'Well, I don't know, do I? Didn't give his name, didn't state his business. He paid up and took away all her things.'

Kate was flummoxed. 'Does her maid know anything?'

'That's the funny thing,' the woman said. 'Miss Vaughan's maid went home to her mother's the evening before, and I've not seen hide nor hair of her since, either.'

'Thank you.'

Kate turned to leave, and the woman coughed expectantly,

but Kate didn't have a penny piece to her name, and felt embarrassed. She tugged at Cecille's arm, and they left hurriedly, hearing an angry snort from the woman as she slammed the door on their backs.

They walked slowly to the waiting trap. Kate was deep in thought, hardly aware of the icy wind tugging at her hat and lifting the hem of her pelisse or of Cecille's chatter.

Luther was behind this disappearance, she felt certain. But what was his motive?

She was very downcast on the journey home, and though she felt mean-spirited in doing so, asked Cecille to excuse her. Her friend left, obviously cross at not being allowed to discuss the mystery of the disappearing aunt.

Later Kate bitterly regretted dismissing her friend so quickly. She longed to see Mansel, and might have persuaded Cecille to obtain the use of the Villiers' brougham to make the longer and more arduous journey to Sketty.

It was evident that Evan wouldn't be her ally against Luther. Now Aunt Agnes had disappeared, Kate was beginning to feel desperate.

Some days after visiting Craddock Street, Kate was summoned one Thursday afternoon to Luther's study. Immediately, she was on the defensive. Obviously, he'd discovered she'd thwarted his plans to keep her cooped up, and she was ready to defend her actions. He stood before the fireplace, thumbs in his waistcoat pockets, and he actually smiled at her.

'Ah, Kathryn. Do sit down. I've some news for you.'

She was taken off guard by his affability, when she'd expected a torrent of angry words. She elevated her nose disdainfully. 'Really?'

'It's about Mansel Jenkins,' he went on. 'He left Swansea for Southampton this morning. He's on his way to war. That's probably the last we'll see of him.'

'Oh, no!' Kate jumped up, her hand clutching at her throat in dismay. He hadn't even said goodbye after all they'd said and meant to each other.

'I thought I'd save you the trouble of conniving at a visit to Sketty,' Luther said sarcastically. 'Incidentally, you may now use the trap whenever you wish.'

Kate hugged herself in misery and despair, hanging her head, feeling her heart would break. She might never see Mansel again. Terrible things happened to men in war. Now she was totally alone.

'Do you hear me?' Luther went on. 'You're free to come and go as you wish.'

What good was that now? Kate thought miserably. Mansel was out of reach, and out of her life for ever. She could never tell him the truth.

'Do you expect my thanks? It was cruel not to let me see Mansel before he left,' Kate cried angrily. 'You had no right to deny me transportation. I'm free to go where I choose.'

'That remains up to me,' he said casually. 'Where did you go with the delightful Cecille the other day?'

Kate folded her lips stubbornly, determined to give nothing away. He probably already knew, anyway, and she'd wager Luther also knew the whereabouts of Aunt Agnes. What devious game was he playing with their lives?

'Well, Kathryn? I'm waiting for an answer.'

Kate threw back her head, her eyes blazing at him. 'Why ask when you already know?'

'Don't be tiresome, Kathryn. You're not as clever as you believe you are.'

'All right then,' she cried. 'You want me to say it out loud. I went to Craddock Street. There! Are you satisfied?'

The sudden and unexpected change in his features made her start, and she stared at him, perplexed. Blood rushed to his face, and a vein began to throb visibly in his temple. His hands were shaking as he reached for the back of a chair for support.

'Craddock Street?' he rasped. 'Damnation! Didn't I forbid you to have contact with that wretched old woman?'

'That was years ago when Evan and I were children,' she said. 'I'm a woman now. I do as I please.'

He didn't rise to her challenge, and she saw something in his eyes which she didn't understand, an emotion she'd never seen in him before.

'So, you saw Agnes Vaughan,' Luther cried, a tremor vibrating in his voice. 'What lies did she tell you? Answer me!'

Kate stared at him, confused, suddenly realising he was unaware of her aunt's disappearance.

'I demand you tell me,' he shouted, spittle appearing at the corner of his mouth. 'Of what did she accuse me? I must know.'

Astonishment keeping her silent, Kate watched her stepfather almost lose control for the first time since she'd known him. Her mind raced. If Luther hadn't spirited Aunt Agnes away, then who was the mysterious man who'd taken her, and wiped out any trace of her whereabouts?

She had to make some response to her stepfather, but instinct warned her not to enlighten him at this time as to what really happened at Craddock Street.

'I didn't speak with my aunt. She was out shopping,' Kate lied glibly. 'I intend to call on her again next week.'

'I forbid it!' Luther stormed. 'You'll make no contact with her – or anyone else outside this house. I'll see to it that Cecille Villiers doesn't visit here again.'

'That's grossly unfair!'

'My previous instructions to Trott stand,' he said, almost choking on his spittle. 'I will not tolerate your defiance.'

'And I'll not be made a prisoner in my own home,' shrieked Kate.

'Silence!' Luther roared, beside himself with rage. 'Silence, damn you!' He clutched at his collar for a moment. 'It's clear your insanity is far worse than Dr Penfold thought,' he went on in a quivering voice. 'Chivers will take you to your room immediately, where you'll remain. A nurse will watch you day and night.'

He pulled at the bell rope nearby.

'You can't do that in this day and age!' Kate cried. 'It's . . . it's unlawful.'

'You're rambling and incoherent, Kathryn,' he said, still trying to catch his breath. 'A possible danger to us all in your mad state. You'll be confined to your bedroom.' He looked triumphant suddenly. 'It's entirely for your own safety. After all, we wouldn't want anything unpleasant to happen to you.'

4

December 1899

With a groan of despair, Kate opened her eyes and struggled up listlessly from under the bedclothes as Ethel knocked and walked into the bedroom, calling her irritating greeting as usual.

'Morning! Good morning.'

Kate scowled, not quite awake. Yet another day of enforced idleness and boredom lay in front of her.

Her first few days of imprisonment had been spent crying for Mansel, worrying for his safety. She couldn't have guessed how much she'd miss him, his tender attention, his friendship.

At last her weeping subsided, and she tried to make the most of what she had. She must have read every book in her father's library in the last two weeks, books brought to her by Ethel or Watkins, the only two people she'd had human contact with, for she'd not been allowed outside this room, the door kept locked from the outside.

'Sleep well, Miss Kate?'

Dispirited, Kate didn't bother to reply, but made herself ready to receive the breakfast tray as usual. Instead, Ethel went immediately to the washstand, placing the large china pitcher of hot water into its bowl. Kate rubbed her eyes.

'Where's my breakfast?'

'The master says you must come down to the dining-room for breakfast this morning, Miss Kate,' Ethel told her cheerfully.

'Are you sure?'

'Shall I come up in ten minutes and help you dress?'

Kate leaped out of bed briskly. A reprieve! She couldn't believe it.

'No, thank you, Ethel. I can manage very well,' Kate exclaimed, hurrying to pour the hot water into the china bowl. 'Oh, but lay out my cream shantung blouse and black alpaca skirt, will you?'

When she walked into the dining-room, her stepfather was already seated at the long table, Chivers in attendance.

Luther glanced up, unsmiling, as she came in, and she hesitated, uncertain for a moment. It wouldn't be the same as eating her breakfast with Mrs Trobert.

'Good morning, Kathryn,' he said solemnly. 'I trust you are now of a steadier frame of mind.'

A sharp retort came readily to her lips, but she bit it back, afraid for her new freedom.

'I'm well, thank you, Luther,' she answered stiffly. 'But I'd rather eat in the kitchen,' she went on. 'I'm used to it.'

'There'll be no more of that nonsense,' Luther said curtly. 'You've no business below stairs. Now, either serve yourself from the chiffonier or sit down and let Watkins bring it to you.'

Defeated, Kate marched to the chiffonier, ignoring the figure of Watkins nearby, and spooned some kedgeree and scrambled egg on to a plate. Her face burned with humiliation that Luther should speak to her as though she were a child, especially in front of the servants.

She saw there were only two place-settings at the table.

'Isn't Evan joining us?' she asked in surprise and disappointment. Her brother hadn't visited her once while she'd been locked away in her room, and she was anxious to know the reason.

'Evan doesn't live at Old Grove House any longer,' he replied casually.

'What?' Kate dropped her fork with a clatter. 'You've turned him out of his own home?' she cried. 'How dare you?'

Luther's mouth tightened in anger at her outburst. 'Don't be absurd, Kathryn,' he snapped. 'Evan has purchased property. It's only right a young man of his age should be master of his own household.'

Kate stared, wondering in bewilderment where her brother had found the money. 'Where's this property, then?'

Luther waved a dismissive hand. 'Some miles out of town,' he said offhandedly. 'You can ask him yourself. He dines here this evening.'

Kate ate in silence, her mind full of new ideas. Evan acquiring his own place could be her salvation. As a bachelor, he'd need someone to run the household, manage the servants. It would be ideal. She'd get away from Luther at last.

When the meal was over, Luther paused in the hall as they parted company.

'Remember what I said, Kathryn. You're not to go below stairs. I hope I'll not find it necessary to confine you again.'

Kate held her tongue with difficulty. She was anxious to see Mrs Trobert, no matter what her stepfather threatened. After witnessing Luther's almost apoplectic fit at the mention of Agnes's name some weeks ago, she was more determined than ever to find her aunt, and was certain the housekeeper knew more than she was willing to let on.

Fearful of meeting Chivers on the back stairs, Kate left the house by the front door, braving the freezing air and the crisp frost underfoot. She crept through the shrubbery that surrounded the house; hid for a moment near the back entrance to make sure the coast was clear, then slipped into the big warm kitchen.

'Mrs Trobert.'

The housekeeper was just about to lower a large ham into a saucepan of boiling water. She started violently at the sudden sound of Kate's voice and the ham fell into the water with a huge splash.

'*Duw annwyl!*' she shrieked.

Kate dashed forward, fearful the older woman had been scalded. 'Are you all right, Mrs Trobert?'

'Miss Kate!' Mrs Trobert swung around. 'You shouldn't be here. The master will be angry. He's given me firm instructions—'

'Are you scalded?'

Mrs Trobert shook her head. 'It's nothing that I haven't had before,' she said, dabbing at her arm with a towel. 'But, Miss Kate, you're running an awful risk. If Chivers sees you, we'll both regret it. I'll suffer more than a scald.'

'I had to speak to you,' Kate insisted. 'My whole future depends on what you know. Where's my aunt?'

Mrs Trobert's gaze slid away. 'Honestly, I don't know, Miss Kate.'

'But you know something,' Kate persisted. 'Did someone call here, a man, asking you for information about Aunt Agnes previously?'

The housekeeper twisted her fingers together, averting her gaze, her lips firmly clamped together. Kate felt angry at her stubbornness, yet at the same time she could sympathise. Luther Templar was a dangerous man to cross, and a servant who disobeyed him could expect no leniency.

'Mrs Trobert.' Kate laid a hand tentatively on the other woman's arm. 'You've known me all my life, surely you trust me?'

'Of course, I trust you, Miss Kate. But I've given my solemn word, and I daren't break it.'

She couldn't press further. It wouldn't be fair. Mrs Trobert, a spinster in truth, although she preferred to be thought a widow, was getting on in age. It would be the end of her if she were turned out on to the street, and Luther was quite capable of doing that. She must find some other means to get at the truth.

Kate dressed early for dinner, full of curiosity about the property of Evan's. Desperate to get away from Luther, she wondered how soon she could move in with her brother. She jumped up eagerly when he walked into the drawing-room.

'Evan, what's this I hear?' she began with a smile. 'You've bought property. When can I see it?'

He looked startled. 'Who told you this?'

'Luther,' she replied, wondering at his vexed expression. Surely, he hadn't meant to keep it a secret from her? She looked up anxiously into his face. 'You know how unhappy I am here, Evan. May I come and live with you? I'll manage your household for you.'

Without replying, Evan walked purposefully towards the drinks cabinet and took out a decanter of whisky, pouring himself a good measure. Kate was surprised. She'd never known him drink before dinner.

'You need someone to deal with the servants,' she went on hopefully.

'I've one maid, and one horse,' he said, turning to her. 'But no carriage, not even a gig. Besides, the property's in a backwater. Fforestfach village is small, a public house or two, and a few cottages. Scarcely any houses or families of consequence.'

'No carriage?' Kate frowned. 'You're very cut off then.' She found this strange. Evan was a gregarious man. Why would he shut himself away like this? Was he that much affected by Luther's accusation of hereditary insanity?

'Very cut off indeed,' Evan agreed quickly. 'You'd be bored to death with no friends nearby.'

'I don't care,' Kate cried. 'I need to get away from Luther. I suffer humiliation and mistreatment at his hands.' Suddenly she was irked by her brother's previous neglect. 'Why didn't you visit me while I was imprisoned in my bedroom?' she demanded sharply.

He looked abashed, yet there was a stubborn set to his jaw. 'I thought it best not to humiliate you further, Kate,' he said evenly. 'Besides, Luther said he preferred I didn't. I can't afford to antagonise him.'

'I see!' Kate was very angry. 'Obviously, he's more important to you than I am.'

'That's not true, Kate, and you know it.' He took a few sips of the whisky, his gaze sliding away from hers. 'The fact is, my house is small, with hardly any facilities,' he went on. 'I'm afraid there's no room for you.'

'But I'm your sister,' Kate said. 'Surely you wouldn't deny me shelter.'

'Don't be melodramatic, Kate,' he said impatiently. 'My property is no more than a hovel compared to the luxury you have here at Old Grove House. You don't realise how privileged you are.'

'If your house is so humble then why did you buy it?' Kate

asked quickly. 'And where did the money come from, Evan? Was all this Luther's idea? Does he run your life for you now?'

'That's enough!' Evan exploded. 'I won't be cross-examined by a mere girl.'

'Evan!' Kate was shocked at his belittling tone. He appeared exactly like Luther at that moment.

The dinner gong sounded, and Kate checked further sharp words. Their stepfather would appear at any minute, and she didn't want him to see there was discord between brother and sister.

'We'll talk again later,' Kate said firmly as she left the room.

'I'll be leaving for Fforestfach immediately afterwards,' he replied quickly. 'I wouldn't be at Old Grove House at all except that Luther insisted I dine here this evening.'

Luther was in the hall and overheard Evan's remark. 'You make it sound a chore, Evan,' he said tersely. 'But I assure you it'll be worth while. I've some news.'

The talk between the two men was desultory as the meal progressed. Kate kept silent, unable to take part in what was mostly shop talk, and wondered when Luther would impart his news. Was it something to do with Aunt Agnes? Whatever Luther had to say about her aunt, it would probably be a lie, she told herself.

Suddenly, her heart skipped a beat at the thought that the news might be about Mansel. Was he wounded? Or dead? At once her appetite deserted her, and she waited on tenterhooks.

When the meal was over, although she badly wanted to get away, Kate remained seated, when normally she'd leave the men to their port.

'When are we to hear this news?' she asked scornfully.

'Impatience is not a good trait in any lady, Kathryn,' Luther snapped.

He sat back in his chair, and Chivers stepped forward with a cigar for his master, and lit it for him. Irritated, Kate feigned a coughing fit, and Luther glanced at her through a cloud of smoke.

'You're in men's territory now,' he said in a mocking tone. 'And must abide by our rules – *my* rules. Like it or not, Kathryn, I control your life.'

Kate lifted her chin, trying to look unconcerned at his words and their deeper meaning. She glanced at her brother for support, but his face was averted. He had deserted her. Beneath her table napkin, her hands were shaking.

'Will you please get on with it, Luther,' she said in a subdued voice. 'I've a bad headache, and wish to retire.'

'Very well.'

With a brief wave of a hand, he dismissed the servants from the room. Kate was relieved to see Chivers leave, but caught the sly glance the man directed at Luther. He'd probably loiter outside, eavesdropping.

As the dining-room doors closed, Luther poured himself a glass of port, then passed the decanter to Evan. Kate noted with annoyance that obviously she wasn't expected to partake.

Her stepfather pushed his chair away from the head of the table, leaned back and crossed his legs.

'Evan,' he began. 'I'm pleased to tell you that the board of directors have decided that you've earned the reward of advancement. As from next week you'll act as assistant buyer to Mr Grimby, with a salary commensurate to the position.'

Evan sat forward, looking astounded. 'Do you mean it?' And then he frowned. 'This isn't some twisted joke, is it, Luther?'

Luther looked pained. 'It's the board's decision, I assure you, and I agree with it. Now, do you accept the position?'

54

'Yes, of course.'

'Oh, Evan!' Kate exclaimed, delighted for him. 'That's splendid, isn't it?'

'There, you see, both of you,' Luther went on with a mocking smile. 'I'm not the ogre you'd make of me.'

Kate wouldn't return the smile. Luther had done the right thing for once, but that couldn't make her like him one iota. Pleased though she was for Evan's piece of good fortune, she couldn't see how it might affect her, and rose to leave.

'I haven't finished, Kathryn,' Luther said quickly. 'Sit down.'

Kate sat, her stomach churning with dread.

'I've decided the business needs new blood,' Luther announced, surprising her. 'I've invited my nephew from Bath to join the family firm as department manager . . . initially.'

'But there's no vacancy,' Evan remarked.

'On the contrary, Evan. Household furnishings needs a new manager now you're risen in the ranks. My nephew will take over there.'

'But has he any experience in the retailing trade?' Evan insisted. 'We can't have just anyone dealing with important clientèle. Our reputation—'

'Simon Creswell, my eldest sister's son,' Luther intoned sharply, 'is a young man of ample ability and impeccable manners. I've every confidence in him.' His expression turned suddenly bitter. 'Despite the fact that his father was a ne'er-do-well, a man of no consequence.'

His eyes gleamed as he looked at Evan before going on with deliberate heaviness. 'My unfortunate sister made a wretchedly low marriage and it was the ruin of her. A warning to us all, eh, Evan?'

Kate was astonished and perplexed to see her brother flush

deeply, and turn an angry glance on his stepfather, but he said nothing.

'However,' Luther went on, 'Simon has risen above his inferior paternal lineage, and I'm inclined to help him. He arrives in Swansea the day after tomorrow, and will take up residence here at Old Grove House.'

'Live here?' Kate exclaimed, outraged at the idea that they were to be saddled with another of Luther's creatures, for that was what this Simon Creswell certainly must be, and she was ready to despise him for it. 'I strongly object to a complete stranger intruding in my father's house.'

Luther looked angry. 'I remind you, Kathryn, Old Grove House, and everything in it, belongs to me, willed to me by your mother.'

Kate fumed in her helplessness. She looked towards Evan, but he was reaching for the port decanter again. Had Luther already robbed him of his spirit?

'Well, Evan,' Kate demanded, her voice rising, 'have you no objection to this nepotistical interloper invading our home?'

Evan slanted another glance at Luther. 'This is business, Kate,' he murmured. 'And after all, Creswell's a relative, of sorts.'

'Stuff and nonsense!' Kate cried angrily. 'He's no kin of *our* family, and he's being foisted on us. It's a trick of some kind.' She jumped up from the table, furious. 'The same kind of dirty trick that sent Mansel packing,' she cried out miserably. 'And ruined my life.'

Luther half rose from his chair, his face paling with rage, then he sat down again, obviously striving for control.

'You're overwrought, girl,' he said tightly. 'You don't learn your lesson easily, do you? Would you like another term of imprisonment?'

Kate swallowed hard, afraid to speak.

'Be glad of Simon's imminent arrival, then,' he said darkly. 'Otherwise you'd remain in your room until the madness subsides. Next time it'll be for a much longer period, believe me.'

'I'm going to live with my brother in Fforestfach,' Kate cried out. 'You've no dominion over me any longer.'

Startled looks passed between the two men; surprise on Luther's face, panic on Evan's.

'It's not possible, Kate,' Evan said haltingly, avoiding looking at her. 'For reasons which I'm not prepared to discuss. You must stay at Old Grove House, where you belong.'

Luther's narrow smile was jubilant at her stunned reaction. 'My dominion, it seems, really *is* inescapable, Kathryn,' he said. 'I suggest you resign yourself to it.'

Kate was so crushed by Evan's rejection she could find no words to reply to Luther's barb.

'I've an important board meeting on the day Simon arrives,' he went on in tones that brooked no disobedience, 'and won't be here to welcome him. You'll do so in my place, Kathryn.'

Kate found her voice at last. 'He'll get no welcome from me,' she cried defiantly. 'I'll have nothing to do with your bloodsucking relatives.'

'Silence your unruly tongue!' Luther crashed a fist on the table. 'Get to your room, and stay there, otherwise I'll be forced to take more drastic action, such as having you committed to a madhouse.'

5

The snow gusted, flakes fluttering against the train's windows like torn tissue paper. It lay quite thick, but the snow and the darkening December afternoon couldn't hide the bleak landscape of heavy industry that stretched along the railway approach into Swansea.

As the train rattled over the viaduct, Simon Creswell craned his neck to see what lay below: row upon row of dismal little houses crammed together in a maze of mean little streets. It looked so depressing, and he felt a shaft of longing for the beauty of the countryside he'd left behind.

He pictured his mother, Mary, in the new, comfortable house her brother Luther had suddenly seen fit to provide for her, with sufficient funds, servants and even a carriage, and his lips tightened with anger. After all the years she'd suffered humiliating poverty, when Luther's wealth might have helped her, it was only now that he'd deigned to come to her rescue. Why was his uncle so suddenly eager to take his nephew under his wing?

Simon slipped his hand into the inside pocket of his coat, fingering the last letter his uncle had sent him. In it Luther's attitude was unmistakably threatening. Mary Creswell would continue to enjoy her new comfortable living only so long as Simon fulfilled Luther's expectations of him, did as his uncle commanded and remained unremittingly loyal.

What was the treacherous old goat up to?

As the train puffed and sighed its way into the station, Simon reached for his two Gladstone bags containing all his worldly possessions.

At least he had the prospect of a job, though working in a shop hardly appealed to him. Still, it was a step in the right direction. In a thriving town like Swansea there would be plenty of opportunity to better himself. He'd take what his uncle offered, bow to his wishes for now to ensure his mother's comfort, but Luther could whistle for loyalty. That commodity had to be earned.

He walked up the long stretch of platform towards the single-storey station building, feeling the cold strike through the thinness of his second-hand overcoat. The front of the railway station gave out on to a busy junction in the High Street. Outside in the swirling snow hackney cabs, as well as private carriages, traps and gigs, were drawn up waiting for train passengers.

Simon hung back, letting the surging crowd thin out. Eventually, a stocky man with a weather-beaten face approached him cautiously.

'Mr Simon Creswell, sir?'

'Yes, that's me.'

'I'm Trott, sir, Mr Templar's groom.' He took the bags then pointed along the street. 'This way, if you please, sir.'

Simon was glad to get in to the comparative warmth of the enclosed carriage, and draw the rug over his legs. He expected a long drive to Old Grove House, but within thirty minutes or so they arrived at their destination.

Simon stepped down from the carriage at the entrance of a large house with a pillared portico. The darkness and blizzard hid much, but Simon was thankful to see the front doors thrown open and light spilling out through the doorway. Eager to be out of the cold, he strode up smartly into the great domed hallway.

He expected to see Luther there to welcome him, but instead a tall, heavily boned man stepped forward with an apologetic cough.

'I'm Chivers, the butler, sir. Allow me.'

He reached for Simon's overcoat and eased it from his shoulders.

'The master regrets his absence, sir. He's detained at the shop,' the man went on in strange, hissing tones. 'I apologise no one's here to welcome you. Miss Kate was supposed to be here, but the young lady appears to be . . . absent also. I do beg your pardon, sir.'

'It's of no consequence, I assure you,' Simon said, a bit overwhelmed at the man's formality.

Chivers snapped his fingers and as if from nowhere a young footman appeared.

'This is Watkins, sir. He'll show you to your room and run a bath. Will you require Watkins to help you dress, sir?'

Simon shook his head vehemently. 'No, thank you. I can manage.'

'Very good, sir,' Chivers hissed. 'Dinner's at eight, but Mrs Trobert will provide a snack, which can be brought to your room after your bath, sir, if that's satisfactory.'

Simon readily agreed that it was, and then followed the footman up the wide staircase, along the gallery overlooking the hall and down a side corridor. He wasn't used to all this bowing and scraping, and felt decidedly uncomfortable.

He was amazed to find that his 'room' was in fact two rooms, a bedroom and a spacious sitting-room, with a fire blazing in the grate. What unexpected luxury. His uncle lived like a king.

The footman was about to open the Gladstone bags.

'I'll see to those,' Simon said quickly. Suddenly he was ashamed of his threadbare belongings.

'Very good, sir,' the young footman said. 'I'll run your bath. Bathroom's two doors down.'

After the hot bath Simon felt pleasantly relaxed. He sat wrapped in his old dressing-gown before his fire, waiting for his snack, feeling bemused. He could hardly believe his uncle meant him to live in such comfort.

He looked about the room: the solid mahogany furniture, the thick pile carpet, the rich brocade window drapes. Such lavishness and style. Suddenly, he was uneasy again, remembering the letter. Knowing Uncle Luther as he did, he realised, with a sinking heart, that all this must come with a very high price to pay indeed. And if he refused to pay it, he had no doubt Luther would see to it that his poor mother suffered.

Kate was determined not to go down to dinner and welcome Simon Creswell into the house, despite Luther's threats of reprisals. Let him do his worst!

She was startled when a brisk knock came at her door and Ethel came in.

'Which dress shall I lay out this evening, Miss Kate?'

'I didn't ring for you,' Kate said.

Ethel looked apologetic. 'Master's instructions, Miss Kate. He says you *will* come down to dinner. He's very angry, so Chivers says, because you weren't there to welcome the new young gentleman.'

Furious, Kate walked to the dressing-table and sat. 'He's no gentleman. He's a bloodsucking crony, after what he can get.'

Ethel looked startled. 'He looks quite respectable to me, Miss Kate, except . . .'

Kate pounced. 'Yes, yes! Go on! Except what?'

'Well,' Ethel said warily. 'I noticed when I showed him into the drawing-room just now that, although he tried to hide them, the cuffs of his shirt are badly frayed, and the leather of his boots look very cracked and worn.'

'Boots!' Kate hooted, and tossed her head. 'He sounds a coarse fellow to me.'

'Oh, no, Miss Kate,' Ethel blurted with enthusiasm. 'Mr Creswell is quite . . .' The maid flushed and looked down at her shoes.

'Well?' Kate demanded.

'Mr Creswell's quite a handsome young gentleman.'

'Oh, you stupid girl,' Kate exclaimed crossly, really put out at the news. 'You'd think a cobra was handsome.' But her curiosity was piqued. 'I'll wear the russet silk tonight.'

That colour made her look older and more mature, she decided. She'd show this intruder she was no naïve and brainless girl to be hoodwinked by a man's looks. And no man could match Mansel in that way.

Her heart flipped in her breast at the thought of her lost love. So many weeks had gone by and no news. But she wasn't ready to give up hope yet. Mansel must come back to her.

Kate squared her shoulders and lifted her chin high before walking into the drawing-room. She was relieved to see Evan was already there with a tall young man in old-fash-ioned-looking evening dress. They were sipping sherry, and talking far too amicably, Kate thought with annoyance. She frowned disapproval as her brother turned at her en-trance.

'Ah! Kate.' He stepped towards her and took her arm to draw her forward. She held her shoulders stiff, and tried to look as haughty as possible. 'This is Simon Creswell, dear. Simon this is my sister, Kathryn. We call her Kate.'

Kate could do nothing but offer her hand. It was grasped securely but briefly.

'Only my friends call me Kate,' she said without smiling. 'And people whom I admire, therefore I'd prefer that Mr Creswell refer to me as Miss Vaughan.'

'I wouldn't have it any other way, Miss Vaughan.'

His firm tones, though deep, were softened by a slight West Country burr. Kate looked up closely at him for the first time, and was disconcerted.

He was taller than she'd first realised, and although there was a half-starved, gaunt look about him, he cut a very impressive figure, even in his outdated clothes. Long straight nose, carved lips; a firm chin that spoke of a strong will, and plentiful brown hair, a lock of which fell over his brow.

'Simon was just telling me something of his life in Bath,' Evan said pleasantly. His hand was still on her arm, and he squeezed it gently, as though in reproof.

'Oh, really,' Kate replied, her tone conveying her utter disinterest. Evan might be ready to welcome Luther's scrounging nephew into their home, but she'd not give him one inch.

'Can I get you a glass of sherry, Miss Vaughan?'

She flashed him a furious glance, and was annoyed to see his large brown eyes showed as much disinterest as her own.

'No, thank you,' she said smartly, and whirled away in a rustle of silk to sit near the fireplace where a log fire burned.

What insolence! Offering her sherry as though she were the outsider; as though he belonged here. She watched him from the corner of her eye, but he turned his back on her, which made her fume.

'Luther tells me we may have the pleasure of your mother's

company at Old Grove House this Christmas-time,' Evan remarked to Simon.

Kate sat forward with a start. Did her stepfather intend to bring the whole sorry Templar clan down upon them?

'I think not,' Simon said. 'My mother's seventy-one and quite frail now. The journey from Bath would be too much for her.'

'I'm sorry to hear it,' Evan replied. 'We'd have liked to meet Mrs Creswell. Isn't that so, Kate?'

He seemed determined to bring her into their conversation. Behind Simon's back, she glared at her brother, yet was curious about the great age difference between Mrs Creswell and Luther, and anyway, Simon Creswell's indifference irked her.

'There's great difference in their ages,' she ventured to remark.

Simon turned to her immediately as though he'd just been waiting for her to speak. 'My mother was the first of ten children,' he explained, 'while Uncle Luther was the last. She was already married before he was born.'

'They're virtual strangers, then,' she said, wondering at the strangeness of such a family.

'Indeed,' he said sadly. 'That's often the way. I, myself, am the youngest of seven children. All passed on now, some before I was born. It's just Mother and myself.'

'She's had a very sad life, then,' Evan remarked. 'To outlive one's children must be the greatest tragedy.'

Simon nodded. 'And she bore it all alone, without family support. There was a rift between my mother and her parents, unfortunately, perpetuated by my Uncle Luther in his turn, until very recently.' He hesitated. 'Not to put too fine a point on it, she was cast out by her family.'

Kate lifted her brows, shocked.

'Oh, not for any impropriety, I assure you, Miss Vaughan,' Simon told her hurriedly. 'She married beneath her, as the saying goes. But she and my father loved each other very much, and were very happy while he lived, even though humblingly poor.'

Kate stared at him in astonishment. He was being very frank; indeed, one might almost say indiscreet.

'Though she was widowed comparatively young,' he went on, gazing at her candidly, 'her family, that is Uncle Luther, wouldn't help her.'

There was unmistakable bitterness in his tone, and Kate caught a fleeting flash of emotion in his eyes. He resents his Uncle Luther, she realised with sudden insight. But that didn't mean he's not in cahoots with him. Thieves often fall out.

At that moment Luther came into the room and strode towards his nephew with an outstretched hand.

'Ah! Simon,' he said in a jocular tone which Kate found jarring, and she stared at him. She could almost believe he was sincere, except she knew him too well. 'I'm glad to see you're making yourself at home. Sorry I wasn't here when you arrived.'

The two men shook hands. Kate studied Simon carefully, but the emotion, clearly visible earlier, was now hidden, his face impassive.

Chivers appeared, announcing dinner was served. Luther strode towards the dining-room, chatting to Simon walking at his side. With a crooked smile at her, Evan gave Kate his arm, and they strolled in behind.

'Do make an effort to be pleasant during dinner, Kate,' he muttered in a low voice. 'For all our sakes. If you can't be pleasant, be quiet.'

Kate had no option but to be quiet as the meal progressed while the men spoke of business, Luther explaining the intricacies of running a successful department store such as Vaughan & Templar. There was eagerness in Simon's face, and he hung on every word spoken by Evan or his uncle, interposing his own questions from time to time.

Kate had difficulty in stifling a yawn at one point, and immediately Simon turned to her.

'And what part do you play in this business empire, Miss Vaughan?'

Kate folded her lips and glared at him, but before she could utter a word, Luther spoke for her.

'Young women of Kathryn's position and breeding can have no place in business,' Luther said. 'I fear they don't have the necessary mental power for such complex matters. No, she's far more suited to her music and watercolouring.'

Kate scowled at her stepfather's deprecating tone.

'I paint myself,' Simon exclaimed, his face brightening as he looked at her. 'Though I favour oils on canvas . . . when I can afford them.'

He smiled suddenly, and she felt the brilliance of it hit her like an unexpected sunbeam, and was momentarily confused. Obviously, Simon Creswell could turn on the charm like a tap.

After that there was a lull in conversation, which seemed to make Luther restless.

'Kathryn,' he exclaimed. 'Old Grove House is becoming far too gloomy of late. We must liven things up for Simon's sake. Do ask Cecille to join us for dinner one evening this week.' He turned to Simon. 'Miss Villiers is entrancing and entertaining. You'll like her. Utterly brainless, of course, but she's sole heir to a brewery fortune.'

Kate was outraged, and rose to her feet, causing the three

67

men to stare at her, and Simon rose, too, clutching awkwardly at his table napkin.

'You barred Cecille from this house for weeks,' Kate cried angrily. 'Now, suddenly, she is permitted for Mr Creswell's entertainment. That's despicable! I, your stepdaughter, was allowed no concessions during my imprisonment.'

'Imprisonment?' Simon glanced around the table, perplexed.

'I doubt Cecille's speaking to me, let alone willing to come to dinner,' Kate went on, 'after the vile way she's been treated, and I can't blame her.'

Luther's face whitened, but obviously he was keeping his anger under control. 'You must excuse Kathryn, Simon,' he said stiffly. 'She's very highly strung, and has been quite ill recently, unable to leave her room.'

'I was locked in for weeks!' Kate blurted. 'Deliberately deprived of my freedom because my stepfather fears a reunion with my aunt—'

'Be quiet!' Luther thundered, rising to his feet. 'And sit down, Kathryn. I'll not allow this outrageous and unladylike behaviour any longer. If you persist, you'll be returned to your room forcibly.'

His eyes glittered dangerously and Kate knew she risked further detainment. That would be too, too shaming in front of the likes of Simon Creswell. Mustering as much dignity as possible under the circumstances, she sat down without another word.

'That's better,' Luther said, and seated himself. 'I apologise for my stepdaughter, Simon.'

Kate opened her mouth to protest but instantly thought better of it. She intended to keep a close eye on Simon Creswell and couldn't do that from behind a locked door.

The meal thankfully over, Kathryn rose to leave the men to their port, but Luther stayed her.

'One moment, Kathryn, I have an announcement.' He waved her to be seated again. 'I think it very fitting that a centenary ball be held at Old Grove House on the last day of the year.'

Kate gasped, hardly able to believe her ears, and Evan looked astounded, too.

'But the last day of the old century falls on a Sunday,' she said incredulously. 'No one will attend a ball on the Sabbath. We'll be a laughing-stock.'

'The occasion will be grand enough to ensure eager acceptance,' Luther replied confidently. 'With the twentieth century upon us, people are less hidebound by convention.'

Kate wasn't convinced, but saw it would be no use to protest further.

'We've not held such an event since before my father's death,' Evan remarked. 'It'll take a great deal of organisation. The ballroom annexe hasn't been used for some time and must surely need a great deal of refurbishing. Is there time?'

'I planned this months ago,' Luther went on rather smugly. 'All preparations are in hand. Invitations will go out to the cream of Swansea society tomorrow.'

'But I've no gown . . .' Kate began, then checked herself.

While she was disturbed that Luther was set on holding the celebrations on a Sunday, she had to admit to a high degree of excitement at the thought of a centenary ball.

Luther's smile was indulgent, yet it made Kate shiver.

'I'm sure Mrs Trobert can be persuaded to accompany you on the train as far as Cardiff, Kathryn, to visit a fashionable couturier. I want my stepdaughter to be the belle of the ball.'

Kate could only stare at him open-mouthed and speechless.

She was certain in her bones that Luther was play-acting. Was it for Simon Creswell's benefit, or was there a deeper, hidden motive in all this false bonhomie?

'You've taken us completely by surprise,' Evan said, voicing Kate's thoughts. There was a certain strained look about her brother's face which she didn't understand.

Luther turned to Simon. 'Is there a friend you'd like to invite to the celebrations?' he asked his nephew. 'Someone from home, perhaps?'

Simon appeared taken aback, as though he hadn't expected to be included.

'Well, there's one great friend of mine,' he replied after a moment. 'His name's Bertram Harrington. He's young, but already is a painter of extraordinary talent and promise. In my humble opinion he'll surpass Turner in time.'

'Tish! And pooh!' Kate exclaimed disparagingly. 'Turner is unsurpassable.'

Simon paused and glanced at her. 'We must discuss the matter at greater length on a more suitable occasion, Miss Vaughan.' She saw he looked quite serious about it.

'But why wait until the New Year?' Luther interposed. 'Why don't you invite Mr Harrington to Old Grove House for Christmas?'

'Oh, yes, do!' Kate cried scathingly. 'Invite the butcher, the baker and the candlestick-maker as well.' She threw up her hands in disgust. 'Let it be open house for all and sundry.'

'Kathryn!'

She stood up defiantly and, after a haughty glance around the table, marched out of the room.

Certain Luther was plotting a marriage between Simon Creswell and Cecille, Kate breezed into the morning-room early the next day, intent on sending a warning letter to her friend. She was annoyed to find Simon already at the bureau, pen in hand. Disconcerted, she turned on her heel and was about to walk out again when he spoke.

'Good morning, Miss Vaughan.'

Kate teetered on her toes, half inclined to leave anyway without reply, but her sense of good manners overcame her impulse.

'Morning,' she replied grudgingly. There was no sense in leaving now they'd spoken. She sauntered further into the room to look through the window.

'Heavy fall in the night,' he remarked pleasantly, half turning in his seat to glance at her. 'I believe we'll see a white Christmas.'

Kate remained silent, but after a moment ventured a glance at him. He'd returned to his letter-writing, ignoring her. Peeved, she lifted her chin.

'You're sending Mr Harrington an invitation already, I suppose?' She sniffed disparagingly. 'No time wasted, I see.'

'Actually,' Simon said evenly, 'I'm writing to my mother. She worries about me – her one remaining child.'

Kate was confused for a moment, noting the unmistakable tenderness in his voice when speaking of his mother, but brushed the feeling aside impatiently.

'She'll be pleased to learn you've fallen on your feet,' she said scornfully. 'Gracious living, and not a farthing spent on it.'

Simon put his pen down and turned in his seat, gazing at her, annoyance in his brown eyes.

'I'm not here for charity, Miss Vaughan,' he said bitingly. 'I'm here to work, to earn my crust of bread.'

'Oh, really?'

'Now, if you'll excuse me,' he went on, 'I'll get on with my letter-writing.'

He turned his back, and, seething, Kate rose and began to pace the room. How dare he take that tone with her?

'Why *did* you come here, Mr Creswell?' she asked pithily. 'What're you after?' She tossed her head. 'Stand up and face me!'

With an angry grunt, he threw down his pen, ink spots scattering on the sheet of paper on the blotter, the letter to his mother. He stood up, tall and straight, then took a few steps forwards, facing her squarely.

'Damnation! Miss Vaughan, you do try a man's patience.' Red patches were colouring his cheeks. 'I'm here to work, honest work.'

Kate lifted her chin in a show of arrogance, although now he was towering over her she wasn't so sure of herself.

'I think you've come to Swansea looking for a rich wife,' she said. 'You and my stepfather are scheming between you.'

'What?'

She wasn't hoodwinked by his look of incredulity. 'You plan to snare Cecille Villiers into marriage,' she rushed on. 'Gain control of Villiers Brewery fortune, not to mention their coalmine at Neath. Don't bother to deny it.'

'That's the most outrageous thing I've ever heard,' Simon growled. There was no softness in his brown eyes now. They were cold and hard like the ground in winter. 'I am grossly insulted.'

'You won't entrap her, you know,' Kate warned. 'Her father sends fortune-hunters packing every day.' She shook her head. 'There's nothing here for you. Go back where you came from.'

Simon remained silent for a moment, though his jaw worked as though he were striving to control an impulse.

'If I'd known Miss Kathryn Vaughan had such vile manners, I'd have thought twice about coming here.'

Kate spluttered an incoherent protest, but Simon talked her down.

'It's none of your business, Miss Vaughan,' he interrupted loudly, 'but Miss Villiers doesn't figure in my future plans.'

Kate stared boldly into his blazing eyes, unwilling to concede defeat.

'Well, it's no good setting your sights on me, Mr Creswell,' she said, her voice rising, more out of chagrin than anything. 'My stepfather must've already warned you. I'm bad stock; tainted blood. I can marry no man.'

6

‘Have nothing to do with Simon Creswell,’ Kate advised
Cecille when she next called. ‘He’s an adventurer and oppor-
tunist.’

They were in Kate’s small sitting-room at the top of the
stairs, taking afternoon tea.

‘Oh, do you really think so?’ Cecille’s eyes sparkled. ‘He
sounds exciting after all. I was beginning to think he’s a cold
fish. He looked right through me at dinner last night.’ She
pouted. ‘And I looked ravishing. Mr Templar said so.’

Kate bit back a caustic retort just as Ethel came into the
room.

‘Beg pardon, Miss Kate,’ she said. ‘I thought you’d want to
know that the guests have arrived.’

‘What guests?’ Kate put down her teacup, frowning.

‘Mr Creswell’s party. They sent one of them telegraph
things this morning. Trott’s just brought them from the railway station.’

‘Why tell me?’

Ethel twisted her hands together, looking uncertain.
‘There’s no one else to receive them,’ she said. ‘Mr Chivers
said I was to fetch you, you being the lady of the house, so to
speak.’

‘Let’s go down and see them,’ Cecille suggested, jumping
up. ‘I’m pining for the sight of new faces.’

'Certainly not!' Kate sniffed stubbornly. 'They're nothing to do with me. They can wait until Mr Creswell gets home.' She lifted a hand airily. 'Serve them tea or whisky, or whatever they want.'

Ethel wetted her lips. 'The lady looks fair done in,' she remarked. 'She asked for water, and wondered if she could go to her room to rest.'

'Lady?' Kate rose to her feet. 'How old is she?' Surely Simon's mother hadn't turned up after all? 'Who are these people, Ethel?'

'A Mr Harrington and his sister.' She frowned. 'They've arrived with masses of baggage, Miss Kate, masses. Trott had to make two trips to fetch it all.'

'He's brought his sister to sponge on us, too?' Kate exclaimed. 'What impertinence!'

'Who are they?' Cecille was quivering with interest.

'Simon Creswell's cronies,' Kate said disparagingly. 'Scroungers and reprobates, probably, descending on us for Christmas like a pack of vultures. What's my stepfather thinking of?'

Ethel was still fidgeting in the doorway.

'Oh, very well,' Kate agreed. 'I'll deal with them.'

She went downstairs, with Cecille and Ethel hot on her heels. The maid hadn't exaggerated about the luggage. Four or five large portmanteaus were stacked in the hall, with some trunks and suitcases.

'Good heavens!' Cecille exclaimed. 'How long did you say they were staying?'

Kate's mouth tightened as she viewed the baggage. 'I'm beginning to wonder myself.'

'They're in the drawing-room, Miss Kate.'

Squaring her shoulders, Kate opened the door and strode

in. Two people were sitting before the fire. The man rose quickly at Kate's entrance and stepped forward.

'Mr Harrington,' she began strongly, determined to be firm. 'I'm afraid Mr Creswell's . . .'

Words died on her lips and she could only blink, spellbound.

Bertram Harrington was of medium height and slight build, but Kate saw only the elegant beauty and sensitivity of his features, and his vivid eyes. Golden hair was swept back from his forehead and fell gracefully to his shoulders.

He gazed back at her expectantly, his eyes the colour of violets, and she still couldn't find her tongue. She didn't need anyone to tell her that here was a true artist.

'I'm afraid you have me at a disadvantage,' he said, his tone soft and cultured. 'I expected to see Simon.'

Kate swallowed her confusion, and tried not to stammer. 'He's still at business.'

She collected her wits, not knowing why she felt so bowled over, except that she'd never seen such beauty in a man before.

'I'm Kathryn Vaughan . . . Kate,' she said, and smiled at him. 'Mr Creswell's uncle, Luther Templar, is my stepfather. I do apologise for neglecting you. Mr Creswell didn't warn . . . I mean, he didn't tell me you were due to arrive.'

'He didn't know,' Bertram Harrington said quickly. 'We made up our minds to come on the spur of the moment. I hope our arrival hasn't inconvenienced you. We did telegraph ahead.'

'Oh, no!' Kate exclaimed enthusiastically. 'No inconvenience at all!' She beamed at him, feeling breathless. 'Your rooms are being made ready as we speak.'

Kate fluttered a hand at Ethel who darted away.

'Meanwhile, make yourselves comfortable,' she rushed on, her gaze riveted on Bertram Harrington's face. 'What am I thinking of? You must be famished. A meal will be served immediately.'

She hurried to the bell rope to summon Ethel again.

'If there's anything at all you need . . .'

Kate dragged her gaze away from him to glance at the woman still seated at the fire, a large black hat obscuring her face.

'Is your sister ill, Mr Harrington?'

Bertram Harrington lifted a hand towards the woman, his voice coaxing. 'Delphine, you must be warmer now. Come and meet our hostess. Miss Vaughan, this is my twin sister, Delphine.'

Delphine Harrington rose, turned towards them and swept off the hat. Golden curls framed her face, silken tresses falling around her shoulders. She was an arrestingly beautiful young woman, her features identical with her brother's.

No, not quite identical, Kate realised, yet couldn't grasp what the difference was. Gazing from one to the other in awe she had to admit she'd never seen such a striking couple.

Delphine moved forward gracefully, a smile curving her lovely mouth, hand outstretched.

'It's an honour to meet you,' she said, in the same cultured tones as her brother. 'Simon didn't say we'd be in such charming company as yourself.'

Kate took the outstretched hand. To her surprise Delphine leaned forward and kissed her cheek lightly as though they were old friends.

'My dear Kate . . . may I call you Kate?' Delphine said in a musical voice. 'It's so gracious of you to extend your generous hospitality to us at this happy season. I know in my heart we'll be the greatest of friends from now on.'

Bemused by Delphine's almost studied words, Kate was suddenly aware of Cecille bobbing impatiently at her side, and remembered her manners to make introductions.

Watkins came into the room and stood expectantly at the open door.

'You rang, Miss Kate?'

Kate asked him to put another log on the fire, and gave instructions for a meal to be prepared for the guests, to be served in the drawing-room where it was warmest.

'Please be seated,' Kate suggested when Watkins had gone. 'You must both be tired after your chilly journey.'

Everyone moved to sit near the fire again where the new log crackled, Cecille manoeuvring herself so that she remained close to Bertram Harrington. Kate viewed her friend's tactics with irritation.

'Have you known Simon Creswell long?' Delphine asked her.

'No. Hardly any time really,' Kate replied distractedly, watching Bertram and Cecille from the corner of her eye. It was then something registered, and she turned to Delphine in concern.

'You're in mourning,' she said, vexed that she hadn't realised before. 'I'm so sorry for your loss. Was it someone close?'

Delphine lifted a lace handkerchief to her mouth and lowered her head.

'Our benefactor, Sir Edwin Blaney,' Bertram answered for her. 'My sister and I were orphaned quite young, you see. Sir Edwin, a distant relative, took us in. His death some months ago is a great loss to us.'

Delphine uttered a little moan.

'Would you like a little brandy, Miss Harrington?' Kate asked solicitously.

Delphine grasped Kate's hand tightly. 'Please, Kate, call me Delphine,' she said, with a little catch in her voice. 'I feel we've so much in common. Besides, Christmas is almost upon us. It's a time to be gay and put aside sad memories. Don't you agree?'

Kate's answering smile was weak. She thought of Mansel. She might as well face the fact that he was out of reach now, probably for ever. He'd left so quickly; been discouraged so easily. Obviously his love for her wasn't strong enough to withstand the misfortune that had come to her.

She flicked a covert glance at Bertram and felt drawn to him. Luther's terrible revelation, if true, must condemn her to spinsterhood, but she wouldn't go into decline. Good friendships were still possible.

They chatted until the meal and a bottle of wine were brought. Kate and Cecille then left to give them some privacy.

'When you're ready,' she said from the doorway, 'just ring for Watkins. He'll show you to your rooms. Dinner's at eight. Simon Cres . . . er . . . Simon will be here then to welcome you, and you'll meet my stepfather.'

In Kate's sitting-room Cecille was bubbling with excitement.

'Have you ever met a man so utterly attractive as Bertram Harrington?' she chortled. 'Oh, Kate, I think I'm in love already.'

'You're prattling like a silly shop-girl,' Kate said irritably. She still felt a little breathless herself. 'He's far too old for you, and far too sophisticated. He's an artist. You couldn't possibly understand him.'

'Oh, and you can, I suppose!' Cecille retorted, tossing her head.

'Don't be silly,' Kate said sharply. 'I've just met him.'

'He's so beautiful, though, isn't he,' Cecille sighed, relenting. 'I do hope he has some money of his own, otherwise my father will never allow him as my suitor.'

Put out, Kate sniffed. 'You're a little previous, Cecille,' she said stiffly. 'I don't believe Bertram's interested in you at all.'

'Sour grapes!' Cecille laughed. 'Actually he remarked that my hair was extraordinary, so there.'

Determined not to be vexed, Kate said, 'What do you think of Delphine Harrington?'

Cecille frowned. 'I don't like her.'

'But that's absurd!' Kate said, but was thoughtful. 'I suppose she *is* a little theatrical in her speech and manners,' she conceded, though felt they were being uncharitable about someone they hardly knew. 'But that's probably just the way she was brought up.'

'Theatrical!' Cecille exclaimed disdainfully. 'She's positively melodramatic. I've never met a person so affected in her manner.'

'You're jealous!' Kate exclaimed with a laugh. 'Because she's so devastatingly beautiful.' She lifted her chin. 'Actually, I think she's quite charming, and we do have a lot in common, losing our parents at a young age.'

'You're only siding with her because she has such a handsome brother. But I saw him first.'

They looked at each other then and giggled.

'Did you notice her extraordinary eyes?' Cecille asked when the laughter had subsided.

'Well, of course. They're identical to Bertram's.'

'No,' Cecille said slowly. 'They're not. There's something missing . . .'

'What nonsense!' Kate said. Suddenly she wanted to change the subject. 'I'll go to Cardiff tomorrow,' she said firmly, 'and order the most exquisite gown for the ball.'

Cecille tossed her ginger head. 'My goodness! You've changed your tune all of a sudden. Not an hour ago you said you wouldn't be seen dead there.' She smiled mockingly. 'Besides, I thought you were still pining for Mansel?'

'Life goes on,' Kate said philosophically. 'One has to make the best of it. And each day brings new surprises.'

Kate was waiting in her sitting-room for the sound of Simon's tread on the staircase, and darted out to accost him as he walked along the gallery past the door.

'You might've had the good manners to tell me your guests were arriving this morning,' she called after him. 'We were completely unprepared. Mr Harrington must've felt unwelcome.'

Simon swung around, taking quick steps towards her.

'Bertram's here already?' He looked pleased. 'That's excellent. But I assure you, Miss Vaughan, I wasn't certain he'd even accept my invitation let alone arrive so promptly.'

'Their rooms weren't ready,' Kate went on archly. 'It was most embarrassing. Miss Harrington – Delphine – was quite exhausted by the journey, too.'

Simon stared at her, his mouth tightening, and the pleasure left his face. '*She*'s with him?' he asked harshly. 'Damnation!'

'I beg your pardon!' Kate exclaimed, taken aback by the suppressed fury in his voice. 'What've you got against Bertram's sister, for heaven's sake?'

The muscles in Simon's jaw worked for a moment before he

spoke, his tone harsh. 'One day Bertram will be recognised as a great painter,' he said. 'If Delphine doesn't destroy him first.'

'That's an outrageous and wicked thing to say,' Kate burst out, aghast at his words. She stared at the dark expression of his face, and then she was angry for Bertram's sake as well as Delphine's.

'What's the trouble?' she went on jeeringly. 'Has Delphine rejected you? Has she seen through that façade of sincerity you assume?'

'Huh! Think what you like,' Simon retorted. 'But, a word of advice, Miss Vaughan. Don't take Delphine at face value.'

'That's rich coming from you,' Kate hooted. 'A common fortune-hunter, out for what you can get.' She lifted her chin haughtily to show that she didn't value his advice, not one penny. 'It's plain that Delphine's a lady of good character and breeding, and I don't hesitate to give her my complete trust.'

'You don't know what you're talking about, you silly child,' Simon snapped. 'As usual,' he added.

'Oh!' Kate was furious at being talked down to. 'I've already warned Cecille against you,' she huffed. 'And as for Delphine, we're the best of friends already.'

His eyes narrowed. 'Careful, Miss Vaughan! Don't make that fatal slip others have made before you.'

With that retort he turned on his heel and strode off along the gallery. Kate glared after him, seething with fury that he'd had the last word. The man was impossible. How much longer must she put up with his odious company in her own home?

Kate ignored Simon's presence at the dining table, and wouldn't even look in his direction. To annoy him, she was as friendly and charming as possible to the Harringtons.

She'd expected to have Bertram all to herself, so was a little put out to find that Luther, without telling her, had invited Cecille to dine with them again that evening.

Later, she was glad of her friend's vapid chatter, for a heavy atmosphere hung over the table, fuelled, it seemed, by a tension between Simon and Delphine.

That beautiful young woman, having thrown off her mourning, was now radiant in a gown of shimmering blue, which set off her wonderful colouring. She chatted amicably and gaily with everyone, but pointedly ignored her brother's friend, much to Kate's enjoyment.

Simon ate sparsely, a morose expression on his face. He *was* a spurned suitor of Delphine's, Kate decided, and now held a grudge against her.

Delphine sat on Luther's left at the table, Bertram on his right. Luther was particularly attentive to the newcomers, his gaze hardly leaving Delphine's lovely face, and obviously found the pair as enchanting as Kate did herself.

She wished Evan had chosen to dine with them that night. He'd have found their company stimulating. She was very glad the Harringtons were at Old Grove House, and for the first time in a long while Kate looked forward to Christmas and the coming of the new century, despite the irritating presence of Simon Creswell.

Simon tapped at the study door, certain he knew why his uncle had sent for him at last.

'Ah! Come in, Simon, my boy,' Luther said. 'Sit down.'

Across the desk, Simon viewed his uncle with scepticism, not deceived by that affable tone. Ever since arriving at Old Grove House he'd been expecting a summons. Now, it seemed, Luther was ready to reveal his true reason for befriending him, the price he'd have to pay for his mother's rescue from poverty and her continued comfort. For her sake alone he must comply with whatever was asked of him.

'Your friends, the Harringtons, are most enchanting,' Luther began. 'People of quality, I would assume, by their high-toned manner.'

He leaned back in his chair, locking his fingers together before him as though about to address a board meeting. Simon felt a spark of irritation at such pomposity.

'In this changing society of ours, with such dangerous stirrings among the working classes,' Luther went on disdainfully, 'it's heartening to realise such gentility still flourishes within the realm, and will continue to do so for many generations.'

Simon resisted a smile at Luther's unconscious snobbery. A fanatical opponent of the burgeoning labour movement, he might have said criminal classes, for in Luther's eyes there was little difference. He was also fishing for information, but he wouldn't like what he'd hear.

'You're right, of course,' Simon agreed lightly. 'But they haven't any money. Not a bean. All squandered by their high-born father not long after they came into the world.'

Luther scowled, obviously understanding Simon's back-handed reference to his own father: low born but no worse than any man of quality.

'How do they live?' his uncle asked.

It was on the tip of Simon's tongue to say that they lived by Delphine's wits, but thought better of it. Luther saw himself as a good judge of character. Let him discover for himself her true nature.

'As you've pointed out,' Simon said, side-stepping a direct answer, 'they're an engaging pair. Because of that they attracted the attention of a distant cousin of their mother, Sir

Edwin Blaney. He provided them with every comfort and advantage, while he lived. Unfortunately, he neglected to provide for them in his will.'

Simon paused to cross his legs, covertly watching his uncle's expression as he did so. Was he already under Delphine's spell? God help him if he was.

'It's difficult for a struggling painter to live by his art, no matter now brilliant his talent,' Simon went on. 'So they're again in straitened circumstances.'

'How unfortunate,' Luther said thoughtfully. 'I do loathe to see fine people brought down through no fault of their own.'

Simon's teeth clenched involuntarily, and his blood began to heat at the thought of his mother's suffering. He was on the point of an angry outburst, and damn the consequences, when Luther spoke again.

'If you've any serious intentions towards Miss Delphine Harrington,' he said, 'I insist you abandon them.'

Simon blinked, surprise dispersing his anger. 'I've no such intentions,' he replied.

Luther looked stern, and his tone was harsh. 'Do you swear it, Simon, on your mother's life?'

Furious, Simon leaped to his feet. 'Damn you, Luther!' he shouted. 'I'll swear by no such thing. And what do you mean by that tasteless remark?'

Impatiently, Luther gestured him to be seated again. 'You're far too sensitive,' he said. 'I merely want your assurance that you don't see Miss Harrington as a future wife.'

This was no idle enquiry, Simon now sensed, and, taking a deep breath to steady himself, sat down. Earlier, after his clash with Kate, he'd decided to keep his own counsel regarding Bertram's sister, but if this was Luther's way of warning off a rival, he was entitled to one caution. Let him take it if he would.

'Delphine is undoubtedly the most strikingly beautiful and alluring woman I've ever met,' Simon said seriously. 'But any man who lets her get her claws into him is a fool.' He stared hard at his uncle. 'I'm no fool, Luther. Remember that.'

'I see.' Luther looked amused at Simon's solemn tone. 'So, she *has* rejected you in the past.'

Simon said nothing. Let Luther, and Kate, too, believe what they would. He wouldn't betray Bertram's confidences. Whatever happened in the future it wouldn't be his fault, he told himself. And in any case, the Harringtons would be gone from Old Grove House after the New Year. No one need ever learn the truth about Delphine.

Simon stood up to take his leave. 'If that's all you need to know,' he said, 'I'll go to my room. I've letters to write.'

'I haven't even begun to tell you what I want of you,' Luther said sharply. 'Do you think you're here because of some meaningless act of kindness on my part?'

'Hardly that, Luther,' Simon replied, resuming his seat. 'Knowing you as I do.'

'Very well, then.'

Luther rose and moved to the fireplace to stand with his back to it. 'I'm going to make a rich man of you, Simon,' he said loftily. 'What do you say to that?'

Simon's smile was mirthless and bitter. 'I'm all for it,' he replied wryly. 'But what dirty deed must I do first?'

'None. You simply marry an heiress,' Luther stated bluntly.

Simon sat forward with a jerk. 'Oh, God! Not Cecille Villiers!' he exclaimed. 'Not that! I'd never stand the chatter.'

Luther was scornful. 'Now, ask yourself, Simon,' he said. 'How would such a marriage benefit *me*?' His smile was crooked. 'No, the bride I have in mind for you is my step-daughter, Kathryn.'

'Kate?' Simon couldn't stop himself laughing out loud at the ludicrous idea. 'She'd never agree. She despises me.'

'Kathryn's wishes are completely irrelevant,' Luther said harshly. 'Oh, she'll have a choice all right. She'll marry you or else spend the rest of her life in a lunatic asylum.'

Simon gave another laugh, but checked it abruptly, seeing the implacable expression on his uncle's face. 'You can't really mean that,' he said in disbelief. Not even Luther would do such an evil and cruel thing to a young girl.

'I mean it all right, and you know it,' Luther said firmly, his eyes glimmering with a fanatical light. 'I'll do what I must to acquire what should've been mine years ago.'

Abruptly he moved away from the fireplace to take agitated strides about the room.

'Kathryn's father, Russell Vaughan, was a dithering fool,' Luther declared with disdain. 'The family business was all but finished when I first arrived. I saw possibilities and seized opportunities.'

He came to stand beside Simon's chair, glaring down at him as though daring him to contradict.

'The business was saved by *my* efforts alone,' he said forcefully. 'My strength, my foresight and my acumen made it what it is today: a flourishing success.'

'I'm sure no one would deny it,' Simon said carefully. 'But I don't see what this has to do with my marrying Kate Vaughan.'

'It's the only way I can get what's mine.' He made a grasping gesture with his right hand, as though pulling something to him, his eyes glittering. 'Those fools on the board hold me back. I must have complete control.'

'But why must I marry Kate?'

'Russell promised on his death that I'd inherit his major

88

share, a fifty per cent holding,' Luther said tensely. 'Instead, he betrayed me. He willed his shares to his children, divided equally between them. They inherit when they reach the age of thirty or when they marry.'

'I see,' Simon said slowly. 'So, as her husband I somehow acquire Kate's shares.'

Luther smiled and nodded. 'You catch on quickly.'

Simon frowned. 'How do you propose I do that?'

'You'll think of something.' Luther smiled, but his eyes were cold, implacable. 'Women are weak vessels, Simon, easily mastered. You'll master Kathryn, or your mother suffers for your failure.'

'All right!' Simon said hastily. 'So, I obtain the shares.' He shrugged. 'What then?'

'Then you immediately sign them over to me,' Luther said. 'I already have Evan's.'

'How?'

'That's none of your business,' Luther snapped.

Simon leaned back in his chair and crossed his legs leisurely.

'Apart from saving my mother from the gutter,' Simon said bitterly, 'why should I do this? What benefit would the marriage be to me?'

'Kathryn's heir to a considerable fortune,' Luther said persuasively. 'I've no interest in her money. I've plenty of my own, more than enough. I want those shares. You can keep her money.'

Simon rubbed his thumb along his jaw, weighing up all the aspects. Such a marriage might free him and his mother from Luther's yoke. It was worth considering for that reason alone.

'And if I refuse?'

Luther shrugged, and strode back to his desk. 'You return immediately to your cold garret in Bath, scraping a living as best you can for the rest of your life,' he said. 'Meanwhile, your mother won't survive another winter without funds.'

Simon held on to his temper. This wasn't the time for being hot-headed. 'Little choice, then,' he commented tightly. 'But, tell me, what's to keep me from taking the money *and* the shares? Perhaps a seat on the board is also included. I might be tempted to renege. I could do you a lot of damage in the boardroom, if I had a mind to.'

Luther smiled. 'I'll take steps to prevent you going back on your word, legal steps. You won't like prison, Simon.'

Simon lifted a brow. 'You've thought of everything.'

'Oh, yes,' Luther said smugly. 'I've been planning this for some time.'

'There is a weakness in your scheme, Luther,' Simon remarked. 'The moment I propose to Kate, the cat'll be out of the bag. Everyone knows we don't get on. Surely, suspicions will be aroused.'

'I'm not a fool,' Luther snapped. 'There'll be no proposal. This is the purpose of the centenary ball. That night, before the assembled cream of Swansea society, I'll announced Kathryn's betrothal to you. *Fait accompli,* my dear nephew.'

'She'll deny it.'

'What? And make a laughing-stock of herself?' Luther shook his head. 'No. She has more pride. Besides, she may be very relieved to learn she can marry after all.'

Simon remembered Kate's strange remark about tainted blood. 'What do you mean?'

'It doesn't concern you,' Luther said dismissively. 'Now, do you agree to comply with my wishes, or will you and your mother return to the bitter cold of poverty?'

Simon rose to his feet. There was no other choice. But Luther was not the only one with plans. Marriage to Kate

Vaughan would place him in a very powerful position, despite what Luther said. There might yet to be way to outwit his uncle. He'd take revenge for his mother and all those years of neglect.

'I agree,' he said solemnly.

7

After dinner a few evenings later, Kate and Bertram were seated close together on the sofa at the furthest end of the drawing-room, deep in conversation.

Simon watched them covertly. They made a very handsome couple; the contrast of Kate's glossy dark head close to Bertram's golden mane was striking. Her hand lay on a cushion beside her and Bertram had surreptitiously covered it with his own.

Simon felt a shaft of jealousy lance through him. It took him by surprise. Yet, after all, he *was* destined to be her husband. But it was more than that. He admired her spirit and courage, and despite her open dislike of him, he sensed there was a deep well of love in her heart. They could be happy, if he could win her over.

His attention was distracted by Delphine's ringing laughter. Seated at the piano, she was singing softly to entertain Luther, standing close by, elbows on the piano, glass of whisky in one hand. His uncle's avid gaze didn't leave Delphine's face.

Serves him right if he gets burned, Simon thought with malice. He'd given Luther all the warning he intended to.

His uncle caught his glance.

'Simon,' Luther said, striding forward. 'I was just saying to Delphine, she and Bertram must visit the shop tomorrow. You can show them around. I'm sure they'll be impressed by the extent and quality of our wares. As good as anything they might see in London.'

Kate rose from the sofa. 'Oh, a visit to the shop would be wonderful,' she exclaimed excitedly, beaming at Bertram. 'I've often wanted to view the place, but have never been allowed.' She glanced at Luther. 'For some reason my stepfather believes it is inappropriate for young female members of his family to be seen on the premises.'

Luther's mouth tightened. 'And I'm afraid you won't be accompanying them on this occasion, either, Kathryn. I don't approve and I have no intention of explaining my reasons.'

Kate felt crushed and humiliated before their guests.

Delphine rose from the piano stool, stepping to Luther's side. She leaned close, placing a hand on the lapel of his evening jacket, and looked up into his face.

'Oh, surely, Luther, Kate can come with us?' she said softly and persuasively. 'I won't enjoy it without her. Oh, please, say she may.'

Luther's implacable expression wavered at her touch, and uncertainty and confusion passed briefly across his face, but he collected himself quickly, and smiled down at her.

'My dear Delphine, of course Kathryn can go, if you wish it. Perhaps I'm overprotective of her. I know she'll come to no harm with you.' He glanced meaningfully at Simon. 'My nephew, too, will keep a close watch. A word with you, Simon.'

Luther strode to the fireplace, and Simon followed, yet kept his attention tuned to the others. Over his shoulder he saw Kate rush gratefully to Delphine, to grasp her hand.

'Thank you for speaking for me,' she said.

Delphine's reply was inaudible, but she placed an arm around Kate's shoulders and drew her towards the piano again to be followed by Bertram.

Although he'd been amused by Delphine's deft handling of Luther, Simon felt uneasy for Kate. Sheltered and guileless, she was vulnerable – a lamb. Bertram wasn't untrustworthy, yet in Delphine's unscrupulous hands his friend was merely clay.

'Is this tour wise?' Simon murmured to Luther.

His uncle raised his brows in surprise. 'They're your friends,' he said bluntly. 'Why object?'

Simon had no answer, at least none he was ready to reveal. He couldn't keep his gaze from straying to the trio at the piano.

'Bertram and Kathryn are becoming far too friendly,' Luther said quietly, following his glance. 'I don't want them left alone together on the tour. They may slip away from the main party. Kathryn is too wilful for her own good. Warn him off without revealing our arrangement.'

'It would be better coming from you,' Simon said, quelling his irritation.

'He's your friend,' Luther snapped.

Simon shook his head. 'Perhaps it's unwise to interfere,' he persisted. 'I'm sure it's merely a flirtation.' But he wasn't at all sure that was true.

'Speak to him tonight,' Luther commanded, an uncompromising cast to his mouth. Then he turned to join the others at the piano.

His pride smarting, Simon gritted his teeth, vexed that he was swiftly becoming a dogsbody. How much longer must he submit? At least until he was Kate's husband, he told himself. Then the tables would be turned.

He decided to speak with Kate first; sound her out, discover her intentions, but cautiously, of course. Surely, she couldn't be falling in love with Bertram so soon after being parted from Mansel Jenkins? He felt a jealous stab again.

* * *

There had been a heavy fall of snow again in the night. Next morning Trott and Watkins were busy clearing the carriage-way down to the road while Kate, muffled up in a cloak and scarf, stood outside near the shrubbery watching them at work. Simon joined her, glad of an opportunity to speak freely without being overheard.

'A chilly morning, Miss Vaughan,' he began, pulling up the collar of his morning coat, wishing he'd waited to put on an overcoat before venturing out.

She turned quickly as he spoke, obviously not having heard his silent approach in the snow. He noted her half smile of welcome freeze as she recognised him.

'Quite,' she said shortly, turning away abruptly to watch the men shovel snow.

'You mustn't hesitate to ask me any question when you visit the shop later,' he went on conversationally, keeping his tone light. 'I can understand your interest in your late father's business.'

She glanced at him. 'It's Luther's business now, as he keeps reminding me,' she said bitterly. 'I dare say it'll be yours one day.'

He was startled. 'What do you mean?'

'You're Luther's heir, aren't you?' she said. 'He has no children.'

'You think he'll never marry again, then?'

She looked doubtful. 'He's too self-centred and hard-hearted to fall in love,' she opined. 'He'd never capture a woman's heart.'

'You may be proved wrong.'

She turned to stare at him. 'Well, you'd hardly wish it,' she said jeeringly. 'His marriage would cut you out of his will, leave you as penniless as you were when you came here, your shirt cuffs fraying, your boot leather cracked.'

Simon felt his face flush at her disdain. 'Has Bertram captured your heart, Kate?' he asked.

Colour came to her cheeks, and she pulled the hood of her cloak around her face, obviously to hide it. She didn't speak, but Simon didn't need her to confirm it, and his heart sank.

'I've known Bertram since boyhood,' he said quickly, 'although we're from very different backgrounds. He's a man of honour, but has no money. Luther would never consider him as a husband for you. The Harringtons will be gone in the New Year. It would be unwise for you to imagine—'

'How dare you!' Kate rounded on him, her cheeks now reddened by anger. 'Your impertinence offends me. You're nothing more than an employee; kindly remember that, Mr Creswell.'

She marched off, leaving Simon shivering in the snow.

Unable to find a moment during the shop tour for a quiet word with his friend, Simon waited until evening. He went along to Bertram's room, and wasn't at all surprised to find Delphine there.

'I'm just leaving,' she said, as she passed him in the door-way, giving Simon a pert smile. 'I just came to warn Bertie not to break sweet Kate's heart with his winning ways. She follows him about like a little pet rabbit. It's too bad of him to tease her so.'

Simon remained silent and unsmiling, standing aside for her to pass in a cloud of heady perfume.

'See you at dinner, Bertie, dear,' Delphine said. 'And try to be nice to that awful little bore, Cecille Villiers. She's dining here – yet again.'

When she'd gone Simon closed the door carefully, and

waited a moment before speaking. He wouldn't put it past Delphine to listen with one ear to the door.

'Delphine has a point, Bertie,' Simon said at last.

'You mean about Cecille,' Bertram said with a wide smile. 'I like her. She's lively.'

'I mean, breaking Kate's heart,' Simon said firmly. 'My uncle has already sent one suitor packing, a very suitable man, too, by all accounts. It'll break Kate's heart if she falls in love with you. Luther will never permit it. He has other . . .'

Bertram was brushing his evening jacket, but looked up expectantly when Simon hesitated, and raised his brows mockingly.

'He has other plans for her, you were about to say? You wouldn't figure in those plans, would you, Simon?'

Simon gritted his teeth in chagrin. They knew each other too well to be fooled; knew each other's most intimate secrets.

'There's Delphine to think of, too,' Simon said, with a meaningful look.

Bertram's expression darkened, and he was silent for a moment. Simon fidgeted. The last thing he wanted was to quarrel with his friend. And whatever happened next it would be his fault for inviting Bertram here in the first place. He might have known Kate would be vulnerable to his looks and charm after what she'd been through.

'The thing is, Simon, old man,' Bertram said at last, with a wry smile, 'I believe I'm falling in love with Kate. She's so fresh and lovely, and . . . untouched. I want to paint her.'

'Delphine . . .'

'Damn Delphine!' Bertram burst out.

'If only you really meant that,' Simon said quickly. Bertram bit his lip and then sighed. 'She's my twin, but I should have a life of my own.' His smile was strained. 'You've been telling me that for years.'

Simon clamped his mouth shut, afraid to say more just then.

Bertram put on his jacket, then looked at his pocket watch. 'You'll have to excuse me, Simon. I've an appointment with Kate in the arboretum.' He looked up. 'Have you been in there? An arboretum under glass; quite extraordinary. I've never seen one before.'

'Stolen kisses under the trees. Very romantic!' Simon snapped, then cursed himself for his transparent outburst. He was aware of Bertram's close scrutiny.

'You're jealous.'

'Nonsense!' Simon flustered. 'I'm thinking about you, and . . . I'm sorry for the girl. She's under Luther's thumb; curtailed in every way.'

'Then she needs all the distraction she can get,' Bertram retorted lightly. 'Let her have some pleasure, even if it is only a few stolen kisses.'

Kate was delighted to see Evan join them for dinner. She'd half expected him to turn up after seeing his open-mouthed admiration of Delphine Harrington on the shop tour earlier that day, and contrived that her brother should be seated next to the beauty at the dinner table. Kate was amused that he did his best to monopolise Delphine, hardly letting Luther attract her attention for more than two minutes together.

Watching them, Kate was wistful. Wouldn't it be splendid if Evan and Delphine made a match of it? Luther could hardly object to Bertram, then. With warmth, she recalled his hand holding hers as they'd sat earlier, murmuring together beneath the feathered leaves of the miniature mimosa in a hidden corner of the arboretum. She firmly put out of her mind her stepfather's dire pronouncement that she could never marry. It simply wasn't true.

'How did you like the shop, Delphine?' Luther managed to get a word in at last.

She turned to him, her lovely face animated. 'Very impressive,' she said. 'I was reminded of Harrods, no less.' She dimpled prettily, and her eyes gleamed. 'It must bring in a tremendous amount of money.'

Luther looked disconcerted at her frankness for a moment. 'It does extremely well,' he said distractedly.

Simon neatly changed the subject by asking Bertram about his painting, and Cecille announced immediately that her father had at last agreed to let her take painting lessons, if Bertram would oblige. Kate was furious with her. The chatter went on until it was time for the ladies to retire to the drawing-room.

'I'll take a turn in the arboretum before retiring,' Delphine announced loudly to no one in particular, but Kate noticed the avid interest of both Luther and Evan, and suddenly felt very uneasy.

Evan entered the faintly lit arboretum with quiet steps, his heart pounding. He had no right to feel this way, let alone come here at this hour to meet a woman he hardly knew. Yet her exquisite face had haunted him since he'd set eyes on her earlier that day. He must see her alone, talk to her, then perhaps this craziness would pass.

He was unaware of her until a little gasping sigh drew his attention to the shadowed leaves of the mimosa, and he stepped quickly that way. She was sitting on a little wooden bench, with room enough for two, a lovers' bench. As she looked up at him her violet eyes were large as though afraid.

'Oh, it's you,' she said breathlessly. 'Thank goodness. For a moment I thought it was Mr Templar.'

Evan frowned. 'Has my stepfather been pestering you?' Fire suddenly blazed in his chest. 'If he has . . .'

'No, no!' She reached out a hand and drew him to the bench and he sat eagerly, his pulses racing at her nearness. 'It's just that – well – he's always at my shoulder,' she went on, her voice quivering. 'I'm – I'm a little afraid of him.'

'He goes too far!' Evan exclaimed, the heat of the internal fire rising in his throat. 'It's insufferable that he should prey on you.'

Delphine clasped his hand. She was trembling and he knew his own hand was not without a tremor in response.

'I'm all right during the day when he's at the shop,' she went on haltingly. 'But in the evenings I can't escape.' She squeezed his hand. 'I feel safe now you're here, Evan.'

'I'll protect you,' he said thickly. 'You needn't fear. I'll have a word with Simon. When I'm not here he can watch over you.'

'Oh, no, please!' Delphine released his hand, and put her trembling fingers against her throat. 'I hate being a nuisance, and I don't want Simon to regret inviting us. I'll be all right.' She paused before speaking again, her voice low and husky. 'If only you were here always.'

'I've my own property elsewhere,' he said. Guilt, like acid, burned his conscience, but he thrust thoughts of Eirwen and the baby out of his mind. The marriage was a terrible mistake, and now he was trapped in it. 'But I promise I'll spare all the time I can to . . . be near you.'

'Oh, Evan.' Her voice was thrilling with emotion. 'You don't know how wonderful it is to be here, in safety and comfort. Bertram and I were becoming rather desperate, you know. We're destitute now our benefactor's dead.'

'How appalling,' he murmured. He couldn't bear to think of her being hounded by deprivation; her fragile and extraordinary beauty wasted by penury. 'How will you manage in the coming year?'

She turned her face away to the shadows, and a quiet sob escaped her, shaking her body. 'I can't bear to think of it, Evan,' she whispered. 'Daren't think of it, or I'll go into decline, I know I will.'

He seized her hand and squeezed it gently. 'That won't happen,' he muttered fiercely, taking the liberty of holding her closer.

He'd never felt this great sweeping wave of emotion for anyone before, and although he'd only known Delphine for a few hours, he couldn't let her go again, not for wife or child. Suddenly he knew, without a doubt, that Delphine, with her extraordinary beauty and presence, was all that could ever matter to him. She was the woman he'd been waiting for, had dreamed of. Eirwen was nothing by comparison. Delphine was his true soul mate.

But what could he offer such a wonderful woman? he thought despairingly. He'd lost his shares to Luther, and owed him a substantial sum. He couldn't sleep these days for worrying about it.

Evan shifted uneasily on the love-seat. Delphine sighed deeply and he tightened his embrace protectively.

It was frustrating and humiliating that he'd no money of his own, except his salary. That had to go for the upkeep of the household in Fforestfach. Eirwen and the baby were a millstone around his neck, yet he wouldn't let them go without.

He'd get his inheritance eventually, he told himself, a considerable fortune by any standards, when Kate saw sense and gave up her shares.

Delphine pressed closer. Her scented hair brushed his lips, and he was seized with longing.

'I'll take your benefactor's place,' he declared rashly. 'I'll have my own fortune – soon.'

Delphine turned her face to him, eyes wide in utter astonishment. 'Evan! Do you really mean it?' Her voice fell to a whisper, and she lowered her glance, moving so that her breast was pressed against his chest. 'What must I do to repay you? I'll do anything you wish.'

'Repay?' Evan felt confused, unsure what she meant.

His heart was beating like a drum as she lifted her face to him. He felt a mad impulse to kiss her glistening upturned mouth, but he resisted, not wanting to frighten her.

'Repayment isn't necessary,' he said in a strained voice. 'I'll protect you against all things, I swear.' He gazed into those fabulous eyes and thought he would drown in their beauty. 'All I have,' he whispered earnestly, his heart contracting with wanting her, 'or will ever have, is yours, Delphine. Take it.'

He was momentarily startled by something that gleamed fleetingly in her eyes. Then, sobbing gently, she leaned her head against his shoulder again, her hair silken against his cheek.

'Oh, Evan,' she murmured. 'God has sent you to me. I'm eternally grateful. Whatever you ask, I won't refuse you.'

Evan, his resolve weakened, was about to surrender to the overwhelming urge when the leaves above them were violently disturbed, and Luther's angry face glowered down.

'What's this, Evan?' he thundered. 'What damnable liberties are you taking with this lady?'

Evan sprang to his feet, Delphine rising with him. She stepped away from him and stood trembling, her arms clasped around herself, staring at him, a blank look on her face. Evan construed she was terrified of his stepfather, and his hackles rose.

'Don't raise your voice,' Evan said tightly, struggling not to shout in turn. 'Can't you see she's frightened?'

Luther's glance flickered over Delphine. 'Yes, frightened of you, you libertine!' he roared. 'How dare you behave in this shameful way? You've already ruined one woman; isn't that enough? Have you no honour?'

'Honour?' Evan hooted. 'That's rich coming from you.'

Luther's eyes narrowed, and the flush on his cheeks turned even darker. 'What do you mean by that?'

'I mean, you've been behaving abominably yourself . . .'

Delphine gave a little moan and tottered forward. Both men sprang to assist her, but it was Luther who caught her as she was about to sink to the floor.

'Look what you've done,' he snarled at Evan. He lowered Delphine's limp form on to the bench, then sat next to her supporting her in his arms. 'Quickly! Call Mrs Trobert or Ethel. Get some smelling salts. Don't just stand there, man!'

'I won't leave her alone with you,' Evan snapped. 'She's had enough of your unwanted attentions.'

Delphine gave a pitiful moan and tried to sit up only to fall back against Luther's arm again. She looked so pale and helpless, Evan was frightened.

'We must do something. She's ill.'

He darted to the bell pull near the door, then rushed back to the mimosa tree, unwilling to leave Delphine for a moment more. He'd promised to safeguard her and he would.

'Help me,' Luther commanded him. 'We must get her upstairs to her room. I'll call Dr Penfold. If anything's seriously amiss, I'll not forgive myself for allowing you to molest her.'

'I did no such thing.' Evan was furious. 'She was appealing for my protection.'

'Huh! The way that shop-girl did, I suppose?' he mocked.

At that moment Chivers appeared beside them.

'Lift her,' Luther instructed the butler. 'Take her to her room. Send Trott for Dr Penfold and have Ethel attend to her. Oh, this is most unfortunate.'

Evan was jostled aside by the butler's bulky shoulders, and Delphine was lifted up, and carried out of the arboretum, while he stared on helplessly.

Luther stalked out behind. At the door he turned. 'I suggest you leave immediately,' he said sternly to Evan. 'Don't return until you're ready to apologise to me and to Miss Harrington. And I want your assurance you'll never force your attentions on her again.'

Much later that night Delphine was in Bertram's room.

'You caused a scene,' he said reproachfully. 'I've already asked Luther's permission to paint Kate's portrait. He was enthusiastic, so there may be a valuable commission here, enough to see us through to the spring. Please be careful you don't lose us that.'

'Huh!' Delphine was dismissive. 'A piffling sum compared to what we will have, and we can have it all, Bertie.' She laughed in obvious delight. 'You should've seen the splendid way I played them off against each other. They quarrelled over me. It was delicious!'

'Delphi, please.'

'We've fallen on our feet here, Bertie,' she went on as though he hadn't spoken. 'Evan's a malleable young fool; very susceptible to womanly blandishments. He's promised me the earth.' Her eyes flashed, and the line of her mouth hardened. 'I'll milk him dry before I'm finished with him.'

Bertram shook his head, looking unhappy. 'Delphi, we're guests here, remember, and lucky to have shelter. For once let's not take advantage. Let's not go too far, as we did with—'

Her laugh was mocking. 'But Evan's ripe for it,' she said. 'Besides, he's no innocent. He's already in a spot of bother with some shop-girl, so I gather.' She looked thoughtful. 'It might be profitable to learn more of that.'

'Must you do this?'

Delphine looked scornful. 'Of course I must,' she snapped impatiently. 'We have to live, and we deserve to live well.' She looked at him, her eyes large and soulful. 'You do want me to be happy, don't you, Bertie?'

'Yes, but Luther Templar's no fool, and neither is Simon.'

'You can talk him round. He admires your amazing talent. Anyway, if he intended to tell them the truth, he'd have done it before now.'

'He's said nothing because he values my friendship,' Bertram said quietly. 'I hate to betray his trust again.'

'Oh, Bertie, for heaven's sake!' Delphine exclaimed angrily. 'Simon's nobody.'

She smiled suddenly, forgetting her anger.

'Evan Vaughan's wealthy, or will be quite soon. He was quivering like a jelly in the arboretum. I swear he was on the point of proposing, and he's known me only hours.' She looked smug. 'By the New Year I'll have him hog-tied. Oh, it's all too easy.'

'Don't underestimate Luther,' Bertram warned. 'Simon's hinted his uncle's a man of granite underneath. He's shrewd, very shrewd.'

'He's an old fool,' Delphine opined strongly, then paused

thoughtfully. 'A rich and powerful old fool, I grant you, but he has his weaknesses.' She gave her brother a knowing look. 'Women – especially women like me – sense these things.' She nodded sagely. 'If I don't trap the stepson then I'll trap the stepfather. Mark my words, Bertie, we're set for life here.' She smiled. 'Or at least until I become bored.'

She shrugged out of her negligee, and stood naked in the gaslight.

'Either way,' she went on confidently, 'before I'm finished we'll have all the money we'll ever need.'

She smiled at him, and climbed on to the bed. Putting a hand against his bare chest, she lifted her face to his, and when she spoke again her voice was low and husky with desire.

'Now kiss me, my darling brother. Show me just how much you love me.'

8

Evan sat at his small desk in Mr Grimby's office, poring over some invoices, but his heart wasn't in it. He'd hardly slept, and couldn't concentrate, his mind filled with thoughts of Delphine, wondering when he'd see her, longing to hold her in his arms again.

He looked up as someone knocked on the open door. It was Simon Creswell with a sheaf of papers in his hand.

'Grimby's not here,' Evan told him distractedly. 'Gone to Manchester on a buying trip.'

Simon came into the room and closed the door carefully.

'I know what happened with Delphine last night, Evan,' he began. 'And I want to warn you—'

'Warn me?' Evan started to his feet, his tiredness turning instantly to anger. 'What the devil do you mean by that?'

'Luther can go to hell as far as I'm concerned,' said Simon tensely. 'But I don't want to see you pay the price, if only for Kate's sake. There's something you should know about Delphine and—'

'What bluff is this?' Evan interrupted harshly. 'Confound it! What's Delphine to you?'

'Nothing.' Simon shook his head vehemently. 'Absolutely nothing.'

'So you say!' Evan felt his jaw muscles tighten in growing

anger. He eyed Simon narrowly, watching his face. 'Did Luther send you? You're doing his dirty work now, I see.'

'No! Listen to me!' Simon burst out. 'Delphine's already caused a rift between you and your stepfather. That's just the start.'

'That's not true,' cried Evan spiritedly. 'She's entirely innocent in the matter. He's been pressing his attentions on her. She's become afraid of him, she told me.'

Simon hooted derisively. 'Delphine afraid of any man? Huh! That'll be the day.'

Evan's hackles rose and he stepped forward threateningly, his hands closing into fists. 'You're insulting,' he rasped. 'I should knock you down.'

'Wait until you've heard me out,' said Simon. 'Delphine doesn't value feelings as we do, she doesn't know right from wrong. She's a strange and dangerous woman—'

'You scoundrel!' Evan bellowed wrathfully. The anger tightening in his chest threatened to burst, and he realised he was a hair's breadth from losing control. 'Kate's right about you,' he went on through clenched teeth. 'You're nothing more than Luther's wretch.'

Simon's face whitened, and Evan was pleased, feeling Delphine was avenged.

'And you're a damned fool,' Simon snapped. 'I thought you were worth saving, but I see I'm too late. She's already snared you. God help you, man.'

With that he turned and left the office, slamming the door behind him.

Evan sat down heavily at his desk, his hands trembling as he tried to gather up the papers strewn there. He was furious, resenting Simon's words. Yet he was ensnared and knew it, but didn't care. Like some beautiful witch, Delphine had taken possession of his mind and his body. His pulses raced wildly and his senses reeled in chaos at the thought of her.

Instinct told him she was capable of unbridled passion, and the notion excited him. His heart contracted, recalling the tingling magnetism of her breast nestling against his chest. He wanted her, desperately, utterly, with a hunger he couldn't explain. He'd never known primal desire like this, not with Eirwen or any other woman, and once experienced he couldn't live without it.

Evan groaned in desperation. He couldn't deceive himself. Delphine would expect marriage, and he'd nothing to offer. He'd commit bigamy to possess her, if he could get away with it. But Luther knew too much for that. Damn him to hell!

The office door opened and Evan looked up sharply, a growl in his throat, half expecting Simon's return, but instead the tousled head of the office boy peered around the door.

'His Nibs wants you,' the lad babbled. 'On the double, mun.'

'What's that!' Evan bellowed, jumping to his feet. The head was quickly withdrawn. 'Jones!' Evan bellowed again. 'Get back in here, you little tyke.'

The boy returned, and stood sheepishly in his crumpled jacket and leggings before the desk. Evan was in no mood to tolerate the likes of him.

'Now, then,' he said tightly. 'Report the message again.'

'If you please, Mr Vaughan,' the boy said, almost primly, 'Mr Templar would like to see you in his office immediately.'

'I should think so!' Evan said. 'This is a caution, Jones. Any more insolence, and you're sacked. Now get out of my sight.'

Evan's temper was more to do with Luther's summons than Jones's impertinence. If his stepfather was expecting an apology he'd be very disappointed. Evan climbed the stairs to the next floor two at a time, his bad mood powering his legs.

In the outer office Miss Collins, Luther's middle-aged secretary and the scourge of all office boys, stood up as he came in. She glared at him imperiously.

'Ah! Mr Vaughan,' she began in a nasal voice, removing the pince-nez from her beaky nose. 'At last. You've kept Mr Templar waiting. He's a busy man, you know.'

She continued to glare at him as though he were guilty of some misdemeanour, and Evan viewed her with distaste, hating her colourless face and her hair scraped back tightly in a bun.

'Well, I won't keep him a minute longer then,' he retorted sarcastically, and strode towards Luther's door.

'Just a minute!' Miss Collins snapped, stepping into his path. 'You know very well you can't just walk in. I must announce you.'

She turned, and Evan heard her corsets creak. Usually he found this amusing, but today nothing would mend his temper.

As he passed her in the doorway, Miss Collins gave him a triumphant stare, but he pointedly ignored her, concentrating on his stepfather, seated at his desk, his face impassive.

'You sent for me,' Evan began curtly.

Luther put his elbows on the desk before him, clasping his hands together, and looked at Evan severely. 'What have you to say to me, Evan?'

'Nothing!' Evan snapped. 'But I demand an apology for your atrocious accusations of yesterday.' He strode to the desk and leaned over, placing his palms on it. 'How dare you order me from my own home. You made me look a fool.'

'Your home is elsewhere than Old Grove House,' Luther

reminded him. 'With your wife and child, or have you conveniently forgotten their existence?'

'That's none of your business,' Evan blustered, not wishing to be reminded. 'I do as I please.'

'Yes, that's the trouble,' Luther mocked. 'With dire consequences.'

He paused a moment then stood up and came around the desk, his hand outstretched.

'Now look here, Evan. I don't want a disagreement. I'm willing to overlook your indiscretion of last night,' he said loftily, 'if you'll assure me you'll cease to bother Delphine.'

Evan ignored the outstretched hand. 'How is she after last night?' he asked anxiously.

'Apparently she was too exhausted to come down this morning, but Ethel assured me she'd eaten breakfast in bed.'

'What did that quack Penfold have to say?' asked Evan bitterly.

Luther's eyes flickered with annoyance. 'He could find nothing amiss, although he hardly stayed with her fifteen minutes.' His mouth tightened. 'What do you have against him, anyway?'

'I hold him personally responsible for my mother's death.'

Luther flinched visibly. 'Nonsense, man!' he blustered. 'She took her own life, damn it!'

'Penfold made no attempt to save her,' Evan shouted heatedly. 'I remember he stood by wringing his hands, doing nothing. He should be struck off. How could you let him come anywhere near Delphine?'

'You were a mere child at the time Alice died,' Luther said, a tremor in his voice. 'You can't know anything of what went on; how we struggled to save her.'

'We?' Evan hooted. 'You did nothing, Luther. I also remember you locked yourself in the study until it was all over.'

A rush of deep hatred for his stepfather swept over him, making his throat and chest burn as though from acid.

'Why weren't you at Mother's bedside, if you were so concerned?' he stormed, and then paused, glaring balefully at the older man. 'You wanted my mother to die, didn't you?' he said tensely. 'Wanted to be rid of her so you could take everything that belonged to my family. And now you're after Kate's shares. How far will you go to get those?'

Luther's face was patched white and purple, and he seemed about to choke. His mouth opened, but several moments passed before he could speak, and then his voice was a mere croak.

'This is an outrage! I won't listen a moment longer. Get out!'

'You'll hear what I have to say,' Evan pressed on. 'Penfold is an incompetent fool – or perhaps worse!'

'What do you mean by that?'

Evan looked into Luther's livid face, but couldn't give an answer because he dared not put a name to his feeling. For years he'd been tormented with the notion that his mother wouldn't have died if the doctor had acted swiftly. Why did Penfold appear to do nothing? But how reliable were childhood memories anyway?

'The point is, Luther,' Evan said, his shoulders drooping, 'I don't want Penfold tending Delphine. Get another man. There's no shortage of medical advice in this town.'

Having had enough, he turned to leave, but Luther detained him. He'd recovered his composure quickly now that Evan had backed down, and looked once more his old arrogant self.

'Just one minute,' he said imperiously. 'You haven't given your word you won't plague her in future. She wants nothing to do with you, man. She told me as much.'

'Liar!' Evan rounded on him, shouting. 'And you're a damned hypocrite, too.'

'Quiet!' Luther hissed urgently, glancing towards the door. 'Collins will overhear. I don't want the nature of our differences known.'

'To hell with that! I don't care if the whole building hears,' Evan shouted belligerently. 'For God's sake, be honest, Luther. Admit you want Delphine for yourself.'

'What if I do?' Luther spat out the words. 'I'm a free man, unlike you. I've much to offer her, whereas you've nothing to offer, not even your name.'

Evan winced as the truth stabbed him through. 'My inheritance is due to me,' he said.

'You forget my conditions,' Luther said. 'Kate's shares first.' He smiled mockingly. 'Not that it'll do you any good with Delphine. She'll not settle for less than marriage.'

He sat down, his gaze contemptuous as he looked at Evan. 'Tend to your wife and child like an honourable man,' he rasped. 'Don't disgrace the Vaughan name any further with your licentious nature – or I'll be forced to make your foolish marriage public.'

'You won't keep me from Old Grove House, not while Delphine's there,' vowed Evan, his voice cracking with tension. 'Or Kate will learn of your underhand plans for her future. She can be very difficult when she chooses.'

He was satisfied to see his stepfather's startled look.

'Has Simon been indiscreet . . .' Luther began, then stopped, realising he'd said too much.

Evan shook his head, smiling bitterly. 'No, he hasn't, but I'm not a fool,' he said. 'I guessed your nephew would have a part to play.'

He stepped closer to Luther and glared into his face across the desk.

'I don't trust you,' he hissed through clenched teeth. 'I couldn't prevent my mother's death, but nothing bad had better happen to Kate, or, by God, Luther, I'll have your head on a chopping block.'

Luther's face suffused with blood again; his mouth opened but he didn't attempt to answer. With one last look of hatred, Evan turned and stamped from the room.

Outside, Miss Collins was just bobbing away from the door as he opened it.

'Did you hear all you wanted, you ugly old battle-axe?' Evan shouted at her as he strode past.

'Well! Really!'

Kate stepped out from her sitting-room as Bertram was about to descend the stairs.

'Bertram?'

He turned back to her with a shining smile, and, taking her by the elbow, drew her back into the room, where they stood close.

'You look so beautiful, Kate,' he said softly, raising her hand to his lips, and her heart did a somersault. 'You must wear that gown when I paint you.'

'Oh, Bertram,' Kate breathed, feeling her face flush with pleasure, and was spurred on to boldness. 'Shall we spend a few moments together in the arboretum before dinner?'

His smile became strained. 'It's unwise, Kate,' he said sincerely. 'We shouldn't be alone together so much.'

'What?' Kate withdrew her hand sharply from his, and stared up at him in disappointment, and he looked uncomfortable.

'Your stepfather doesn't wish our friendship to continue,'

he said regretfully. 'As a guest under his roof I daren't displease him. If I'm forced to leave,' he went on with a catch in his voice, 'I may never see you again.'

Kate felt confused as two powerful emotions battled within her: rage at her stepfather for interfering in her life once again; and an overpowering longing for Bertram to sweep her into his arms.

'He's actually forbidden our friendship?' she asked tremulously, fighting the desire to reach up and put her arms around his neck.

'Not in so many words to me,' Bertram explained. 'But Simon's made it plain that Luther disapproves.'

'Simon!' Kate cried in wrath, stepping away from him. 'How dare he? That man's behaviour is intolerable.'

'He means no harm, Kate,' Bertram said quickly. 'Simon's a man of honour.'

'I'm sorry, Bertram,' Kate exclaimed crossly. 'I know he's your friend, but I'm certain he'd betray you if he could profit by it. He's too much like his uncle.'

There was a murmur of conversation in the gallery outside and a rustle of silk. Kate moved quickly to the door and held it ajar. Two people passed and continued down the staircase.

'It's Delphine and my stepfather,' she said when they'd passed.

'I must join them,' Bertram exclaimed quickly. 'Or she – Luther may become suspicious. Wait here a moment before following.'

'Bertram!' Kate blurted, turning to him. 'I can't bear this.'

With a little sigh, he bent his head and kissed her quickly on the cheek.

'If only things were different,' he said huskily. 'I feel I've waited for you all my life, wanted you all my life.'

'Then fight for me!' Kate cried out passionately. 'Defy Luther, Simon, everyone who'd stand in our way.'

With a deep moan, Bertram gathered her up in his arms, pulling her to his chest, but almost instantly he held her away again, shaking his head.

'Kate, you don't understand,' he said miserably. 'And I can't explain. I've no money, and then there's Delphine . . .'

'Delphine will have no trouble finding a husband,' Kate said desperately, clinging to him.

He gave a hollow laugh. 'She'll never let . . .' He stopped speaking, and moved away from her clutching hands. 'Kate, my dearest one, it can't be.' He gave a groan. 'I should've listened to Simon. The last thing I want is to break your heart.'

'Bertram . . .'

'I'm going down,' he said firmly, moving to the doorway. 'It's for the best, Kate.' Then he was gone.

Kate stood clenching her fists in anger and frustration. She wouldn't let Luther or Simon ruin her chance of happiness. She'd find some way to defeat them; and with a determined step she went down.

Evan came into the hall, fresh snowflakes on his hat and shoulders. She ran down the remaining stairs to greet him.

'Evan! I'm so glad you're here,' she exclaimed with relief. 'I must talk to you.'

'Good evening, Kate,' he said offhandedly.

'Come into the library a minute,' she urged. 'It's Luther and Simon Creswell. They're trying to come between me and Bertram.'

Evan looked distracted. 'Where is Luther?' he asked, an edge to his voice.

'In the drawing-room,' she said. She tugged at his arm. 'Please, Evan, I must talk to you in private.'

He glanced at his pocket watch. 'Excuse me, Kate,' he said harshly. 'I must see Luther, the sooner the better.'

Alarmed, Kate grasped his arm before he could move away. 'Evan, whatever's the matter? You look so grim.'

He paused for a moment before answering. 'He's forbidden me to come to Old Grove House because of Delphine.'

'What?' Kate was astonished. 'He can't do that.'

'He already has.'

'Why?'

'You wouldn't understand, Kate.'

'Don't talk down to me, Evan,' she said sharply, smarting under his tone. 'I'm not a child.'

'All right,' he conceded. 'Luther's ordered me to stay away from Delphine, because he plans to take her for himself.'

Kate stared open-mouthed for a moment, and then laughed at the absurdity of the idea.

'Luther and Delphine! It's preposterous. He's old enough to be her father. She can have any man she wants,' Kate said with sudden insight. 'Why on earth would she choose him?'

'He's obsessed with her,' he said tensely. 'He sent Simon to warn me off. He denied it, but I'm certain Luther was behind it.'

'Simon Creswell again! Oh, that man!' Kate was furious. 'Is there no end to his meddling? He had the effrontery to warn me off Bertram, too.' She grabbed at his lapel, suddenly afraid for the future. 'Oh, Evan, what're we going to do? How can we outwit him?'

He put his hands to his face, covering his eyes, and shaking his head, as though in anguish.

'Evan, what is it?'

'Luther has a hold over me,' he said at last, distress etched on his features. 'I've made a grave mistake, Kate, which I bitterly regret.' He lifted his hands in protest as Kate opened her mouth to speak. 'No! I can't discuss it.'

'Perhaps I can help.'

'My dear girl.' Evan shook his head sadly. 'You can't even help yourself. Luther has plans for you, too, and I can't stop him.'

'What?' Kate was suddenly frantic. 'What do you mean?'

Evan shook his head, his shoulders drooping.

'What secret are you keeping from me, Evan?' Kate cried. 'Do you really believe we have tainted blood?'

Without answering, Evan looked past her, as if seeing another place and another time.

'Evan! You're frightening me!'

He looked down at her, and smiled sadly. 'Don't be afraid, Kate.' He smoothed the back of his index finger against her cheek. 'Aunt Kate,' he said softly.

She frowned, perplexed. 'Why do you call me that?'

The dinner gong sounded loudly in the hall and Evan seemed to snap out of a reverie. 'Come on,' he said firmly, taking her arm. 'Luther the Ogre awaits and I'm ready to do battle.'

Luther sprang to his feet, knocking over his glass of wine, which ran in a dark red pool on the white damask cloth before him.

'That's enough! Get out!' he roared at Evan, throwing down his napkin. 'Damn you, sir, for insulting me at my own table.' He lifted an arm and pointed to the door. 'Get out of my house and stay out.'

'I won't leave, blast you!' Evan shouted back, already on his feet, his plate of food barely touched. 'You'll have to put me out forcibly.' He was scarcely aware of the shocked faces around the table. 'Get your bully-boy Chivers to manhandle me, if you dare. Show your guests your true character.'

Luther was livid and speechless. He swayed, and then sank on to his seat, his face mottled white and red.

'Evan, please!' Kate cried out, rising, and Simon pushed back his chair, too, as though ready to restrain her.

'It's all right, Kate,' Evan said, his breath catching jaggedly in his throat. 'I've said all I'm going to say to him.'

His gaze flickered over her, and then rested on Bertram Harrington sitting alongside.

'Harrington,' he blurted tensely. 'If you've any regard for your sister, watch over her while she's under the roof of this bloodsucking tyrant.'

There were gasps around the room, and with one last look into Delphine's wide eyes, Evan hurried away. He was aware that Chivers followed him out. The butler went immediately to open the door of the cloakroom near the front entrance.

'Your hat and coat, sir?' he hissed, a faint smile lifting his mouth.

'No! Blast you!' Evan shouted in rage. 'I'm not leaving. I've every right to be here.'

With that he rushed upstairs and went to his suite of rooms.

Evan spent the next few hours either sitting thoughtfully, weighing up his position, or pacing about his sitting-room, undecided on what to do next. He knew he'd never sleep that night and couldn't bring himself to go to bed.

Just before midnight there was a light tap at the door, and Evan groaned in exasperation. The last thing he wanted tonight was to face Kate's questions or her tears. On impulse, he extinguished the lamp, hoping she'd believe he'd retired for the night.

The tapping came again immediately and someone quietly

spoke his name. In utter astonishment he recognised Delphine's voice and rushed to open the door.

She stood there in a flowing lace negligee, her blonde hair cascading around her shoulders. He could only stare at her loveliness, faintly illuminated in the dim light of the hallway.

'Delphine!'

'Must I stand here all night, Evan?' she asked softly.

Without waiting for an answer, she moved past him, her body brushing lightly against his as she went by. His mouth suddenly dry, Evan hurried to relight the lamp.

'What's wrong?' he asked quickly, turning to face her. 'Is it Luther?'

'No, dear Evan,' she said softly. 'I was so worried about you, I couldn't sleep. I had to come and see for myself.'

'You shouldn't be here,' he said unevenly. 'You might be seen. It could be misconstrued, and your reputation . . .'

She stepped closer, looking at him from under her lashes.

'Do you really want me to go?' She made a little moue. 'Am I not welcome in your bedroom?'

'Oh, Delphine, my dear.' He couldn't resist that look, and moved closer, gently grasping her upper arms. 'You know I long to be with you constantly.'

'Then don't worry about my reputation,' she said softly. 'I had to speak to you,' she went on, her eyes sparkling in the lamplight. 'You're so brave, defying Luther. The man's a tyrant. I do admire you so much.'

He felt the warmth of her skin beneath the lace of the negligee, and a longing to embrace her almost overwhelmed him. But he kept his head.

'Thank you,' he said sincerely. 'Your concern is very precious to me.'

'Oh, your fire's still alight,' she exclaimed, moving quickly towards the fireplace and sinking on to a chair. 'Mine's gone out. May I linger here a while, Evan?'

On impulse he knelt at her feet, grasping her hands. 'Stay as long as you wish,' he answered softly. 'It's wonderful just to look at you.'

'And I feel safe here with you,' she whispered, leaning close. 'I was afraid walking through the passageways. My heart was fluttering, and still is.'

She clasped both his hands suddenly and brought them to cover her breasts.

'Feel how my heart beats, Evan, my dear.'

'Delphine!' Evan's throat closed as a wave of desire for her washed over him and through him.

'Evan, let's not waste a moment being together,' she whispered in a gush of words. 'We long for one another, desire one another. Why deny ourselves?'

Evan's senses were inflamed yet he was also confused. 'I'm not sure what you mean,' he whispered hoarsely.

She released his hands, and reaching forward, stroked his face gently. 'Yes, you do,' she said lightly. 'You know exactly what I mean.' Amusement sparkled in her eyes, and for a moment he thought she was laughing at him. 'You've promised to be my benefactor, Evan,' she went on huskily. 'And that gives you certain intimate privileges.'

He rose to his feet, disconcerted. 'I'm not a man to take advantage of a woman in any circumstances,' he said, and then thought of Eirwen, feeling suddenly guilty.

Delphine rose too, and standing very close to him, her hands on his chest, she tilted her head back to look up into his face. 'But you've promised me so much,' she said, her voice low and husky. 'And I know you're a man of your word; you'll keep your promise.'

Evan gazed down at her tempting mouth, so willing and ready for him. 'I'll do anything for you,' he said hoarsely. 'Give you anything you desire.'

'Will you buy me a new gown for the ball?' she asked, and leaned heavily against him. 'I've no money, you see,' she went on, a pathetic sob in her voice. 'I've nothing, Evan, except your patronage.'

'Oh, don't call it that,' he exclaimed. 'It's friendship; no, it's love, Delphine. I know this seems very sudden, but I do love you. I'd ask you to marry me this moment, except . . .' He paused, mortified, unable to put the truth into words.

She seemed to sense his distress, and put both her hands to hold his face. 'Don't fret, my dearest,' she whispered. 'We'll find a way. Just kiss me, and love me.'

His desire spiralling out of control, Evan gathered her into his arms, kissing her passionately.

'I'm yours, Evan, yours alone,' she declared in a low thrilling whisper. 'The lover I've waited for all my life. Take me now.'

Sweeping her off her feet, he carried her eagerly to his bedroom. Everything, and everyone else in the world was forgotten.

At nine o'clock the next day the morning-room was very quiet. The snow, lying thick on the ground, seemed to deaden every sound outside and even inside the house. Simon, sitting at the bureau writing to his mother, was glad of the calm after the family storm of the evening before. But how much longer would it remain so, with Evan Vaughan refusing to see sense in his quarrel with his stepfather?

The door opened and he turned quickly in his chair, expecting Kate to put in an appearance. Instead, it was Delphine who stood in the doorway, looking very elegant and as beautiful as ever. He was surprised to see her, since she hardly ever rose before midday.

'Good morning, Simon,' she greeted him. Her tone had a studied warmth as though they were old and very dear friends instead of bitter enemies.

'Morning.' He tried not to speak gruffly, watching her mistrustfully. 'You're up early. Is anything wrong?'

'Is anything right in this house?' She laughed lightly at her own joke, then took a seat near the fireplace. 'I'm not over that awful scene we witnessed at dinner last night,' she went on. 'Have you *ever* seen such bad manners, not to mention bad taste.'

'If this household isn't to your good taste,' he replied with sarcasm, 'why don't you leave?'

'Don't be absurd, Simon. I find life at Old Grove House most entertaining.' She pursed her lips prettily, looking up at him from under her lashes. 'And perhaps profitable, too.'

Resolutely, Simon put down his pen, rose and walked to the fireplace. He'd been waiting for a chance to talk to her without either Luther or Evan hovering at her shoulder.

A teasing smile played gently around her lovely mouth. 'You hate me, don't you, Simon, because of Bertram?'

Simon felt his jaw tighten in anger. 'Don't you realise you're destroying him,' he said tensely. 'He could go on to greatness. Let him go, Delphine, for pity's sake.'

She raised her brows, and a mocking smile twisted her lips. 'You're not lecturing me on morality, are you, Simon dear?'

His shoulders drooped, seeing the light of defiance and deep scorn in her eyes. Hers was the power, and she wouldn't relinquish it on a plea from him.

'Would it do any good?' he asked dispiritedly.

'Hardly.' She laughed. 'I do as I desire; always have and always will.'

Simon clenched his teeth in exasperation and helplessness. How can one reason with a being who has no concept of right or wrong?

'You're up to your old tricks, Delphine,' he said tightly and with very little hope. 'And, as usual, someone's going to get hurt.'

'Well, it won't be you, will it, Simon?' Her tone was acid. 'I realised long ago that you're immune.'

'I've seen what you've done to Bertram and other men.'

She gave a high laugh. 'Bertram is as happy as any man can be,' she said. 'He's rapidly reaching the height of his powers as a painter. Right now he's enjoying a harmless flirtation with a pretty girl and . . . he has me.'

Simon didn't trust himself to speak for a moment. When his anger was more under control, he asked, 'What if Bertram wishes to marry?'

Delphine's eyes flashed with the iridescence of fire opals. 'My brother will *never* marry,' she said with intense conviction. 'He'll never leave my side. I won't allow it. We've always been together and always will be. He's part of me, and nothing and no one on this earth will separate us.'

Simon felt a shiver of horror run up his spine at the implacable look in her eyes as she spoke. And then she smiled, lifting her head in supreme confidence.

'I'll marry, of course,' she went on lightly. 'I'll marry a man of wealth and power, who'll give me anything and everything I ask for.'

'So, you're already hunting Luther Templar?' he said after a moment.

Delphine smiled sweetly. 'Oh, Simon, you really believe you know me, but don't try to put words in my mouth. I haven't set my cap at any man, yet.'

Simon shook his head in disbelief. 'You don't fool me,' he said, unable to hide his distaste. 'I've seen your diabolic designs before, so don't pretend Luther isn't in your sights. But why torment Evan? He and his stepfather are at each other's throats,' he said bitterly. 'And all because of you.'

'Totally untrue.' Delphine's tone was peevish. She waved a hand airily. 'I've not encouraged either of them.'

'The way you didn't encourage Sir Edwin, I suppose?' Simon said scornfully. 'You set that family at war, and drove him to suicide.'

'That wasn't proved,' she said quickly, then checked herself. 'I mean, it isn't true. Sir Edwin was ill. His death came as a great shock to me.'

He shook his head. 'Was that because you and Bertram were the losers?' he said sarcastically. 'Sir Edwin's will must've come as an even greater shock.'

She appeared not to hear, her expression closed and pensive. 'I'm not the cause of a rift in this house,' she said stubbornly. 'Some very strange remarks were made at dinner last night.' She glanced up at him, eyes wide. 'Didn't you think so?'

'Do what you like with Luther,' he said wrathfully. 'But, for God's sake, leave Evan alone. He's too good a man for you to destroy.'

'I believe he's already married,' Delphine said. She pursed her lips, looking thoughtful. 'Luther knows it, and is using it against him in some way. He made some very pointed comments about marital responsibility and facing up to mistakes,' she said reflectively.

'There's enough strife in this house already,' Simon said sharply. 'Your meddling can only harm Kate.'

'Oh, your innocent little Kate has no idea what's going on,'

Delphine said waspishly. Her glance at Simon was narrow and shrewd. 'Are there any family secrets I should know about? Indiscretions with shop-girls, for instance?'

'None!' Simon exploded. 'And if there were I'd hardly tell *you.*'

'Temper, temper!' Delphine scolded. 'A real gentleman wouldn't show his feelings so plainly. You've a lot to learn, Simon.'

'Not from the likes of you,' rasped Simon.

But she was impervious to his sarcasm he realised. Her eyes were half closed, her mouth a tight line in a rather scheming expression. It momentarily marred her beauty.

'You'd be wise to cultivate my friendship,' she warned, her tone hard. 'I could be mistress of this house one day.'

Simon eyed her contemptuously, not trusting himself to say what was in his mind.

She looked smug. 'Meanwhile, I'll have to be content with the next best thing.' She flashed a coy look at him. 'Married or not, Evan's ready for a mistress. He's been very generous to me so far. Very generous.'

'What?' Simon was shaken, and stared at her in vexation. 'You just told me you weren't encouraging him.'

She laughed. 'I lied.'

'Damn you!'

Delphine's smile was malicious, as though pleased at his reaction. 'Evan really hates his stepfather, doesn't he,' she went on with amusement. 'Hates him with cold venom. He looked as though he could kill him last night. Such deep passion he has, and so easily manipulated.'

She raised a hand to pat the satin ribbons laced in her hair, and then stood up as though to leave, but instead turned to him, frowning.

'Oh, yes,' she went on. 'And what was behind Evan's remarks about Dr Penfold and some sleeping powders? For a moment, I thought Luther would have an apoplectic fit.' Her smile at Simon was radiant. 'I find Old Grove House fascinating.'

9

Christmas 1899

Kate was happy that Simon Creswell was spending Christmas in Bath with his mother, but was livid to discover that Luther had invited Cecille Villiers to share their Christmas at Old Grove House. She recognised a deliberate ploy to check her friendship with Bertram.

'We shouldn't, you know,' Bertram whispered to Kate on Boxing Day morning as she drew him quickly behind a silk screen in the music room, hearing the echoes of Cecille's resonant tones calling to them through corridors and passages of the house. 'She's your guest,' he said. 'It's most unfair and impolite.'

'Nonsense!' Kate proclaimed resolutely. 'She's Luther's guest. Let him entertain her.'

Bertram laughed softly. 'I fancy he's otherwise occupied.'

Cecille's voice came nearer and Kate moved closer to Bertram, glancing up at him frankly.

'She won't find us,' she said in a determined whisper. 'I want you all to myself.'

'Oh, my dearest Kate.'

His hand was warm in the small of her back, drawing her nearer still and she felt a pleasurable thrill as his lips brushed lightly against hers.

She'd never felt such excitement as this, not even with Mansel, and, a little giddy, she leaned heavily against him, his arms immediately encircling her. He kissed the top of her head, and she sighed with contentment. She must somehow prompt him to ask that one important question.

'A girl might almost believe she's loved,' she said boldly, leaning back and gazing into his incredible eyes. His gaze faltered and Kate was disconcerted enough to speak plainly. 'Bertram, am I just some passing fancy to you?' Disappointment made her tone sharper than she intended.

'Oh, no, Kate.' He looked dismayed. 'I swear on my soul, you mean a great deal to me.'

'Great enough to last a lifetime?' she asked meaningfully. 'You can guess my feelings for you, Bertram. Surely there's nothing to keep us apart.'

He took a step away from her, his face clouded with concern. 'Kate, I've already told you, my life's complicated, my future uncertain. I dearly wish to make a claim on you, but I can't, at least, not yet.'

'But why?'

'Please don't ask me to explain.' His expression was agitated. 'Just believe no one means more to me than you do.'

Piqued, Kate turned a shoulder, and lifted her chin. 'I suppose I must be content with that?'

'Yes, Kate, for the moment.' He stepped closer again, and put an arm around her. 'In the New Year I may find myself in a new position financially. I pray so.'

Kate swung round in his embrace. 'But *I* have money, Bertram,' she said in agitation. 'When I marry I'll receive my inheritance. We'll live in great comfort, I promise you.'

'That depends entirely on your stepfather,' Bertram reminded her sadly.

'But . . .'

Bertram stilled her lips with a gentle finger. 'Kate, we must wait. Have patience, my dearest girl.'

Simon returned from Bath the day before the ball. His face was pale and drawn and Kate guessed his mother's health had not improved.

The centenary celebrations were to be held on the Sunday as planned. Kate still wondered nervously if any guests would turn up. If the ball were a disaster, her family would be scorned by the whole town. Living in hope that Bertram would propose at the ball, Kate invited Cecille to spend the Saturday night at Old Grove House so that they could prepare for the occasion together the following day.

Hardly able to contain themselves with excitement, Kate and Cecille waited until most of the guests arrived. Very few had refused the invitation on religious grounds, it seemed, and Kate thought it indeed a sign of the changing times.

Bertram was waiting at the bottom of the staircase for Kate, his eyes full of admiration. She almost forgot herself, aching to fly into his arms.

When he escorted her into the ballroom, she couldn't help gasping with appreciation at the finery of it. She hadn't been in this part of the house for years, not since her childhood. Luther had refurbished everything splendidly, and obviously at great expense. For a moment she felt grateful to him. Her parents would have been thrilled to see Old Grove House so full of life and gaiety. The evening was proving to be a tremendous success.

Kate danced time and again with Bertram, and felt deliriously happy in his arms. There was one more dance before suppertime, when Kate noticed Cecille standing alone near the entrance of the ballroom and felt a surge of guilt.

'Bertram, would you dance with Cecille, just this once?' she asked persuasively. 'I'll sit out for a while.'

Bertram sighed. 'If I must,' he agreed, and moved reluctantly away.

Kate took a seat against the wall, and was content to survey the room as the orchestra struck up a waltz. Luther danced by with a laughing Delphine in his arms. Evan stood at the edge of the floor, his face a mask of fury as he watched the pair, and Kate felt a twinge of disquiet at the malevolence on her brother's face.

Abruptly, her disquiet turned to alarm when she saw Simon Creswell making a beeline for her. Surely he wasn't going to ask her to dance? To her dismay he bowed and offered his hand.

'May I have the pleasure, Miss Vaughan?'

She was tempted to refuse, but was conscious that guests sitting nearby were observing them so she stood up, to be led unwillingly to the floor. She felt stiff and awkward in his embrace, although he held her at almost arm's length, as if any contact would be displeasing to him, and Kate ground her teeth in annoyance.

They moved in silence for a few minutes, and then Bertram sailed by with a beaming Cecille in his arms. It was too much for Kate to bear.

'I'm surprised to see you here, Mr Creswell,' she remarked acidly. 'With your mother so ill. Obviously filial obligation isn't a strong point with you.'

She felt his arms tense.

'You've a razor-sharp tongue, Miss Vaughan,' he hissed between clenched teeth. 'Careful you don't cut yourself.'

Kate was furious and would have left him standing there, but his hand clasped hers more tightly, and his arm imprisoned her waist like a band of steel, drawing her closer.

'No, Miss Vaughan,' he said harshly. 'You won't humiliate me so easily.'

They whirled around to the music a few more turns before he spoke again.

'I don't want to be here tonight, Miss Vaughan,' he said with deep bitterness. 'I've no choice but to obey Luther's command.'

His hand trembled as he spoke, but his grasp didn't loosen. They danced on to the end of the waltz in silence.

As the music came to an end he bowed briefly to her, turned and walked away. Instantly Bertram was at her side, and, immediately forgetting Simon Creswell, Kate turned to him, smiling, and grasped his arm.

'Bertram, take me in to supper.'

Throughout the supper recess a soprano of great talent entertained the guests. Kate was anxious for the dancing to start again, longing to be held in Bertram's arms. When everyone had drifted back to the ballroom, Kate was surprised to see her stepfather on the orchestra's rostrum, apparently about to make an announcement. Curious, she drew Bertram nearer to the crowd of expectant guests as they stood before him.

'Ladies and gentlemen,' Luther began. 'Tonight we'll see in a new century with hope in our hearts that the present conflict with the Boers will soon end, and peace be restored. Let's also hope the new century brings prosperity to us all.'

There were cries of 'Hear, hear!' and 'Bravo!' as servants moved among the guests with trays of glasses filled with champagne.

Kate watched her stepfather with scepticism, then became aware that Simon Creswell was standing at her side, but she didn't look at him.

'On this auspicious eve,' Luther went on grandly, 'I've a special announcement to make. A very worthy young man has asked for my stepdaughter's hand in marriage, and I am delighted to give my blessing on the match.'

Kate spun round to Bertram, her mouth open in astonished delight. 'Oh, Bertram, darling, how wonderful . . .'

His eyes were wide. 'Kate. I . . . I . . .'

'The young man in question,' Luther continued loudly drowning out Bertram's stammering, 'is my esteemed nephew, Simon Creswell. Please all raise your glasses in a toast to this happy young couple now betrothed in marriage.'

Amid the clinking of crystal glasses and calls of congratulations, Kate was rooted to the spot, unable to move or think clearly. She was vaguely aware that Bertram eased his hand from her grasp, and that someone else's arm closed around her waist.

Her breath caught in her throat with shock, and she struggled to take in air, pulling against the arm that held her. She had to get out of here into the cold night air or she'd faint. The orchestra struck up a chord as the dancing started again.

'Don't make a scene here before all these people,' Simon hissed in her ear, holding her fast to him, attempting to swirl her into the rhythm of the music. 'You'll make a laughing-stock of us all.'

'Let me go!'

'Quiet, you little fool!' He twirled in a head-spinning circle, pulling her along with him, and she was forced to follow his steps. 'Luther's got us into this mess; we must go along with it – for now.'

'I'm going to faint,' she murmured weakly. The wonderful evening had turned into a nightmare.

'Don't you dare faint,' Simon instructed her fiercely, hissing close to her ear. 'I forbid it.'

'What?' Abruptly her senses returned at his overbearing tone, and she stiffened in his arms. 'How dare you dictate to me?'

'Smile! You little idiot! We're in love. And we have the eyes of the room on us.' He beamed widely at a dancing couple passing close.

'I don't care!' Kate said though clenched teeth. 'I want to get out of here.'

'We can't,' he muttered, swirling again, and Kate's head spun. 'It'll be midnight in half an hour. We've got to stick it out until after the turn of the century. For God's sake, have some courage, Kate.'

Her head snapped back and she stared up into his face. 'I haven't given permission for you to use my first name,' she said haughtily.

'Don't be absurd,' he muttered, his expression impatient. 'We're engaged to be married.'

'Over my dead body!'

He looked down at her sharply and then his lips twitched. 'You know, you're quite pretty when you're cross. I've noticed it before.'

'You humbug!' Kate grated, following his dancing steps instinctively. 'You conniving scoundrel! You knew this was going to happen, didn't you?'

'Yes.' His tone was hard with anger. 'But I'm in Luther's trap. I was given as much choice in the matter as you.'

'I don't believe you,' Kate declared. 'It's my inheritance, isn't it? That's what you're after.'

He looked down at her with mocking eyes. 'What else! It'd be a brave man who'd marry such a sharp-tongued shrew without *some* incentive.'

'Oh!' Kate gasped in shock and fury. 'Oh!'

'I'm sorry, Kate.' He did sound regretful, but she was in no mood to forgive. 'You sting me with your unfounded insults,' he went on, 'so I sting back. Let's call a truce, at least until after midnight.'

Kate had nothing further to say to him. She tried to turn off her mind and be aware only of the music and the glittering chandeliers above their heads, moving her legs like an automaton. Would this night never end?

A minute before midnight the music stopped, the guests standing about the ballroom in anticipation of the vital second when the century would turn. The huge grandfather clock in the hall began to strike out the preliminaries. Someone opened some French windows nearby, when cold air rushed in but no one seemed to mind, except Kate.

And then the first stroke of midnight sounded. Simultaneously, the ringing of church bells could be heard throughout the town, drifting in on the crisp night air. Suddenly the whole room went wild, with people milling about, hooting out joyful 'hurrahs', hugging and kissing each other with abandon.

Imprisoned by Simon's grip, Kate stood very still, numbed and chilled by a unimaginable coldness deep within her being. She felt removed from the merriment around her. It sounded far away. She could see no reason for rejoicing. At this moment she could see no future, even; none that could be endured, anyway.

Cecille rushed past, clinging to Bertram's hand as she dragged him along.

'Happy New Year, Kate!' she screamed in Kate's face. 'Happy New Century!'

Kate felt suddenly sick with dismay, and she looked up bewildered into the face of the man whose hands held her.

'Welcome to the twentieth century, Kate,' Simon said quietly.

The orchestra were playing 'Auld Lang Syne'; people began to sing and join hands. Kate wrenched herself from Simon's grip.

'I'll never marry you,' she cried out passionately. 'I'll die first.'

She turned and rushed away through the throng, resisting the many hands that tried to pull her into the expanding ring of merrymakers. She had to get away from all the laughing and celebration; away from people. She wanted to flee into the freezing night air and perish in the cold. Instead, she fled to the sanctuary of her bedroom.

The turning of a brand-new century hadn't changed the world overnight after all, Simon found. On the very first day, the staff of Vaughan & Templar, High-Class Emporium, had to be about their business as usual, no matter how hung over they were from the previous night's revelries.

He'd drunk quite a bit of champagne after Kate had abandoned him on the dance floor, and now had a splitting headache. The look of utter devastation on her face after Luther's announcement had remained with him all night.

She'd rather die, she'd said. That hurt. What with the memory of that and the champagne, he'd not slept a wink.

He could hardly see for the pain as he made his way to his small office in the household and furnishing department at ten minutes to nine, and had just hung up his bowler and muffler, and seated himself carefully at his desk when young Jones put his head around the door.

'Morning, Mr C,' said the boy jauntily. 'Bad head, is it? I'm selling headache powders, see, penny each. Want one?'

Despite his pain, Simon couldn't help grinning. 'Get out, you cheeky article.'

'Please yourself, mun. Oh, by the way, Miss Collins says His Nibs wants to see you, sharpish.'

'Out!' Simon stood up quickly, and a shattering pain shot through his skull. 'Wait a minute!' he went on, wincing. 'I *will* have one of those powders, after all.'

Simon's head felt no better as he opened the door to Luther's office. He hoped there was nothing very serious on his uncle's mind. The way his head felt he couldn't guarantee he wouldn't lose his temper completely, and that might spell the end for his mother.

'Good morning, Simon,' Luther began cordially enough.

Simon squinted at him through the pain. His uncle seemed to be in a very good mood now he had Kate exactly where he wanted her.

'Is it?'

'Undoubtedly, my boy!' He paused, as though in after-thought. 'How's your dear mother?'

'Weak,' Simon replied gloomily. 'It's her heart. The winter's cruel. I'm afraid she'll catch this terrible influenza sweeping the country. It's claimed the lives of many healthy people already.'

'What will be, will be,' Luther muttered in a disinterested tone, and Simon ground his teeth at his uncle's lack of feeling for his own flesh and blood.

'This weakness of the heart is a fault in our family,' Simon said with a rasp. 'You should be careful yourself, Luther.'

'Nonsense! I intend to live for ever. And why shouldn't I? Everything's going exactly as I planned.'

'Not for Kate,' Simon remarked with sarcasm. 'She was overwrought last night. It came as a great shock to her.'

Luther's lips tightened, but only momentarily. 'She should be grateful,' he said. 'An arranged marriage is better than ending up an arid old spinster.'

'I doubt she thinks so,' Simon said, easing himself on to the chair before Luther's desk. 'She swears she'll never marry me.'

'Huh! She has little choice.' Luther's voice was harsh. 'However, you must talk her around. I'd rather she came to it willingly than being forced.'

Simon didn't reply. The whole matter of swindling Kate out of her inheritance was becoming more and more distasteful. If it wasn't for his mother he'd tell Luther to go to hell.

'Simon, I'd like your opinion on a very private and personal matter,' Luther said confidentially. 'It must go no further, you understand.' He stood and began to pace the room. 'No mention of it to Kathryn, and certainly not to Evan. Do I have your word?'

Simon agreed, watching him with curiosity. There was an air of excitement about him, and he seemed almost younger.

'I've decided to marry again,' Luther said. 'I intend to ask Delphine Harrington to be my wife.' His eyes glinted as though expecting opposition. 'As her friend, do you think she'll accept me?'

Simon's heart sank. He was astonished that such a sharp-witted man as Luther could be taken in so quickly and easily by a lovely face and cunning mind. Delphine was much more foxy than he realised.

'This is a very sudden decision,' he said hesitantly. 'You know absolutely nothing about her or her background.'

Luther frowned. 'Are you implying Delphine is my social inferior?'

Simon shook his head, then wished he hadn't. Suddenly his headache was much worse. 'No, far from it. Her lineage can't be faulted, but that's not the issue, Luther. Delphine isn't what she seems.'

'Damnation, Simon!' Luther exploded. 'You're jealous.'

'It's not jealousy,' he denied strongly. 'It's a warning. Delphine is beautiful and charming, but there're depths to her, dark fathoms, of which you couldn't conceive. Consider this carefully.'

'You speak as a lover might,' Luther persisted in fury, obviously jealous himself.

Simon shook his head sadly. Clearly, Delphine already had power over Luther, and he could guess her tactics. It would be a strong man who could resist her physical charms, her willingness for intimacy. Better men than Luther had succumbed. If he hadn't known the truth before meeting her, he might have surrendered himself.

'Luther, I'm not exaggerating when I say that marrying Delphine could mean a great deal of misery for you, and possibly the downfall of our family.'

'You're an unprincipled blackguard!' Luther roared. 'How dare you defame that lady's name. If my control of the business didn't depend on your marriage to Kathryn, I'd send you packing, you and your decrepit mother.'

Seized with wrath, Simon leaped to his feet. 'That's unforgivable!' he stormed, the pain in his head forgotten in his rage. 'Perhaps you and Delphine deserve each other. So, go right ahead. Marry her and be damned to you!'

10

On the third day of the New Year Kate decided it was time to confront Luther Templar. She was angry with herself for putting it off for so long. He might think he'd won, but she'd show him she still had some fight in her.

Ethel was dusting the banisters on the staircase.

'Tell me immediately my stepfather returns from business,' she instructed the maid.

'He hasn't gone to business,' Ethel said. 'He did go in for an hour last Monday, but hasn't been to the shop since. He told Chivers he'd be working from home from now on.'

Kate was astonished. Luther had never missed a day at the shop since she could remember, not even for illness. He was never ill.

'Where is he now?'

'Inspecting the stable roof, Miss Kate.'

Kate fetched her cloak and, pulling on galoshes, made her way to the stables. Snow was still piled against the foot of the hedges.

Luther and Trott were standing by watching as Prosser, the old gardener, clung precariously to a ladder, while at the same time trying to put a rope around a huge branch that had imbedded itself in the stable roof.

As Kate approached with quiet steps, Luther was muttering furiously. Prosser finally succeeded in securing the rope, and descended shakily to the ground. His face was white and Kate guessed it wasn't only from the cold.

'You should've felled that rotten tree last summer,' Luther shouted at him angrily. 'Look at the damage, man! The cost of repairs will come out of your wages.'

'That's not fair!' Kate exclaimed, outraged at the injustice of it.

'Kathryn!' Luther whirled at the sound of her voice, surprise then impatience crossing his face. 'Be quiet. It's none of your business.'

She clenched her teeth, annoyed at his deprecating tone. 'It is!' she retorted rebelliously. 'Prosser's not to blame. It's your own fault for not getting some help for him. He's been with us for years, and it's getting too much for him.'

'No, no, Miss Kate.' Prosser stepped forward, alarm on his lined face. 'Still do my job, I can. I don't want no help.'

'You see!' Luther's smile was sneering. 'Your interference could've cost Prosser his job, Kathryn. Kindly leave staff matters to me; after all, it's my property.'

He turned back to the two men.

'Prosser, get that branch down so the damage can be assessed. Trott, help him. And have the rest of that damned tree felled today. I want no more damage, or you *will* be out of a job, Prosser.'

'Are the horses all right?' Kate asked anxiously as she fell into step beside Luther as he walked away.

'Frightened,' he answered. 'But Trott managed to calm them quite quickly last night, apparently. Luckily, his quarters are on the other side of the building or we might've lost a good groom, as well.'

They walked on in silence for a moment, then Luther paused and looked at her, hardly bothering to hide his irritation.

'I'm inspecting the grounds this morning, Kathryn. You won't want to accompany me, I'm sure. You'd better get back to the house.'

'No, I want to talk to you,' Kate insisted.

His eyes narrowed for a moment. 'Very well.'

He marched on, his steps more hurried, but Kate was determined to keep up with him, despite the treacherous path under her feet. She was glad they were outside, where the sly Chivers couldn't overhear.

'I won't do it, you know,' she blurted defiantly. 'I won't marry Simon Creswell, and nothing on earth will make me change my mind.'

He stopped abruptly and stared at her. 'I command it,' he said harshly.

'Huh!' Kate lifted her chin and her hood slipped back a little, the cold morning air biting into her skin. 'Command all you want, Luther. I refuse, and you can't force me. This is the twentieth century.'

He pursed his lips and stared hard at her as though weighing her up. It was such a calculated look that Kate shivered.

'You will, Kathryn,' he said in a confident tone. 'You see, you have two choices. You'll marry Simon willingly or spend the rest of your life in a mental institution.'

'Oh, not that old threat again!' Kate scoffed. 'I'm not in the least intimidated.'

He stared at her in silence, but something in his eyes warned her he'd go to any lengths to get his way, and her heart contracted with sudden fear.

'You'd never get away with it,' she said shakily.

'Of course I would.' Luther smiled mockingly. 'In fact, it'd be very easy in the face of your mother's suicide. I've Dr

Penfold under my thumb. He'll do exactly as I say or go to prison.'

Kate's jaw dropped open. 'Prison? What's he done?'

'Never mind the details,' Luther snapped. 'Penfold breaks the law very seriously almost on a daily basis.'

'I don't believe it,' Kate spluttered. 'My father would've known.'

'Your father was an incompetent fool!' Luther blazed.

Kate felt hot blood rush to her face at this insult. 'At least he wasn't a liar and a cheat,' she cried out furiously. 'You said I could never marry or have children, now you're forcing me into this unwanted match. Admit your lies, Luther. Admit my mother did *not* commit suicide. How did she really die? Tell me that! Because you know.'

Luther's lips turned purple with rage. 'Silence!' he roared, his eyes blazing. He seemed unable to say more for a moment, then he gasped, 'I'll tolerate no more defiance.' He appeared to struggle to take a breath.

'I've reached the end of my rope with you, my girl,' he rasped, his expression vicious. 'Your disobedience ends now.' He wagged a finger in her face. 'Listen to me. Unless you agree to marry Simon this instant, Penfold will be fetched. You'll begin the rest of your life in a padded cell this very night.' His gaze was menacing. 'Well, what's it to be?'

'I hate you!' Kate screamed at him in impotent rage. 'You'll pay for this, Luther Templar, I swear it.'

Slithering and sliding in her haste to get away, Kate fled back to the house, and rushed through the back entrance into the big kitchen. Mrs Trobert, stirring a large stewpot on top of the range, turned as Kate came barging in.

'Whatever's the matter?' she asked. 'Has one of the horses been hurt?'

Kate stared at the housekeeper miserably, on the point of blurting it all out, but she hesitated. It wouldn't be right to discuss Luther's treachery with a servant, even one as faithful as Mrs Trobert. If only there was another woman she could confide in. If only Aunt Agnes would reappear.

Kate boycotted both luncheon and dinner, being content with meagre snacks in her bedroom. Some time later when she was thinking of going to bed, someone knocked at her bedroom door. Kate was momentarily disconcerted, wondering if Simon Creswell was audacious enough to come to her room. She opened the door a crack to see Delphine standing there.

'May I come in, Kate?'

Delphine swept past her in a cloud of exquisite perfume and a rustle of silk skirts. 'My dear!' she began. 'Where have you been hiding yourself all day?'

'I'm indisposed,' Kate said hesitantly.

Delphine gave her a knowing glance. 'You're upset, of course you are,' she said. 'But we women must learn to ride out the adversities men throw at us, and turn them to our advantage.'

Kate was flummoxed at such flowery words. They sounded like something out of a novel. 'I don't know what you mean,' she said hesitantly.

'Kate, I *know*.' Delphine's smile was condescending. 'You can't bluff me, my dear. I caught a glimpse of your face right after Luther announced your betrothal. You were shocked – devastated.'

Kate sat on the bed, letting her shoulders droop. Delphine sat beside her, putting an arm around Kate's shoulders.

'Let me be a sister to you,' she murmured persuasively. 'Tell me everything.'

'I'm doomed,' Kate began, feeling a sob rise in her throat at the relief of at last being able to talk to someone who understood. She went on to tell Delphine of Luther's threat and his falsehoods.

'He lied when he told my fiancé, Mansel, there was madness in my family,' Kate sobbed. 'But now he insists I marry that odious Simon.'

'I see,' Delphine said slowly, patting Kate's hand.

'My mother didn't kill herself,' Kate wailed, suddenly beset by a sense of powerlessness and grief. 'But Luther knows more about her death then he admits to, I'd swear to it.'

Delphine's expression was eager and alert. 'Tell me more,' she urged, her eyes gleaming.

Kate had poured out her heart, her suspicions and her dreads, and Delphine was sympathetic.

'My poor child,' she cooed. 'You're badly used. But consider. Will marriage to Simon be so terrible? He's handsome, and quite cultured . . . for a man of his low class.'

Kate was startled at Delphine's deprecating tone. 'I thought he was your friend.'

Delphine gave a tinkling laugh. 'Hardly. He's my brother's friend. We barely tolerate each other for Bertie's sake. Nevertheless, I think he'll make a good husband for you.'

Kate jumped up quickly, offended. 'But I don't trust him,' she exclaimed in dismay. 'He's cunning and devious, like Luther.' She wrung her hands in misery. 'Besides, I love Bertram, and he loves me. He wants to marry me, he said so.'

Delphine straightened her back, and her violet eyes glittered, while her smile was suddenly a little strained. 'Oh, my poor girl!' she began in a subdued tone. She rose from the bed, and grasped Kate's hand tightly. 'Kate, I'm sorry to have to tell you this, but Bertie's promised in marriage to another.'

'What?' Kate snatched her hand away to clutch her throat in disbelief. 'No, that can't be true.'

Delphine shook her head sadly. 'It's true. He's been engaged to be married for two years now. A young woman in Bath; the daughter of a baronet, no less.'

Kate shook her head again, speechless, and could only stare at her companion.

'They'd have been married long ago,' Delphine said confidentially, 'but for some difficulty with the father over a dowry.' She nodded emphatically. 'Bertie's totally devoted to her, and they plan to marry quite soon.'

Kate still refused to believe it, remembering the touch of Bertram's lips on hers, and the warmth of his hand on her arm. 'But he'd have told me,' she cried. 'Bertram's too considerate to lead me on.'

'Did he ever tell you unequivocally that he loved you?' Delphine asked archly.

Kate hesitated, reviewing in her mind everything Bertram had ever said to her. She couldn't remember him saying those actual words. 'Not in direct terms, no,' she admitted, feeling tears smart behind her eyes. 'But he wouldn't deliberately deceive me. He knows I love him. I've made it plain.'

Delphine put her arm around Kate's shoulders. 'My dear,' she said. 'I'm ashamed to admit Bertie's been trifling with your affections, and I'm cross with him for it.' She kissed Kate's cheek. 'It's too bad of him, but then, he's a man, and all men are deceivers. It's their nature.'

She was betrayed at every turn. Distressed, Kate put her hands up to cover her face to hide her irritation with Delphine's studied words, as though she were play-acting.

'What am I to do?' Kate moaned. 'I love him.'

'Take my advice,' Delphine said in a practical tone. 'Marry

Simon Creswell and be mistress of your own household. If you're clever, and I believe you are, Kate, you'll find a way to manage him and have things your own way.'

'I despise him.'

'Despising a man has never been a bar to marriage,' Delphine said. 'In despising him, you'll remain in control. It's love that renders a woman helpless in marriage.'

Kate lay awake that night. It broke her heart to know Bertram's words of love were false, but she had to accept that now, for why would his own sister lie?

She had little choice now but to marry Simon Creswell. There was nothing else she could do. But she could lay down some rules for this forced marriage.

Next morning, waiting in the doorway of her small sitting-room, she called quietly to Simon as he passed by.

'Mr Creswell.'

'Kate. You're up early.'

She lifted her chin at his familiar greeting, even more determined to take charge of the interview. 'Please come into my sitting-room a moment,' she said stiffly. 'I want a word with you.'

'Certainly.'

Kate closed the door behind them. He smiled mockingly.

'Is that wise? People might talk.'

'Don't be facetious,' Kate said sternly. 'This is serious.' She hesitated a moment before going on, knowing she must trust him up to a point. 'Luther's ready to carry out his threat to have me committed,' she went on shakily, the mere idea making her stomach churn. 'Unless I marry you.'

To her annoyance his lips twitched again.

'Ah! A very difficult choice, I appreciate that,' he said lightly. 'But I suggest you settle for the sham marriage.'

She ground her teeth in fury at his amusement. 'You're enjoying my climbdown, obviously,' she snapped. 'It must make you feel very superior.'

His mouth tightened, his humour gone. 'I like it no better than you,' he retorted quickly. 'As I've explained before, Luther has me in a vice.'

Kate swallowed hard, wondering if she were about to make a grave mistake, but could see no other course of action. 'Then let's make a bargain,' she suggested. 'Our marriage will be in name only.' She lowered her eyes, twisting her fingers together nervously, feeling her cheeks flame at what she must say next. 'I'll not expect you to demand your – marital rights. It'll be as you say, a sham marriage.'

'You needn't fear to bear children,' he said frankly. 'There's no such condition as hereditary insanity. Luther lied.'

A wave of relief washed over her at this confirmation of what she'd known instinctively. 'I've always known it in my heart,' she said. 'He lied about my mother's suicide, too, didn't he?' she went on hopefully.

Simon shook his head. 'I know nothing of that,' he said. 'He confided in me about Jenkins, but little else. My uncle plays his cards very close to his chest.'

She regarded him steadily, wondering why he'd revealed as much as he had, and suspected deep reasons of his own.

'Thank you for telling me, but it makes no difference,' she went on disdainfully. 'We'll live separate lives. We'll never be . . . intimate.'

He didn't respond for a few moments, but looked at her with a steely glint in his eyes. When he spoke his tone was harsh.

'So, you don't want children at all.' His lips tightened. 'A strange attitude for any woman.'

Kate flashed a punishing glance at him. 'I certainly don't want *your* children,' she retorted hotly.

'So be it!' he growled. 'That'll suit Luther very well.'

'What do you mean?'

'You play right into his hands, Kate. It'll please him that no descendant of the Vaughan or Creswell families can dispute any heirs he might acquire.'

Kate blinked. 'Heirs? Luther has no heir except yourself.'

Simon pursed his lips, studying her. 'That'll change soon,' he said. 'Luther swore me to secrecy, but you've a right to know. He intends to marry Delphine. No doubt he hopes for an heir.'

'What?' Kate was startled. 'But Delphine said nothing of this to me when she came to my room late last night.'

Simon's eyes narrowed. 'What did she want?' he asked sharply.

Kate's nostrils flared at his impertinence. 'That's none of your business,' she snapped. 'The point is, she didn't mention it.'

'Perhaps he hasn't asked her yet,' he said, his mouth tightening at her sharp tone. 'Delphine's devious and experienced. She's guessed his intentions, all right. Huh! She's been scheming towards it from the moment she got here. Either Luther or Evan. She's not the least choosy.'

Kate was astonished and somewhat shocked. 'You make her sound like . . .'

'Like a hussy?' he suggested wryly.

Kate nodded, staring at him silently. Simon's mouth set in a grim line.

'That's a polite word for her, Kate,' he said seriously. 'Evan should disentangle himself. You must persuade him.'

'He's not entangled with her, as you put it,' she said hotly. 'You make it sound sordid.'

'You are too young and innocent to understand men,' he said flatly. 'Or women like Delphine Harrington.'

She was confused at his meaning, and felt naïve and unworldly for a moment, but then rallied. After all, she'd no reason to believe he spoke the truth about Delphine, or about anything else for that matter.

'Evan wouldn't behave dishonourably,' she said stubbornly. 'Besides, his affections are his own affair. I won't interfere, and neither should you.' She tilted her chin defiantly. 'You're not family, Mr Creswell, kindly remember that.'

'Not yet,' he retorted with a smile that irritated her. His gaze was steady on hers, and Kate found she had to look away. 'You still don't trust me, do you?' he went on, a hint of rancour in his voice.

'Of course not.' She spoke sharply. 'Could anyone blame me under the circumstances? I'd be a fool to trust Luther's man an inch.'

'I'm *not* his man,' Simon growled. 'Not by choice, anyway.' He paused. 'I'll prove it,' he said quickly. 'There's something else you should know. Luther plans to get his hands on the shares your father left you in order to gain total control of the business.'

'That's not possible,' Kate exclaimed in disbelief. 'My father's will is watertight.'

'Oh, Luther has it all worked out.' Simon's smile was cold and resentful. 'After we're safely married, I'm to persuade you.' He tilted his head. 'With dire threats, of course, to hand the shares over to me. In turn I'm forced to make them over to him.' He hesitated, looking at her keenly. 'Do you realise he's already acquired Evan's shares?'

'How?'

'By duress, or even blackmail.'

'Preposterous!' she exclaimed. The idea that Evan could be blackmailed was ludicrous.

'It's true, I tell you,' Simon insisted. 'Evan's been indiscreet apparently.' He held up a hand to silence her. 'I know no more than that. You must ask your brother.'

'I don't believe it!' she declared loyally, then hesitated thoughtfully.

'If you'll help me, Kate, we can beat Luther at his own game,' he went on eagerly. 'Marry me and hand over the shares. I'll take the seat on the board and whip up opposition against Luther, or even defeat him altogether. What do you say?'

Kate stared at him, astounded at his audacity and his belief that she could be tricked so easily. 'Oh, you are a devious devil,' she blurted at last. 'And you must think me a complete fool.'

'How can you say that when I'm trusting *you* completely, Kate,' he said in deep seriousness. 'If my uncle learns that I've revealed his plans, my mother and I are finished, put out on the street.'

'So you say!' Kate scoffed, though still uncertain of her ground.

'Damnation!' Simon exploded. 'Why are you so obstinate?'

'Because I'm not the silly young girl you take me for,' Kate flung back at him. 'Make no mistake, Mr Creswell, I've agreed to marry you only because Bertram, the man I love, is engaged to another. If he were free I'd never marry you, no matter what threats are made.'

Maybe that was idle bravado, and easy to say now, but she didn't care.

'Bertram? Engaged to be married?' Simon looked mystified. 'What're you talking about?'

'Delphine told me,' Kate said, a lump rising in her throat. 'It was she who helped me make up my mind about marrying you.'

'Oh, did she?' Simon looked angry.

She was ashamed to be weeping in front of him, but couldn't help it. 'I wish someone had told me straight away that Bertram belongs to another,' she sobbed, staring up at him accusingly through her tears. 'I might not have fallen in love with him.'

Simon's returned stare was unsympathetic. 'You fall in love too easily, Kate,' he said with impatience. 'First Mansel Jenkins and now, within weeks, your affections turn to Bertram. What kind of love is this that flits so easily from one man to another?'

Kate gasped at his insolence. '*What?*'

'You've no idea what love is,' he said disdainfully. 'You're merely playing at it like a silly schoolgirl.'

'How dare you?' Kate was furious. 'You're insufferable, and entirely without feeling and human decency. God help me if I'm to be joined for life to such an uncaring monster.'

As she rushed out of the room towards the staircase, she heard him follow.

'Kate! Wait a moment.'

She turned to face him, giving him a killing glance.

'A lifetime in a lunatic asylum is becoming more and more attractive,' she sneered. 'At least I'd be protected from you.'

11

On a cold evening in the middle of February, Kate waited for Simon in the hall and handed him the black-edged letter, which had arrived in the afternoon mail. Guessing what it meant, Kate thought it too cold-blooded, even for Simon Creswell, to leave it on the hall table for him to find. He took it from her with shaking fingers and tore open the envelope.

'It's obviously bad news,' she ventured.

'It's from my mother's housekeeper,' he said quietly, his face suddenly drawn and pale. 'She has passed away.' He paused and swallowed hard, and she saw he struggled to control his feelings in front of her. 'Influenza,' he went on raggedly. 'Her poor heart couldn't stand it.'

'I'm so sorry,' Kate said, meaning every word, and feeling a shaft of pity, despite their continued animosity. The pain of her own mother's terrible passing was forever fresh in her mind and heart.

He glanced at her briefly before his gaze returned to the letter. 'I leave for Bath tonight,' he said sombrely. 'I won't return until after the funeral.'

'Shouldn't you wait until morning to travel? The weather's so poor.'

He took his watch out of his waistcoat pocket. 'No. There's a train at nine o'clock tonight. I want to get there as soon as possible,' he said resolutely. 'But first I must speak with

Luther.' He paused and gazed at her keenly. 'When I do return we must talk.'

Kate bridled. 'About what?'

'Things have changed with my mother's passing. It affects you, too.'

Kate frowned, lifting her chin. 'I don't see how.'

'I've no time to explain now,' he said shortly and walked away in the direction of the study, leaving Kate to grind her teeth in consternation.

Not bothering to knock, Simon walked straight in, and his uncle looked up in surprise.

'This'd better be important,' Luther said. 'I don't like interruptions when I'm doing the household accounts.'

Simon felt rage engulf him. 'Is the death of your own sister important enough?' he rasped.

'What?'

'My mother will no longer be a burden on you,' Simon went on harshly. 'She's gone where your neglect can no longer hurt her.'

Luther got to his feet. 'Mary's dead? You have my deepest sympathy, Simon.'

'Oh, have I!' he said raggedly. 'Pity you didn't have sympathy for her when she was alive and in dire need. I can never forgive you for that, Luther.'

'You're overwrought, my boy,' Luther said. 'That's understandable, and I'll overlook your outburst this one time.'

Simon felt exasperated. 'I leave for Bath on the hour,' he said tensely. 'I'll probably be away a week. I take it you have no objection to me being away from my department?'

'Certainly not, Simon.' He gave a small cough as though in apology. 'I'm afraid I won't be able to attend the funeral. Pressure of business.'

'You mean you won't take the trouble to pay your last respects to your remaining sister,' Simon said wrathfully. 'Huh! It's no more than I expected.'

Luther looked angry. 'Obviously, you're much more upset than I realised, but there's no call for impertinence.' His mouth twisted in mockery. 'You needn't expect to inherit anything from her,' he said. 'She was, after all, no more than a pauper, thanks to your father.'

Simon couldn't trust himself to reply, and, turning on his heel, left the room. But his heart was full of vengeance. Somehow he'd pay Luther back for all the misery his mother had suffered; somehow he'd bring Luther to his knees.

Evan reached the crossroads at Fforestfach at mid morning, and walked his horse slowly, afraid of a slip in the icy ruts in the track. He cursed the need to come here today, and was reluctant to arrive at his house. He wouldn't have made the visit at all if his aunt didn't demand it, writing to him at Old Grove House almost each day to complain. He must put a stop to that before Luther discovered his arrangement with her.

Evan was edgy and bad-tempered. Aunt Agnes would rebuke him for his long absence, and Eirwen would be clinging. He cursed under his breath again, dreading the coming reunion with her. He couldn't bear to think of her open face and rosy cheeks, and wondered how she'd ever captivated him. Now he thought only of Delphine, day and night, and his need to be with her burned like an eternal flame.

His house, situated on two acres of land, abutted the fields of a small farm, and lay a quarter of a mile behind the Marquis Arms public house, and was approached through an archway between some ancient stone cottages, and down a long, narrow, winding lane.

Arriving at last, he quartered his horse in the single stable behind the house and made his way in through the kitchen door. Megan, Aunt Agnes's maid, was at the sink rinsing some crockery. She looked up startled to hear his footsteps on the flagstone floor.

'Oh, sir, I didn't know you were due to arrive.'

'Where's Miss Vaughan?' he asked abruptly, noticing the coldness of the room, and the lack of cooking aromas.

'In the sitting-room, sir.'

'And Mrs Vaughan?'

'The mistress has gone to the farm, sir.'

Evan was astounded at such foolishness. 'What, on foot in this weather?' he snapped.

He made his way to the front sitting-room and strode in. At the sight of him, his father's sister, Agnes Vaughan, rose awkwardly from a rocking-chair with the aid of a stick, and faced him squarely, her eyes, so like Kate's, flashing with anger.

'So!' she began, her tone reproving. 'You've deigned to put in an appearance, have you?'

'I'm my own master, Aunt,' Evan said pithily. 'And answer to no one.' His conscience told him he was in the wrong, yet he couldn't help excusing himself. 'The shop takes up a great deal of my time.'

'The shop! Huh!' Agnes's lips tightened. 'You talk as though it were your own,' she said scornfully. 'It's Luther Templar's shop now. He controls everything.' Her lip curled. 'Even you, I dare say.'

'He doesn't control me!' Evan blurted, but his words sounded hollow even to his own ears. 'You insult me, Aunt, even though I provide you with free board and lodge.'

'For your own convenience,' Agnes retorted sharply. 'Who else would keep your wife company in this out-of-the-way place, I'd like to know.'

'It's necessary,' Evan said sourly. 'You must see that.'

'No, I don't see it,' she snapped, her glance contemptuous. 'You're weak like your father,' she went on. 'And swayed by your own interests and desires, as he was, otherwise he wouldn't have let that scoundrel Luther gain so much power.' She stared at him fixedly. 'Beware of your base desires, Evan, lest they lead you to destruction.'

He was startled. 'What do you mean by that?' he demanded, feeling suddenly uneasy. She couldn't know anything of the way he behaved with Delphine in the privacy of his rooms, yet he felt apprehension at her choice of words.

'I still have my contacts,' Agnes said sharply. 'Through my maid's weekly visits to her parents in Beach Street. I know what's going on.'

He was vexed. 'I'd rather Megan didn't visit town,' he said quickly. 'She may be recognised, and questions asked about your whereabouts. It could be embarrassing.'

Her glance was sharp. 'I don't understand your fear of your marriage being made known,' she said. 'You could've done better in a wife, socially, I'll admit, but there's nothing shameful in the union. With careful tutoring Eirwen can take her place by your side in society.'

'No! I don't wish it.'

Evan was too quick to respond, and his aunt's eyes narrowed.

'So, there *is* truth in what I've heard,' she said sharply. 'I might've known it was more than pride.'

He was immediately wary. 'What do you mean?'

The creases around her mouth deepened in a look of

disapproval. 'I hear your stepfather's entertaining guests from Bath,' she said. 'A handsome brother and sister.' She paused, and he was uncomfortably aware of her shrewd study of his face. 'They say the woman's causing strife between you and Luther,' she went on stonily. 'There's rivalry for her favours.'

'Unfounded lies!' Evan burst out furiously.

'You dally with her,' Agnes insisted bluntly. 'While your wife and child scratch for sustenance and warmth.'

'This is preposterous,' Evan bellowed heatedly, feeling sweat break out on his forehead. He flicked it away quickly with shaking fingers.

She was staring at him fiercely. 'Good God, man!' she cried out. 'Not even you'd be fool enough to take a mistress under Luther's roof, the very woman he wants for himself.'

'Who are these gossips?' Evan shouted. 'I demand to know.'

'Servants chatter among themselves. There's little that goes on in any house that they don't know about. Megan reports it all to me.' Her glance was stony. 'I see by your face it's all true.'

'None of it's true,' Evan lied desperately. 'I swear.' He paused, his heart sinking. 'I hope Eirwen's heard nothing of this.'

'I'm old, but not an idiot,' Agnes snapped angrily. 'Nor am I a meddler. But, remember this, Luther's a man you cross at your peril.'

Evan was badly shaken. He didn't need to be warned about Luther. And he was concerned about gossip, even at servant level. If his aunt could find out so much so easily so could his stepfather. Luther wouldn't hesitate to take revenge and see him in the gutter, a ruined man.

'While you entertain yourself with another woman,' Agnes went on bitterly, 'your family suffers.'

She pointed a rheumy finger at the fireplace behind her,

where small logs burned brightly, though not giving out much heat.

'The coal merchant's refused to supply us,' she said. 'He hasn't been paid since before Christmas. These local trades-people won't wait for their money, as they do in town. After all, we're outsiders.'

'This is outrageous,' Evan said, feeling his face heat up again with humiliation. 'I'm a landowner. How dare they refuse.'

Agnes's faint smile was mocking as she shook her head.

'This is the twentieth century,' she said. 'Apparently, we landed gentry aren't so awesome as we once were.'

'All the same, it's an impertinence,' Evan blustered to hide his guilt.

He had neglected his responsibilities for Delphine's sake. She was demanding, but he couldn't deny her anything when her soft silken body yielded to his.

'I've a good mind to take my business elsewhere,' he went on feebly.

Agnes gave an exclamation of impatience. 'It's only through Eirwen's ingenuity we've something to burn at all,' she said pithily. 'She borrowed a horse from the farm and dragged some fallen logs up from the copse. She had to chop them herself.' Her tone was suddenly scathing. 'Since you didn't see fit to provide us with a handyman.'

He was flabbergasted at Eirwen's resourcefulness. She had more spirit than he thought, and would certainly make trouble for him if she learned of his affair with Delphine.

'I'll see to it directly, Aunt,' he said quickly, anxious to avoid any such vexation.

He felt coldness around his heart. Delphine mustn't hear of his marriage, either. Accommodating to his every pleasure as she was, she obviously wanted and expected marriage. He couldn't bear it if he lost her now, not after experiencing the boundless passion of her lovemaking, and her expertise in pleasing a man.

'I'm glad to hear it,' Agnes said with disdain.

'And, of course, you must have a man about the place,' he hurried on. 'Someone local. Perhaps you'll make enquiries in the village, Aunt?'

'Very well.' She sniffed. 'I'll send Megan up to the Marquis Arms later. The landlord's been helpful to us.'

Evan looked around him, suddenly at a loss, and longing to leave, but knowing full well he couldn't, not until he'd spoken with Eirwen.

'Well, I'm here,' he said, spreading his hands in a mocking gesture. 'But where's my son and wife to greet me?'

'Russell's in his cot in her bedroom,' Agnes said. 'It's warmer in bed for a baby in this weather. Meanwhile,' she went on harshly, 'Eirwen is begging some provisions from the local farmer's wife.' She folded her lips in disgust. 'To think a Vaughan must stoop to that. Luckily, your wife doesn't suffer from pride. What she lacks in social graces she makes up for in common sense.'

'Beg?' Evan was bewildered. He'd never thought of Eirwen as a true member of his family, and the idea upset him.

'It's not only the coal merchant who's refused further credit,' Agnes said sharply. 'Your misplaced pride and your neglect hurts us all, even your own son, Evan.'

Evan's conscience was stung. He realised if he didn't make amends soon, his aunt would lose patience altogether, and might leave his house. Eirwen couldn't manage without her, and would undoubtedly come looking for him at Old Grove House. The thought brought cold sweat to his brow.

'I'll leave household expenses in your hands, Aunt Agnes,' he said in a placating tone. 'You'll get an ample amount each month.' He'd do this even if it meant he spent less with his tailor. 'And please inform me if you need more.'

Agnes raised her brows, her tone frosty. 'Does that mean your wife won't see you again for some time? Your son hardly knows you, Evan. You didn't even bother to come to visit him on his first birthday.'

He'd forgotten and had nothing to say in his defence.

'I can't understand how you can ignore him,' Agnes went on, her expression softening. 'He's so like your father in looks. He'll be an asset to the business, in time.'

Evan wetted his lips but said nothing. There were years yet before he need worry about that. He reached for his hat on a nearby chair, and gave a little bow to his aunt. She looked astounded and then angry.

'You're not leaving without seeing them, surely?'

'I've clients waiting . . .'

At that moment the door opened and Eirwen came into the room, carrying Russell in a woollen shawl. Her face lit up at the sight of her husband, and she hastily put the baby down on a deep armchair nearby.

'Evan, my dearest! You've come home at last.'

She ran to him, and before he could prevent it threw her arms around his neck, placing her lips against his, then, stepping back, lifted the baby into her arms again.

'Do you want to hold your son, dearest? It's such a long time since you've seen him.'

She held the child out, and reluctantly Evan took him and held him against his chest.

'Oh, *Duw! Duw!*' Eirwen exclaimed distractedly. 'I've nothing tasty for your dinner, *cariad*. That dratted butcher wouldn't let me have even half a pound of best pork sausage.' She sniffed disparagingly. 'Haven't been paid, he said. I told him straight, I did. Married to a rich man, I am, I said, so he was talking through his straw hat.'

She giggled at her own joke, the roses in her cheeks deepening in hue. Her prettiness, which once entrapped him, now seemed commonplace, even tawdry. He turned his gaze away from her in sudden aversion and bitterness, and filled his mind instead with images of the porcelain flawlessness of Delphine's skin, imagining the silkiness of her breasts under his fingers.

'All bills will be settled,' Agnes said heavily. 'Isn't that so, Evan?'

He snapped out of his reverie at her words. 'Yes, yes. It'll be put right,' he confirmed. Still not looking at Eirwen, he went on, 'Don't worry about dinner. I can't stay today. Pressure of business won't wait, you see.'

'But I haven't seen you for weeks.' She looked crestfallen. 'We've not . . . been alone for so long,' she went on meaningfully, and then glanced briefly towards Agnes in embarrassment, her cheeks flushing. 'I am your wife, Evan.'

'Eirwen's right,' Agnes said. 'A husband's place is at his wife's side. The daily journey into town from here would be little trouble to you if we had a horse and carriage. The new handyman can act as groom.'

'What new handyman?' Eirwen asked, looking from one to the other.

'It's true.' Agnes nodded, her lips thinning. 'A handyman *and* the bills paid. My goodness!' Her tone was scathing. 'We'll hardly know ourselves.'

'A carriage is out of the question,' he declared firmly. 'We can't stable two horses.

'A small trap, then,' Eirwen said. 'Or even a gig.' She

gripped his hand tightly. 'Oh, please, Evan, dear,' she urged. 'I could drive that myself, and even go to market in town.' She tossed her head. 'I'll show these local traders I'm not a woman to be trifled with.'

'Allow a woman to drive herself!' Evan handed his son back to Eirwen, and stared at her in consternation. 'Hardly proper behaviour, Eirwen,' he said, his tone stern and reprimanding. 'You're not in the Valleys now.'

'Evan!' Her face flushed bright red. 'How can you speak to me like that? What's happening between us? Are you tired of me already?' Her eyes flashed in sudden pique. 'My father warned me this could happen.'

'Then you should've listened to him,' he flashed back. 'And saved us both a lot of regret.'

'Oh!' Eirwen covered her mouth with her hand, her expression shocked. Evan was conscious of his aunt standing by watching everything.

'I'm sorry,' he apologised, more to Agnes than Eirwen, and turned to leave.

'You can't go like this,' Agnes said, censure in her tone. 'You can't just walk away without an explanation of your abominable behaviour towards Eirwen. She has a right to know your intentions.'

Evan was exasperated. This visit was a disaster, and he wished fervently he'd ignored his aunt's letters of complaint.

'I refuse to explain myself in my own home,' he said brusquely. 'Especially to you, Aunt Agnes.'

'Home!' Eirwen exploded, her cheeks reddening. 'This isn't *your* home, Evan. You're never in it.' She folded her arms across her breast, and looked at him defiantly. 'For two pins,' she said, 'I'd take Russ and go to my parents in Trehafod. At least I'd not go cold or hungry.'

'Do as you damned well please,' he thundered. 'I'd rather you went.'

Eirwen looked shocked. 'What's changed you, Evan?' she asked plaintively. 'I love you still. Why are you so angry with me?'

She seized his arm, but he didn't want to look at her. He wished she would go back to the Valleys, and leave him in peace, and then he could forget all about her and the child.

'Don't press me, Eirwen,' he said impatiently. 'I won't be questioned like this. I'm going.'

He went hurriedly, glad to forget her. Eirwen stood between him and what he desired most in the world. But nothing would keep him from Delphine, not even death.

Evan dined at his club in the High Street, and arrived home just after eleven, going straight to his rooms, expecting Delphine to come to him as usual. He was about to undress when someone tapped at the door and Chivers walked straight in.

Evan stared at the butler, annoyed. 'What're you doing about at this time of night?' he said sharply. 'I didn't ring.'

'No, sir, but I want a word with you.'

'Whatever it is it'll have to wait until morning,' Evan said dismissively, loosening his tie.

He removed his cufflinks and then sat down to remove his shoes. Chivers didn't retreat but closed the door and stood waiting silently.

Evan glanced up at him, irritated. Why was the man lingering? Damn it! Delphine might arrive any minute.

'That'll be all, Chivers.'

Chivers cleared his throat, but still didn't go.

'I said clear off!'

'It's about a letter I found in your wastepaper basket,' Chivers said, ignoring the outburst. 'Very careless, that was.'

'What?' Evan frowned, perplexed. 'What letter?'

'From your aunt, sir, mentioning your wife and child.'

'What?' Evan jumped up. 'What the devil are you talking about, man?'

Chivers pursed his lips. 'Well, sir, knowing how the master feels about Miss Agnes Vaughan, you wouldn't want him knowing you've been harbouring her.' The butler's smile was sly. 'Then there's the little matter of you putting a common shop-girl up the spout and marrying her. You don't want that gossiped about, do you? Five guineas, sir, and I'll see the letter's destroyed and my mouth stays shut.'

'You blackmailing bounder!' Evan shouted, although he was furious with himself for not destroying that last letter as he had all the others. 'You'll not get a penny piece out of me. Show the letter to Templar, if you dare. He won't pay you either.'

'Others might. Miss Harrington won't take kindly to you having a wife already,' Chivers said. 'Not after her being so generous with her . . . friendship, so to speak.'

'Damn you to hell!' Evan roared. 'Get out of my sight before I take my fist to you.'

Delphine waited until midnight to go to Evan's room. She was flitting like a ghost along the gallery at the top of the main staircase when a dark shape emerged suddenly from the shadows of a doorway, carrying a candle.

'Will you take my light, miss?'

She stopped in her tracks, momentarily disconcerted at being caught out, and then was angry.

'Are you spying on me, Chivers?' she hissed back at him.

'Well, it wouldn't be the first time.' His tone was offensive.

'You'll regret it, I promise you,' she said.

He gave a low scornful laugh, and Delphine's hackles rose.

'I mean it,' she murmured. 'I have your master just where I want him. You'll be dismissed at a moment's notice if I ask it.'

'I don't think so,' he drawled confidently. 'I know too much about Mr Templar.' He sniggered softly. 'You'd give your eyeteeth to know what I know.'

She was interested but wouldn't show it, and stared at him, lips tight.

'Besides, you're not too fragrant yourself,' he went on when she didn't speak. 'With your almost nightly visits to Mr Vaughan.'

Her breath caught, but she kept silence, realising his game was blackmail. Her mind raced ahead, weighing up options.

'And even more interesting are your late-night visits to your brother's room. It's often dawn before you leave him. What'll the master make of that, I wonder?'

That was too much for her.

'You creeping cobra!' Delphine spat out the words, her hands clawed, ready to rake his face with her fingernails.

'Incestuous whore!' he hissed back, venom in his tone.

Delphine gasped at his audacious words, and felt a chill. Chivers was dangerous. He could ruin all her carefully laid plans with a few careless words, and suddenly she was afraid, a new and unpleasant experience for her.

'You've no proof,' she whispered, when she'd got her breath back. 'It's my word against yours.' She swallowed hard and went on hesitantly. 'What is it you want anyway?'

'Huh!' He looked her up and down, his tone scornful. 'You've got nothing I want, except money.'

'What?'

'I'm selling, not buying,' he said sarcastically. 'I've a letter here, addressed to Evan Vaughan.' He took it out of his pocket, and waved it under her nose. 'The master would like information about the party who wrote it, but I reckon you'd pay for proof that Mr Vaughan is already married.'

Delphine was interested, despite anger at his insolence. 'What's your price?'

'Five guineas.'

'Don't be absurd! I've no money.'

'That's a pity. Looks like the old man will get all the gossip. At least I'll be in his good books for a while.' There was a new threat in his voice.

'All the gossip?' she asked slowly.

'Templar thinks he's clever, but he doesn't know half what goes on. It's my duty to tell him.'

Delphine tightened her lips. Of course he wouldn't keep his mouth shut.

'All right!' she said. 'I don't have any money, but what about this?' She slipped a bracelet off her wrist. 'I swear it's worth more than five guineas. It's gold, and those are genuine sapphires.'

He examined the bracelet by the flickering light of the candle, while she held her breath, awaiting his verdict.

'All right,' he said at last. 'It's a deal.' And handed her the letter. She glanced at it.

'How do I know this letter's genuine?' she asked, looking up, but Chivers had already melted into the darkness.

Delphine stood for a moment in the silence and shivered. Chivers could still betray her. Luther Templar must be snared within the next few days; somehow she must manoeuvre him into a proposal of marriage.

But she hadn't finished with Evan, either. Chivers would be back for more, and Evan would provide the money to pay him off.

12

Standing at his mother's graveside one last time before returning to Swansea, Simon's thoughts were not on his mother
but on Kate. He'd thought long and hard about their separate
situations over the endless week before the funeral.

He had the power to walk away now. He'd be penniless
again, but at least he'd be his own man. The idea of penury
didn't bother him too much. After all, he'd been poor all his
life, and he was still young, with no responsibilities now he was
alone.

Kate was still in desperate circumstances however. He
didn't doubt for a moment that, should he back out of the
agreement, Luther would find another suitor for Kate,
possibly some unscrupulous scoundrel who'd ill-treat her.
He might even carry out his threat to have her put away, or
worse.

He couldn't walk away from that possibility with a clear
conscience, Simon decided. Besides, the need to avenge his
mother still burned in his heart, and Kate might yet help him.
Once married, he'd do his utmost to persuade her to hand over
the shares. He'd take great pleasure in watching Luther squirm
when he took the seat on the board.

He would go ahead with the marriage, and if Luther were at
all suspicious of his motive, Simon would assure him he was
bent on getting his hands on Kate's considerable fortune.

Luther wouldn't question such incentive. It would make perfect sense to him.

He made a point of avoiding Luther when he arrived at Old Grove House later that night, and the next morning set off early for the store without having breakfast. He wasn't surprised mid morning when the door of his small office opened and Luther stood there, an uncertain expression on his austere features.

'Simon, why haven't you been to see me?' Luther began pompously. He came further into the room and closed the door carefully behind him. 'How were things?'

'Don't pretend you're remotely interested,' Simon replied cuttingly, rising to his feet. 'Otherwise you'd have been at the funeral.'

Luther stared at him, mouth pinched in annoyance, and then he raised his brows, conceding. 'You're right,' he said flatly, his eyes glinting. 'I'm not at all interested in Mary, dead or alive.'

Simon gritted his teeth, suppressing an angry outburst. Luther was uncertain of his intentions and was trying to get him off balance.

His uncle moved to a chair nearby and sat, his gaze shrewd. 'Let's not beat about the bush, Simon,' he said evenly. 'I expected you to come storming in to see me last night, bringing our agreement to an abrupt end.' He paused, and then continued as though it were an afterthought. 'Now I can't use your mother as a lever.'

Refusing to be unsettled, Simon steeled himself not to react. Instead, he resumed his seat, leaning back leisurely in his chair and taking his time to cross his legs comfortably.

'Why would I renege on our agreement?' he asked, smiling. 'Marriage to Kate is obviously to my best advantage.'

His uncle's returned smile was thin and mirthless. 'You fence with me,' he said, his tone amused. 'Careful, Simon, I am a swordsman extraordinaire.'

'Really?' Simon drawled. 'Assassin would be closer to the mark, I think.'

With a roar, Luther leaped to his feet. 'Damn you!' he shouted. 'You go too far. I can dispense with you at a moment's notice, send you back to obscurity. Remember, my influence is extensive. I can ruin you wherever you go.'

'That would be incredibly stupid,' said Simon calmly. 'You need me.'

'I need no one,' Luther exploded, his face reddening in fury. 'I've come this far without help, and I mean to go on and have it all.'

'Have a care,' warned Simon. 'Your raised voice carries outside this room. Do you want the whole store to hear our business?'

Luther took a deep breath, steadying himself. 'It's of no consequence to me whether Kathryn marries or not; whether she lives or dies,' he said in a now modulated tone. 'And as for you, I can find another candidate to replace you just like that,' he hissed, snapping his fingers. 'Or have her certified within hours.'

Simon gazed at him as if unimpressed, though inwardly he felt a new repugnance for his uncle's undisguised callousness. He was right to be afraid for Kate's safety.

'My dear uncle,' Simon said calmly. 'You're under a misapprehension altogether. Our agreement still stands. I'm as keen as you are for this marriage to take place.'

Luther's expression was stony. Simon saw he was unconvinced, and hurried to explain himself. He stood up and came around the desk.

'I intend to get my hands on Kate's inheritance any way I can,' he went on. 'I've been poverty-stricken all my life, and I'm tired of it. I deserve better; I deserve the best, and I'll have it, even if it means marrying a shrew like Kate Vaughan.' Simon extended a hand to him. 'I suggest we shake hands on it, Luther, so there'll be no more misunderstandings.'

Luther looked genuinely surprised at the gesture and his frankness. He grasped Simon's hand, and after shaking it relaxed visibly.

'There's hope for you yet, Simon,' he said with a cunning smile. 'I'm glad to see you're a man who can dispense with the need for love in marriage. It never pays.'

Simon raised his brows. 'Then why are you set on marrying Delphine if you don't love her? She has no money or property. What can be your purpose, I wonder?'

'My motives are none of your concern,' Luther rasped in anger. 'And if you know what's good for you, you won't mention it again.'

Simon shrugged. 'As you wish.'

Luther strode towards the door, where he turned before opening it. 'The wedding ceremony will take place in April,' he stated pompously. 'You can tell Kathryn that funds are ready for her trousseau.'

Simon wetted his lips before making another move in his secret game. 'I've been looking at some property in Sketty village,' he said casually. 'Funds should also be made ready for its purchase. Kate and I will want to move in immediately after the wedding. A honeymoon is out of the question.'

Luther's eyes narrowed, and a cunning expression crossed his face. 'You're far too eager, Simon, and not as clever as you think,' he said. 'After you're wed, you and Kathryn will continue to live at Old Grove House where I can keep an eye on you both.' He gave a chuckle. 'I'm a long way from trusting you, especially with a large sum of money until after the ceremony.' He paused a moment to regard Simon keenly, and then went on with an air of magnanimity. 'However, once the shares are safely in my grasp, you may live where you wish, and do with your wife as you will.'

'That *is* generous of you,' Simon said, an edge to his voice. 'What do you suggest I do about Kate?'

'You'd do well to get rid of her as soon as is decent,' Luther advised decisively. 'I'm sure Dr Penfold will oblige.' He paused again, his eyes narrowing in suspicion. 'Unless, of course, you *do* have feelings for her.'

'I assure you, Kate's money is all I care about,' said Simon casually. 'I see myself as a gentleman of leisure from now on.'

Luther pursed his lips thoughtfully. 'You have no interest in the business then?'

'None whatsoever,' Simon lied blithely. 'You're welcome to it.'

There the matter rested. But Luther was a wily fox. From now on Simon knew he must appear to be in favour of any proposal Luther made, no matter how unscrupulous.

The next morning, feeling much easier in his mind now that he'd spoken with Simon, Luther was settled in his study with some correspondence and invoices brought to the house by Miss Collins.

He glanced briefly at her as she sat at a small desk near the window, pencil and notepad ready for his dictation.

'That order to Lassiter's for lace curtain materials, has it been fulfilled on time?' he asked her, surveying papers on the desk before him.

'No, Mr Templar.'

'Cancel it,' he instructed brusquely. 'Place it elsewhere.'

'Yes, Mr Templar.'

Someone tapped faintly on the study door, and Luther glanced up frowning, annoyed at being disturbed.

'Come in,' he called loudly. But no one entered and the tapping came again.

'Shall I answer it, Mr Templar?' Miss Collins asked eagerly, rising from her chair.

'Yes! Yes! But be sharp. I haven't got all day,' Luther said without looking up, and waved a hand impatiently.

Miss Collins scuttled to the door and jerked it open.

'Yes? What do you want?' she asked in scratchy tones. 'Mr Templar's very busy.'

'Oh! I'm so sorry!' The words were accompanied by a strangled sob, and Luther recognised Delphine's voice immediately.

'Delphine!'

He rose hurriedly, scattering the papers, and went quickly around the desk to the door. She stood there, shoulders hunched as though in misery, holding a lace handkerchief to her mouth, her eyes glistening with tears. Luther was immediately concerned.

'My dear! What is it?'

'It's really nothing.' She half turned away. 'I don't want to be a nuisance, Luther,' she whispered.

She was unsteady on her feet, and he quickly put his hand under her elbow, drawing her to a chair. She looked up at him forlornly, her expression one of despair, and his heart contracted with a sudden longing to hold her and protect her from all harm. No woman had ever had that effect on him, and this new and intense feeling awed him.

'Delphine, my dear, you must tell me what's bothering you.'

She glanced pointedly at Miss Collins hovering close by, and then lowered her head, touching her lips again with the handkerchief.

Abruptly Luther turned to his secretary. 'Take your refreshment now, Miss Collins,' he told her sharply. 'Go along to Mrs Trobert in the kitchen.'

Miss Collins was watching Delphine with round eyes, as curious as a cat's. 'Shall I help the young lady to her room first, Mr Templar?'

'You're dismissed,' Luther told her cuttingly. 'I'll ring when I want you.'

'Yes, Mr Templar.'

When Miss Collins had closed the door behind her, Delphine rose, and took a shaky step in that direction.

'I mustn't take advantage of your kindness,' she murmured in agitation. 'You're such a busy man, and my troubles seem trifling now.'

She swayed again and Luther stepped forward to support her, his nostrils filled with her perfume. Even in distress she was glorious, he thought, his mouth drying at her nearness. He wondered if this were the ideal opportunity to tell her what was in his heart, ask her to be his wife.

'You must think me a silly weak woman,' she said, leaning on his arm. 'But I didn't know who else to turn to. My brother's so preoccupied with painting Kate's portrait, I rarely see him. Too often, I'm alone and . . .'

'Has someone been pestering you?' Luther asked, feeling his hackles rise at the notion. 'You must tell me everything.'

A little sob escaped her. 'Oh, Luther, I don't want to be the cause of any more discord between you and Evan. I'm sure he doesn't realise he's harassing me.'

His grasp tightened on her arm. 'The bounder!' he exclaimed wrathfully. 'Tell me what he's done.'

'Don't be angry with me, please,' she said tremulously. 'I try
to avoid him, but he pursues me with such ardour. I'm at my
wits' end, and so I come to you.' She looked up pleadingly into
his face. 'You're so strong, Luther. I know you'll protect me.'

'The swine!' he muttered between clenched teeth, and
before he could prevent it, words spilled out. 'He's a married
man with a child. He has no right to approach you.'

Delphine gasped in dismay, her hand clutching at her
throat. 'Oh, mercy me!' she exclaimed in distress. 'I'd no
idea, Luther, I swear it.'

'Of course you didn't, my dear,' he said soothingly. 'How
could you know? However, it's a union he's ashamed of and
now bitterly regrets.'

'I've never given him a moment's encouragement, I assure
you,' Delphine said, her eyes wide. 'You must believe me.'

He patted her arm. 'I do, my dear. Evan's an unprincipled
cad. No woman is safe from him.'

Anger engulfed him. He'd punish his stepson for this, and
he didn't deserve Luther's silence or discretion any longer.

'It's because of his unfortunate marriage that I'm forced to
withhold his inheritance,' he confided. 'Although I had intended to let him have the money shortly.' He coughed,
recovering his discretion. 'That is, when a certain transaction
is completed to my satisfaction, but he'll not get a penny now
until he's thirty. The young fool's already in debt to me up to
his ears.'

Delphine breathed a deep sigh, and looked a little calmer.
'How honourable and wise you are, Luther,' she said softly,
her eyes wide, her admiring gaze fixed on his face.

Wanting to impress her further with his power over his

stepson, he went on, 'I may even foreclose on his property. It's what he deserves after hounding you, my dear.'

She gazed at him earnestly; her lips parted as if in awe, and seizing his hand, she held it tightly. 'I was right in coming to you for help,' she murmured. 'If only there was a way I could repay your kindness.'

As he looked deep into her eyes, he was filled with a suppressed excitement, as though something momentous were about to happen. The moment had come to speak his heart. Then her glance slanted away, and he was uncertain again.

'Evan came to my room last night,' she confessed, her voice muffled as though with shame. 'And forced his way in.'

'What!'

'I fought him off,' she said quickly, her frank gaze returning to his. 'Nothing happened. I told him point-blank that there could never be anything between us because . . .' Delphine turned her face away slightly, as though she were unable to meet his glance. 'Because my heart aches with love for some-one else,' she ended, in a whisper.

Luther felt the muscles in his face stiffen with shock and jealousy. Had he left things too late or had Simon been deceiving him all along?

'Who is this man you love?' he asked, his voice harsh with displeasure.

Hesitantly, she looked up at him through her lashes, a flush blooming on her cheeks, and she smiled. 'Oh, Luther, can't you guess?' she said softly. 'Haven't I made it obvious over the weeks, with every glance, every accidental touch? You must have sensed it, my dear.'

He stared at her, not understanding, and her smile faltered, humiliation etched on her face.

'You think me a brazen hussy!' she cried in distress. 'No better than a common scullery drudge.'

She tried to turn away from him, but his grasp on both her forearms was firm.

'Oh, dear God,' she went on miserably, her face averted from his. 'I'm ashamed and mortified. You must think the worst of me for speaking so plainly.'

Luther felt winded as her meaning dawned on him, although hardly believing it. And then his heart swelled with delight and eagerness.

'Delphine!' he exclaimed. 'Oh, my dearest! I think no such thing. I've been a blind fool.'

'You're not displeased with me, then?' she murmured nervously, and stepped closer to him. 'I couldn't bear it if you were.'

'Displeased!' He laughed. 'I'm overwhelmed with joy.'

He encircled her in his arms, his pulses racing as he looked deep into her eyes and saw flames flicker there that he'd not noticed before.

'There's a question I've longed to ask since first we met,' he said quickly, his breathing laboured now with excitement. 'But I was afraid – afraid you'd refuse me.'

'Luther, don't tease me, please,' she breathed, her hands clutching at the lapels of his coat. 'I want only to please you and you alone, so ask your question, my dear man.'

He held her close, scarcely able to believe this was happening: all he'd dreamed of for months. The words tumbled from his lips in his excitement.

'Dearest, Delphine, will you do me the great honour of becoming my wife?'

He held his breath, waiting for her answer, but instead she pulled away, tears in her eyes.

'Luther, I'm not worthy of you,' she said and hung her head.

'Not worthy?' he repeated jovially, and, placing a finger beneath her chin, raised her face. 'Why, the very opposite is true. You're the daughter of a baronet. I've no claim to noble family connections.'

'But I've nothing to offer a man like you,' Delphine said. 'I've no wealth to bring to the marriage. All I have is my love and myself.'

'That's all I'll ever want from you,' Luther said eagerly. 'I've wealth and power, and it's all yours, my love, if you consent to be my wife.'

Delphine stepped closer, and looked up into his face. Her lips were but a kiss away, and Luther trembled from the powerful tide of desire that rose within him.

'You'd share it all with *me*?' she said in wonder, her eyes large and so innocent. 'No one has ever been so generous to me in all my life.'

Luther held her fast to him. 'There's nothing I wouldn't do for you, Delphine,' he declared, his voice throbbing with an emotion he'd never known before, and for a moment he was frightened at the power of it. 'Nothing I wouldn't give you. Ask what you will. I'll strive to fulfil your every wish.'

With a shuddering sigh, Delphine placed her lips against his, her arms entwining his neck. Luther held her close, relishing the exquisite sensations she aroused in him. He'd not felt like this since his youth. Let no man try to take this from him.

At last Delphine drew back her head, laughing. 'I will marry you, Luther, my love,' she said. 'And I swear I'll be yours and yours alone as long as you live.'

She lifted her face to his, and their lips met again in a long kiss so passionate he was momentarily astonished, and then, eager for more, so eager, desire made his head swim. Stirred powerfully, his hunger grew, reaching right into his soul.

Finally, Delphine tilted back her head, and looked into his eyes, her gaze troubled. 'Luther, dear,' she said hesitantly. 'Would you think it strange if I ask you to keep our engagement secret from everyone for the time being?'

He was surprised and disappointed. 'But why, beloved?' He wanted to tell the world; especially boast about it to Evan.

'It's Bertram,' she said with a catch in her voice. 'He's so possessive and jealous. He's already made me promise never to marry and leave him. I'm afraid of what he'll do when he knows I've broken my promise.' She moved closer to Luther as though for protection. 'There are depths to my brother that even I fear.'

Luther hesitated, disturbed by her words, and Delphine lifted her hand to his cheek.

'Dearest, you said you'd grant my every wish.'

He smiled, unable to resist that look. 'So I did!' he said, and kissed her again. 'It's our secret, but I'll make discreet plans straight away. Shall we make it a June wedding?'

Delphine laid her head against his shoulder. 'That would be perfect. I can't wait to be your wife.' She looked up at him. 'Shall *I* be mistress of the household, or is that Kate's prerogative?'

'As my wife you rule all you survey,' Luther said, laughing. 'Be free to make any changes you see fit. This house needs a woman's touch.'

'But will Kate object?' Delphine asked dubiously. 'She doesn't like me, you know. She's very jealous, though I don't know why.'

Luther was annoyed with his stepdaughter. 'Kathryn has no say in this household,' he said sternly. 'She's here only by my sufferance, as is Evan.'

'You're a compassionate man,' Delphine said. 'That's one reason why I love you so.'

He kissed her cheek, and immense joy warmed his heart at her words.

'Kathryn's wilful and rebellious,' he said. 'But I hope marriage will tame her.'

'Well, I'm only too happy to be her friend, if she'll let me,' Delphine said. 'After all, she'll be my stepdaughter and I feel responsible for her welfare.'

'You're very generous and sympathetic,' Luther said. 'She really doesn't deserve you.'

'It's my nature,' Delphine said softly. 'The mothering instinct is strong in me.'

'Let's hope she appreciates it.' He held her at arm's length for a moment, smiling. 'As from today, you're the lady of the house,' he said. 'I leave it all to you.'

She moved into his arms again and snuggled close. 'Oh, Luther, you make me so happy.'

That night, making sure Chivers was nowhere about, Delphine went to her brother's room in triumph. Evan was probably still waiting for her, but let him wait.

'The old fool's succumbed at last,' she said gleefully, sliding into bed next to him. 'He's asked me to marry him, promised me the earth. We'll be rich, Bertie, rich!' She paused, sliding a hand across his shoulder. 'Of course, Evan's not to know yet.'

She was sure of Evan's devotion, and while he wasn't important to her plan any longer, she hadn't finished exploiting him. She laughed.

'When he knows I'm marrying Luther there'll be hell to pay.'

'So, you've got what you want,' Bertram replied bitterly. 'I hope it'll make you happy, but I doubt it. There's no happiness for us, not after the way we've lived, the things we've done. Sir Edwin killing himself was our fault.'

She was piqued by his ungrateful attitude. 'Don't censure me, Bertie,' she snapped. 'Not after all these years. Do you think I like being pawed by Luther? He's nothing more than an obnoxious old man.'

'Then why do it?' He sat up in the bed. 'Delphine, I'm sick to death of it all,' he said desperately. 'Weary of your scheming, plotting and lying.'

'I'm doing it all for you,' she retorted. 'For us.'

'I don't want it. My work's affected. The portrait of Kate isn't going well. Her innocence makes me ashamed.'

'Well, I feel no shame,' she answered sharply. 'Why should I? I live as I choose.'

When he didn't reply, she touched his face tenderly.

'Things will be different when I marry Luther,' she assured him, her voice softening. 'We'll share the spoils. We'll travel and you can paint. I'll arrange a good exhibition for your work in London, Paris, anywhere you like. My dear! You'll be lionised as a great artist. Isn't that what you've always wanted?'

'But at what price?' he blurted.

She was impatient. 'There's no price. It's ours to take.'

'I want nothing from these people,' Bertram flared angrily, turning his back on her. 'And all I want from you, Delphine, is my freedom.'

'Freedom!' She was stung and hurt. 'You make me sound like a jail warden.'

He turned to face her, his face pale. 'So you are!' he said, his voice quivering. 'You've imprisoned me in this loathsome relationship since we were children.' He took a gasping breath, as though forcing himself to go on. 'When we were young orphans, homeless and penniless, I took comfort in our love, although even then I knew it was wrong.'

Seething, she flung the words back at him. 'How can our love be wrong?' she cried. 'It's kept us strong and united against the world. Together, we're invincible.' She shook her head. 'Nothing is wrong, Bertie, if it works to our advantage.'

'You're destroying me, Delphine,' he pleaded. 'You've taken away my decency and self-respect. When you marry Luther, I'll return to Bath.'

'You'll never leave me!' She was scornful and confident. He was the first male she'd ever dominated, her first trophy. 'You'd never survive without my strength.'

'I want to live my own life,' he said desperately. 'Find real love, and not be ashamed any longer.'

'It's that Vaughan girl, isn't it,' Delphine hissed in fury. She'd known Kate was a threat as soon as she'd set eyes on her. 'Have you slept with her?'

Her fingers convulsed into claws at the thought of him with another woman.

'No,' Bertram said, shaking his head. 'I want to, but I respect Kate too much to take advantage.'

'Respect!' Delphine's lips stretched in scorn. 'A respectable woman. Huh! How utterly boring.'

She looked at him under her lashes, still furious at the thought of him with Kate. 'You stay well away from her,' she said malevolently.

'It's too late anyway,' Bertram said miserably. 'She belongs to Simon.' His eyes flashed. 'But I can find someone else to love. Let me go, Delphine!'

Delphine's throat closed up and she almost choked on her

fury. 'I'll see you dead first,' she hissed at him, raking her fingernails viciously across his bare chest. 'Dead, and rotting in your grave. You belong to me, Bertie. No other woman shall have you.'

13

'This is a farce!' Kate exclaimed angrily, pulling at the neckline of the wedding dress. 'A complete farce.'

'Please, Miss Vaughan!' Miss Clarke, the dressmaker, on her knees pinning up the hem, glanced up in irritation. 'Please don't pull the lace like that. It's so delicate, it'll tear. And it isn't paid for yet,' she mumbled in an undertone.

'You look wonderful, Kate,' Cecille said. 'I wish it was me getting married.'

'I wish it was you, too!' Kate retorted hotly. 'You can have Simon Creswell and welcome to him.'

Beautiful as the dress was, she wanted to tear it off in protest.

'To think in a matter of two days you'll be a married woman,' Cecille went on. 'Oh, how exciting. How romantic.'

Kate was even more cross, and twitched her skirts.

'Cecille, you're an empty-headed, silly girl, and I've no patience with you. I don't love Simon, so how can it possibly be romantic?'

'If you don't keep still, Miss Vaughan,' the dressmaker snapped, 'the dress won't be ready and you'll have to walk down the aisle in your underslip.'

'Where is the groom?'

'He's taken himself off to some hotel until the wedding,' Kate said. 'It's all for appearances sake, of course. The hypocrite.'

'You're next, Miss Villiers.' Miss Clarke got awkwardly to her feet, her face flushed. 'Last touches to your bridesmaid's dress. Miss Harrington should be here, too, for her fitting.'

'I'm surprised you asked Delphine to be a bridesmaid,' Cecille said pertly.

'I didn't,' Kate said bitterly. 'Delphine made all the arrangements; chose the materials, picked the designs. I've had no say in anything. I wanted Evan to give me away, but Luther insists it's his prerogative.'

'Bertram will make the handsomest best man,' Cecille said. 'You won't mind if I set my cap at him, will you?'

Kate bit her lip but didn't reply, hurt that Bertram was quite ready to see her marry another man without protest. He knew very well she despised Simon, and what she felt for him.

Two days later Kate awoke with a fearful headache, matched by a dreadful stomachache. She sat on the edge of the bed, telling herself that she simply couldn't get married today. When Ethel came in to tell her that a hot bath had been drawn, Kate was irritated by the maid's obvious cheerfulness.

'Lovely day for a wedding, Miss Kate,' she announced, throwing back the window drapes. 'Happy is the bride that the sun shines upon.'

'That'll be all, Ethel!' Kate said in a dangerous tone, wishing she were lost in the jungles of Africa or stranded on the baking sands of the Sahara. She wished for any fate, except marriage to Simon Creswell.

Miss Clarke came after breakfast, and made a great to-do of getting Kate into her dress, fussing with hems and flounces, and last-minute stitching, until Kate wanted to scream.

Ethel dressed her hair, and Miss Clarke had just fixed the bride's headdress and veil in place on Kate's trembling head when Evan knocked on her door, looking extremely handsome in his grey morning suit. As he came into the room she flew at him in panic.

'Evan! You must stop the wedding!'

There were gasps from Ethel and Miss Clarke, and Kate turned to them, her cheeks bright.

'Leave me,' she ordered, hearing the hysteria in her own voice. When they'd shuffled out, Kate clutched desperately at Evan's lapels.

'Evan, I mean it. I can't go through with this travesty. I'm throwing my life away for nothing. You must help me.'

He pushed her away. 'Kate, this is nonsense,' he said sternly. 'Of course you'll marry Simon. You must.'

'Must?'

He hesitated, his face flushing. 'For my sake,' he said.

'Your sake?'

'Stop repeating everything I say, for heaven's sake.' He sounded very angry and Kate stared at him.

'I will if you start making sense,' Kate retorted furiously. 'How does my marriage to Simon affect you? What're you keeping from me, Evan?'

For a moment he looked as though he wouldn't answer, and Kate tugged at his coat impatiently.

'I'm in considerable debt to Luther,' he said at last. 'But he's promised to let me have my inheritance straight away if I make sure you marry Simon.'

'But that's despicable!' Kate was outraged. 'How could you agree to such a thing?'

'I've little choice.'

Kate folded her lips in anger at his attitude. 'You surrendered your shares to him,' she accused. 'And now he's after mine.'

Evan looked taken aback. 'Who told you that?'

'Simon.'

'What else did he tell you about me?'

'Nothing,' Kate snapped. 'What else is there?' Her eyes narrowed as she studied his guilty expression. 'What're you hiding?'

'Simon's a good man,' he said confidently. 'He won't ill-treat you, he's promised me that.'

'Oh!' Kate was enraged. 'I see. An agreement between gentlemen, is it? Do I mean so little to you that you'd throw my happiness away for some debts?'

Evan glanced down, unable to meet her eyes, and scuffed his shoe on the carpet. He looked like a small boy caught out in a misdemeanour.

'Luther could foreclose on me; take my property,' he muttered. 'You don't realise what a disaster that would be.'

'Meanwhile, I have an imminent disaster of my own,' she snapped. 'Simon Creswell for a husband.'

Evan turned and strode towards the door.

'There's nothing I can do, Kate. Nothing. Everything will work out for the best. You'll see.'

The church of St Mary's was a mass of flowers. It was the wedding Kate had always dreamed about. It was the groom that was all wrong. Walking down the aisle on Luther's arm, Kate was dazed, feeling it was all happening to someone else.

Ahead, she could see Simon Creswell, tall and elegant in his morning suit, and Bertram standing next to him. Both men turned to watch her approach the altar.

Kate sent a pleading glance to Bertram, but he looked away, embarrassed. Her heart sinking like a stone, Kate knew she could fight the inevitable no longer. What was the point of struggling, when no one would save her?

She stumbled over the marriage vows, knowing each word was a lie.

'I pronounce you man and wife.'

The words rang through the church and through Kate's head, like echoes of misfortune, striking a chill throughout her body, and she felt numb.

'You may kiss the bride.'

Kate went rigid, dreading his touch, as Simon leaned towards her, but conscious of the eyes of the congregation on her, reluctantly offered her cheek. His lips merely brushed her skin.

'Have courage,' he whispered in her ear. 'It'll be over soon, and then you can go back to being Miss Kate Vaughan in all but name.'

The reception was in the Mackworth Hotel in the High Street. Kate sat next to Simon at the top table, silent and unsmiling as the chatter from the numerous guests buzzed around her.

As best man Bertram got up to speak, but appeared to have little to say. As he resumed his seat, Luther stood, and Kate's hackles rose, angry to sit and do nothing while he spouted hypocrisy in wishing her happiness.

'Ladies and gentlemen,' he began. 'I have an announcement of my own.'

Kate stared up at him in surprise.

'Of course we all wish the happy couple a splendid future,' he went on pompously. 'However, I'm delighted to announce my own impending nuptials.'

There were gasps of surprise throughout the room, and Kate saw Evan half rise to his feet, his face white.

'Yes, I'm to be married,' Luther went on.

He turned to Delphine and held out his hand and Kate was astonished to see a fleeting expression of consternation on her lovely face. After a moment's hesitation, she took Luther's hand and rose to stand beside him.

'Miss Delphine Harrington has done me the great honour of consenting to be my wife,' Luther declared with a great deal of pride. 'The wedding is to be in June.'

There was a great angry shout of protest. Evan was on his feet, marching forward, an enraged expression darkening his face. He stood in front of Delphine, staring at her pleadingly.

'Say this isn't so,' he begged, his voice ragged with emotion. 'You don't love him, Delphine. You can't. For God's sake, tell me he's lying.'

She shrank back behind Luther, clutching at his sleeve, a look of terror on her face.

'Don't let him near me,' she cried out. 'I'm afraid of him.'

Kate stared open-mouthed, appalled at what was happening. There were shouts and murmurs from the guests. Simon jumped to his feet, as did several other men. Kate rose too.

'Evan, what're you doing?' she cried, distraught. 'You're making a spectacle of yourself, of all of us.'

He ignored her, but leaned across the table, arms outstretched towards Delphine.

'You belong to me,' he called out in a terrible voice. 'No other man shall have you, I swear it.'

Delphine gave a little scream and shrank back, a handkerchief to her mouth.

'You reprehensible scoundrel!' Luther thundered, stepping in front of Delphine. 'How dare you insult a lady in this outrageous manner? Stand back, sir, stand back!'

Simon and Bertram came forward and grasped Evan by his arms, pulling him away.

'Take your hands off me!' he cried.

He struggled violently with the two men who held him. There was uproar among the guests, and Kate felt her face burn with shame and humiliation. This was the worst day of her life.

'Evan!' Simon hissed, trying to subdue him. 'This isn't the time or place.'

Evan shrugged off their grasp and staggered back, eyes blazing, and he looked out of his mind.

'Damn you to hell, Luther!' he bellowed fiercely. 'You've taken the only woman I'll ever love, and you'll pay for it, I swear.'

There were further gasps and angry murmurs among the guests. Kate wished the ground would open up and bury her, and prayed Evan would leave without saying another word.

With one final stare at Delphine, Evan turned on his heel and marched out; the room buzzed with excited conversation.

Simon signalled to Luther and Delphine to sit down, and then faced the guests.

'Ladies and gentlemen, I apologise for my brother-in-law's outburst. It's all a misunderstanding.'

There were a few titters and guffaws in the room, and Simon's expression darkened.

'If any guest feels uncomfortable in the circumstances, my wife and I will understand if they wish to leave now.'

Silence answered his words.

'Very well,' he went on. 'Champagne is being served in the adjacent room. Perhaps you'll all assemble there, where the celebration of our wedding will continue.'

Guests began to drift towards the other room and Simon

came back to Kate's side, his face still dark. He took her arm, his grip unnecessarily tight, to lead her out, but Kate held back.

'I can't stand another minute. How can I face anyone after that?' Kate cried in a trembling voice. 'I want to go home.'

Simon's lips thinned in anger. 'You always run away from unpleasantness,' he said sharply. 'Well, you're not going to today. You'll go in there, smile and hold your head high.'

'I won't!'

Simon's jaw worked as if struggling not to shout. 'You're my *wife* now,' he said acidly. 'You'll do as I tell you, and like it.'

His grip on her arm was uncompromising. Seething with impotent fury, Kate had no choice but to obey.

Her steps were leaden as she moved reluctantly among the guests. Simon stayed close, always at her elbow, not letting her retreat one inch. Her face ached from trying to smile, when she was crying inside. Her marriage to Simon was disaster enough, but Evan's unbelievable behaviour had made it the worst calamity she could have imagined. After two hours Simon had a quiet word with Bertram, and then drew Kate aside.

'We can leave now,' he said quietly.

'Oh, thank God!' she replied, feeling weakness in her legs. 'I couldn't have stood another moment.'

'You can expect more histrionics from your brother,' he said dryly. 'Luther's announcement has stirred up a hornet's nest, and Delphine isn't pleased, either.'

'I thought that, too,' Kate said with interest. 'What does it mean?'

'We'll discuss it at home,' he said curtly.

Kate was determined to go straight to her bedroom as Simon handed her down from the hansom cab outside the house.

Chivers opened the door to them and gave a little bow, a decided smirk on his face, which Kate found offensive.

'Good evening, Mr Creswell, Mrs Creswell. Please accept best wishes from all the staff.'

'Thank you,' Simon said curtly. 'Send Ethel to help Mrs Creswell change.'

'Very good, sir.'

Hand firmly under her elbow, Simon steered Kate towards the staircase.

'I can call the maid myself, thank you,' she muttered crossly. 'And I hardly need your help to climb the stairs.'

'Let's not give rise to tittle-tattle,' he answered, through clenched teeth. 'At least wait until we're in the privacy of our bedroom before having our first marital disagreement.'

'Our bedroom?' Kate stopped abruptly, seized by alarm and then anger again, and whirled to face him. 'We have an agreement, remember,' she flared. 'You promised you wouldn't make marital demands on me.'

Simon glanced back along the corridor. 'I won't discuss our private life here,' he hissed, taking her arm to move her forward, but she snatched it away.

'So, you've gone back on your word,' Kate blazed. 'I might've known!' She lifted her chin defiantly. 'Well, I can promise you this, I won't submit willingly. You'll have to take me by force.'

'Oh, be quiet, woman, for pity's sake!' Simon looked exasperated. 'My God! You're making me regret the marriage already.'

He grabbed her arm again and pushed her forward.

'Don't you manhandle me, you – you ruffian!' Kate squawked, suddenly frightened. She wasn't ready for what must come next. He propelled her along to the end of the corridor where double mahogany doors faced them.

'But this is Aunt Agnes's old apartment,' Kate said in confusion as Simon opened the doors and pushed her inside. 'These rooms haven't been used for years.'

The double doors gave into a small vestibule, leading off from which were more doors. Simon marched through the nearest one, and Kate followed, more out of curiosity than anything else. She halted in the doorway, realising with dismay that they'd entered the bedroom.

She expected to see the familiar dark drapes and heavy early Victorian furniture, the style her aunt favoured. Instead, nothing was as she remembered it; everything was changed, new furniture, new drapes, all very tastefully and expensively done.

In fright she stared at the magnificent double bed in golden wood. Simon followed her gaze.

'No one's going to molest you or force you,' he assured her tetchily. 'I'm a man of my word.'

'So you say!'

She averted her eyes as he took off the tailed coat of his morning suit and reached into a nearby wardrobe to take out a dark red silk smoking jacket, and put it on.

She found it annoying and suspicious that he seemed so at home in this suite, while she was uncomfortable still in her wedding dress. She longed for a hot bath, and a pot of hot tea.

'Who but you could've ordered this move?' Kate asked angrily.

Simon's glance was scornful. 'You can be incredibly dim-witted at times, Kate. Don't you understand what's happening? I thought today's fiasco would've opened your eyes.'

Suddenly, she spotted photographs of her parents on a table beside the double bed, which she normally kept at her own bedside. She darted forward and picked them up, putting them under her arm possessively.

'These are *my* personal possessions,' she said indignantly. 'You had no right to order them moved out of my room.'

'I didn't,' he snapped, pushing past her to stride into the vestibule again, and opened a different door.

She followed him into the large sitting-room, where tall windows gave a view over the treetops to the sea, and flopped on to a nearby chair. The headdress was making her head hurt, and the pull of the lace train on her shoulders felt like a ton weight.

'Well, someone's responsible,' she said feebly.

'It was Delphine's doing, of course,' Simon snapped.

'What?' Kate was slighted. 'That woman! How dare she take over without so much as a by your leave? She's no right. What's it to do with her?'

'Huh! Everything, apparently,' Simon said, then paused looking at her. 'Don't you want to get out of your finery?' he asked. 'I certainly want to be rid of this collar.' He put a finger around the edge of it. 'It's strangling me.'

'Don't change the subject,' Kate snapped. 'Why're the servants taking orders from Delphine?'

'Apparently, Luther called the staff together before breakfast this morning,' Simon said, 'and informed them that Delphine's now mistress of Old Grove House.'

Kate stared, feeling thoroughly outraged. She'd assumed, on her marriage, she'd take over the running of the house. Instead a stranger was taking her mother's place.

'Nothing will stop Delphine now,' Simon said thoughtfully. 'She has your stepfather exactly where she wants him – eating out of her hand – and she'll dare to do anything.'

'Luther's not a man to be manipulated,' Kate said. 'How does she do it?'

'Manipulating men is Delphine's greatest talent,' he said dryly. 'They look into those violet eyes, and believe anything she tells them. You believed her that Bertram is betrothed to someone else.'

'You mean he isn't?' Kate stood up abruptly, feeling a swell of renewed anger rise in her breast. 'You knew that all along,' she accused with a wail. 'And choose now, *after* we're safely married to tell me. How despicable!'

'What difference would it make?' Simon rasped. 'Our marriage had to go ahead, whether you knew or not.' He took a deep breath. 'Besides,' he said quietly, 'I thought knowing the truth would've made you more unhappy.'

'How do you think I feel now?' she blazed at him. 'Trapped! That's how I feel. I love Bertram, don't you understand?'

Ethel tapped at the door and came in. Kate felt her face flush with embarrassment at their raised voices, and wondered how much she'd heard and understood.

'Not now, Ethel,' she said tetchily, avoiding the maid's gaze. 'I'll ring when I'm ready.'

With a startled glance of curiosity at both of them, the maid withdrew.

'Now you've set tongues wagging,' Simon remarked. 'They'll know below stairs we're having our first quarrel.'

Kate gave a bitter laugh, feeling emotionally exhausted. 'Does it matter what the servants think after the pantomime we put on for our friends and acquaintances today,' she said wearily. 'We'll never live that down.'

But she knew he was right. Nothing would have changed Luther's mind. Bertram was as much out of reach as Mansel

Jenkins. But why had Delphine lied about him? There was so much she didn't understand, and needed answers.

'I want plain speaking from now on, Simon,' Kate said sharply. 'I insist on knowing the truth about everything. I'll *not* be kept in the dark.'

To her surprise he made no objection, but nodded agreement.

'Start by explaining why Evan's so incensed,' she went on, and then hesitated. 'Are they lovers, he and Delphine?'

'Of course they are,' Simon said. 'I don't think Luther realises it yet. Delphine's very clever and she's playing a dangerous game. People will get hurt. It's happened before.'

'If you knew they spelled trouble why did you bring them here?' she asked angrily.

'I invited Bertram alone,' Simon responded quickly. He paused, a look of resignation on his face. 'Although I might've known she'd never let him out of her clutches.'

'What a strange thing to say.'

'Delphine is a strange woman.'

'She's also a liar,' she said with derision. 'But she won't bamboozle me again, nor will she dictate to me either, stepmother or not.'

Kate walked towards the bell rope near the fireplace, and gave it a few tugs.

'I'll have my things moved to my own room straight away.' She glanced at him enquiringly. 'Shall I ring for Watkins to move you?'

Simon was standing near the window looking at the scenery.

'No. I'll keep these rooms. Look at this splendid view, Kate.' He turned his head to look at her and waved a hand, beckoning her forward. 'We can see Mumbles Head from here, and the lighthouse. Come and see.'

Kate held back stubbornly. He was being too friendly; too like a husband, and she still didn't trust him.

'I've seen it,' she said shortly. 'I'm going to my own room now. When Ethel comes, please give her my instructions.'

'Yes, Mrs Creswell,' he said with irony.

Kate would have flounced out at that point, but her train was so heavy she could hardly turn. Yet she was determined to have the last word.

'As you said, Simon, now I can get back to being Kate Vaughan again, in *all* but name.'

14

Evan sat in the library of his gentleman's club early next morning, a copy of that day's *Cambrian Leader* on the reading stand before him. The paper was full of news and reports on the war in South Africa, but his mind couldn't take in anything of it. He saw only images of Delphine's blank expression and Luther's triumphant smile as their nuptials were announced.

Misery was like a heavy stone in the pit of his stomach. How could she betray him after the passionate ways they'd shown love for each other, after all they'd meant to each other? He felt so angry with her for not denouncing Luther's plans straight away, and hatred for his stepfather was as bitter as poison in his mouth.

He'd behaved foolishly, he realised, having slept on it, and had stayed away from the shop, unable to face anyone. And yet, what man would blame him for reacting so strongly in the face of such deceit?

A discreet cough interrupted his thoughts. He looked up to see the day porter standing near his chair.

'Excuse me, Mr Vaughan, sir, but a messenger called with a letter for you.'

The porter held out a silver tray on which was a small white envelope. Evan picked it up, and immediately whispers of Delphine's distinctive perfume entered his nostrils. He almost let the letter slip from his fingers. He dismissed the man with a wave of his hand, and placed the letter on the reading stand, staring at it, his emotions mixed.

How dare she have the effrontery to write to him after what she'd done? He'd never forgive her, and he wouldn't forgive Luther either. Some way or other he'd take his revenge, but he must bide his time.

Hesitantly, he fingered the envelope, wondering what she could possibly say that would excuse her. On impulse he raised the envelope to his nose, breathing in the heady fragrance.

Memories of their passionate nights together flooded his mind, stimulating his senses. His pulses raced as he recalled how willing and eager Delphine was to gratify his every desire, every appetite. How could she do those intimate things and *not* love him?

She didn't want this marriage to his stepfather, he decided. Luther was manipulating her as he did everyone. Anger swelled against his stepfather again, and feverishly he tore open the envelope.

Evan, my dearest love, I beg you not to cast me off without a second thought. I must see you. Have mercy . . .

She'd be at the home of a dear and trusted friend, Mrs Sybil Jenkins of Eversley House, Sketty, at two o'clock that afternoon. She begged him to call on her there, so that she could explain the truth behind Luther's shocking announcement.

Evan put the letter carefully in his wallet.

When Kate came down to breakfast she saw there had been changes overnight. Luther was in his usual seat at the head of the table, but Delphine, normally a late riser, now occupied the chair at the other end, in Alice's place.

'Good morning, Kate,' Delphine greeted, without a smile. 'Chivers tells me you slept in your old room last night, your first night as a bride. Hardly a good start to a marriage.'

Sending Delphine a disdainful glance, Kate went to the chiffonier and spooned some hot porridge into a bowl, splashing milk on to it, her hand shaking with fury.

'It's none of your business,' she said stiffly as she took her place at the table. 'You're still a mere guest in this house, remember.'

Delphine looked furious, and Luther glanced sharply across at Kate.

'That'll do, Kathryn!' he barked. 'My future wife can make whatever changes she sees fit. She can hire and discharge servants as she pleases.' He looked down the table at her, and smiled. 'She has my complete confidence, and will even attend to the daily checking of the household accounts.' His glanced snapped back to Kate. 'If you require any domestic funds, ask Delphine.'

Kate ground her teeth, enraged, but said nothing. Instead she sent the now mollified Delphine a stinging glance. Simon was to blame for letting this viper into the house, and she wouldn't forgive him for it.

'Where's your husband?' Luther asked.

'I've no idea,' Kate said loftily. 'We live separate lives.'

Mid morning Ethel came into the small sitting-room at the top of the stairs to tell Kate that Mrs Trobert wanted to speak to her urgently.

'Miss Harrington deals with everything now,' Kate said pithily. 'Speak to her.'

'No, Miss Kate – er, I mean, Mrs Creswell . . .'

'Miss Kate will do,' Kate said quickly.

'It's private, Mrs Trobert said.'

In the kitchen Mrs Trobert looked decidedly nervous when Kate walked in. She told Ethel to go about her work with brush and dustpan in the bedrooms, and sent the boot boy and scullery girl packing, then carefully closed the door to the servants' hall, probably afraid of Chivers.

'I thought you should know,' Mrs Trobert began in a hoarse whisper, 'that a personage of our acquaintance, who's not welcome in this house, intends to make a visit.'

'Aunt Agnes!' Kate's eyes were wide with excitement.

'Shush!' Mrs Trobert glanced about nervously. 'My job hangs by a thread, mun. I'm sure Miss Harrington's looking to get rid of me.'

'Tell me about Aunt Agnes,' Kate urged, though she didn't mean to be unsympathetic.

'She'll be calling here one afternoon in the week to see Mr Evan, so I'm told by her maid Megan.'

'Of course, she doesn't know he's not here,' Kate said, biting her lip in frustration. 'We must get word to her.'

'Can't be done, Miss Kate,' the housekeeper said. 'Megan wouldn't say where Miss Vaughan's hiding herself. Sworn to secrecy she is, on the pain of dismissal.' Mrs Trobert nodded emphatically, to show how serious the situation was.

'Then I'll see her when she comes,' Kate said.

'Oh dear!' Mrs Trobert wrung her hands. 'What a to-do! If the master finds out, it's all up with me. End my days in the workhouse, I will.'

'That won't happen. He won't find out,' Kate said, though she was hardly reassured herself. Nothing in this house was certain any longer. 'We'll be very careful.'

At that moment the door from the servants' hall burst open

and Ethel came running into the kitchen, nose red, face streaked with tears.

'Sacked, I am!' she wailed, throwing up her hands. 'She's finished me, and accused me of stealing. Pack my things straight away, I must, and get out tonight.'

'What?'

Ethel sank on to a chair and putting her arms on the kitchen table laid her head on them, sobbing noisily. Kate hurried to her, putting her arm around the girl's shoulders.

'It's started,' Mrs Trobert cried out, clapping both hands to her cheeks, her expression fearful. 'The purge! She won't stop at Ethel. We'll all be gone by Michaelmas.' Mrs Trobert paused. 'Except Chivers; him and her are as thick as cronies.'

Kate patted Ethel's shoulder, as sobs racked the maid's body.

'Pull yourself together, Ethel, for goodness' sake,' she said firmly. 'And tell me what's happened.'

Ethel lifted a blotchy face, her expression pathetic. 'It's that sapphire bracelet Miss Harrington always wears,' she said. 'Every morning I lay it out for her to wear, with a pair of sapphire earrings; her favourites.'

'Struts around like Lady Muck,' Mrs Trobert commented. 'Down here every five minutes, giving me orders. She wants me out, I know it.'

'I haven't seen the bracelet in her jewellery box for a while,' Ethel went on. 'And then this morning I noticed the earrings were missing, too.'

'If anyone's a thief around here, it's that Chivers,' Mrs Trobert opined darkly. 'Don't know why the master ever took him on, a man like that, shifty-eyed brute.'

'Well, I didn't want to get the blame for losing them,' Ethel said quickly, wiping her nose on the hem of her apron. 'So I thought I'd tell Miss Harrington, in case she hadn't noticed.'

'Don't know the first thing about cooking, she don't,' Mrs Trobert chimed in. 'But down she comes early this morning, telling me I overcooked the hams for luncheon the day before yesterday.'

The housekeeper stared at Kate, her fingers clutching at her throat. 'This household's going to the dogs, Miss Kate. Something terrible is going to happen. Feel it in my bones, I can.'

'Please, Mrs Trobert!' Kate said impatiently. 'Let Ethel explain.'

The maid gave another sob and a huge swallow, before going on. 'Miss Harrington was in the west corridor talking to Chivers,' she said. 'I waited until he'd gone.' She glanced at Mrs Trobert. 'Because we know what he's like, don't we?'

The housekeeper nodded emphatically, and opened her mouth, but Kate forestalled her.

'Do go on, Ethel!'

Ethel wiped at her nose again, this time on her cuff.

'As soon as she saw me, she flew in a rage, and said I was spying on her.' The maid looked up at Kate, her reddened eyes as round as saucers. 'You could've knocked me down with a feather duster.'

'Spying?' Kate was thoughtful.

'I explained about the missing jewellery,' Ethel went on. 'And next thing, she's screaming at me, saying I'm a thief, and giving me the sack; telling me to be out of the house by suppertime.' Ethel's face crumpled in misery again. 'I got nowhere to go. My family live in Aberystwyth.'

Kate patted the girl's shoulder. Delphine wouldn't get away with this.

'Stop crying, Ethel, you're not going anywhere,' she said. 'I'll have a word with Mr Templar myself.'

But she couldn't do that until evening now that Luther was once again working at the shop, and there was luncheon to get through, with Delphine queening it at the head of the table. In the dining-room, Delphine and Bertram were already seated, with Chivers in attendance serving the meal. She was annoyed they'd not waited for her.

'The luncheon gong sounded ten minutes ago,' Delphine said sharply. 'Don't be late in future.'

Kate didn't bother to reply but sat down, laying her table napkin over her lap as Chivers put a plate in front of her.

'You've sacked Ethel,' she said bluntly. 'I'd like to know why.'

'It doesn't concern you,' Delphine snapped. 'But if you must know, the girl's a common thief. She's stolen the sapphire bracelet Bertram gave me last birthday, and some sapphire earrings.'

'If you're so certain she's a thief why didn't you call the police and have her taken into custody?' Kate asked pithily. 'But you couldn't because it's a lie.'

Delphine's fine features were marred with a sneer. 'I'm sure Luther wouldn't want another scandal,' she said. 'Not straight after the atrocious behaviour of your brother yesterday. The man's a raving lunatic, shaming us like that. I've given him no encouragement, none.'

Kate ground her teeth in ire. Instead, she glanced at Bertram's face, tight with strain, and felt pity for him.

'Yet,' Kate persisted, 'you must be anxious to get the jewellery back, since they're a precious gift from your brother?'

'Oh, she's already disposed of them,' Delphine said. 'A

common little trollop like that will have all kinds of criminal connections.'

'We'll see what Luther has to say,' Kate retorted.

Delphine's smile was confident. 'You can try, Kate,' she said ungraciously. 'But you'll be wasting your time.'

She put her napkin on the table, and rose.

'I'll be out visiting friends most of the afternoon,' she said to the butler. 'Mrs Trobert has her instructions about dinner. See they're carried out to the letter, and make sure that wretched girl is packed and ready to leave before I get home. Is that clear?'

'Very good, madam.'

Kate wasn't finished with her. 'You accused Ethel of spying on you, Delphine,' she said loudly, watching the butler's face. 'What have you got to hide, I wonder?'

Chivers's expression gave nothing away, but, to Kate's surprise, Bertram gave a little cry of distress. Without looking at her, he stood up and hurried from the room.

Delphine's mouth was pinched with anger. 'I'm warning you, Kate,' she said ominously. 'Don't cross me. Your future lies in Luther's hands, and I have great influence over him. Don't think Simon can save you. He's just a pawn in Luther's game, while I am the all-powerful queen.'

Sybil Jenkins was much younger than Evan expected. She simpered, giving him knowing glances as though they shared a secret and he took a dislike to her.

'Oh, Mr Vaughan,' she began, fluttering her hands. 'I've heard so much about you from dear Delphine, and, of course, my stepson, Mansel.'

Evan's smile was stiff. Somehow he'd failed to connect the name, and was discomfited.

'Your dear sister, Kathryn, was a favourite at Eversley House,' Sybil gushed on. 'Especially with my husband, Maldwyn. We were devastated when their understanding was called off.' She paused meaningfully. 'We never knew why.'

'It's a mystery,' Evan murmured, straining not to show his dislike.

'And now she's married,' Sybil went on, her expression expectant.

'Yes, well,' he said, and tried a feeble quip to hide his consternation. 'The course of love is often very strange.'

Sybil astonished him by clapping her hands in excitement. 'Oh, the course of love – how thrilling!' she chortled. 'And to think I'm helping little cupid at this very moment.'

Out of his depth, Evan glanced at Delphine for help.

'Sybil's a dear friend, and very sympathetic to our situation, dearest,' Delphine said gravely. 'I've confided in her that we're deeply in love, but fate is against us. She's only too happy to give us a safe meeting place.'

'You're very kind, Mrs Jenkins,' Evan said, unsmiling.

'Well,' Sybil went on, patting her hair self-consciously, looking from Evan to Delphine. 'I'll leave you two lovebirds alone.'

She fluttered from the room, giving them a backwards glance and a giggle as she went. Evan breathed a sigh of relief as the door closed on her figure.

'What an absurd woman,' he said. 'How can you bear to be friends with her?'

'She serves a purpose,' Delphine said, and then smiled quickly when he stared at her. 'But let's not waste time, my darling.'

She darted forward to kiss him, and he steeled himself not to respond as ardently as he longed to. She looked up into his face.

'You must think I've betrayed you,' she went on timorously. 'But things aren't what they seem.'

'I want to believe you, Delphine, but what was I to think, suddenly finding out you're to marry my stepfather? It was a damned shock.'

'I know, my dear and I'm sorry.' Taking his arm she drew him to the sofa. 'Look, sit down, let me explain the terrible predicament I'm in.'

'I'd rather stand,' Evan said, resisting.

He wanted a steady mind and heart, and her nearness made him vulnerable. She looked up at him.

'You're still angry with me,' she said reproachfully. 'I don't deserve it, really I don't. What I did, I did for you, to save you humiliation and ruin.'

He stared. 'What?'

'It's true,' she went on miserably. 'Luther made it quite plain what would happen if I refused him.'

'Tell me everything.' Evan sank on to the seat next to her, and she moved closer to him.

'A week ago Luther asked me to marry him.' She looked at him in alarm. 'Out of the blue!' she exclaimed, as though he were accusing her of betrayal. 'I vow I'd no idea he had marriage in mind.'

Evan took her hand, and patted it reassuringly. He was well acquainted with Luther's chicanery.

'I was gracious, of course,' she said, putting a handkerchief to her mouth. 'But refused his proposal, and said I loved you and that we were to marry.'

Evan's heart contracted guiltily, and he opened his mouth to speak, but Delphine forestalled him.

'We've never discussed marriage,' she said modestly. 'But I knew you'd propose eventually, after all we've been to each other.' She lifted her candid gaze to his. 'Marriage is your intention, darling, isn't it?'

Evan cleared his throat in embarrassment and indecision. He should tell her now about Eirwen and the trap he was in, but he still couldn't find the words. Delphine appeared not to see his confusion, but went on speaking.

'Luther was seething with anger and jealousy,' she said. 'And he told me something then, Evan, which I flatly refused to believe, until he showed me proof.'

Evan held his breath; his heart almost stopped beating as he looked into Delphine's frank gaze.

'He said you were in debt to him, a considerable amount, and he showed me the papers you'd signed when you bought that property.'

'You knew about the house in Fforestfach,' Evan cut in quickly. 'I told you myself.'

She nodded, her violet eyes flashing briefly. 'Yes, you did, and I wondered why you never took me there.'

Evan swallowed. 'Delphine, my dear, there's something I must tell you—'

'He also told me,' Delphine interrupted quickly, her voice trembling as she placed a hand on his arm, 'you're already married, Evan, and have been for over a year. And there's a child—'

She stopped abruptly, her hand covering her mouth, and stared at him.

'It was such a blow, Evan,' she whispered at last. 'I felt dirty and degraded, remembering the nights we shared, the things . . . the things you made me do.'

Evan was suddenly frantic at the look on her face. 'Delphine, please, let me explain.' He grasped her hand tightly. 'I didn't mean to deceive you or cause pain. And I certainly didn't mean to dishonour you. I fell in love, utterly, recklessly. Please forgive me, my darling.' She sobbed and he rushed on. 'Don't let this come between us.'

'This wife of yours,' she said. 'Do you love her?'

'No!' Evan protested loudly. 'I hate her! I love you.'

She lifted her gaze. 'Then, my darling,' she whispered, 'my sacrifice is worth it to save you.'

'Sacrifice?'

She clutched his hand.

'Luther gave me a terrible ultimatum,' she said, a tremor in her voice. 'I must be his wife, or he'll foreclose on your property and ruin you into the bargain.'

'The swine!'

'He said the fate of your wife and child were in my hands. I love you too much, Evan. What else could I do but agree?'

'Damn him to hell!' In rage, Evan slammed one fist into the other. 'I could kill him.' He stared at her. 'You can't marry him, Delphine. It's too much to ask.'

'I have to.' She shook her head. 'But it'll make no difference to us. Being his wife won't end my love for you.'

She stroked his cheek, and Evan felt desire swell within him. He'd never let her go.

'Evan, come back to Old Grove House where you belong.'

He twisted his head away from her touch. 'No, I daren't be under the same roof as Luther now,' he said raggedly. 'I might be tempted to do him a mischief for the way he's treated you.'

'We must be clever,' Delphine said persuasively. 'Before he relieves you of your position at the shop, which he's also threatening, pretend you're resigned to the fact that he's won me over. He's conceited enough to believe it.'

'No.'

She leaned into him, putting her soft face against his. 'But think, my love,' she said coaxingly. 'What sweet revenge it'll be to make a cuckold of Luther under his own roof. How you'll enjoy that; how we'll both enjoy it.'

Unable to control the impulse, he grasped her in his arms and kissed her.

'I'll try to persuade him to let you have your inheritance,' Delphine breathed after an ardent moment. 'Then you'll be independent.'

Evan groaned with despair. 'How will I bear watching you with him?' he asked desperately. 'See him kiss or caress you?'

'You'll bear it, my love,' she said. 'Because you know everything I say and do with him is false.'

She pressed her open mouth to his again, her small sweet tongue probing until his senses reeled.

'You alone have my undying love,' she whispered huskily at last. 'Now and for ever.'

15

Kate found Ethel still crying in her room at the top of the house, and re-engaged her as her personal maid. It was the first independent financial thing she'd ever done and she was pleased at outwitting Delphine. Then she was unnerved, realising she hadn't the means to pay the girl's wages. She'd have to appeal to Simon for help. This wasn't a happy thought.

She went reluctantly to his rooms that evening. He was standing in the bedroom doorway and couldn't have looked more surprised to see her.

'Well, a visit from my wife in our married quarters.' He raised his eyebrows. 'I *am* honoured.'

Kate didn't like his mocking tone. 'Save your sarcasm for the underlings at the shop,' she said pithily. 'I'm here on domestic business.'

'Oh, really?'

He disappeared into the bedroom, leaving her standing there, and Kate was furious. She followed him, biting back angry words, struggling to remember she needed his help.

He took off his tailed coat, draping it on the shoulders of the wooden valet standing at the end of the bed, and removed his waistcoat.

'Don't walk away when I'm speaking to you,' she snapped. 'Manners aren't your strong point, are they?'

His expression showed impatience as he removed his collar stud and then the celluloid collar. He flung it down on the bed as though it were a rat that had had him by the throat, and then pointed at it.

'That's the first thing I'll abolish when I'm a director,' he said gruffly. 'No one should have to put up with that torture for hours on end.'

'Is that what Luther promised you for marrying me?' Kate asked edgily. 'A slice of the business. Talk about blood money.'

He gave her a pitying glance then sat on the bed to remove his shoes.

'Well?' he asked with irritation. 'What's this domestic business that needs my attention?'

'I've hired a personal maid,' she said arrogantly. 'You can afford her wages, I presume?'

He paused in the act of pulling off a shoe and looked up at her in exasperation.

'You've done what?' he snapped. 'Why? You have Ethel.'

She related the drama of the morning.

'I've re-engaged her, and Delphine's furious,' Kate said. 'As my husband I expect you to back me up.'

Simon let the shoe drop on to the floor with a thud.

'So, I'm your husband only when it suits you.'

Kate glared at him.

'I won't let Delphine have the last word. You must support me.'

Simon took off the other shoe in silence, and then stood up, sliding his braces from his shoulders.

'I'm not sure I can afford a maid,' he said at last. 'Especially since I've just put a deposit on some property in Sketty. A nice house, not too large. Very good views.'

Kate's mouth dropped open, and for a moment she was speechless. Simon removed his cufflinks and unbuttoned his shirt.

'How do you expect to pay for that?' she asked at last.

His answering smile was wry. 'I'm counting on your inheritance.'

'How dare you take that for granted?' Kate spluttered. 'That money's mine. You won't see a penny piece of it.'

Simon looked annoyed. 'You haven't got the money yet,' he snapped. 'You'll need me to negotiate with Luther. He's too cagey a bird for you to deal with.'

'Huh! I've managed until now without your help.'

Simon's lip curled with scorn. 'Oh, yes, you're doing so well you can't even pay your own maid.'

'And you can't afford fine property,' Kate flared. 'You'd better call the deal off.'

His expression was suddenly serious.

'We need to get away from this house, Kate,' he said. 'What happened this morning is just the beginning. You'll never be happy while Delphine is mistress here.'

'This is my home,' Kate stormed. 'I won't be driven out by Delphine or anyone else.'

'I think you will, Kate.'

He undid the buttons of his trousers' flies, and Kate stared.

'What're you doing?'

'I'm changing for dinner, what else.'

Kate looked askance at him. 'Can't you do the decent thing and wait until I'm gone?'

'You *are* my wife, Kate,' he said blithely, letting the trousers fall around his ankles. 'Have you forgotten so soon?'

With an exclamation of fury, Kate turned and fled.

★   ★   ★

'The dining table's hardly the place to talk business,' Luther said, as he poured himself a glass of port and then passed the decanter to Simon.

'On the contrary,' Simon replied, grasping the decanter firmly by the neck. 'I understood most deals are struck across the damask cloth.'

'We have guests,' Luther said, glancing apologetically at Bertram.

'Hardly that now,' said Simon. 'Bertram's family, or will be soon.'

Bertram rose. 'I'll join the ladies, if you wish.'

Luther waved him to be seated again, but Simon spoke up.

'I'd be obliged if you'll leave us, Bertram,' he said. 'We've known each other too long for you to be offended.'

Luther looked annoyed as Bertram smiled and left the room.

'You take a high hand, Simon,' he said brusquely. 'Have a care.'

'You don't hold back when it comes to business,' Simon said flatly. 'And neither do I. You've taught me well.'

Luther's smile was crafty. 'Flattery will get you nowhere.'

Simon sipped his port, waiting a moment more before beginning.

'The only business that interests me at the moment, Luther,' he said at last, 'is Kate's inheritance. I've kept my side of the bargain. I married the girl. Now it's your turn to make it worth my while.'

'You're in a great hurry,' Luther remarked tersely. 'You haven't been married a week yet.'

'A bargain's a bargain.' Simon's smile was bitter. 'You wouldn't give a debtor a second chance, why should I?'

'You think I'm in your debt?'

'You know you are.'

Luther shifted in his seat. 'The thing is, Simon, I don't trust you.'

'All I want is the money,' Simon said earnestly. 'I'm buying property. You said yourself that once you have the shares, I can do as I please.' He smiled broadly. 'I'm anxious to begin.'

He sipped his port again, allowing Luther to digest his words.

'Kate's no real wife to me,' Simon went on frankly. 'I need amiable female company.' He smiled. 'I can't do that on the pittance I receive as a salary.'

'You were happy to take it,' Luther snapped. 'You had damned little when you came here.'

'True.' Simon nodded. 'But now I've married a Vaughan, a family of wealth and property, and should take my rightful place in Swansea society; enjoy myself, find some willing female entertainment.'

Luther smiled. 'And you will, my boy,' he said jovially, although Simon wasn't taken in. 'As soon as you've signed the legal documents I've prepared.'

'Documents?' Simon put down his glass of port, and sat upright. 'What documents?'

'My safeguard,' Luther said. 'I'm not the fool you take me for, Simon.' He laughed. 'You're too like me, shrewd and not a little unethical. Your signature will ensure the shares are passed to me without fail, or you face litigation.'

'Surely we don't need this legal claptrap,' Simon protested.

There was no way Luther could make this shady exchange of shares legally binding. No lawyer worth his salt would condone or compound the questionable bargain they'd made. No court would ever give credence to this swindle. These so-called legal documents were a bluff, but Luther's fears must be quelled.

'I want only the money,' Simon repeated, emphasising sincerity in his voice.

'Then you won't object to signing?'

'Of course not,' Simon assured him, rising. 'Let's do it now. You have the papers in your study?'

In the study, Simon took up the pen, but hesitated long enough to show some concern before adding his signature. Beside him, Luther appeared to relax visibly.

'Good! That's settled then,' he said.

He gathered up the papers and, opening a small safe in the corner, put the documents inside. He slammed the door and spun the dial lock.

'Splendid,' he went on, returning to the desk. 'I'll contact the family lawyers first thing in the morning. Kathryn will receive her inheritance within a week.' He smiled. 'And within a fortnight I'll have that damned board of directors exactly where I want them.'

Mr Walters, the Vaughan's family lawyer, rotund and be-spectacled, opened his attaché case and removed a sheaf of papers. He glanced at Kate, sitting on the other side of the desk in Luther's study, and smiled.

'This is a very important day in your life, Kathryn,' he said. 'You've become a very rich woman. You'll need guidance in the management of your fortune, and I'm sure Mr Templar will provide that.'

Simon gave a small cough and stepped forward. 'As Kate's husband I'll provide all the assistance she needs,' he said in a firm tone. 'I'm sure my uncle has no objection.'

Mr Walters peered at him over the top of his spectacles, a glint in his eye, and Simon realised the lawyer was suspicious of him.

'Mr Templar has a great deal of experience in financial matters,' he said, looking down his nose at Simon.

'I'm equally as astute,' Simon said, an edge to his voice. 'And I have the right.'

Mr Walters sniffed. 'Of course, as the husband it is your prerogative,' he conceded stiffly. He glanced at Luther. 'I must, by duty, invoke the codicil of Russell Vaughan's will, that you, Mr Templar, as executor, unequivocally approve your stepdaughter's marriage. Do you so approve, Mr Templar?'

There was a slight hesitation and Simon held his breath. He wouldn't put it past his uncle to squirm out of their arrangement at the last minute, if he'd found a better plan, and his mouth went dry.

'I so approve,' Luther said at last.

Mr Walters slid a document across the desk. 'Your signature, Mr Templar, if you please.'

That done, it was Kate's turn to take up the pen. To Simon's surprise, she turned to glance at him, a question in her eyes, and in that moment he thought she might yet trust him. He nodded imperceptibly, and Kate bent her head, the pen scratching the thick parchment.

Mr Walters rose. 'Congratulations, Kathryn. I'll make all the necessary arrangements, and send you copies of documents,' he said. 'Funds will be at your disposal by the end of this week.'

'The shares certificates, too?' Simon asked quickly.

Mr Walters stared at him, his mouth tightening. He grasped Kate's hand. 'My dear, may I speak a word of caution?' He flicked another glance at Simon. 'A young woman of your tender years can easily fall prey to unscrupulous people, and your fortune is large enough to tempt anyone—'

'Have no fear, Mr Walters,' Simon cut in sharply, stepping forward. 'No one will take advantage of my wife. She's in good hands.'

When Mr Walters had gone, Kate and Simon were about to leave the study, too, when Luther spoke, his tone harsh. 'A word, Simon.'

Simon hesitated until Kate was across the hall well out of earshot, and then glanced back at his uncle, holding the door ajar.

'Later, Luther,' he said casually. 'Kate and I must talk.'

Luther's mouth was pinched in anger. 'Very well, but remember, I have your signature on a very damning document. Don't even consider duping me, I warn you,' he said darkly. 'Or you'll face more than poverty, you'll face prison.'

Kate was in her small sitting-room when Simon tapped at the door and stepped in. She'd been expecting him, and guessed what was feverishly on his mind: her money. She looked up from the crochet work she was doing, her glance scornful.

'Shouldn't you be back at the shop, earning your bread?'

'That's a very uncharitable thing to say to one's husband,' he said without rancour. 'Especially when he's protecting you from unscrupulous people.'

Kate couldn't help a smile. He really believed he could charm the money out of her.

'And who'll protect me from you?' she asked scathingly. 'I've already said, you won't see a farthing of it. So I hope Luther's paying you well for your trouble in marrying me.'

'I'm not in Luther's pay, and I'm not interested in your money, either,' he said tersely. 'It's the shares I want. Without them I can't take the seat on the board. If I'm to fight Luther I must have them.'

Kate lowered the crochet into her lap. 'All you men think alike,' she said coolly. 'Because I'm young and female it follows I must be a fool.'

'Huh! No one could ever believe that of you, Kate,' Simon said sarcastically. 'Not with that acid tongue of yours.'

Kate was livid. 'You're conniving with Luther,' she burst out angrily. 'Planning to give the shares to him. He's already tricked Evan in some way, but neither of you will trick me.'

'So what'll you do with them?' Simon asked impatiently. 'Sit on them until they're useless?'

'I may make them over to Evan,' Kate said, lowering her glance to the crochet again.

Her fingers trembled with anger and she could hardly hold the crochet hook. It infuriated her to accept that, as a woman, she was banned from what was her rightful place, when she had as much gumption as any man.

'Then Luther *will* get hold of them,' Simon said harshly. 'He's strangling your brother with debts. And with their rivalry over Delphine, Evan can't move against him. If he could, he'd have done it before now.'

He came and stood before her, towering above her, and Kate felt intimidated.

'I alone can fight Luther,' he said persuasively. 'Contact Walters tomorrow and make arrangements for the transfer to me.'

Kate flung down the crochet work, and stood up, face to face with him, although she had to hold her head back to look him full in the eye.

'And what about this property you're buying in Sketty?' she blurted angrily. 'Who's to pay for that I'd like to know? You're a liar, Simon Creswell, and not a very clever one, either.'

His expression was dark. 'I'm doing that for you, woman!'

he barked. 'The time's coming when life at Old Grove House will be impossible. 'You'll need to get away.'

'Liar!'

Simon's jaw worked in anger, but he held his tongue. Kate continued to stare defiantly into his eyes. It was just beginning to sink in what her new wealth really meant. She could leave here any time she wanted. A stab of unhappiness punctured her defiance. She'd never abandon her home to the likes of Luther and Delphine. And she wouldn't submit to Simon Creswell either.

'Is that your last word?' he asked with a tremor in his voice.

'It certainly is!'

Simon's mouth stretched into a thin angry line. 'The lawyer's right,' he said abrasively. 'You *are* an empty-headed, wilful little fool, and something tells me you'll be very sorry for obstructing me.'

One afternoon a week later, Ethel told her she was wanted urgently in the kitchen. Kate's heart missed a beat, feeling sure it was Aunt Agnes, and at last she'd learn the truth about her mother's death.

She'd been in possession of her inheritance for two days and already ownership of the shares was weighing heavy. Simon never let an opportunity go by without attempting to persuade her to hand them over to him, and she was growing weary of it. He was persistent, if nothing else. It struck her, now, that her aunt was the very person to give the advice she needed.

In the kitchen an elderly lady sat in the chair near the range, a cup and saucer in her hand, while a walking-stick leaned against the wall nearby. She was dressed in black and wore an old-fashioned poke bonnet. Her face was lined, but her eyes were bright, and, looking into them, Kate was reminded immediately of her father.

'So, there you are, Kathryn Vaughan,' the lady said, her voice strong and surprisingly full of vigour. 'Come closer, my poor old eyes are fading.'

Kate went forward eagerly and grasped the hand that was held out to her. 'Aunt Agnes, at last you're here,' she cried. 'Where have you been all this time? Why did you disappear? Are you all right?'

'Steady! Steady!' Agnes said. 'We can't talk here. Mrs Trobert's at risk every moment. You must get me into your rooms without being seen. I'm told the present butler is a rogue of the first order.'

Kate wrung her hands. 'How can I do that?'

'There's that old iron staircase on the back wall of the west wing which goes up to the nursery,' Mrs Trobert said helpfully. 'And the nursery is right above Mr Creswell's quarters.'

'Quite right!' Agnes exclaimed. 'I used it often when I lived here.'

Kate eyed the walking-stick. 'It'll be too much of a climb for you, I'm afraid.'

Agnes struggled to her feet. 'Not when you're as determined as I am,' she said stoutly. 'I'm here on a mission, and I'll be damned if I'll go away without completing it.'

Kate warmed to her aunt and liked the free way she talked. With the aid of the stick and Kate's arm, Agnes made her way slowly through the shrubbery to the west side of the house. Ivy covered most of the wall, but the staircase was still there, although a little rusted in too many places. It must be as old as the house itself, Kate thought, swallowing her dread that it might give way under their combined weight. But Agnes appeared to have no such fear. She grasped the rail and hauled herself on to the first step.

'Give me a hand, young Kathryn,' she gasped. 'I'm not so agile as I used to be.'

It was a long and painful climb to reach a half-landing, and Kate saw they were outside the French windows of Simon's bedroom. She pushed gingerly on the catch and to her relief it gave under pressure, and she helped Aunt Agnes inside.

'Oh, mercy me!' Agnes panted, sinking into a basket chair near the bed. 'I'll never be able to climb down again.' She looked at Kate hopefully. 'What I need is a good stiff drink.'

In Simon's sitting-room Kate found a bottle of brandy and gave two fingers of the golden liquid to her aunt.

'Oh, that's better,' Agnes said after taking some eager sips. 'Now let me look at you, Kathryn. Ah! Yes, you've grown into a beautiful young woman.'

'Call me Kate,' she said quickly. 'Only Luther calls me Kathryn and I hate it.'

'Oh, yes, Luther,' Agnes said, her eyes narrowing. 'May he rot in hell.'

'Aunt Agnes!' Kate was shocked at the venom in her aunt's voice.

'It's what he deserves,' Agnes said adamantly. 'We'll talk of that later, but now I want to ask you about your brother, and why he's deserted his wife and child?'

'What?'

Agnes nodded, as though confirming a private notion. 'He hasn't told even you. He's ashamed.'

Kate grasped Agnes's hand. 'Tell me everything,' she urged. 'Much depends on me knowing the truth. But before we talk, you must eat and drink. I'll get Ethel to bring something from the kitchen.'

★   ★   ★

As Agnes made a meal of chicken breasts cooked in wine, and some roasted potatoes and parsnips, she explained where she'd been living since disappearing from the town. Kate listened in astonishment and growing concern as she learned of Evan's young wife, Eirwen, and his son, Russell, and the isolated house in Fforestfach.

'There was a time when he neglected the bills, leaving his poor wife to scratch for sustenance,' Agnes said, deep disdain in her voice. 'Until I shamed him.'

'I can hardly believe it of him,' Kate said.

'He hasn't been near us for months,' Agnes went on tiredly, placing her knife and fork carefully on her now empty plate. 'Eirwen is threatening to return to her people in the Rhondda, taking Russell with her. I can't allow it. That child's a Vaughan, and must take his place in the family.'

'I agree,' Kate said thoughtfully. 'But Luther may not want that. Did you know he plans to marry? I dare say he hopes for an heir.'

'I know all about it,' Agnes said. 'Luther's fiancée is the very same woman Evan's been messing with. I suspect she's a trollop.'

'She's a baronet's daughter,' Kate said.

'A high-born trollop, then.' Agnes's tone was sour. 'I heard about the scandalous scene at your wedding.'

Kate was vexed and flushed with shame. The county knew their family disgrace, and a great swell of anger rose in her heart against Evan.

'I won't keep quiet much longer,' Agnes said firmly. 'Evan must face up to his responsibilities.'

'He'll get a tongue wagging from me, too, when I see him,' Kate said wrathfully. 'He's gone into hiding, and hasn't even been to his duties in the shop, so Simon tells me. I'm surprised Luther isn't kicking up a fuss about that.'

'He'll have his dark reasons,' Agnes said, loathing in her voice.

'Why do you hate my stepfather so much?'

Agnes was silent for a moment, her gaze turning inward as though looking into the past. And then she spoke.

'Because I believe he murdered your mother.'

Kate stared, knocked back by the words, and was then unsure she'd heard properly. 'Murdered?' The word was alien on her lips. 'But Luther says she killed herself – that she was insane.'

'Alice Vaughan never killed herself!' Agnes's nostrils flared with anger. 'She was very unhappy and lived to curse the day she married him, but if she'd had any such intentions I'd have known. We were as close as sisters, despite the difference in our ages.'

She took Kate's hand and squeezed it tightly. 'Believe me, my dear,' she said gently. 'Your mother was the sanest person I've ever known and she loved her children too much to leave them alone with that tyrant.'

'But Dr Penfold was here the night she died,' Kate said, feeling confused. 'Surely he would've known if Luther was responsible.'

'That charlatan should never have been allowed near Alice,' Agnes said heatedly. 'He should be struck off.'

'Why?'

'Never mind.' Agnes looked away. 'I blame myself for not insisting on seeing her that night, but Luther ordered me out of her rooms.'

She raised a handkerchief to her lips, pain in her eyes as she looked at Kate almost beseechingly. Finally she found the strength to go on.

'The following morning, when I learned Alice was dead, I knew it couldn't have been a natural death.'

'Oh, Aunt Agnes, how terrible! What did you do? What could you do?'

Agnes held her head up, her expression drawn and tired. 'I accused him to his face of causing her death!' she said stalwartly. 'In front of the doctor and Roberts, the old butler we had then.'

'What did he say?'

'He was in a terrible rage. I thought he'd have a seizure,' Agnes said. 'He cursed me, foul language, then threw me out, bag and baggage.' Agnes gave a sob. 'The only home I'd ever known.'

She paused for a moment, handkerchief to her mouth again, overcome by painful memories. After a moment, she seemed to rally, though Kate saw that her aunt was close to exhaustion.

'It was Mrs Trobert who got rooms for me in Craddock Street,' she went on quietly. 'Through a cousin of hers.'

'Why did Mother marry Luther?' Kate asked in wonder. 'It couldn't have been for love.'

'I begged her not to,' Agnes said, her voice trembling. 'But Luther was charming in those days and persuasive – the devil! And she felt you and Evan growing up needed a father.'

'But why kill her?' Kate asked, a sense of horror stealing over her at the very thought.

'Alice stood between him and what he's connived to get ever since he joined the business: total control,' Agnes replied. 'She wouldn't make over her shares, you see. When she died he inherited everything, except what your father left you. He found he couldn't touch that.'

Kate was silent, recalling Luther's repeated threats to have her committed. She always knew he was ruthless; now she realised he'd stop at nothing to get his way.

'Luther's evil,' Agnes said, as though reading her thoughts. 'And evil attracts evil.'

Kate thought of Delphine. They were two of a kind, perhaps.

'This husband of yours, Kate,' Agnes said. 'Who is he?'

Kate felt a shiver go up her spine. 'He's Luther's nephew.'

'I must meet him.'

'Is that wise?'

'I'll know immediately if he's set in Luther's mould. For your sake, Kate, I hope he's not.'

She thought of the unrelenting way he'd tried to acquire her shares since they'd married. 'Simon's after the shares Father left me,' Kate said quietly.

Was history repeating itself?

Agnes's eyes glinted, and her lips were set in a straight line. 'Be careful, my girl,' she said.

The clock in the sitting-room chimed five times.

'It's so late,' Agnes said suddenly. 'I must leave before Luther returns.'

She tried to rise from the basket chair, but sank back exhausted.

'I should never have climbed those stairs in my state,' she said. 'Oh! Kate, how will I get home tonight?'

Kate's mind was already made up. 'You'll spend the night here.' She pointed to the double bed. 'I'll call Ethel, and between us we'll get you settled. You need a good night's rest.'

'Luther will be furious with you if I'm discovered. I'm so sorry, Kate, my dear, to bring this trouble on you. I may have put you in serious danger, but I had to come. Evan must see reason.'

'Don't fuss yourself so,' Kate said. 'I'm very glad you came. Now I know the truth.'

Ethel, already sworn to secrecy, helped Agnes to undress and she was put into Simon's bed. Food and drink would again be smuggled in later when Kate and the rest of the family were at dinner. Luckily, as Ethel remarked, it was Chivers's day off, and usually he didn't return to the house until midnight.

'How did you get here?' Kate asked her aunt as she adjusted her pillows to a more comfortable position.

'It's Megan's day to visit her parents,' Agnes said with a sigh. 'We caught the horse bus from Carmarthen. In Swansea, Megan got us a hansom, and dropped me at the gates.' She paused, looking perplexed. 'How I'll get back I don't know.'

'Leave that to me,' Kate said confidently. 'I have a plan.'

Here was a chance to test Simon's motives and allegiance. She risked betrayal, but at least she'd learn whether he could be trusted with her shares.

Kate was waiting for Simon in his sitting-room when he returned from business. She put down her crotchet work as he came in, and stood up.

'Good. You're back,' she began pleasantly. 'What sort of a day have you had?'

He stared at her in total astonishment. 'I beg your pardon?'

She pointed to a chair nearby. 'I've put your clothes there. You can change in the dressing-room.'

His glance strayed from her face to the clothes neatly laid out and back to her face, puzzlement changing to suspicion. 'What's going on, Kate?'

'Nothing. I'm just being helpful.'

'Helpful to whom?' he asked. 'Certainly not to me. You hate my guts.'

Kate grimaced. 'Don't be vulgar.'

He glanced towards the vestibule, his head cocked, listening intently. 'Why can't I go into the bedroom?' he asked.

Kate wetted her lips. 'Who says you can't?'

'You're as transparent as a pane of glass, Kate.' He whirled about and strode towards the vestibule, Kate at his heels.

'Wait a minute!' she called. 'Don't go in! I'll explain if you'll just wait.'

'What are you hiding?' he asked brusquely. 'Who are you hiding?'

He flung the bedroom door open and marched in, stopping short at the sight of the figure in the bed, grey hair loosened, spread on the pillow. Agnes was still asleep and unaware.

'Who is she?' he asked, his voice hushed.

'My father's sister,' Kate murmured. 'My Aunt Agnes.'

He silently signalled her outside. Kate went, a little breathless now at what she'd done. In the living-room she turned to face him, apprehension making her heart skip a beat.

'What's she doing here, and in my bed?' he asked bluntly.

Kate wetted her lips again. 'She came to see Evan.' She frowned at him. 'Did you know he was married?' she asked sharply.

'I was beginning to suspect it. But what's that got to do with your aunt being in my bed?'

Kate explained Agnes's mission.

'She's an old lady,' Kate said stubbornly. 'And she's exhausted. There was nothing else I could do. No one must know she's here, especially Luther.'

'I see.' He turned his back and walked away, to look through the window, his thumb rubbing his jaw.

Kate swallowed hard, looking at his tall frame and square

shoulders, waiting for some response. When he didn't speak, she asked, 'Are you going to betray us?'

He turned back to her with a look of contempt. 'That doesn't deserve an answer,' he said curtly. 'What happens in the morning?'

Kate darted towards him eagerly. She'd thought it all out while she'd been awaiting his return. 'Ah, well,' she said. 'That's where you come in, Simon.'

'What?'

'We need the coach and groom to take her back to Fforestfach,' she explained patiently as though to a child. 'I can't order it, but Trott will obey you.' She looked up at him hopefully. 'You could bribe him to keep his mouth shut.'

He looked astonished again and then perplexed. 'Is all this subterfuge really necessary?'

Kate bit her lip, undecided. Should she tell him everything Agnes had told her about her suspicions of Luther? Simon had professed to be prepared to topple Luther in the business, but was that a bluff? Were they in cahoots instead, scheming to get her shares any way they could? Were they even ready to see her dead, too?

She thought of the old lady in bed in the other room and felt her mouth go dry, knowing she had no choice but to trust him.

'Do you believe your uncle is capable of murder?' she asked flatly.

He stared at her without speaking, and Kate nodded.

'Yes, that's what Aunt Agnes is accusing him of: the murder of my mother,' she said quietly. 'When he thought I'd spoken to her last year he almost had a fit, right in front of my eyes. He's frightened of her, so he's guilty of something.'

Simon was thoughtful. 'Tell me everything you know or can remember about Dr Penfold,' he said.

They were still discussing plans for the following morning when the dressing gong sounded.

'I'll change now in the dressing-room,' Simon said. 'But we'll exchange rooms tonight. You sleep here in case your aunt needs you, but I'll be back early, before the servants bring the hot water.'

'Oh, Simon.' Suddenly afraid, she caught at his arm. 'Is it going to be all right? If it's true that Luther killed my mother, we're dealing with a desperate man.'

16

—◆—

'Now we must be swift, so I'll carry your aunt downstairs, while you keep a look-out.'

They were in Simon's rooms, dressed and ready to leave. It had been tricky, with servants bustling about in the earlier part of the morning, but Ethel had managed to avert discovery by endeavouring to be everywhere at once, and Kate was grateful to her.

'Can Trott be trusted?' She was anxious.

'There's no time for questions or second thoughts,' he said impatiently. 'Let's hope Chivers isn't snooping about the shrubbery.'

'Ethel says he's occupied in the wine cellar.'

'We'll use the iron staircase,' said Simon. 'Trott will bring the coach around the back. He's taking a big risk, you know, Kate. The man could lose his job.'

'Only if we're caught.'

They went into the bedroom. Aunt Agnes was sitting in the wicker chair, dressed, and looking much better than she had the afternoon before.

'Aunt Agnes, this is . . . my husband, Simon Creswell.'

Agnes's glance was sharp as she looked him over, obviously weighing him up.

'You're a fine-looking man,' she said bluntly. 'But handsome is as handsome does.'

Simon's smile was wry. 'And I'm pleased to meet you, too, Aunt Agnes,' he said. 'Now, with your permission, I'll sweep you off your feet.'

Kate preceded them down the iron stairs. As Simon began his descent with his burden, the stairs seemed to vibrate under their feet, and Kate felt her heart leap in fright. It was quite a drop to the gravel below, and she wouldn't want to trust herself to these stairs too often. The metal creaks and groans continued until Simon reached the ground. Kate noted he looked a little shaken, too.

Almost immediately Trott appeared with the coach. Aunt Agnes was helped inside. Kate scrambled in too, with Simon right behind her.

'Oh, what a relief,' Kate said.

'We're not in the clear yet,' Simon warned. 'We may be seen going down the carriageway. We must have a tale ready, one that Luther will believe.' He snapped his fingers. 'I've got it! I'm taking you to view the property I'm buying in Sketty.'

'Sharp-witted, I see,' Aunt Agnes remarked, eyeing him speculatively. 'And ambitious.' She glanced at Kate. 'You didn't tell me he's set to be a landowner already.'

'Not with *my* money, he isn't,' Kate said emphatically, and Simon gave a loud sigh.

With several steep hills to climb, it was almost an hour before they reached Fforestfach, and Aunt Agnes had fired one question after another at Simon throughout the journey. She was quiet and thoughtful when they reached the opening to the lane that led to the house.

Trott pulled up the coach at the roadside outside the Marquis Arms, and jumped down from his seat to speak to Simon through the window.

'Daren't take the coach down that track, sir,' he said, touching his hat. 'Too narrow. Beg pardon, sir.'

'Quite right, Trott,' Simon agreed. 'We don't want any suspicious damage.'

Simon helped Agnes from the coach, and would have lifted her up again, but she pushed his arm away.

'I'm not a helpless cripple, young man,' she said. 'I'll walk down the lane. I've done it before.'

She pressed something into Trott's hand, and Kate thought she saw the flash of a whole sovereign.

'You've been a good servant to the Vaughans, Trott,' she said. 'I hope you always will be. Miss Kate needs all the help she can get. Do you understand me?'

'Yes, Miss Vaughan, ma'am.'

'Wait for us,' Simon said to him. He glanced at the pub's doorway, a typical village tavern, the doors always open and sawdust on the floor.

'You can wet your whistle,' Simon said to him. 'But make sure it's just the one.'

Trott's weather-beaten face broke into a grin, and he touched his hat again. 'Yes, sir. Count on me.'

The walk down the lane was slow, as Agnes hobbled along.

'You mustn't expect much, Kate,' the old lady said, puffing a little. 'We're not grand at Glasfryn, but Eirwen does the best she can and it's comfortable, if not fashionable.'

Kate felt a mounting excitement at the idea of meeting her sister-in-law and nephew. She could hardly believe it was true that her brother had an established family. Why had he kept his secret from her?

For some reason they approached the house through the kitchen garden, where potatoes and cabbages grew, together with other vegetables, and entered by the door to the kitchen.

A young woman with thick brown hair flowing over her shoulders stood at the sink, peeling potatoes. She looked up, startled, as they came in, her eyes round with surprise. At the sight of Agnes, she let the potato and knife drop into the water and rushed forward, wiping her wet hands down the front of her apron.

'Agnes! Oh, *Duw! Duw!* There's worried I've been. Are you all right, *cariad*?'

She clasped the older woman tightly for a moment and then led her to a chair nearby, hardly glancing at Kate and Simon.

'Don't fuss, my girl,' Agnes said, though Kate could hear emotion in her voice, and knew instinctively that these two were fond of each other.

When seated, Agnes made introductions. 'Eirwen, this is my niece, Kate, and her husband, Simon Creswell.'

Eirwen nodded in Simon's direction, her head dipped respectfully. Kate stepped forward eagerly, and held out her hand. Shyly, her cheeks rosy with embarrassment, Eirwen took it, and to Kate astonishment, curtsied.

'Don't curtsy,' Agnes rebuked sharply. 'Kate's your sister-in-law, not your employer. You're a member of the Vaughan family now. Hold your head up, my girl, and be proud.'

'Yes, Agnes,' Eirwen said dutifully.

Kate grasped her hand in both of hers, and then, impulsively, kissed her cheek.

'I'm so pleased to meet you,' Kate said. 'I'd no idea of your existence, otherwise I would've called on you before this.'

'That's kind of you,' Eirwen said, lowering her gaze, and Kate could see she was having great difficulty with the meeting.

'Where's Megan?' Agnes asked. 'Isn't she back yet?' She glanced at Kate. 'I gave permission for her to stay with her parents last night, but I expected her to return first thing.'

'Oh, she did,' Eirwen assured her. 'She's down at the farm, buying some milk.' She smiled at Kate. 'My boy, Russell, is a proper little guzzler when it comes to milk,' she said proudly.

'I'm longing to see him,' Kate said, pleased that Evan had named the baby after their father.

'Oh, *Duw!* What am I thinking of?' Eirwen exclaimed. 'Receiving guests in the kitchen. Please come into the parlour, and I'll make some tea.'

She helped Agnes to her feet and they followed her out into a long wide passage, painted in gloomy colours of dark green and brown. Several doors led off, and Eirwen took them through to a room at the front of the house, with a window that overlooked the track to the road. The roof and smoking chimneys of the public house could just be seen through the trees.

As the main reception room, it was hardly fashionable or rich in decoration, but, as Agnes had told them, it looked comfortable enough, and even at this time of the year a fire burned in the large old-fashioned grate.

'Sit yourselves down,' Eirwen said, her cheeks still flushed. 'I'll bring some tea, and I made some Welsh cakes this morning.' She looked a little abashed. 'Perhaps they'll be too plain for you,' she said uncertainly.

'They'll melt in the mouth,' Agnes said, reassuringly. 'Eirwen is a wonderful cook, Kate, and an excellent mother.' There was a certain pride in her voice.

'Can I see the baby before we have tea, please?' Kate asked.

She was excited at the thought of holding a baby for the first time in her life, and this one was her nephew. The idea made her want to laugh in pleasure.

'I'll fetch him,' Eirwen said eagerly and dashed from the room.

'She's such a pretty girl,' Kate said when Eirwen had gone. 'Why has Evan kept her hidden? It's such a shame.'

'The man's a fool,' Simon opined bluntly, the first words he'd spoken since they'd entered the house.

'I quite agree with that assessment, young man,' Agnes said. 'Eirwen makes the best wife for any man; a real homemaker, which is more than can be said for that useless creature Luther is marrying.'

'Useless?' Kate looked astonished that her aunt would have an opinion of a woman she'd never met.

'Ethel told me all about her, and a few things she's probably never told you,' Agnes said. 'I believe Luther is making a grave mistake, which he'll find out to his cost.'

'You're a lady of discernment,' Simon said. 'You're quite right about Delphine Harrington. My uncle will regret he ever met her, but let him discover that for himself.'

Kate was irked by the deep meaningful glance that passed between Agnes and her husband.

'What's going on?' she asked. Irritation turned to anger when they were silent. 'Don't treat me like a child,' she exclaimed heatedly. 'What're you keeping from me?'

Before either could reply, Eirwen came into the room, a bright-eyed baby in her arms. At the sight of the child Kate jumped up, her anger forgotten.

'Oh! Let me take him,' she said excitedly, gathering the infant eagerly into her arms.

A strange and exhilarating sensation went through Kate's body as she held the plump child against her breast, and looked into his face. The fragrance of his beautiful skin, unknown and yet so familiar, was in her nostrils, and suddenly a great yearning engulfed her. She carried him to a chair and sat, cuddling him close. He burbled at her, looking intently into her face with intelligent eyes so like Evan's; it was remarkable.

'He's so beautiful!' she exclaimed in wonder. 'How can Evan ignore him so?' Immediately she spoke the words she regretted them, and glanced up at Eirwen, apologetically. 'Eirwen, I'm sorry. That was inconsiderate of me. You must think me very callous.'

Eirwen sank on to a chair nearby. 'But it's the truth, isn't it, Kate?' she said miserably. 'He's deserted me for another woman. He must think me a fool not to guess it. How can I stay in his house? I'll return to my people in Trehafod.'

'Oh, please!' Kate cried. 'Don't do that, I beg you. I'll speak to Evan myself. He must put this foolishness behind him. He still loves you, I know he does, and how could he not love his child?'

She clasped Russell to her and kissed his silken cheek. He spluttered his secret language at her, and made a grab for her hat. Kate's mouth went dry with a deep and unfamiliar emotion, accompanied by a longing so intense she almost moaned at its grip on her.

'He's adorable,' she whispered, and kissed his head. Suddenly, she felt like weeping. This wonderful experience was denied to her. Never would she hold her own child in her arms. Her marriage was a sham.

She glanced up at Simon, and flushed to find he was observing her intently. As their eyes met, he smiled. She thought to see mockery in his look, but instead was surprised to see understanding, and indeed a longing of his own.

'Would you like to hold him, Simon?' she asked generously, though she hated to give up the child. She wanted to keep him for ever.

Simon took the boy from her, and sat nearby, jigging him on

his knee, and to Kate's surprise made strange unintelligible noises at him, which Russell seemed to appreciate, for he spluttered and giggled in response.

Kate saw her aunt was watching Simon intently, her gaze sharp and watchful. Probably Agnes could make no more of him than Kate did herself. He'd obviously not had the benefit of a true gentleman's education, but he conducted himself well.

Yet what lay in his heart? That's what Kate continually wondered, especially over these last twenty-four hours since she'd learned of Luther's inner evil. Could Simon really be taken at face value? Her common sense told her not.

Eirwen was admiring her hat, and Kate dragged her thoughts away from the man she'd married to look more closely at her sister-in-law.

For the wife of a Vaughan of Swansea, Eirwen was shabbily dressed, and Kate was again gripped by displeasure at the thought of her brother's callous attitude.

Drawing Eirwen to one side of the room, she encouraged her to talk about their daily lives at Glasfryn, and was appalled at the arduous nature of it. Something must be done.

Speaking to her aunt quietly as they were about to leave, Kate said, 'I'll send my dressmaker to Eirwen, and bear the cost myself. She'll have decent gowns and a coat, too. I'll ask Evan for repayment.'

'It won't please him.' Agnes shook her head. 'He has only his salary, and I suspect his lady-love has prior claim on that.'

'I don't understand why he's not received his inheritance, now he's married,' Kate said.

'I don't doubt Luther withholds it for purposes of his own.'

Kate nodded thoughtfully, feeling she already knew what they were. Evan had done his best to persuade her to surrender to Luther's demands, and still her stepfather did not have his way.

'You needn't take responsibility for Eirwen on yourself, Kate,' Agnes said, breaking into her thoughts.

'But I do,' Kate said. 'She is my sister-in-law, part of my family now, and I have precious few relatives. I won't let her be treated like some shop-girl any longer.'

Ethel took her place at the refectory table in the big kitchen, her mouth watering at the aroma of steak and kidney pie, just finishing off in the oven. Except for Chivers and young Ben the Boots, most of the others were already seated, knives and forks at the ready.

There were sighs all around as Mrs Trobert turned from the range with one big pie dish, and carried it to the table.

'Where is he?' Trott asked, nodding towards the empty chair at the head of the table.

'Down the cellar, where else,' Mrs Trobert replied with a sniff. 'Treats it like his own lately.'

She put the pie dish down in front of Chivers's chair, and turned to the range again where a second pie waited, and brought that to the table, too.

'Hope he won't be long,' Watkins said, eyeing the pies hungrily. 'The grub's getting cold.'

Chivers's tall, bulky frame appeared from the door leading to the cellar, carrying two wine bottles under his arm. He turned and locked the cellar door carefully then brought the bottles to the table. Mrs Trobert gave a loud sniff again, as she took her seat at the opposite end of the table.

'Them's the fifth this week,' she said severely. 'You're very free with the master's cellar since Miss Harrington took charge.'

Chivers rounded on her angrily. 'Shut your face, you old bat,' he snarled. 'And keep your nose out of my business.'

Mrs Trobert gasped, and there was a general murmuring at the table.

'That's no way to talk to a lady,' Peters said, lifting his bony shoulders in disgust.

'Pipe down, you old cadger,' Chivers snapped. 'You shouldn't be here anyway. Always on the cadge, you are.'

'Leave him alone,' Mrs Trobert said, as Peters seemed to shrink with mortification. 'He's been here longer than you have.'

'When are we going to have the grub?' Watkins asked with irritation.

'Yes,' agreed Bessie plaintively. 'Don't forget I still got to wash up all the crockery after you lot have gone to bed, and it's half nine already.'

Chivers looked around the table, serving spoon in hand. 'Where's that bloody boy?'

As if on cue Ben, the boot boy, came in from the scullery, and marched straight to his place at table between Ethel and Trott.

'Wash your hands first, you dirty little tyke,' Chivers bellowed. 'You come in late again, and you'll go to bed hungry.'

At last Chivers dished out the portions of pie while Ethel fetched the vegetables and gravy boat from their warming place on the range. Chivers opened the two wine bottles and poured a glass for each man. Grudgingly he poured half a glass each for Mrs Trobert and Ethel. Young Bessie and Ben were not allowed any.

Ethel savoured hers. Whatever it was, it was lovely, and went well with the steak and kidney pie. Mrs Trobert had made bread pudding to follow. The men had a second glass of wine each.

'Nice drop of stuff,' Watkins remarked.

'Should be,' Chivers grinned. 'Cost a bob or two, I can tell you.'

Ethel glanced at Mrs Trobert's face and saw unbridled disapproval, but the older woman managed to hold her tongue, and Ethel was thankful. She'd enjoyed the food and wine. Unpleasantness at the table now would give her indigestion to go to bed with.

'Yes, this here wine's all right,' Trott agreed, with an air of a man who knew what he was talking about. 'But it isn't a patch on the drop of ale I had yesterday in that pub in Fforestfach. That was nectar, that was.'

Chivers was immediately alert. 'What pub?'

Trott looked around the table, crestfallen.

'What pub, I said?' Chivers thundered.

'Mind your words, Trott.' There was a warning in Mrs Trobert's voice.

Chivers looked from one to the other. 'What're you buggers getting up to behind my back?'

Ethel felt the tension rise, and one look at Mrs Trobert's face made her speak up, though she quailed inside, having never had the nerve to challenge the butler before.

'The only one who's up to something is you,' she said loudly, marvelling at her new confidence.

Staring at her as though he couldn't believe his ears, Chivers pushed back his chair, the legs scraping on the flag stoned floor, and stood up to his full height. 'Hey! I don't take backchat from a chit of a girl,' he thundered. 'You're sacked!'

'You can't sack me,' Ethel said. 'My wages are paid by Mr Creswell.'

'Then you've got no business being at this table, eating the master's food.'

'Yes, I do!' she burst out. 'Miss Kate says I'm entitled to have all my meals. She pays towards my keep, as well you know.' She tossed her head, the exhilaration making her face heat up. 'Now then!'

Chivers spluttered incoherently for a moment, then he rounded on Trott.

'What bloody pub?'

With an apologetic glance at Mrs Trobert, Trott shrugged, as though to show his helplessness. 'I was taking her home, wasn't I,' he said. 'Her, Miss Vaughan.' He glanced again at Mrs Trobert. '*Duw! Duw!* The old girl's aged, hasn't she, Mrs T. I remember when she could tackle a coach and pair, as good as any man.'

'Agnes Vaughan?' Chivers asked incredulously. 'Agnes Vaughan was here, in Old Grove House?' He looked down the table at Mrs Trobert. 'This is your doing, isn't it?' he said. 'You brought that old witch here.'

Mrs Trobert got to her feet. 'She's not a witch,' she blurted. 'The master hates her cos she knows too much.'

Chivers's face creased in a nasty smile of satisfaction. 'Heads are going to roll for this,' he said pleasantly. 'When I tell the master what's been going on, you're for the chop, Mrs T, and not before time either.'

'You can't tell him,' she cried. 'I've got no other home to go to.'

'Then you'll have to sleep in the gutter, won't you,' he snapped back. 'Beg for pennies down by the museum with the rest of the down-and-outs.'

He turned his gaze to Ethel. 'And you can pack your things and get out of your room, too,' he said. 'The mistress is getting a new maid as well as a new cook. The new girl'll want your room.'

He sat down looking pleased with himself.

'We'll get some willing females around here for a change.' He downed the last of the wine. 'Something a man can stay in nights for.'

His hard glance fixed on a stunned Ethel. 'Have your bags packed by eight o'clock tomorrow morning,' he said, and jerked his thumb in Mrs Trobert's direction. 'You're finished here, same as this old scarecrow.'

Ethel was late fetching the hot water, and Kate noticed immediately the maid's tear-stained face.

'What's happened now?'

Ethel wrung her hands. 'Oh, Miss Kate, something awful,' she began with a gulp. 'Last night, that stupid man Trott gave the game away to Chivers about Miss Vaughan. He told the master first thing, and Miss Harrington's been down and given Mrs Trobert the sack on a hour's notice.'

'Oh, no!' Kate clamped both hands to her mouth. This was her doing. Hastily, she got out of bed and reached for her wrap.

'Nasty she was, too,' Ethel went on, helping her into it. 'Said some spiteful things about Mrs Trobert's cooking; refused to give her a reference.' Ethel's face crumpled again. 'What's Mrs T going to do? She's got nowhere to go.'

Kate pulled herself together, remembering she was now a woman of considerable means. Mrs Trobert, a family retainer of long standing, wouldn't suffer.

'Tell her not to worry,' Kate said firmly. 'And she's not to leave the house, no matter what Miss Harrington says. I'll not have it!'

Ethel fidgeted. 'There's something else,' she said. 'The mistress has told me to leave my room; wants it for the new maid, so I've got nowhere to sleep as from eight o'clock this morning.'

'Mistress?'

'That's what the servants have to call her now. She'll soon be mistress, won't she, Miss Kate, when she marries the master?'

Kate's lips were pinched with anger. 'Go straight to Mr Creswell's rooms,' she commanded the maid. 'I don't care whether he's dressed or not. Tell him I want to see him here immediately.'

Ethel left, and while she was gone Kate paced her bedroom floor, anger and frustration stiffening her stride. Simon was right. Delphine wouldn't be satisfied until the whole household had been turned upside down. It was obvious she meant to be rid of all the old staff and replace them with . . . who and what? And why? What was she planning in that dark scheming mind of hers?

There was a tap at the door and Simon came in. Kate stared at his tousled hair and unshaven face. She'd never seen him like that before. He also looked quite cross.

'What's the meaning of this summons, Kate?' he asked tetchily. 'I'd hardly got out of bed.'

'You must do something about Mrs Trobert,' she began. 'We can't let her be thrown out on to the street.'

'What?'

Kate explained about Trott's foolishness.

'Well, what am I supposed to do?' Simon asked.

'See that she's housed and comfortable, and doesn't starve.'

He raised his brows. 'I'm already paying Ethel's wages,' he reminded her. 'And trying to buy the house in Sketty. I'm not made of money.' He sniffed. 'Unlike my lady wife.'

'There's no need to throw that in my face,' she said stiffly. 'I'll provide funds, if you'll make all immediate arrangements.'

He went and sat on the bed, yawning widely. 'I suppose I can have breakfast first?'

Without thinking, Kate sat down next to him. 'Ethel will have to sleep in your dressing-room from now on,' she said thoughtfully. 'Delphine's had her evicted for a new maid.'

'Now, just a moment,' Simon retorted quickly. 'I don't feel that's quite proper. After all, she's your maid.'

'She's got to sleep somewhere.'

'We must exchange rooms,' Simon said firmly. 'You take my quarters, with Ethel.' He looked around. 'I'll sleep here.'

Kate thought about it for a moment. It seemed reasonable.

Simon gave a little cough. 'This is quite cosy, isn't it,' he remarked. 'Just the two of us.' He smiled at her. 'Why don't I ring for breakfast to be served here this morning?'

Kate rose hastily from the bed, her cheeks growing hot.

'Our business is concluded,' she said sharply, not looking at him. 'You can return to your quarters.'

'What a pity.' He sounded disappointed. 'And speaking of business,' he went on, carefully. 'Have you thought any more about making your shares over to me? Every day you delay gives Luther more room to manoeuvre.'

'Oh, really?' Sceptical, Kate turned to glare at him.

'He's planning expansion,' said Simon quickly. 'Some mad scheme to open a branch in London, of all places. It's far too risky, and some board members are worried. Others are crumbling under pressure. I need to be on the board to stop him in his tracks.'

'I'm still not convinced of your sincerity,' Kate said. 'Not to mention your integrity.'

'That's uncalled for,' Simon said angrily, springing to his

feet. 'Perhaps you'd rather see the business run into the ground?'

'Of course not.' Kate shook her head. 'Luther's been managing it successfully for years. Why should anything go wrong now?'

'He's tried to set these plans in motion many times before,' Simon said. 'The board was too powerful to let him, but slowly power is passing to Luther, through Evan's shares, and winning over less cautious members.'

'And you think *you* can stop him?'

'I know I can if only you'll trust me.'

'I'll think about it,' Kate conceded. 'But first Mrs Trobert must be helped.'

Kate was taken by surprise when Evan showed up for dinner the following evening. She stared at him across the table, and then looked around at the others seated there. No one but her seemed taken aback to see him or remarked on his rather subdued attitude.

Luther conversed with him about business matters as though nothing untoward had passed between them, and even Delphine gave him a polite smile.

Kate was so angry with her brother, and couldn't begin to forgive him until she'd spoken to him bluntly. And blunt she'd be, especially about his treatment of Eirwen. Throughout dinner Kate wouldn't look at him again, let alone speak, but was determined to corner him at the earliest opportunity.

'This beef's overcooked,' Evan remarked suddenly, and to Kate's astonishment, Delphine seemed to bridle, as though she'd prepared it herself.

'Mrs Perkins, our new cook, isn't used to the range yet,' she said coldly. 'Chivers assures me she has the highest references.'

'But you haven't seen these references yourself, Delphine?' Simon asked sharply.

Delphine's cheeks flushed, and it was the first time Kate had ever seen her unsettled.

'Luther has total confidence in Chivers's integrity and judgement in these matters,' she said stiffly. 'Isn't that so, Luther, dearest?'

Kate caught the strange little smile that twisted Evan's mouth for a moment.

'It is, my dear,' Luther said, smiling back at her. 'It's a relief to know my household is in your capable hands. I'm sure Mrs Perkins will settle in.' His smile disappeared and his mouth tightened. 'Mrs Trobert's disloyalty and devious behaviour couldn't be tolerated. We're well rid of her.'

Kate caught Simon's warning glance and held her tongue.

When Delphine rose to leave the men alone with their port, Kate was forced to rise, too. In the hall Delphine turned to her.

'Shall we take just a little brandy together in the drawing-room, Kate?' Delphine smiled sweetly.

Kate's lips tightened. 'I don't think so, Delphine,' she said stiffly. 'Not after the disreputable way you tried to get rid of Ethel.'

'She's a thief!' Delphine said harshly. 'I'm astonished you've kept her on.'

'That's my business,' Kate retorted. 'You could've saved Mrs Trobert's job, if you'd wanted to, but obviously you intend to make a clean sweep of the servants.'

'My dear, there's nothing I could do about that wretched old woman,' Delphine said plaintively. 'Luther's mind was made up, and I'm a mere kitten in his hands.'

Alley cat, more like, Kate thought, and longed to say so.

'You may be my future stepmother,' she said disdainfully, 'but we'll never be friends.' Kate stared haughtily into the other woman's face. 'I don't like you, Delphine. You're trash!'

Delphine's nostrils flared and a sound came from her throat like that of an enraged cat. With a look of triumph, Kate turned away and abruptly marched off, feeling better for having spoken her mind at last.

She hurried to her little sitting-room, deciding she wouldn't go to bed until she'd had sharp words with Evan, too. Simon was the first to appear on the stairs and Kate called him inside.

'Did you know Evan was coming here tonight?'

'Yes,' he admitted. 'He came to the shop today. He's made some kind of an apology to Luther and Delphine.'

'And what about us?' Kate flared. 'Is he ready to beg our forgiveness?'

'The damage has been done,' said Simon, resignation in his tone. 'There's no advantage in raking it up again; no point in quarrelling with him.'

'And what about his poor wife?' Kate asked indignantly. 'He didn't take his eyes off Delphine all through dinner. He's obsessed. It's disgraceful! I'm going to tackle him about it, no matter what you say.'

Half an hour later, Kate looked over the balcony. Evan was crossing the hall when Delphine suddenly appeared from out of the shadows beneath the staircase and approached him. They kissed briefly. Kate withdrew her head, shocked. When she peeked again, he was climbing the stairs alone.

She stepped out in front of him as he passed in the gallery.

'So, you've decided to show your face again,' she began belligerently, vexed and dismayed at what she'd just seen. 'I don't know where you get the nerve. What sort of man are you?'

A scowl appeared on his face, and he tried to step past her, but she grasped his arm.

'Don't you dare ignore me,' Kate cried wrathfully. 'I want an apology for the abominable way you behaved at my reception.'

'It had nothing to do with you, Kate.'

'What?' She was furious. 'You ruined my wedding day!'

'Huh!' Evan's lip curled. 'You said the marriage is a charade. You didn't want to go through with it, remember?'

'I didn't expect to be made a laughing-stock in public, either,' she answered tightly. 'I haven't had one invitation to dine out since, not one.'

'I'm sorry,' he said briefly and offhandedly. 'Now, excuse me, Kate. I'm tired.'

'No, I won't excuse you,' Kate snapped. 'Explain why you've kept the existence of your wife and child from me.'

Evan's body stiffened as though she'd struck him across the face. 'What?'

'I've been to Fforestfach,' Kate said defiantly. 'I've met Eirwen and Russell. How could you desert them?'

Evan grabbed her arm and hauled her roughly into her sitting-room, his expression livid.

'How dare you meddle in my life?' he growled. 'How dare you judge me?'

'Aunt Agnes judges you,' said Kate. 'And she has cause.' She swallowed hard, shaken by the violence in his eyes. 'I saw you in the hall just now. Delphine's making a fool of you, Evan. Can't you see it?'

'Who else knows about Eirwen?'

'Simon does.'

'Damnation! Did you have to tell him?'

'Simon helped me get Aunt Agnes home,' Kate said. 'I don't know what we'd have done without him.' She paused. 'Why did you give your shares to Luther?' she asked, accusation in her voice. 'And why is he withholding your inheritance? What's his asking price?'

'It's none of your damned business, Kate.'

'I think it is,' she snapped. 'You're aiding and abetting him in trying to defraud me of *my* shares.'

Evan gave a bitter laugh. 'I don't have to. Simon's doing that. He's Luther's lackey.'

Kate was confused. Simon had helped with her aunt, but was he really helping himself?

'I'll have some bills for you to settle shortly,' she said abruptly, wishing to change the subject until she'd had more time to think about Simon's motives.

'What bills?' he asked, frowning.

'Dressmaker's bills,' she replied swiftly. 'Eirwen must be fitted out according to her station in life, the wife of a Vaughan of Swansea. I've sent Miss Clarke to her.'

'Cancel it!' Evan shouted.

'So! You refuse,' Kate cried in anger. 'Then I'll pay them myself, and shame you.'

She stepped away from him and looked him up and down. He was a stranger and it was Delphine's doing.

'No sister-in-law of mine will be seen in clothes fit only for a shop-girl,' she said defiantly.

'She *is* a shop-girl, damn it,' Evan snarled. 'She isn't good enough for me. I was trapped into marriage.'

'Oh! I see!' Kate tossed her head angrily. 'Well, she was good enough to take to bed, wasn't she?'

He looked stunned and Kate rushed on.

'Eirwen was good enough to amuse yourself with until Delphine came along.'

'Be quiet!' he thundered.

'I won't!' Kate shouted back, thoroughly worked up. 'You need the brutal truth to bring you to your senses.'

'I won't stand for this.' He turned away, but Kate shouted after him.

'You fool!' she shrieked. 'You threw Eirwen away like an old shoe when you'd finished with her. And for what? For a woman who's thoroughly bad.'

He turned back to face her, his expression dark. 'You're going too far, Kate,' he said, a dangerous warning note in his voice, but she wouldn't stop now.

'Delphine's behaving no better than a harlot!'

Fury flashed across his face and he lifted a hand. Kate thought he was about to strike her and she flinched.

'Go on then,' she panted. 'Strike me! Has she dragged you down that far?'

Remaining silent, he lowered his hand, his face white, but Kate was still filled with wrath.

'You're despicable,' she said in a low voice. 'I'm ashamed to call you brother.'

17

'I've some interesting news for you,' Luther said. 'I thought you'd like to know that Mansel Jenkins has been wounded in battle. I don't know how serious it is.'

Kate gave an involuntary cry, shaken at the news. She was aware of Simon's glance and tried to hide her feelings. She'd made sacred vows, even if the swearing of them had been forced on her, and to have tender feelings for any man other than her husband would make her no better than Delphine. Yet her heart ached for Mansel.

'Is this why you've summoned us here to the study?' Simon asked, anger in his voice. 'Jenkins's war exploits don't interest either of us.'

'No,' said Luther brusquely, and made a steeple of his hands to peer imperiously at them over his fingertips. 'You're both here to discuss your financial arrangements.'

Kate sat up straight and glanced suspiciously at Simon.

'It's come to my attention, Kathryn,' Luther went on, 'that you're frittering away your fortune on absurdities such as gowns for Evan's pitiable wife.'

'She's not pitiable,' Kate bridled. 'Surely my brother hasn't complained?'

'No, I intercepted the bills.'

Kate's mouth dropped open in astonishment. 'You did

what?' She stared at him. 'How dare you. You've no right to go through my post let alone open my letters.'

'This is my house, Kathryn.' Luther looked down his nose at her. 'Anything that goes on here is my business. This irresponsible conduct must be stopped. I've arranged for Mr Walters to call tomorrow.'

He stared at her, his eyes narrowed. 'It's my opinion you're mentally incapable of tending to your finances in a sensible way,' he went on. 'Therefore Walters will arrange power of attorney for Simon with immediate effect.'

Kate was speechless, and Luther continued.

'This will also give him access to your company shares, of course.'

She stared at Simon. 'So, you're behind this!' she said through clenched teeth. 'I might've known.'

Simon shook his head. 'I assure you, Kate—'

Furious, Kate jumped up from her chair. 'Don't bother to lie. You've been after those shares since our wedding day. You've told me a pack of lies. I knew I couldn't trust you.'

Simon rose to his feet and tried to take her arm, but she shrugged him off angrily, admonishing herself for believing he might be genuine.

She swung around to glare at Luther. 'I won't sign anything,' she said adamantly. 'And Mr Walters won't be party to underhandedness, so there's nothing you can do.'

Luther rose, looking wrathful. 'You've defied me once too often, Kathryn,' he thundered. 'I'll have you put away, and this time I really mean it! You'll stay institutionalised until you rot of old age. Now, get to your room and stay there until you see reason.'

'Now, just a damned minute!' Simon exclaimed hotly, stepping forward to place both palms on the desk. 'Don't you speak to Kate like that. She's my wife. You have no power over her any longer.'

Kate was surprised and impressed by his vehemence, even though she was wary of him.

'Thank you, Simon,' she said shakily. 'That's the first time anyone's stood up for me.'

'You little fool,' Luther burst out. 'Do you think he has any real regard for you? It's your fortune he's after.'

'I know that,' Kate flung back at him. 'I'm not such a fool as you think.'

Simon might be a rogue and a fortune-hunter, too, but what he said was true. As Simon's wife, Luther could no longer dominate her. She was free of him at last. And if she couldn't outwit Simon Creswell in the long run, then she had no right to the name Vaughan.

Luther's furious glance turned to Simon. 'I warn you, you're skating on thin ice,' he said through clenched teeth. 'We have an agreement.'

'I married Kate, didn't I?'

'I have your signature, Simon, remember that.'

'I'll not stand by while my wife is coerced into signing away her birthright,' Simon said fiercely. 'In future please keep out of our financial affairs.'

'I see! Now I know where I stand,' Luther said ominously. 'Well, Simon, you won't be surprised when I tell you you're sacked from your position as department manager at Vaughan & Templar.'

Simon looked stunned, and Luther smiled narrowly.

'We'll see where your so-called principles will get you,' he said triumphantly. 'In a few weeks you won't be able to pay your tailor or even afford the fare of a hansom cab.'

'I'll find other employment,' Simon said truculently.

'I don't think so!' Luther said. 'Not in this town. I've too much influence. Your name will be blackened, I'll see to that.'

'I've had enough of this,' Kate cried. 'Come along, Simon.'

She whirled about and stalked out, Simon at her heels, closing the study door after him, and in the hall Kate turned to him.

'What'll you do now?'

Simon put his hand to his face and rubbed his jawline hard. 'I don't know,' he said. 'Losing my job is a facer.' He looked puzzled. 'And unexpected. I didn't think he'd go that far.'

'What did Luther mean when he said he had your signature? Is it on a document of some kind?'

'It's nothing of importance,' Simon said, with a dismissive wave of his hand. 'What's worrying me is losing my income. I'll have to let the house in Sketty go. Damnation!'

'I've been thinking about that,' Kate began carefully. 'Luther will continue to spy on me, and things can only get worse once he marries Delphine. It would be sensible to have my . . . our own place.'

Simon beamed at her.

'But, understand me,' she went on hastily, 'I won't desert my home here unless provoked beyond endurance.'

'I agree,' Simon said eagerly. 'Well, that's one thing off my mind. With your permission I'll see the vendor tomorrow, and press for completion.'

'There's one other matter,' Kate said. She'd made up her mind to use Simon as he'd used her. 'Take me to see Mr Walters at his offices tomorrow. I'm ready to make the shares over to you, Simon.'

'What?'

'On one condition,' she went on hastily at his elated expression. 'You sit on the board only as my deputy, and you'll sign an affidavit to that effect. Is that understood?'

Simon frowned. 'No, I don't understand. I need a free hand, Kate.'

'Well, that's my condition. Take it or leave it.'

'You still don't trust me,' he growled.

'You're right. I don't doubt you'll further your own schemes once on the board,' she said, thinking of the mysterious document Simon must have signed. 'To make sure it's not at *my* expense I want to be consulted before any moves are made against Luther.'

Simon smiled. 'Why won't you take my word?'

Kate was scornful. 'Because I'm no fool. You'll sign the affidavit.'

'Very well, Kate, I agree to your condition.' He smiled ruefully. 'What choice do I have, now I've lost my employment?'

Kate gave a laugh, visualising Luther's face when he finally realised they'd outwitted him.

'Luther can sack you, but he can't stop you receiving a director's salary,' she said.

'Are you sure this is what you want, Kate?'

She glanced up at him, bemused by the strange timbre in his voice. 'Yes, I'm sure.'

Simon watched Kate climb the staircase and, when she was out of sight, returned to the study. Luther looked up and smiled when Simon entered, closing the door carefully after him.

'Did our ruse work?' Luther asked, leaning back in his chair.

'Yes.' Simon nodded, taking a seat before the desk. 'She took the bait, hook, line and sinker. By this time tomorrow the shares will be mine.'

'Excellent, my boy, excellent.'

'I think you went too far in sacking me,' Simon said peevishly. 'That could've proved damned awkward for me if Kate wasn't convinced. I could've been left without an income at all.'

'It was the perfect touch,' Luther said. 'She might've been suspicious if I hadn't.'

He chose a cigar from the box on the table and indicated Simon should take one, too.

'I'm impressed, Simon,' he went on. 'I congratulate you on your brilliant strategy. I couldn't have devised a better plan myself.'

The following evening, Simon was waiting for her in the sitting-room.

'Ethel didn't tell me you were here,' Kate said huffily.

'Why should she?' Simon retorted. 'We're married. This is our apartment.'

'Our business arrangement hasn't changed anything between us,' she said. 'Please continue to keep your distance.'

Simon stood up, giving an exaggerated sigh. 'Would you like to see the property we've bought?' he asked. 'I can take you tomorrow.'

'Property *I've* bought,' she corrected. 'And no, I don't want to see it. The purchase was merely expediency. I've no interest in it.'

With that she allowed Simon to escort her down to dinner.

Later Simon followed his uncle into the study. Luther, rubbing his hands, went immediately to the bell rope, and then sat on a sofa, indicating Simon should be seated too.

'Tonight, my boy, thanks to you,' Luther said jovially, 'I finally fulfil an ambition I've nursed for many a year, and we drink to it.'

Chivers appeared.

'The champagne, Chivers, as smart as you can,' Luther said.

When the door had closed on the butler, Luther turned another beaming smile on Simon. 'Total control of Vaughan & Templar has been my goal since joining the company,' he said. 'And now my position is unassailable.'

'And Kate's twenty-five per cent . . .' Simon paused. 'My twenty-five per cent will achieve this for you.'

Luther leaned back against the cushions, a reflective expression on his face. 'For years I've battled those faint-hearted fools on the board. Most of them are in their dotage, and resist change to protect their fat dividends. Yes, the company's made them rich men, but they refuse to look to the future.'

Chivers entered with a bottle and two glasses on a tray. Wordlessly, he uncorked the champagne and poured the foaming liquid into the glasses, offering them to the two men.

When they were alone again Simon tasted the champagne.

'Russell Vaughan left you in a weak position then?' he asked.

'A mere ten per cent,' Luther said with disgust. 'That was my holding. The five men on the board hold forty per cent between them, so even with Evan's twenty-five I was always outvoted. The company's progress has been held back for years.'

'Yet it's been doing so well,' Simon said. 'Business is booming.'

'We can do better,' Luther said adamantly. 'We'll expand right into the heart of the nation: London. A branch in the capital will put us on the map.'

Simon took another sip of champagne. 'Won't that spread us too thin?'

'Rubbish!' Luther glared at him. 'You sound like those old fogies in the boardroom.'

'It's still risky.'

'I intend to take personal charge of a purpose-built store in a fashionable area of the city,' Luther said grandly. 'I'll sell this house and buy a place in London. Delphine's all for it. She'll be the toast of London society, mark my words.'

Simon put his glass carefully on the low table before him. 'I don't think so,' he said.

Luther started forward, turning his head sharply, and stared. 'What did you say?'

Simon leaned back, crossing his legs, enjoying his uncle's startled expression. This was the moment he'd waited for with such eagerness. He allowed himself a mocking laugh.

'Did you really believe I'd give up a seat on the board?' he asked. 'Give up a director's salary and fat profits?'

For once Luther was speechless, and continued to stare.

'Yes, you were right not to trust me.' Simon nodded, smiling. 'I warned you I'm no fool, even though I've had no gentleman's education.'

'You swore an oath.' Luther's voice was hoarse with disbelief.

'I lied.'

'You signed that document.'

Simon laughed again. 'Luther, we both know it's worthless. You can't enforce that without exposing your own double-dealing with both Kate and Evan.' Simon's expression hardened. 'Your only hold over me died in February. I went through with the marriage to Kate just to reach this moment; just to watch you squirm.'

'What do you want, Simon?'

'I want a partnership, fifty-fifty, based on a legally binding agreement.'

'Out of the question!' Luther leaped to his feet and, ignoring the half glass of champagne, strode to the drinks cabinet and poured himself a large whisky.

'Then I'll take my seat on the board,' Simon said, 'and oppose everything you try to achieve. I'll turn the board against you. You said yourself they'll not stand losing their juicy dividends. By the time I've finished they'll vote you out.'

'You can't do this to me.'

'Yes, I can, Luther,' Simon rasped, rising to his feet. 'You gave me the power.'

Luther swallowed the whisky in one gulp, and then turned to glare at Simon, his face mottled. 'With twenty-five per cent you don't have as much power as you think.'

He sounded desperate, Simon thought with satisfaction, but knew Luther's devious mind was already at work to find a way out.

'The other board members won't trust a Johnny-come-lately like you.'

'What, after you let me marry your heiress stepdaughter?' Simon smiled. 'You'd have done better to let Kate marry Mansel Jenkins. You manipulated him easily enough.'

'I warn you, you won't get away with reneging on our agreement.'

'We never had an agreement,' Simon snapped. 'I've been lying through my teeth all along.'

Luther went to his desk and sat, putting his elbows on top and arranging in hands in a steeple. He looked at Simon over the top of his fingertips, his expression dark. Thwarted, Luther was a dangerous man.

'All right! How much will you take for the shares? Ten thousand, twenty?'

'Princely!' Simon exclaimed. 'If it was just the money I might be tempted, but it's not. I'm after revenge for my mother. I want your head on a plate.'

To Simon's astonishment, Luther smiled.

'So that's it!' He gave a deep laugh, and sounded relieved. 'For a moment I thought you wanted the company for yourself after the threats you made to oust me.'

'They weren't idle threats, Luther,' Simon warned, feeling unsettled at his uncle's sudden change in attitude. Was there a loophole he'd overlooked, one that Luther could slither through?

'Look, Simon, my boy,' Luther said, rising to his feet. 'You're trying to enter a world for which you have no aptitude or experience. You're clever, I grant you, and plausible. But the cut and thrust of the boardroom is not for the uninitiated. You'll be out of your depth within a month.'

'You can't flannel me, Luther,' Simon said. 'I'll take my place on Monday, and I intend to make my presence felt. You'll agree to my terms eventually. Yes, the boot is on the other foot now.'

Luther pursed his lips as though considering Simon's words, while Simon marvelled how quickly his uncle had recovered from the shock of realising his ultimate goal was still out of reach.

'I see you need to be taught a lesson,' Luther said. 'Very well, Simon, take your place and do your damnedest. I've waited years already. I can wait a little longer. We'll see who the board votes out first.'

Luther turned to leave then spun on his heel to glare malevolently at Simon.

'But remember this, I fight dirty and I take no prisoners. No one cheats me and gets away with it.' He smiled mockingly. 'I always win in the end because I don't care who or what must be sacrificed.' He raised his brows. 'Do you really have the stomach for a bloody battle?'

18

June 1900

The preparations for the wedding of Luther and Delphine had the house in turmoil for weeks. Rooms were redecorated and refurbished, quite unnecessarily, Kate thought.

Apparently Delphine wouldn't consider visiting a couturier in Cardiff for her wedding gown, but insisted that designers be brought from London at tremendous expense. Kate wondered at her stepfather's patience with his extravagant bride-to-be.

Delphine magnanimously suggested that Kate might wish to take advantage of the visit of the London haute couturière to have a decent outfit and gown made for the wedding.

'Madame Nivaro is above and beyond anyone else,' Delphine said. 'My stepdaughter mustn't look a dowdy provincial in front of my fashionable friends.'

Tight-lipped, Kate declined, and called in Miss Clarke instead.

The big day came at the end of June. The wedding took place at St Mary's Church, with a reception at the fashionable Metropol Hotel in Wind Street, after which the couple left for Italy, where they were to spend a month. Meanwhile, guests danced the night away at a ball at Old Grove House.

The week before, Evan had taken himself off to his club again, and wouldn't return, he said, until the extravaganza was over. There was a calmness, even smugness about him, which Kate found disquieting.

'Don't drag our name through the mud again,' she warned him. 'I've hardly any friends left.'

'Don't worry, I won't show my face,' he replied, and left.

Kate awaited the ceremony with dread, but to her relief Evan kept his distance, and nothing untoward happened. But she had other things to worry her. More than anything else she hated the prospect of Delphine as her stepmother, there being no more than seven years difference in their ages. Besides, Kate didn't know how much longer she could endure Delphine controlling the daily life of Old Grove House, and, therefore, her life. As the new Mrs Luther Templar, Delphine's dominion would be absolute, powerful enough to force her from the only home she had ever known.

The one bright prospect for Kate was Luther's absence on the honeymoon, and she made plans to take advantage of it.

'I'll invite Aunt Agnes and Eirwen to spend a week at Old Grove House,' Kate told Simon as they descended the staircase together to join the guests at the celebrations.

'Don't do it,' Simon said impatiently. 'There's too much friction between Luther and me already. Why antagonise him more? And what about Evan?'

But Kate was determined to do as she pleased. 'I don't care what my brother feels.'

Kate wrote to her aunt the very next day suggesting the visit, and received an acceptance almost by return. At the end of the week Simon fetched them from Fforestfach, bag and baggage.

Kate was in the hall to welcome them, ignoring Chivers standing at the back, near the entrance to the servants' quarters. Let him see and hear all he wanted, she thought. With the master and mistress away there was nothing he could do.

She went forward and eagerly took baby Russell from Eirwen's arms.

'I've engaged a nursery maid, Blodwyn, for the duration of your stay,' Kate said, kissing his silken cheek. 'That'll give us time for long chats and outings.'

Eirwen was silent, staring about her as though mesmerised. She turned widened eyes on Kate. 'I'd no idea the house was so grand,' she said, and looked round at Agnes uncertainly. 'I shouldn't have come. Evan won't like it, and I'll be out of place.'

'Rubbish!' Kate dismissed her fears quickly. 'It's fitting that you and Russell should be here. You're members of the Vaughan family.'

Watkins appeared to deal with their baggage and show them to their rooms, where Blodwyn took charge of the baby. Kate went along to her sister-in-law's room later.

'When you're settled, Eirwen, ring the bell there,' Kate said, pointing to the bell rope alongside the fireplace. 'One of the servants will show you to the drawing-room. We'll have some tea and plan our days ahead. Don't worry about Russell. Blodwyn's very experienced. Her references are impeccable.'

'Oh! I can't!'

'What?'

Eirwen wrung her hands. 'I can't call servants to me and order them about, mun. I'm no more than a servant myself.'

'Eirwen, that's nonsense!' Kate was taken aback. 'You're Mrs Evan Vaughan. You should be used to the idea by now.'

Eirwen bridled. 'Oh, you think so, do you?' she said. 'Well, I've spent *my* married life so far chopping wood, cleaning out fires, yes, and scrubbing floors, even when I was carrying my baby. I don't feel like Mrs Evan Vaughan, I can tell you.' She sniffed miserably. 'And I've seen nothing of my husband for

275

months.' She flopped on to a chair nearby and put her face in her hands, sobbing.

Kate went quickly and put an arm around her sister-in-law's shoulders. 'Oh, Eirwen, I'm sorry for my thoughtlessness.' She felt renewed anger against Evan. How could he be so callous? 'I'm hoping this visit will put things right for you.'

'It's too late for that.' Eirwen shook her head. 'Evan doesn't love me any more. There's someone else, I'm certain, and I think I know who she is. I'm not such a fool as people believe.'

Kate was distressed. She'd hoped that, faced squarely with his responsibilities, Evan would come to his senses.

'You mustn't think it's too late,' Kate said. 'I'm sure Evan will see sense before long.'

Ethel saw to Eirwen's needs, dressing her hair and helping her choose something to wear from the various outfits Kate had purchased, and Eirwen finally composed herself enough to appear in the drawing-room. She paused before the fireplace and gazed up at Kate's portrait hung there.

'Oh, Kate, there's lovely that is,' she said, genuine admiration in her voice. 'It does you justice, too.'

Kate was pleased. 'Simon believes Bertram will be as great as Turner one day,' she said. 'You'll meet him at dinner.'

Eirwen fidgeted in her chair. 'I won't come down to dinner,' she said tremulously. 'A fish out of water, I'll be. Won't know which knife to use.'

'Then you must learn,' Kate said quickly. 'It's only the family dining tonight. You'll sit next to me. I'll guide you. Remember, you're Mrs Evan Vaughan.'

The dinner gong sounded five minutes before Kate and Eirwen entered the drawing-room. Simon and Bertram were already there, chatting to Agnes about the portrait. Eirwen blushed helplessly as she was introduced to Bertram, and it was only Kate's supporting arm around her waist that prevented her from curtsying.

'Can I get you an aperitif, Mrs Vaughan?' Bertram asked, as Eirwen seated herself on the sofa.

'No, thank you,' she said awkwardly. 'It'll go straight to my head on an empty stomach.' She glanced around in consternation, her face aflame again. 'Oh, pardon me for mentioning my stomach in mixed company.'

'We've all got stomachs, Eirwen,' Aunt Agnes said bluntly. 'Empty or otherwise.'

'Yes, and my stomach wishes Chivers would call us for dinner,' Simon said quickly. 'I'm ravenous.'

Eirwen looked a bit bemused, but relaxed a little, and Kate was just congratulating herself, when the door opened, but it wasn't Chivers announcing dinner. Instead Evan appeared.

'Good evening, family,' he said, strolling in, a smile on his face as though pleased to surprise them.

He halted as his glance fell on Aunt Agnes, and his smile froze. His gaze travelled to the other figure on the sofa, and he blinked as though not able to believe his eyes.

'Eirwen!' He stared, his face turning pale. 'What the hell are *you* doing here?'

Her cup and saucer rattled on the tray as she discarded them and rose hastily to her feet.

'Evan, love.' She ran towards him, her arms outstretched as though to embrace him. 'It's been months . . .'

With an oath he pushed her away. 'Keep back,' he snapped harshly. 'You're making a spectacle of yourself, as usual.'

Eirwen recoiled, her hand going to her throat. There was shock in her expression and Kate felt it, too. She rose hastily, and Evan rounded on her.

'What's the meaning of this, Kate?' he stormed. 'I demand an explanation.'

Simon rose, taking a step forward, but he kept silent, though his eyes were watchful.

'Eirwen's here by *my* invitation,' Kate said firmly. 'She and Aunt Agnes are spending a few days at Old Grove House.'

'What?' He turned back to glare at Eirwen. 'Are you mad, woman?' His furious glance turned on Agnes. 'How could you allow this, knowing my feelings?'

'I see nothing wrong in your wife visiting her relatives,' Agnes said defensively. 'Particularly by invitation.'

Evan glared at her for a moment then turned wrathful eyes on Kate. 'What right have you to meddle in my life, Kate? I warn you, I won't stand for it.'

'I'm not meddling. I'm trying to help.'

'Damnable presumption!' Evan spluttered.

'Don't speak to my wife like that, Vaughan,' Simon said abrasively. 'She's hardly committed a crime.'

'Keep out of it, Creswell,' Evan snarled. 'This is between my sister and myself, and none of your business.'

'Look how elegant Eirwen is in her new gown,' Kate said, quickly fearing a quarrel between the men, for Simon's face had darkened dangerously, and a pulse throbbed ominously in his throat. 'I thought you'd be happy to see your wife and son.'

'Happy?' Evan's mouth twisted. 'I'd be happy never to see either of them again. I wish they were both dead.'

'Evan!' Eirwen looked devastated. 'You don't mean it!'

'Yes, I do! Every word.'

'I say, Vaughan!' Bertram said in a shocked voice. 'That's a big strong.'

Evan glared at him. 'Be bloody glad she's not your wife,' he barked.

'Oh!'

Eirwen put both hands to her mouth and stared at him. She looked stricken to the heart and Kate was stunned at the virulence of her brother's attack. Aunt Agnes struggled to her feet, her expression angry, and Kate knew she must speak up.

'For God's sake, Evan,' she exclaimed. 'What're you thinking of, treating your wife in this monstrous way?'

With an incomprehensible mutter, Evan strode to the sideboard and poured a measure of whisky. He took a long swallow of his drink, and then pointed a shaking finger at Eirwen.

'She manoeuvred me into marriage,' he accused bitterly. 'Trapped me with her loose ways.' His face contorted with anger. 'I'm not even certain Russell's my child.'

Kate gave a gasp of utter disbelief, which was echoed by Agnes, and they exchanged horrified glances.

'Oh, my God!' Eirwen ran to the sofa and collapsed on to it, sobbing. 'May heaven preserve me from his evil tongue.'

'I've never witnessed such appalling behaviour in my life,' Agnes said tremulously. 'Your father would be ashamed of you.'

'It's me that's shamed,' Eirwen whimpered. 'And it's me that was led astray, too.' She gulped down a sob, her face streaked with tears. 'I was a good girl until I met you, Evan Vaughan.'

'You were good, all right,' Evan snapped. 'Good for one thing only, throwing yourself at me shamelessly.'

Eirwen sprang up from the sofa, her cheeks red, and Kate could see she was angry at last.

'How dare you talk to me like that in front of these people?' she cried, lifting her chin proudly. 'My parents are God-fearing people, big in the chapel back home. And I knew nothing about men until I met you.' She twisted her fingers together, her face crumpling again. 'The other girls said you were up to no good, showering me with gifts. I wish I'd thrown them back in your lying face.'

'You ungrateful bitch,' Evan stormed. 'I married you, didn't I, more fool me. I should've paid you off, as Luther suggested.'

It was all too much for Kate. Her blood boiled at his treatment of Eirwen, who was innocent of any wrongdoing.

'You hypocrite, Evan!' she burst out. 'You stand there, so sanctimonious, accusing Eirwen of the very thing you're doing yourself. I saw you and Delphine kissing shamelessly in the hall the other night.'

There was a stunned silence, and Kate put a hand to her mouth. She turned to look at her sister-in-law, who was staring at her husband, her mouth open, and then Eirwen glanced around at everyone in the room.

'What kind of a house is this?' she asked in distress. 'What kind of people are you?'

'Eirwen,' Kate stammered. 'I'm sorry. I shouldn't have said that in front of you.'

'There's glad I am you did,' Eirwen said, nodding. 'Now I know for sure. My husband's a cheat and a lecher.'

'Kate's mistaken,' Evan said, embarrassed. 'My kiss for Delphine was no more than one of affection for a future stepmother.'

'You liar,' Eirwen screamed wrathfully. 'You're not even man enough to admit it when you've been caught red-handed.'

She flicked her skirts around and stalked towards the door.

'You wanted to be rid of me and you will be,' she announced. 'Going home to Trehafod, I am, immediately, me and Russ.' She stood at the open door and glared at her husband. 'Never see your son again, you won't, Evan, so don't come begging, mind. If you do my father'll probably take a pickaxe to you.'

'Good riddance!' Evan said churlishly as the door slammed closed.

'You don't know what you've done, you fool,' Agnes said irately. 'You've turned your back on your own child. No good will come of this, Evan. Mark my words.'

'We'll see,' he retorted. 'Meanwhile, I'm selling the house in Fforestfach, Aunt, so you'd better look elsewhere for a home.'

'You can't turn out Aunt Agnes just like that,' Kate spluttered.

Evan gave her a baleful look. 'You betrayed me,' he said. 'I've nothing more to say to you, Kate.'

The drawing-room door opened suddenly and Chivers stood there. 'Dinner is served,' he announced to a silent room.

With one final malevolent glance at Kate, Evan strode out.

Bertram offered his arm to Agnes to escort her in to dinner. Kate followed on behind, and was surprised as Simon put his palm gently under her elbow.

'Don't blame yourself,' he said quietly. 'I think Eirwen knew the truth all along, and would've gone eventually. You just helped her make up her mind.'

'What about Aunt Agnes?' Kate asked. 'I'm responsible for making her homeless.'

'No such thing,' Simon said. 'There's the house in Sketty. She'll be comfortable there, and I'm sure she'll like it much better than that barn in Fforestfach.' He hesitated, and Kate realised something else was on his mind.

'What is it?'

'I'm dreading Luther's return,' Simon admitted anxiously.

281

'He's sure to be suspicious of Evan's marriage break-up. His affair with Delphine has been openly spoken of. If Luther learns of it, he'll ruin your brother for sure. Evan's playing with fire, Kate, and we could all be burned yet.'

19

Kate and Simon escorted Eirwen, Russell and Aunt Agnes back to Fforestfach the following morning. When they reached the house Trott took charge of their luggage, and Kate made one last plea.

'Please reconsider, Eirwen,' she said as Simon helped them step down from the coach. 'It isn't right that Russell should be separated from his father.'

Eirwen gave her an impatient glance as Simon handed the baby into her arms again.

'It's never been any other way, has it?' she rejoined with spirit. 'Evan doesn't want us. I may be just a simple girl from the Valleys, but I've got my pride.'

'But how will you live?'

'Oh, I'll manage, don't you worry,' Eirwen said with a toss of her head. 'My mam'll look after Russ.' Her smile was bitter. 'There're some advantages not being a lady, mind,' she said. 'There's plenty of work for the likes of me, in service for instance.'

Kate was shocked to think of the wife of a Vaughan of Swansea earning a living by waiting on others. But as Eirwen had already told her, Evan had let his wife work like a servant since they'd wed.

'Eirwen, I'm sorry for Evan's treatment of you.'

Eirwen's eyes flashed. 'So you should be, Kate,' she burst

out. 'If you hadn't interfered, I'd have won him around eventually. This woman Delphine is only a passing fancy.'

Kate was so flabbergasted at Eirwen's self-deceit she was speechless. They moved towards the front door, but Eirwen turned to them, her features stiff.

'You needn't come in,' she said gracelessly. 'We can manage now.'

Kate stopped, feeling she'd been slapped in the face, and didn't know which way to gaze, though from the corner of her eye she saw that Agnes looked apologetic. Simon touched the old lady's arm.

'You can move into the house in Sketty any time, Agnes,' he told her. 'I'm at your disposal.'

Agnes smiled up at him. 'I won't leave until Eirwen is safely away,' she said. 'She's sending for her father today.'

One morning a week later Ethel brought morning tea as usual, her fresh face agitated. Gloomily, Kate ignored her as she hovered at the bedside, in no mood to deal with domestic problems.

Evan hadn't returned to Old Grove House, and told Simon he'd do so when Luther arrived back. Kate was bitter about her brother's attitude. After all, whatever troubles he had he'd brought on himself by his outrageous behaviour.

Ethel coughed apologetically, shifting her weight from one foot to the other, until Kate was forced to acknowledge her.

'What is it, Ethel?'

'It's Mrs Perkins's birthday,' Ethel burst out. 'She's in the kitchen now showing off a present she's been given.'

Kate felt irritable. 'Ethel, I hardly think—'

'It's a bracelet!' Ethel interrupted excitedly. 'Exactly like the one belonging to Miss Harrington – er, Mrs Templar; the one she accused me of stealing.'

Kate stared. 'You're mistaken.'

Ethel shook her head vehemently. 'No, I'm not, Miss Kate, and what's more, Mrs Perkins says Chivers gave it to her. They're courting, you know?' Ethel gave a nervous giggle. 'Or, at least, that's what Mrs Perkins calls it. My mam would call it something else.'

Kate said nothing, but sipped her tea. Even if Ethel was right, and it was the missing bracelet, there was nothing she could do about it. As mistress of the house, Delphine must deal with that.

'I reckon Mrs Templar knew all along who had the bracelet,' Ethel went on, her lips narrowing in ill-concealed anger. 'And that's not the only thing. Chivers makes free with the master's wine cellar, his cigars and anything else that's going. Mrs Templar knows about his thieving ways and does nothing.' She shook her head. 'Miss Kate, this is becoming a very rum household, indeed.'

'I've finished Cecille's portrait,' Bertram announced as they sat in the drawing-room before dinner. 'I must say Villiers was very generous with my fee.'

'You're worth every penny, and he knows it. He's a very shrewd man,' Kate assured him, glancing at her own painting hanging over the fireplace. 'Cecille must be thrilled.'

Bertram looked down into his glass. 'I'm leaving Swansea, Simon,' he said quietly. 'Before Delphine comes back. I'll go to France to paint. The commissions I received from Templar and Villiers have given me enough to live on, modestly, until I can find a patron.'

'My dear old friend,' Simon exclaimed, rising to his feet,

and moving towards the other man, hand outstretched. 'I'm delighted to hear the news. I've wished it for so long.'

Bertram rose and they shook hands, but Kate was aghast at the prospect of losing him.

'Wished it?' Kate exclaimed in astonishment, shooting an accusing glance at Simon. 'What're you talking about?' she cried, dismayed. 'Bertram can't leave us. This is his home now. He'll find a patron easily enough in a town of this size.' She shook her head emphatically. 'You mustn't go, Bertram. I . . . we need you here.'

'Kate!' Simon said sharply. 'You don't understand. Bertram must go. It's . . . vital.'

'Huh! What nonsense!' she said dismissively. 'Bertram, I beg you to think again about this. You're my only friend.'

Bertram gave an embarrassed glance towards Simon. 'You have Simon. I can hardly be more your friend than he is.'

'Yes, you are!' she insisted. 'And I need you. Let's not pretend,' she went on sharply, not looking at Simon. 'You know as well as I do my marriage is one of convenience – convenient to Luther Templar.' She hesitated before going on. 'Delphine and I will never be friends. Bertram, you and I have so much in common. Please say you'll give up these plans.'

'Kate, you don't know what you're asking.' Simon's face was dark with anger. 'This might be his last chance to escape.'

'Escape from what?'

A strange look passed between the two men. She thought she saw wretchedness in Bertram's eyes, and pity in Simon's, but the moment passed too quickly for her to understand the glance properly.

'Will neither of you speak?' she asked pithily.

'I value your friendship, Kate,' Bertram said quietly. 'And I'll stay if you wish it, and if I can be of service to you as a friend.'

'You're a fool, Bertie,' Simon said raggedly. 'A sacrificing fool.'

In August Luther and Delphine returned from Italy. Kate anticipated their arrival with bleakness. Her stepfather was devious and unscrupulous, and she was convinced that if he found a way to hurt her or her family he wouldn't hesitate.

The hall was filled with boxes and portmanteaus when Delphine came home, looking more beautiful than ever. Luther seemed relaxed and extremely pleased, Kate thought, after parading his lovely wife through the fashionable salons of Rome. Kate wondered how long his good humour would last. It proved to be short-lived indeed.

The first hint of trouble came during the afternoon when she spotted two members of the board of directors, whom she'd met at Luther's wedding reception, being shown into his study. In Luther's absence, Simon had attempted to have him voted off the board as chairman. It had failed miserably, and now came retribution. Kate wished Simon were home, so he could be present at the meeting to defend his actions. When he did return she hurried along to his room to warn him.

'I've been expecting it,' he said blandly. 'I'll just have to ride out any attempts to get rid of me. Luther has enemies on the board as well as cronies.'

When Luther finally made his appearance later in the drawing-room, Kate rose hastily to her feet, disturbed by the dark expression on his face.

'Chivers tells me that Agnes Vaughan has been staying under this roof,' he began angrily, glaring at Kate. 'Not to mention that common little baggage Evan married.' He hooked his thumbs into his waistcoat pockets. 'You've disobeyed my wishes, Kathryn.'

Kate bridled. 'I've every right to entertain my family in my own home,' she replied airily.

'This is your home only as long as I allow it,' Luther shouted. 'It's my house and I'll not have the likes of that carping old woman in it. You took advantage of my absence. That's despicable.'

'I agree,' Delphine chimed in quickly, walking forward to stand next to her husband. 'God knows what else has been going on here, with thieving servants about.'

'That's unfair, Delphine,' Kate cried. 'And I have something to say to you on that very subject.'

'Silence!' Luther bellowed. 'You'll push me too far one of these days, Kathryn.' He gave Simon a dark look. 'It seems you're teaching your wife the same conniving ways you employ against me. Your tactics in the boardroom failed.'

'I did no more than you'd do yourself,' Simon said calmly. 'What you're planning in the company is bad for business.'

'I'll be the judge of that,' Luther snapped. 'And I think the result shows the board trusts me more than it does you.'

Simon's lips tightened, but he said nothing.

Luther's attention turned back to Kate. 'I'm extremely displeased, Kathryn,' he said severely. 'You'll be punished for your disobedience.'

Kate stared as he pulled at the bell rope nearby, and Chivers appeared immediately as if already waiting outside the door. Luther pointed at Kate's portrait above the fireplace.

'Chivers, take that down from the wall. Burn it.'

'Very good, sir.'

'No!' Delphine stepped forward, shock on her face. 'Luther, you can't do that. Not Bertram's art.'

'What a mean-spirited action,' Simon exclaimed angrily. 'What do you hope to gain by it?'

Luther ignored Simon's outburst, but smiled at his wife. 'Bertram will have many more commissions from me, my dearest,' he assured her soothingly. 'A portrait of yourself will hang here in pride of place. And Bertram can do one of me, too. I also have a fancy for a painting depicting Old Grove House. That would look very fine in the dining-room. Don't you agree, my angel?'

Delphine seemed mollified, and placed a hand against his chest. 'And will Bertram be paid handsomely for his great art, my dear?' she asked, a provocative smile curving her lips.

'Of course!'

'Shall I remove the painting now, sir?' Chivers asked.

'When dinner's being served,' Luther said. 'Utterly destroyed, Chivers, you understand?'

'Leave it to me, sir,' Chivers said, and left the room.

Bertram, who'd been silent all through, rose to his feet. 'I say, Luther, let me have the portrait, instead,' he said. 'I don't wish to see it destroyed.'

Luther looked annoyed. 'I'm sorry, my boy,' he said stiffly. 'I know it must be painful to see your work treated so, but Kathryn's betrayal warrants the harshest punishment. I won't reconsider.'

'You barbarian!' Kate burst out, unable to contain her anger any longer. 'And a Philistine, besides. To destroy a piece of art of this calibre just to spite me is unforgivable.'

'You have the gall to insult me in my own drawing-room,' Luther shouted, his face turning red. 'Damned treachery, after what you and your scheming husband have done between you.'

Trembling with anger, Kate looked appealingly at her husband. 'Simon, escort me to my quarters, please. I will not dine in this man's company.'

He came forward and took her arm, but instead of moving to the door he held her back. 'No, Kate,' he said loudly. 'Old Grove House is your home, you were born here.' He sent Luther a defiant look. 'We won't be ousted, not from here or the boardroom. We'll dine here tonight and every night, and be damned to you!'

Luther stared silently at them, bristling with anger, and Delphine's eyes flashed hatred at them. The summons to dinner came to interrupt the awkward moment, but everyone hesitated to take the first step.

'I'm not finished fighting, Luther,' Simon said defiantly. 'Depend on it. I'm sorry Kate has lost the painting. However, I'm not sure it was yours to destroy, and I'll be seeking legal advice in the matter, you can depend on that, too.'

Kate took breakfast in her quarters the next morning. When Ethel came later to collect her tray, she'd made up her mind to adopt Simon's attitude, and fight on.

'Ethel, are you certain about Mrs Perkins's bracelet being the same one that was stolen?'

'I'd swear to it in a court of law,' Ethel said confidently.

'Let's hope it won't come to that,' said Kate, and went in search of her new stepmother.

Delphine was at the bureau in the morning-room, busy with invitation cards. She looked up as Kate came in, her expression hardening, and turned back to her task without a word of greeting. For the first time in her life under the roof of Old Grove House, Kate felt like an interloper, and resentment bubbled up.

'I've something important to tell you, Delphine,' she burst out.

'If it's about the portrait,' Delphine replied offhandedly, 'I've nothing more to say.'

'It's not that,' Kate said. 'It's about your stolen sapphire bracelet. I know where it is.'

Delphine's pen scratched jarringly on the card, and a spray of black ink disfigured the cream parchment. She gave an exclamation of annoyance. 'Oh, look what you've made me do!'

Kate was intrigued by her sudden fluster. 'Don't you want to know who's got it?' she asked. 'You made enough fuss when accusing Ethel of theft. Or perhaps you know already?'

Delphine turned from the desk, a look of annoyance on her face, and her eyes were wary. 'I'll admit that was a mistake,' she said huffily. 'But one never knows with these common servant girls.'

She turned to the desk again, and Kate walked to the window to stand with her back to it to get a better view of Delphine's face.

'Well, aren't you anxious to have the bracelet returned to you?' she said challengingly. 'After all it must be worth quite a sum of money.'

Delphine flung down the pen, exasperated. 'This is tiresome, Kate. Can't you see I'm busy with dinner invitations for next week,' she said sharply. 'Besides, that bracelet will never be seen again. I dare say the thief disposed of it that very same day.'

'On the contrary,' said Kate triumphantly. 'You'll find it on the wrist of your own cook, Mrs Perkins. Chivers gave it to her as a birthday gift.' She gave Delphine a narrow smile. 'Now, I wonder how he got hold of it.'

A flush coloured Delphine's cheeks. 'Are you suggesting he stole it?'

Kate shook her head. 'Chivers is much too shrewd for that, much too cunning.' She paused, giving Delphine a fixed stare.

'I don't believe it was stolen at all. Perhaps it was given to someone as payment for services rendered.'

The remark was a shot in the dark, but it had an astonishing effect on Delphine. She rose awkwardly from the desk, upsetting the pile of cards, which scattered on the floor. She seemed too upset to notice.

'What are you suggesting?' she asked bitingly, her voice rising from its normal self-confident tone. 'Are you saying *I* gave the bracelet to Chivers?'

Kate shifted her weight uncomfortably. She didn't know what she'd meant, but instinct told her there was a mystery here, which Delphine didn't want solved.

'Well, did you?' Kate bluffed her way on. 'If he stole it, Luther must be told, and Chivers must be sacked immediately. We can't have thieves and liars in the house, can we, Delphine? You said so yourself.'

Delphine's mouth worked for a moment but she uttered no words. Kate was quick to take advantage of her uncertainty.

'It's common knowledge in the servants' hall that he makes free with Luther's cellar and heaven knows what else in the household. Perhaps he takes cash, too.' She paused. 'Since you now deal with the day-to-day household accounts you must've noticed such discrepancies. Why haven't you said anything to Luther?'

'How dare you question me like this?' Delphine blustered. 'I'm mistress of this house now. I do as I please.'

'He's not a man who'd tolerate anyone cheating him in any way,' said Kate meaningfully. 'We've already seen his revenge can be swift and merciless.' She lifted her chin, her expression challenging. 'It's time he inspected the accounts again, and it's my duty to warn him.'

Delphine took a step forward, her expression thunderous.

'You interfering little wretch!' she rasped. 'Don't get in my way or I'll make you sorry.'

Her expression and tone were so vicious that Kate was startled and unable to speak. Delphine took a deep breath as though to compose herself.

'You're skating on thin ice yourself,' she went on in a calmer tone, although her hand trembled as she lifted it to finger the string of pearls adorning her throat. 'You've more to lose than I have, you and your fool of a brother.'

'Evan has nothing to do with this,' Kate said guardedly, suddenly less sure of herself. 'You've done him enough harm already. His marriage has broken up because of you. I warn you, Delphine, keep your claws out of my brother.'

Delphine laughed but there was no humour in it. 'Evan is a weak malleable fool,' she scoffed, her face aglow with malice. 'He belongs to me. I treat him as I like, and I'll continue to do just that so long as he amuses me. When I'm finished with him, I'll throw him off.' She paused, sending Kate a feline smile. 'Like a dead rat.'

Kate was shocked at her outspoken callousness, and unnerved, too. Delphine's frankness showed she saw no real threat in her stepdaughter, and Kate at that moment felt helpless.

'You're contemptible!' she said feebly. 'I called you a harlot to Evan and I'm right. You've the morals of an alley cat.'

Sparks came from Delphine's eyes. 'Careful what you say,' she hissed. 'I can easily throw Evan to the wolves now; use him as pawn against you,' she went on. 'His position is very vulnerable. I can persuade Luther to sack him. What will he do then, eh?'

'If you do that, Delphine,' Kate said angrily, finding her spirit again, 'I'll tell Luther about your affair with Evan.

There's enough evidence. I saw you kissing in the hall one evening, and I'm certain Chivers will tell all he knows for the right price.'

Delphine's features were stony, hatred gleaming in her eyes. 'Luther will never believe you or anyone else,' she said. She lifted her chin arrogantly. 'I have sexual power over him; that's a power a puerile girl like you can never understand.' Her expression was mocking. 'You don't know the first thing about men, you pathetic virgin bride.'

Kate's face flamed. 'How dare you!'

Delphine stooped to gather up the invitation cards, and then sat at the desk again, turning her back on Kate. 'Close the door as you leave,' she commanded tersely.

Kate swallowed down her anger, still smarting at Delphine's jibe. 'You've not heard the last of this,' she said stiffly. 'One of these days Luther will realise the woman he married is rotten through and through. No better than a street whore!'

Delphine's answer was a scornful laugh that echoed in Kate's ears as she hurried away.

20

'I really don't understand you,' Cecille said, watching Kate as she sat before the dressing-table, putting the final touches to her appearance. 'You're married to one of the handsomest men in Swansea, yet you're still a vir—'

'Don't say it!' Kate interrupted loudly.

Two weeks had passed since her spat with Delphine, yet her stepmother's taunt still hurt. She'd confided in Cecille, but now wished she hadn't.

'It's no one else's business but mine,' she went on sulkily, readjusting the neckline of her gown. 'Besides, my marriage is one of convenience, forced on me by my stepfather. I don't love Simon.'

'Still,' Cecille said. 'Aren't you just a wee bit curious about – well, that side of marriage?'

Kate tossed her head. 'Not in the least!'

'Well, I am,' Cecille declared. 'I can't wait to be married. I hope someone proposes soon, preferably Bertram. I'll bet he's had lots of women.'

'Oh, really! Cecille,' Kate exclaimed, disturbed at the idea, reminded of Delphine's shameless behaviour. 'We'd better go down,' she went on stiffly.

Yet another of her stepmother's dinner parties this evening.

Kate had endured so many over these last weeks, and was growing weary of putting on an act for appearances sake. It was galling to watch Delphine perform like the Queen of Sheba, taking homage from her devoted subjects. She'd wormed her way into most spheres of Swansea society, and Kate was astonished at the high tone of the guests who often sat at Luther's generous table.

'I was surprised to see Lord and Lady Perrisford dining here last week,' Cecille remarked as they descended the stairs. 'Socialising, when their only son was killed at Kroonstadt last April.'

'Life goes on, I suppose,' Kate said, and sighed despondently.

Despite what she'd said to Cecille, she wished her relationship with Simon *were* on a different level. She missed Eirwen's baby, Russell, and knew a child of her own might make all the difference in the world to her life and her future.

As they entered the drawing-room a woman's booming laugh greeted them.

'Oh, no!' Cecille whispered with annoyance. 'That dreadful Mrs Gilbertson's here. If she prattles on about the Swansea Women's Freedom League again tonight, I'll walk out. I really will.'

'I'm thinking of joining the league,' Kate said staunchly. 'It's about time women stood up for their rights. I admire Mrs Gilbertson.'

'I don't understand why Delphine invites her so often,' Cecille insisted huffily. 'The woman's hardly top drawer.'

The drawing-room at Old Grove House, crowded with chattering guests, sparkled in the light from several gas chandeliers. Kate nodded politely to Cecille's parents, and her smile was stiff as she greeted a bejewelled Sybil Jenkins. She'd found it difficult and embarrassing when the Jenkinses had first come to dine, but was gradually coming to terms with their frequent presence at Old Grove House.

'What's the matter with your brother?' Cecille murmured in her ear. 'His face is like a thundercloud.'

Evan was standing before the fireplace, a glass of whisky already in his hand; his expression showed he was barely keeping his temper under control. Wondering what upset him, Kate surveyed the rest of the room and then got the shock of her life.

Her head spun giddily as she recognised Mansel Jenkins deep in conversation with Delphine near the French windows, and stared at him transfixed, hardly able to believe her own eyes. She'd thought of him so often, though feared never to see him again. Now suddenly here he was, and no one had thought to warn her of his coming.

His tall figure, thin and wan, unlike his former robust self, leaned heavily on a walking-stick. He was so changed a wave of compassion for him washed over her.

'Oh! I say, Kate!' Cecille had spotted him, too. 'I didn't know Mansel was home. You never said. Doesn't he look dreadful?'

'Cecille, I need some punch,' Kate said hastily. 'Will you go and fetch me a glass?'

'What? Before dining?' Cecille looked into her face. 'Kate, you've gone as white as a sheet. Didn't you know he was coming to dinner?'

'Cecille, please!'

With a sulky moue Cecille flounced away towards the punch bowl.

Tension mounted in her breast as she stared at the man who'd jilted her so cruelly. Bent on waging a war of nerves on

297

her, Delphine had deliberately kept quiet about his home-coming. Kate wondered how she'd get through the rest of the evening, what she could possibly say to him.

As she watched, Delphine put her hand against Mansel's chest in a manner that suggested she knew him well. Kate was affronted, and took a step forward, intending to interrupt their tête-à-tête.

But someone grasped her arm and held her back.

'So that's the man who threw you over.'

Startled, Kate spun on her heels to look up into Simon's frowning face.

'I see Delphine has him buttoned down already,' he said contemptuously. 'He's obviously the credulous fool I took him for. He should be careful she doesn't add him to her trophies.'

'That's a beastly thing to say!' Kate exclaimed. 'And Mansel wasn't to blame for the breakdown of our engagement. Your uncle's dishonesty was solely responsible.'

Simon's expression was scornful. 'You're a strange woman if you don't feel some bitterness at being jilted,' he said. He studied her face, frowning. 'Did you know he was coming here tonight? Has he been in touch with you?'

'It's none of your business if he has,' Kate parried heatedly, angry with him. 'My relationship with Mansel is my affair.'

'And I'm your husband,' Simon said angrily. 'He can't mean anything to you now, so take that absurd hankering look off your face, woman. You're making an exhibition of yourself.'

Kate stared up into Simon's infuriated eyes and was sur-prised to feel confusion. She glanced again at Mansel and suddenly the months rolled back. She remembered the plea-sure of his company, the warmth of the kisses they'd shared; she remembered the way she'd loved him, and the pain of his going away. Any chance of warmth and love in her life had left with him, and she felt lonely and unwanted. But he was back now.

'I loved him, so,' she said simply. 'I think I still do, despite everything.'

Simon gave an angry growl. 'Huh! The way you thought you loved Bertram?' he said heavily.

'You always belittle my feelings.'

'Because they appear shallow to me.'

'How dare you!'

Wilfully, she tried to pull away from his grasp on her arm but he held fast.

'Kate, listen! I didn't mean that,' Simon said quickly. 'Even if we're married in name only, I can't have my wife throw herself at another man, just because they were once engaged.'

Kate bridled. 'I'm not throwing myself at him. I haven't even spoken to him since last autumn.'

'People are watching you,' Simon warned. 'And your face gives away your thoughts so easily.' He hesitated. 'Everyone knows he deserted you, so have a care how you behave.'

'Let people think what they like,' Kate snapped. 'It doesn't bother me.'

That was a lie. She still hadn't forgiven the so-called friends and acquaintances who'd snubbed her after Evan's behaviour at her reception. Simon was right. It mustn't happen again, yet she was angry with him for reminding her.

'Obviously, you can't ignore the man,' Simon said. 'But when you speak to him I ought to be with you.'

'No, Simon.' Kate shook her head vehemently. 'Mansel and I have things to say to each other, things that are personal and private. Remember this,' she went on quickly when he opened his mouth to protest. 'I'm your wife, but you don't own me.'

'I'm not trying to,' Simon snapped. 'Oh damn! Here comes Mrs Jenkins. Be careful, Kate.'

Sybil Jenkins sailed forward and was on them in a moment. Without preamble, she took Kate's arm and drew her away from Simon, giving him a frosty glance.

'Despite what's happened in the past, Kate,' Sybil said as she led her away, 'you should acknowledge Mansel now.' She glanced about her. 'The whole room's agog. There'll be talk if you cut him dead.'

'I've no intention of cutting him dead,' Kate replied with a defiant backward glance at Simon. 'I'm anxious to talk to him.'

With Sybil leading the way Kate approached Mansel and Delphine, who looked annoyed at the intrusion. Kate raised her gaze to his face, hardly knowing what to expect, but his returned glance was so cold, it struck right through to her heart like a splinter of ice.

'Mansel, dear, here's Kate,' Sybil said unnecessarily, getting a look of irritation from Delphine. 'You must both seem reconciled for appearances sake.'

There was an awkward silence, and then Sybil turned away.

'Will you excuse us, Delphine?' Kate said sharply.

Delphine remained where she was and glanced up at Mansel, who smiled faintly at her, and, with a lift of her shoulder, she turned on her heel and glided off. But even with her going the awkwardness didn't lift, and Kate felt tongue-tied for a moment, her embarrassment growing every second.

'Mansel, I'd no idea you were home,' she burst out at last. 'How are you?'

His lips thinned. 'Do you really care, Kate?' he said tightly. 'According to my stepmother, you've never once enquired after my wellbeing in South Africa.'

She was astonished at the attack, and annoyed at his unexpected hostility, as though he were the injured party.

'Is that so surprising?' she said sharply. 'After all, you deserted me without one word of explanation.' She felt a sob begin to erupt at remembered pain, and lifted a trembling hand to her throat in an attempt to prevent it. 'Why didn't you write to me, Mansel? You broke my heart.'

He looked confused, as though caught out in some way. 'Luther's revelation distressed me so much,' he said. 'I didn't know what I was doing, Kate. I was upset. I fled.'

'Yes,' said Kate bitterly. 'All the way to South Africa. You preferred to face the Boers than me.'

'It was such a shock.' His voice faltered. 'I needed time to think.'

'Really? Then maybe you just didn't love me enough, Mansel,' Kate cried in distress. 'You gave up so easily.' She lifted her handkerchief to her mouth. 'Perhaps you were even glad of an excuse to escape?'

'That isn't true, Kate,' Mansel said. 'I do – did love you.' His face tightened in bitterness. 'And if we'd married I wouldn't have gone to war and wouldn't be wounded.' He touched his thigh tentatively. 'I've a shattered leg for my trouble.'

'I – I'm sorry,' Kate said, suddenly concerned. 'Was it very bad out there?'

He turned his head away. 'I don't want to talk about it,' he replied brusquely. 'The war's over for me. I'll never fight again; doubt if I'll ever ride a horse again. I just want to forget it.'

'I hope you don't blame me,' said Kate quickly, upset at his reproach. 'It was Luther's doing entirely. It was as much a shock to me as it was to you. None of it is true, of course. It was just a ploy to split us up.'

Mansel's face darkened as he glanced across the room at her stepfather. 'Yes, and I intend to get an explanation from him,' he said. 'But in private. There's been enough talk.'

'Tackle him by all means,' agreed Kate. 'Though whether he'll tell you the truth is another matter.'

'What do you mean?'

'My stepfather's a devious man,' she said. 'We're all pawns in this game of power he's playing.'

He turned his gaze back to her, reproach still in his glance. 'I was devastated to learn you'd married someone else, Kate, and so soon after my going to war. You might've waited for me.'

Kate gave a laugh of astonishment. 'After you jilted me so cruelly?'

Mansel's expression darkened.

'Anyway,' Kate went on hastily, 'Luther left me no choice. But I'm sure he'll have a plausible explanation for that, too.'

'It seems underhandedness runs in your family,' he said tersely.

Kate was stunned at the slur, and suddenly realised that the change in him went deeper then his physical being. He was an embittered man, obviously looking for someone to blame for his misfortune.

'What are you getting at, Mansel? Why are you attacking me like this?'

Mansel's mouth tightened. 'Did you think it a joke to buy the house I built for us in Sketty?' he asked bitterly. 'Did it amuse you? It was insensitive, and I'd thought better of you, Kate.'

She stared at him, her mouth open in bewilderment. 'I don't know what you're talking about.'

'Don't try to make out you didn't know,' he said scornfully.

'I didn't,' Kate protested strongly. 'I bought the house on my husband's recommendation, sight unseen.'

'Huh! Very trusting, I'm sure,' Mansel retorted. 'And who *is* this husband of yours, anyway?'

'I am Simon Creswell,' Simon announced, suddenly appearing at her elbow. 'I'm Kate's husband.'

He held out his hand, but Mansel hesitated to take it.

'I suggest we make a show of good humour,' Simon said grimly. 'To silence wagging tongues.'

Reluctantly, his expression bleak, Mansel grasped Simon's hand briefly.

'Creswell.' He appeared to consider. 'I don't think I know the family.'

'Simon is Luther's nephew, from Bath,' Kate told him pointedly. She was straining not to erupt with anger. He must have known all along that the house in Sketty belonged to Mansel. Why had he kept it from her?

'Your father tells me you were wounded at Mafeking,' Simon said conversationally. 'Bad luck, especially when Boer resistance was so quickly overwhelmed on that occasion.'

Mansel nodded, his face sombre. 'Stray bullet,' he said dully. 'Shattered my right leg. Ironic, really, when I'd survived the hell of Kroonstadt in April.'

There was an uncomfortable silence again, while Simon shifted his weight from one foot to another and Mansel stared over Kate's head. It was a relief when Delphine moved to his side.

'You've hogged his company for too long,' she said gaily. 'Come along, Mansel, my dear. Mrs Gilbertson is longing to meet a war hero.'

As soon as they were alone, Kate rounded on her husband. 'How dare you keep me in the dark about the house in Sketty. Why didn't you tell me the vendor was Mansel's agent?'

'Because I knew you'd reject it out of hand,' Simon replied

stubbornly. 'It's an excellent property and we've got it at a very good price. Besides,' he went on quickly as she was about to retort, 'I gave you a chance to view it before purchase, if you remember.'

'Is there no end to your deceit?' Kate asked furiously. 'What else are you keeping from me?'

'Nothing,' he snapped. 'Don't take your spite out on me, Kate, just because Mansel didn't go down on bended knee to beg your forgiveness.'

'Oh!' Kate was outraged. 'That's an unpardonable remark, and so like your bad manners.'

She whirled away to find a quiet corner where she could collect her shattered feelings and calm down after Simon's petty onslaught, wondering how she could excuse herself from the dinner table. Someone came to stand close by and she looked up to see her brother.

'What did our glorious hero have to say for himself?' he asked resentfully. 'Delphine's making a damned silly fuss of him. Hero or not, I'll knock him down if he as much as lays a finger on her.'

More likely the other way about, Kate thought grimly.

'Delphine's not your concern,' Kate snapped impatiently. 'Let her husband worry about her admirers.'

Dinner was announced before Evan could reply. With no way to escape, Kate quickly took Evan's arm, not wanting to allow Simon to escort her into the dining-room.

When the ladies rose from the table much later to leave the men to their cigars and port, Kate waylaid Delphine in the hall, out of earshot of the other ladies.

'Why didn't you tell me Mansel Jenkins was coming to dinner?' she asked sharply.

'Why should I mention it to you?' Delphine arched her brows with disdain. 'The Jenkinses are *my* friends, not yours.'

'I was once engaged to Mansel,' Kate cried. 'I've a right to know.'

'The marriage would never have worked.' Delphine smirked. 'Mansel's too much of a man for a milksop like you, even in his present weakened state. He'd have been out looking for fresh meat within a month.' She threw back her head and laughed. 'A married virgin: it's too hilarious for words! You know, of course, that you're the butt of many a crude joke in the fashionable salons of Swansea.'

'You alleycat!' Kate cried, mortified. 'I know what you're trying to do. You want to add Mansel to your trophies.'

Delphine pouted prettily. 'How very astute of you to realise that.'

'You can't fool Luther for ever,' Kate said tensely. 'And heaven help you when he finds out.'

Delphine's smile was mocking. 'Luther's putty in my hands,' she said. 'After an hour in my bed he'd sell his soul to the devil if I asked him to.'

'You're a vile creature,' said Kate with disgust. 'Don't try your disgusting wiles on Mansel. He's a good man. So was my brother before you got your claws into him.'

'Oh, yes, Evan's very gallant, isn't he,' she sneered. 'Getting that miserable shop-girl into trouble, and then casting her off when something better comes along.'

'You poisoned his mind!' Kate accused heatedly.

She took a step forward, seized by an overwhelming urge to rake her fingernails across Delphine's perfect features. Somehow she held back, staring into the other woman's scornful eyes.

'You're like some horrible cancer that needs to be cut out,' Kate hissed. 'I wish you were dead!'

Delphine's face blanched at the words and Kate was shocked too by what she'd said in the heat of the moment. She was about to apologise when Delphine suddenly struck her across the face, the force of the blow sending her head snapping back painfully, and Kate clapped her palm to her cheek, speechless with astonishment.

Delphine's look was baleful. 'You'll pay for that remark,' she rasped. 'And pay dearly. You've made a bad enemy in me, Kate, and you'll be sorry. You wish me dead, but it'll be you who's sorry to death when I'm through with you.'

In the dining-room Simon sat at the now cleared table with the other men. He let Chivers refill his glass with port, but refused the cigars the butler was handing round.

He eyed Mansel Jenkins sitting opposite. There was a strained look on the man's face as though he were still in pain. Simon wanted to feel sympathy, but couldn't. He was as knocked back by Mansel's return as Kate was, and was troubled to think she might be still in love with him. Simon's heart felt heavy at the thought, and he wished fervently that Delphine hadn't brought Jenkins here. What was her game, anyway?

Simon took a deep breath. He longed with all his heart to please Kate, even though she mistrusted him, and knew Mansel Jenkins could drive an even bigger wedge between them, but there was nothing he could do about it.

Luther nodded to Chivers and the butler left the room. At once Mansel rose to his feet with some difficulty and stood leaning on his stick.

'Templar,' he began. 'I'd like a word with you in private. May we withdraw to your study? I'm sure these gentlemen won't mind your absence for a short while.'

'Wait now, my boy,' Luther said with forced joviality. 'This is no time to talk business. Sit down, sit down. Have some more port.'

'It's not business,' Mansel said tersely. 'There's a private matter I need to discuss with you.'

Luther looked uncomfortable. 'I can hardly desert my guests, Mansel,' he said. 'Can't it wait until another time?'

'No, it won't wait!' Mansel's fist crashed down on the table. 'And if you persist in putting me off I'll have to speak out here before these gentlemen.'

Luther got hastily to his feet. 'Kindly behave civilly to me as a guest should,' he said with dignity, although his hand was shaking as he lowered his glass to the table. 'And sit down.'

'Very well,' Mansel continued, though he remained on his feet. 'I'll ask my question here and now, and let the others make of it what they will.'

'This is neither the time nor the place—' Luther began.

'When I asked for your stepdaughter's hand in marriage last autumn,' Mansel went on doggedly, 'you fobbed me off with a tale of her mental illness, which caused me to break my word to her.' A sob escaped him. 'To my undying shame.'

There were murmurs of embarrassment around the table, and Mr Jenkins rose to his feet. 'Mansel, my dear boy, what're you doing?'

'Leave me be, Father,' Mansel said raggedly. 'I'll have this out now. It's because of this man's lies I went to war, and am now a broken man.'

'That isn't my fault—' Luther interposed, but Mansel cut across his words.

'You lied, Templar!' Mansel stormed. 'You told me Kate could never marry or bear children because of a serious mental disorder inherent in her family. Yet she's now married to your nephew. I'm entitled to an explanation, at least. You ruined my life with your lie.'

'It wasn't a lie,' Luther asserted strongly.

There were murmurs and rumbling around the table and Luther glanced about him, obviously disconcerted.

'It was a medical mistake,' he went on hurriedly. 'Made by that quack, Penfold. I'd no idea he was a scoundrel and an incompetent fool.'

There was a subdued oath from Evan. 'You let that rogue treat my mother,' he said. 'What harm did he do her?'

As though exhausted, Mansel sat down heavily, and seemed to sink on to his seat, leaning back, his face white. The confrontation had obviously taken it out of him.

The other men stared at Luther, and he looked from one to the other like a wily fox.

'The villain duped me completely,' he lied without a blink of his eye, but there was a film of sweat on his upper lip. 'Later I heard talk and sought a second opinion, only to find that Penfold had made a grave error.'

'Or else perpetrated a fraud,' Simon cut in quickly, looking at his uncle.

'Good gracious!' Mr Villiers exclaimed suddenly, rising to his feet. 'I've just remembered. Penfold's my family's medical man. I must see about a change at once.'

'Penfold should be struck off!' Luther cried out, banging his fist on the table. 'The blackguard should be run out of town.'

'We need incontrovertible proof of his misconduct,' Mr Jenkins said. 'And that may not be easy to find.'

'I can help you there,' Simon announced casually.

Everyone stared at him. Simon noted Luther's glance was particularly intense.

'I've been investigating Penfold in my spare time, for my

own reasons,' he said, looking pointedly at Luther. He shook his head. 'He's indeed an evil man, committing many heinous crimes against young boys.'

There was a sharp intake of breath from Luther, and astonished gasps and glances of horror around the table.

'The doctor's notorious among the working-class people of the town,' Simon went on. 'And is greatly feared.'

'This is dreadful,' Evan said. 'And to think that a man like that has had access to this house.' He glanced at his stepfather. 'I trust you didn't know of his activities, Luther?'

Luther huffed in outrage. 'I most certainly did not,' he exclaimed loudly, staring round at his peers. 'Like the rest of you, I took the man at face value. He seemed like a gentleman.'

'Oh, he's a gentleman by birth,' Simon said. 'And for that reason might think himself safe from retribution.'

'Scandalous!'

'I'll speak to my brother-in-law, the assistant chief constable, tomorrow,' Mr Jenkins assured them. 'This man must be put behind bars.'

'Hear, hear!'

Simon nodded his approval. 'When apprehended Penfold might reveal some surprising names.'

'What's that?'

'It's very possible members of our own class are shielding him,' Simon explained. 'Either because they share his appetites or, more likely, he's useful to them in other ways. He's wide open to blackmail, of course. Don't you agree with me, Luther?'

His uncle's glance was venomous.

There was a chorus of denial around the table.

'No! Never!'

'Not one of us.'

'Impossible!'

Simon kept his gaze steady under Luther's furious glare.

'It doesn't bear thinking about, does it?' he said. 'That one of our kind could stoop so low.'

There was an outbreak of excited talk. Mr Villiers and Mr Jenkins moved away from the table to speak together in low voices. After one malevolent look at Simon, Luther moved hastily to join them. He couldn't afford to appear the odd man out, now the witch-hunt was on.

Simon glanced at Mansel, sitting silent and unconcerned with the turn of events. It looked as though he was still in love with Kate, despite his treatment of her. But was he gentleman enough not to take advantage of her strange marriage?

The irony of their situation struck him as ridiculous and sad. Mansel was free to tell her how he felt, while her husband was forbidden by a promise not to do so.

But how does a man tell his wife of convenience that she's his world; she's all he lives for? How can he make her love him?

21

---◆---

'Are you at home to Mr Mansel Jenkins, Miss Kate?'

Kate rose hastily, abandoning her easel and paints, and turned a flushed face towards Ethel standing patiently in the doorway.

Mansel was here! She'd thought of no one else all morning, unable to forget his cold look, going over all that she'd said to him and blaming herself for his unfriendliness.

'Are you sure it's me he's come to see?'

She was certain he'd never want to speak to her again.

'Oh, yes, Miss Kate.' Ethel nodded enthusiastically. 'Asked for you, he did. Brought a lovely bunch of flowers. I'll put them in a vase and bring them up to you.'

'Show him up straight away,' Kate said eagerly, patting her hair self-consciously. 'Don't keep him waiting a minute longer.'

When Ethel left, Kate rushed to a mirror. She looked pale and tired, and hadn't slept much, thinking of him, regretting all that had happened subsequently, especially her marriage. Anger with Simon hadn't subsided. It had made her restless.

Kate came forward with outstretched hands as Mansel came in to the sitting-room, and her cheeks flushed with warmth.

'Mansel, I'm so glad to see you.'

He took her hand and raised it to his lips, and she felt a thrill race up her spine. There was still something between them, and they both knew it.

'I didn't know whether I'd be welcome,' he said in a low voice. 'But I've come to apologise for my boorish behaviour. Can you ever forgive me, Kate?'

'Oh! Mansel!' She clasped his hand in both of hers, pressing his fingers warmly. 'There's nothing to forgive. We found ourselves in a very awkward situation.'

She was about to blame Delphine for that, but decided to say nothing to him against her stepmother, uncertain how deep their acquaintance went. Instead she smiled reassuringly, and drew him towards the fireplace.

'Please sit down,' she said, almost shyly. 'Would you like some tea?'

He sat on a sofa and she ventured to sit beside him.

'Perhaps later,' he said seriously. 'We must talk, Kate. There's so much I want to say to you.'

'And I to you, Mansel,' Kate said sincerely.

'Kate, my dearest girl, I do regret all that's happened,' Mansel said, his voice shaking with feeling. 'I was a fool, a blind, credulous fool. When I think of all we've lost, you and me, I'm desolate.'

Kate hung her head, overcome with emotion, too. 'Neither of us is to blame,' she murmured. 'There were forces at work against which we were helpless.'

'But that's behind us now,' he said hopefully. 'I'm home.'

'Oh, yes!'

Kate dared to move a little closer to him on the sofa, her heart beating wildly. The horrors he'd been through had taken their toll, but he was still handsome, still dashing, and she remembered how they'd been together; remembered the day he'd taken her to view the house he'd built. In the room that was to be their bedroom, he'd kissed her passionately. He'd loved her then. He still loved her, she was certain.

She desperately needed to be loved, desperately longed to satisfy the yearnings of her body and soul. She was tired of her lonely life, a life without love. Despite Luther's cruel wiles, true love wasn't broken so easily. Luther hadn't destroyed what they had.

She grasped Mansel's hand. 'I didn't enquire about you, Mansel, because Luther kept me a virtual prisoner,' she said breathlessly. 'But a day didn't go by without a thought of you, and I prayed nightly for your safety. I knew one day you'd return to me.'

He brought her fingers to his lips again. 'And you were constantly in my thoughts, dearest Kate,' he said. 'You don't know how bitterly I regretted my swift departure without speaking to you first.'

She leaned a little closer still, wanting his kiss, to feel his arms about her.

'You're so lovely, Kate. I left behind a young girl, but I return to find a beautiful woman. You were mine by promise before you were Creswell's.'

'I'm still yours, Mansel, dearest.' Kate breathed quickly, but was disappointed that he'd not responded in the way she longed for. 'You don't know how I cried for you. My life was unbearable, and I was so lonely and hurt.'

She hadn't meant to say that because it sounded like a reproach, and she didn't blame him for what happened, not really.

'And I was punished for it, Kate, tenfold,' he said tremulously. 'I don't deserve your forgiveness.'

'We deserve all the happiness we can find,' she said decisively. 'No one can stop us now.'

She reached out a hand to touch his face, and he leaned towards her, his gaze on her mouth. Kate held her breath, waiting, but suddenly he sat back, looking at her as though stricken.

'Kate! What're we doing?'

He rose awkwardly and, taking his stick, began to walk about the room in jerky agitated strides, while Kate stared in dismay at his changed manner.

'Mansel, what is it?'

'I've no right . . . we've no right saying these things to each other. You're a married woman; Creswell's wife.'

'Not in my heart,' Kate said quickly. 'We're married, but I'm not his wife . . .' Embarrassment flooded her face with warmth. 'I'm not his wife in the biblical sense.'

He stared at her in astonishment for a moment, and Kate's embarrassment deepened. Delphine's cruel taunts echoed in her mind. Would Mansel laugh at the absurdity of her situation, too?

'Nevertheless,' he said, his expression thoughtful. 'I feel like a cad. I could very easily damage your reputation, Kate. I've done you enough harm already, leaving you to your fate.'

He moved unsteadily to the door. 'I must go.'

Kate rose hastily, shattered by the transformation in him. 'No, don't go, Mansel, I beg you.'

'Kate, I must, for both our sakes.'

Then he was gone. Kate stood stock-still staring at the closed door for several minutes, unable to believe he'd deserted her once again, for that's how it felt. That was her last chance of knowing love. Coldness settled over her at the realisation that once again it was denied her.

*   *   *

'Why did you bring Mansel Jenkins here?' Simon asked Delphine, catching her alone in the hall after dinner. 'What're you trying to do,' he went on angrily. 'You're never happy unless you're destroying something or causing pain for someone, in this instance Kate.'

She was at the foot of the staircase, about to go up, but turned slowly to look at him, a mocking smile curving her mouth.

'I'm mistress of Old Grove House,' she said. 'I don't explain myself to anyone, especially not to you.'

Simon ground his teeth at her arrogance. 'You knew it'd be a terrible shock for her. It was a cruel trick, Delphine.'

Her mouth tightened. 'Kate's not the delicate flower you think,' she said irritably. 'She's got steel in her, that one. I've seen it in her eyes, and she has an acid tongue.' She gave him an appraising look. 'If you're worried Mansel will take her from you, don't.' She laughed. 'I've already ensnared him. He's mine in every sense. He won't look at another woman now.'

Simon felt revulsion, seeing the blatant lasciviousness in her expression. 'Bertram, Evan and now Mansel.' He grimaced. 'You disgust me.'

'There'll be others,' she said nonchalantly. 'You can depend on it.' With a dismissive lift of her shoulder, she turned to climb the stairs.

'You're playing with fire,' Simon said quickly. 'Luther's not a man to be crossed without taking revenge.'

She laughed again, looking down on him. 'There's not a man alive that I can't twist to my will,' she said scornfully, then paused to give him a poisonous look. 'Except you.'

When Mansel Jenkins called on her again the following afternoon, Kate didn't know what to think or feel, and received him tremulously. He looked apprehensive as he came into the room.

She rose, but remained quiet, waiting for him to speak, to explain himself.

'I wouldn't have blamed you if you'd refused to see me,' he began. 'I'm not a coward, Kate. I believe I've proved that on the battlefield, but when we spoke yesterday of things close to our hearts, I admit I was suddenly afraid.'

'Afraid of me?'

He smiled. 'No, of myself. You should be *my* wife, not Creswell's. I feel badly cheated. Suddenly, I wasn't sure what my motive was in coming to see you.'

'Motive?' Kate shook her head. 'But surely your motive is love as mine is? We're only taking back what was taken from us, Mansel.'

'You're right,' he said, and came towards her with uneven strides, his free hand outstretched to take hers. 'My dearest Kate. I've missed you so badly these long terrible months, and thought never to see you again. Now we're together, I'd be a fool to let our strange circumstances matter.'

'Oh! Mansel!'

She took the initiative, and reached up to kiss him. As their lips met, he dropped his stick and embraced her with a little groan of longing, and Kate gave herself over to the joy of being in loving arms at last.

They stayed talking together most of the afternoon, and over tea she persuaded him to tell her of his experiences in South Africa.

'War changes a man, Kate,' he said sadly before taking his leave, this time with a fond kiss. 'I'm not the man you once knew. I can never be that man again.'

'I'm just thankful you're home at last,' Kate said. 'Please come again tomorrow, if you can.'

He smiled and kissed her again. 'I'll be here,' he said softly. 'Nothing can keep me away now.' He clutched at her urgently, and held her against his chest. 'Though what is to become of us, Kate, my dear, I don't know.'

Neither did Kate, but she wouldn't let her newfound happiness be spoiled by doubt and worry.

Later that day, as Kate was putting away her needlework, she heard a woman's raised voice in the vestibule, and the next moment the door was thrown open and Delphine stalked in. Kate looked at her in astonishment.

'How dare you entertain *my* friends behind my back,' Delphine raged, her face contorted in her fury. 'You deceitful little slut!'

'What!' Kate couldn't believe her ears. 'What're you talking about?'

'Mansel Jenkins has been to see you alone here twice, and I know what's going on,' Delphine said explosively. 'Mansel's mine. Understand? Mine, not yours. Don't think you can entice him away with your little-girl charms. His tastes are a pinch more spicy.'

Kate stared for a moment dumbfounded, then recovered her voice. 'Get out of my rooms, Delphine,' she commanded loudly. 'Get out, now.'

'Mansel's promised—' Delphine began angrily, but Kate cut across her words with anger of her own.

'I won't discuss Mansel's visits,' she said wrathfully. 'Who visits me is none of your business.'

'Your husband will get to hear how you entertain men behind his back, while denying him his rights to your bed,'

Delphine threatened, her face darkening. 'Be warned, Kate, you're no match for me.'

'You can tell Simon anything you like,' Kate snapped. 'Mansel's home and we're determined to be together. Our love's strong enough to face any condemnation.'

Delphine stared open-mouthed for a moment, then, whirling, marched out of the room.

'The mayor and his lady wife are dining here tonight, among other dignitaries,' Ethel said as she helped Kate from the bath. 'You've got to admit the house has livened up since the master married.'

Kate said nothing, still upset after her quarrel with her stepmother. Delphine had implied that she and Mansel were lovers, but Kate refused to believe it.

Ethel helped her into her satin bloomers, and tied the ribbons in her matching basque. She'd just padded into the bedroom when the door flew open and Simon stood there, his face dark with fury. He glared at Ethel.

'Get out!' he thundered.

Ethel dithered, staring from Simon to Kate and back again, while Kate, conscious of her dishabille, tried to grab at a wrap on a chair nearby.

'Are you deaf, girl?' he bellowed, and, lifting a hand, pointed at the door. 'Do as you're told. Get out.'

'Stay where you are, Ethel,' Kate cried defiantly. 'What's the meaning of this, Simon?'

Simon scowled at Ethel. 'I pay your wages, girl,' he rasped. 'Get out or you're sacked.'

With a frightened glance at Kate, Ethel rushed out of the room, but Kate hoped she hadn't left the apartment, for she was very alarmed at the wild expression on Simon's face.

'How dare you burst in here unannounced and uninvited,' Kate said tensely, her trembling fingers clutching at the wrap as she held it in front of her. 'Get out yourself.'

In two strides he reached her, and, snatching the wrap from her grasp, flung it aside. Kate put both hands up to cover her décolletage.

'You hussy!' Simon exploded. 'Don't try to hide yourself like an innocent. I know the truth.'

'What?'

'You've denied me, your own husband, but you've given yourself willingly to Mansel Jenkins.'

Kate's head was spinning and his words didn't make much sense, but she saw an opportunity to make the situation plain to him. The farce was over. She wasn't going to dissemble any longer.

'Mansel and I love each other,' she said defiantly. 'We never stopped loving each other.'

'You're *my* wife.'

'Oh, you can't pretend that means anything to you,' Kate cried scathingly. 'Your marriage to me is merely a means to an end for you, money and power. Well, you've got what *you* want. Now I'll have what I want, and that's Mansel. I want a husband who'll really love me, who'll give me children.'

'I've never denied you children,' Simon blurted out furiously. 'It was your decision to live apart.'

'I won't stand here like this arguing with you,' Kate cried. 'Get out of my bedroom.'

'No!' Simon looked around him wildly. 'You brought him in here, didn't you? He made love to you in our bed.'

Kate's mouth dropped open. 'How dare you!'

'You admitted as much to Delphine,' Simon said raggedly.

'She's a liar.'

'No.' Simon shook his head vehemently. 'She wasn't lying. She was totally incensed when she spoke of it. You've done something unforgivable to her, Kate. You've stolen one of her trophies.'

'It's not true,' Kate said, trembling, and then felt stubborn. 'But even if it were,' she went on derisively, 'it's no concern of yours. I don't belong to you.'

He took a step towards her, his eyes aflame. 'You belong to me all right. I'll kill any man who says different.'

Kate stared. 'You're talking like a madman.'

'Maybe I am.' He ran trembling fingers through his hair. 'Good God, Kate! How much do you think a man can stand?'

He took another step forward and Kate was frightened by the wildness in his eyes.

'Stay back, Simon,' she warned, edging away. 'Don't come any closer.'

His mouth tightened aggressively. 'I'll have what's mine,' he said harshly. 'I won't be denied any longer.'

Before Kate could turn and run for the safety of the bathroom, he sprang at her, his arms closing around her, and he held her tightly to his chest. Kate fought fiercely, trying to wrench herself from his unwanted embrace, but he was too strong.

'He shan't have you, Kate. You're mine,' he said hoarsely, his breath warm on her cheek. 'No man will have you but me, your husband.'

Frightened, she struggled even harder. 'Let me go, you beast,' she screamed. 'Ethel! Ethel!'

But Ethel didn't appear to save her. There was no one to save her.

He grasped her chin and held her face up to his. 'Kiss me,' he commanded throatily. 'Kiss me.'

Kate squirmed to release her face from his grasp, writhing this way and that, but though she struggled, his mouth found hers, his lips passionate and demanding as he held her in a vice-like grip.

She couldn't believe what was happening, and was astounded at the fervour of his kiss. Mansel never kissed her like that. She'd have been shocked if he had.

Suddenly the kiss was at an end, and the next moment, with a gasping sob, he'd lifted her into his arms, and carried her towards the bed.

'Stop this!' Kate cried, kicking her legs frantically and beating at his chest and shoulders with her fists. 'Stop this! Put me down. You've no right.'

'I've every right. I'm your legal husband.'

He threw her on to the bed, and then struggled out of his coat. With a terrified sob, Kate tried to scramble away, but she wasn't quick enough. He caught her and held her fast, pinning her to the bed.

'You went to bed with him,' Simon rasped, his face flushed with passion. 'You'll go to bed with me now, willing or not.'

He covered her body with his own, and held her face between his hands to kiss her again. Kate tore at his hair, scratched his face, but although she knew she must have hurt him, he released her mouth for only a moment.

'My beautiful Kate,' he said throatily. 'I've dreamed of nothing but this since I first saw you.'

'I hate you!' she flared.

'You *will* love me,' he answered huskily. 'You will!'

He wrenched at the shoulder strap of her satin basque, and the fabric tore, exposing her breast. He stared down at her nakedness, suddenly stilled, as though mesmerised.

Kate kept very still, too.

'Mary Creswell would be very proud of her son now, wouldn't she,' she panted; her heart was fluttering like a wild bird. 'Ravishing a defenceless woman, even if I am legally your wife.'

He gave a gasping sob and looked at her with a stricken expression. Slowly he raised himself up from her and sat on the edge of the bed, still staring at her. He looked pale and winded, as though someone had punched him in the diaphragm.

Kate took advantage of the moment to scramble off the bed, and snatched up the wrap lying on the floor. She pulled it around herself to cover her exposed breast, and, rushing quickly to the door, flung it open.

'Get out!' she said, drawing in a lungful of air. 'You're a brute, and certainly no gentleman.'

'Wait . . .'

'I said get out, Simon!' Kate bawled, hearing hysteria in her voice. 'Before I call the footman and have you thrown out.'

'I'm sorry, Kate, so very sorry.' He stood up, his clothes dishevelled, fingernail scratches reddening his cheek. 'But you drove me to it, you and that damned snivelling coward, Jenkins.'

'He's not a coward,' Kate said hotly. 'He fought valiantly for his country. He wouldn't do such a dishonourable thing as you've just done.'

'He came sniffing around another man's wife,' Simon retorted hotly. 'I call that dishonourable, and damned cowardly, too.'

'Just go, will you. I can't bear to look at you. You disgust me.'

'Don't take that uppity tone with me, woman,' he snarled, suddenly looking dangerous again, and she cringed. 'I was sorely provoked.' He put both his hands to his head, confused. 'I didn't know what I was doing. Your attitude is unfair, Kate.'

'Oh, I'm unfair, am I?' Kate sparked. 'It's unfair to resist when you burst in here and try to . . . to . . .'

'What?'

'Rape me!' she blurted.

'Rape? Good God, Kate!' Simon looked horrified. 'It's not true. What kind of an animal do you take me for? I'd horse-whip any man guilty of that.'

'Don't deny it! You tried to take me against my will,' Kate said stubbornly. 'If that isn't rape I don't know what is.'

'Now, look here, Kate—'

'No, you look, Simon,' Kate flared. 'You've made my mind up for me. I'm going to sue for divorce. I'll marry Mansel at last. We belong together.'

His mouth dropped open and he stared at her, shocked. 'You can't do that. Think of the disgrace. You'd be a ruined woman. And Jenkins would fare no better.'

'Nonsense!' Kate said, tossing her head. 'This is the twentieth century. Society's moving towards a much more open attitude to such things now,' she said haughtily. 'Soon women will have rights equal with men.'

Simon shook his head fiercely. 'I'm not concerned with what society thinks or does,' he shouted. 'Damn society!'

'Don't raise your voice to me,' Kate shrilled, frightened again.

A vein throbbed in his temple, and he glared at her. 'I won't divorce you,' he said darkly. 'And you've no grounds to divorce me. I've not been unfaithful, and don't ask me to provide false evidence because I won't.'

'I have legitimate grounds for divorce.' She felt her face flush. 'Our marriage has never been consummated, and I'm willing to have that proved by a medical examination. The marriage will be annulled.'

He glanced towards the bed, his expression angry. 'I'll deny it,' he said. 'And anyway, Mansel Jenkins has put paid to those grounds.'

'Mansel's not my lover,' Kate said triumphantly. 'As Delphine's always taunting me, I'm a married virgin.'

'If you think divorce will be easy, you're deceiving yourself,' Simon said harshly. 'Jenkins won't like it, and neither will his family.'

'I'm divorcing you, Simon, so get used to the idea.'

'Kate, please.' Simon took a step towards her. 'I was . . . am jealous. I believed Delphine. You can't blame me for behaving like any outraged husband.'

'I suggest you gather what assets you can, while you can,' Kate said, striving to quell the quiver in her voice. 'When I divorce you, you'll have nothing. Not even the seat on the board. Now, get out of my sight.'

Two days passed before Mansel called on her again. She'd delayed writing to her lawyer about divorce proceedings, feeling that Mansel should be told first, and she wanted to explain the grounds again. She flew into his arms as soon as Ethel left the room, taking his kiss eagerly.

'You're trembling, Kate,' he said, holding her away from him and looking into her eyes. 'Is something wrong?'

'Simon and I have quarrelled,' she said.

He looked startled. 'Oh, I say!'

'I've told him everything about us,' Kate said soothingly. 'The marriage was never consummated, and so I'm suing for an annulment.' She reached up and stroked his face. 'I'll be a free woman, Mansel. We can marry at last.'

He stepped back, staring at her in dismay. 'An annulment is as bad as a divorce,' he said.

'Divorce isn't so unusual these days,' Kate hurried to assure him, disturbed by his manner. She'd thought he'd be pleased they could be together at last. 'And I'm sure it can be done quietly.'

'Quietly?' He looked profoundly shocked, and Kate's heart quivered. 'That it should be done at all is an abomination,' he said severely. 'No, Kate, it won't do at all.'

'But it's the only way,' Kate said. 'I can't stay married to Simon, not now.' She hesitated before explaining. 'He tried to force himself on me,' she said, her voice quivering. 'He tried to rape me.'

Mansel raised his eyebrows. 'He *is* your husband, Kate,' he said matter-of-factly. 'A man expects his conjugal rights.'

'What?' She stared in disbelief. 'You condone what he did? I can't believe it, Mansel.'

'It's hardly a matter for divorce,' he said tersely. 'You must put the idea right out of your head.'

'But, Mansel, how can we be together if I do nothing?'

Without answering, he turned and hobbled across the room, his strides erratic and angry, to stand for a few moments before the fireplace, leaning on his stick. Kate stared at the uncompromising stiffness of his shoulders, and her heart sank.

'Why don't you answer?'

He turned back to face her. 'A man in my position can't marry a divorced woman, Kate,' he said, as though reasoning with a child. 'You must see that.'

'No, I don't! Why not, Mansel?'

He looked impatient with her. 'The scandal would be too damaging,' he said. 'Personally and for business. My father's offered me a partnership at last. He won't stand for divorce.'

'But it's not a divorce as such. It's an annulment,' Kate said. 'There's little disgrace in that, I'm sure. It happens all the time, and in good families, too, when a daughter elopes with the wrong sort of man.'

'There'd be talk, vicious talk. I'd have to leave Swansea,' he said. 'And what if, out of spite and revenge, Creswell were to counter-sue, citing me as co-respondent?' Mansel shook his head vehemently. 'No. No. It's unthinkable. My father's prominent in Church circles. He might even cut me out of his will.'

He stared at her stonily.

'I'll have nothing to do with it, Kate.'

'And what of me?' Kate cried, unable to accept he was spurning her again. 'I deserve some thought, surely?'

He looked thoroughly put out. 'You foolish girl,' he snapped. 'Don't you understand? My whole future would be at risk. It's out of the question.'

Kate clasped her hands tightly together, feeling the heat of embarrassment flood her face and neck.

'Why did you come to see me so often this past week?' she cried. 'Even speaking of love to me. If you can't marry a divorced woman, what are . . . what were your intentions, Mansel?'

Mansel looked defensive. 'To be honest, I . . . I don't know,' he muttered.

'Oh!' Kate was mortified. 'Your intentions were dishonourable then? You never intended to marry me.'

He remained silent, his gaze sliding away from hers. 'I don't know, I tell you,' he burst out angrily. 'I've not been myself since the war. I told you I'm a changed man.'

'I see!' she said, feeling her misery would choke her. 'So, I'm to excuse your dishonourable behaviour because you're a war hero.' She turned from him to hide her tears. How could she have been so naïve?

'It was seeing you again, Kate,' he said, to excuse himself. 'All the old feelings rushed into my head, confusing me. Memories took hold of my heart. After all I've suffered I wasn't thinking like a rational man.'

Incensed by these thin excuses, Kate whirled to face him again. 'Simon's right about you,' she cried. 'You are a snivelling coward. Now, go, Mansel. Get out! I never want to set eyes on you again.'

'Well, that's a bit awkward to manage,' he said stiffly. 'Delphine's a family friend. We'll be dining here often. We're bound to run into each other.'

'Do the decent thing and stay away.'

He moved painfully to the door, and then turned to look at her. 'Really, Kate!' he said irritably. 'I don't see why I should deny my friends over a trifle. After all, we were never intimate.'

'You philandering cad!'

'That's a bit strong,' he retorted hotly as he stood in the doorway. 'You're behaving like a spoiled child. I'd no idea you could be so petty.'

Stunned at his effrontery, Kate could only stand with her mouth open, staring as Mansel left, closing the door quietly behind him.

22

———◆◆◆———

September 1900

Kate sat in the house in Sketty, taking tea, while her aunt sat opposite, her expression cool.

'Well,' Aunt Agnes began huffily. 'I was beginning to think you'd disowned me, Kate.'

Kate shifted uncomfortably in her chair. 'I'm sorry I've neglected you. I've had my reasons for not calling here.'

'Tsk! I can't understand your lack of curiosity, for the life of me,' Agnes said irritably. 'You buy a house you've never seen, and never wish to see, by the looks of it, even though it's also the home of your last aged relative.'

'I have been here before,' Kate said quietly. 'With Mansel Jenkins.' She glanced down at her cup. 'We were to live here.'

'Ah! Now I see.' Her aunt's tone softened. 'Then why buy it if it holds sad memories?'

Kate's lips thinned. 'That's Simon's doing,' she said angrily. 'He dealt with the purchase, and deliberately didn't tell me the truth. He's a conniving scoundrel as well as a dishonourable brute.'

'What?' Agnes stared at her.

Kate felt her face flush with embarrassment.

'I've come to ask your advice,' she began tremulously, reluctant to speak out. Mentioning divorce to a lady of her aunt's generation would probably open up a flood of ridicule. She straightened her shoulders, ready to do battle if necessary.

'Well?' Agnes frowned at her hesitation.

'I want to divorce Simon. I'm seeing my lawyer tomorrow.'

Agnes's fingers jerked convulsively, sending her cup and saucer tumbling on to the carpet, spilling tea.

'What?' Her aunt's tone was scandalised. She stared at Kate. 'What did you say?'

'He's a monster, Aunt,' Kate cried defensively.

'What utter nonsense, girl,' Agnes said angrily.

'I won't be talked out of it,' Kate exclaimed stubbornly. 'Simon's behaved abominably. We agreed to live separate lives, yet some weeks ago he molested me in my own bedroom.' Her voice rose at the memory. 'He tried to rape me!'

Agnes snorted. 'I'm surprised he's been as patient with you as long as he has,' she said. 'Not many men would pander to a woman's silliness.'

'What?' Kate couldn't believe her ears. 'Silliness?'

'Yours isn't the first arranged marriage, Kate,' Agnes snapped. 'Many of them work out well. But it's up to the woman.'

'I'm damned if I'll accept it,' Kate retorted stubbornly. 'Or submit, either.'

Agnes sniffed. 'It's not natural, Kate, an unconsummated marriage,' she said decisively. 'And I dare say it's unhealthy, too. A woman needs release from her . . . emotions, as does a man.'

'Well! I never thought to hear such talk from you,' Kate exclaimed. 'It's a strange sentiment from a spinster!' she blurted then was immediately sorry.

Agnes's lips tightened for a moment. 'A spinster I may be,' she said. 'But I'm no virgin.'

'Aunt Agnes!' Kate was shocked, but her aunt looked defiant.

'I'll tell you the story one day, perhaps,' she said. 'But for the moment we're discussing your life. Kate, I believe Simon has deep feelings for you. Don't throw love away on a whim.'

'Huh! What nonsense,' Kate said scornfully. 'He married me for money, and made no bones about it, either. Then he has the effrontery to become insanely jealous of Mansel Jenkins.' Kate tossed her head. 'When, plainly, he has no right to be.'

Agnes's eyes narrowed. 'What has Mansel Jenkins to do with this absurd divorce?' she asked.

Kate ran her tongue over her lips nervously. 'Mansel came to the house to see me several times and I received him in my apartment.' She paused, feeling foolish. 'We spoke of . . . of love, and what had happened between us previously.'

'You silly girl!' Agnes exclaimed in agitation. 'What were you thinking of? You're a married woman.'

'I don't *feel* like a married woman,' Kate blurted. 'I thought you'd understand, Aunt. Like any other woman I long to be loved, yet I'm trapped in a loveless marriage.'

'Now you're whingeing like Evan,' Agnes snapped.

'His problem was of his own making,' Kate retorted hotly. 'I was forced into it. All my feelings for Mansel flooded back, and he feels . . . felt the same.' Kate hesitated, embarrassed again. 'At least I thought he did.'

'Ah ha! I see!' Agnes's glance was a knowing one. 'You frightened him off with your talk of divorce?'

Kate couldn't look Agnes in the eye. 'He was beastly to me,' she admitted.

'So!' her aunt said severely. 'You foolishly dally with another man, and you're surprised your husband reacted the way he did?'

331

'I'm *not* Simon's property to do with as he sees fit,' Kate cried angrily. 'He's no right to force himself on me, and I despise him for it.'

'I'm sorry to hear you say that,' Agnes said, looking gloomy.

'Money, money, money,' Kate rushed on in anger. 'That's all he thinks of. It's the motive for everything he does.'

'Well, I disagree,' her aunt said forcefully. 'Obviously, I know your husband better than you do yourself.'

'What?'

'I've become very fond of Simon these last months. While you've neglected me, Kate,' Agnes said, looking grim, 'your husband has visited me every week since I've lived here, sometimes twice a week. It can't be for my money as I have none.'

Kate stared in astonishment, and felt put out. 'He's never mentioned this to me.'

'He's been generous, too,' Agnes went on. 'He provided me with a pony and trap, and a boy to drive it, so that Megan and I can visit town whenever we choose.'

Kate was flummoxed. 'I'd have provided those things if you'd asked . . .'

'Ask? Beg, you mean,' Agnes snapped. 'I didn't have to ask Simon. He's a very thoughtful and understanding man. In my opinion Luther Templar did you a favour in arranging the marriage.'

'Aunt Agnes! You go too far,' Kate said sharply. 'Simon Creswell is *not* the man I want for a husband.'

'Take my advice, you unwise child,' Agnes said impatiently. 'Cling to him. He'll be the making of you. And forget Mansel Jenkins. He's a lost soul, anyway.'

'What do you mean?'

Her aunt looked undecided, as though regretting her hasty comment.

'Give Simon a chance, I beg you, Kate. He loves you, I'm certain of it.'

Kate hurried to the door intent on getting away quickly. She needed to think. As she was about to close the door her aunt called to her.

'Kate, say nothing to Evan about Delphine and Mansel. He's a jealous hot-headed young fool, and may do something we'll all regret. The woman's not worth it.'

'I think the hour is up, my boy,' Luther said, stretching, and Bertram laid his brush aside and stepped back reluctantly from the easel.

'When can you sit for me again?' he asked.

Luther stood and, stepping down from a small wooden platform, straightened his waistcoat and shot his cuffs.

'Not for some time, I fear,' he replied. 'I've some business in London. I'll be away three, perhaps four weeks.' He smiled at the brief expression of irritation on his brother-in-law's face. 'I promise I'll sit immediately I return.'

'Will Delphine accompany you to London?'

'No, she'd find it tiresome,' Luther said, a note of regret in his voice. 'My business commitments will be intense. There'll be no time for pleasure, and Delphine must be always amused.' He smiled indulgently. 'Swansea will give her all the society and entertainment she needs.'

He glanced round the nursery, which Bertram was now using as a studio, and at the many canvases leaning against the walls.

'You'll not be idle, I think, while I'm away,' he said. 'I know you have several commissions from my friends.'

'Yes, indeed.' Bertram smiled faintly. 'And I won't neglect your own. There's a great deal of work to do yet on the background.'

Luther looked at the many canvases again, and then strolled towards some in the corner of the room. Bertram quickly stepped forward to block his path.

'Those are unused,' he said hastily and steered Luther to another wall, where many canvases leaned one against the other.

'You've enough here to make an exhibition,' Luther said. He fingered them, some framed, others in stretchers, and suddenly felt inclined to be generous. 'When I return I'll arrange an exhibition for you in London,' he said magnanimously. 'I'll have much influence there before the month's out.'

'If I'm to have your patronage, Luther,' Bertram said quickly, 'I'd prefer to live and study in Paris.' He flushed. 'I've still much to learn.'

'As you please, my boy,' Luther said munificently, as his fingers touched a gilded frame that seemed familiar. He lifted it out and stared at it, while Bertram gave a little cough of embarrassment.

'I couldn't let it be destroyed, Luther,' he said apologetically, as Kate's lovely young face stared back at them from the painting. 'I gave Chivers twenty pounds to return it to me.'

'The rascal!' Luther said, but discovered he wasn't angry.

His dream of a mercantile empire bearing his name was coming true despite Simon's attempts to oust him. He could afford to be lenient with Bertram, although he couldn't afford to appear weak.

'Kate mustn't know of its existence,' he warned Bertram. 'I'd prefer you get it out of the house. Sell it. Mansel Jenkins would probably give you a good price, eh? A portrait of his lost love.'

Bertram looked uncomfortable, and Luther wondered at it,

but had no time to probe the matter. There were many arrangements to make for his trip to the capital.

Again he wished Delphine were accompanying him. How would he bear it for a whole month, not to see her beauty and feel the warmth of that lovely body in his arms?

And yet his dream, his long-awaited dream was coming true. Delphine would still be his when he returned.

That evening Kate sought out Simon, her mood vexed after her talk with her aunt. She knocked and walked straight in to his rooms. He was sitting in an easy chair reading a newspaper, but jumped up at the sight of her, his face turning dull red.

'Kate! At last you acknowledge me.'

'This isn't a social visit,' she told him imperiously. 'I can't forgive or forget your disgusting behaviour towards me.'

He stepped forward, hands outstretched. 'Please, please forgive me.' He appeared distressed, but she didn't believe it. 'I can't go on like this,' he went on. 'You've ignored my existence for weeks. Isn't that enough punishment for my foolishness?'

'Not in my book!' she exclaimed indignantly. She straightened her back and drew her lace wrap more firmly around her bare shoulders. 'No punishment is adequate for your crime.' She sniffed. 'You should be horsewhipped, in my opinion.'

He took another step forward. 'And I'd gladly take the punishment,' he said eagerly, 'if it meant your forgiveness.' When she didn't answer his shoulders dropped. 'So, why are you here, Kate?'

'I'm told you've been worming your way into my aunt's affections like a poisonous snake.'

His lips twitched. 'Well, am I a worm or a snake? I can't be both.'

Kate's mouth tightened in ire. After insulting her he had the audacity to make fun of her. His moods changed so quickly from remorse to humour she doubted the sincerity of either.

'Without consulting me you provided Aunt Agnes with transport.' Kate's eyes narrowed with anger. 'That was just to put me in the wrong, wasn't it,' she accused. 'What a mean, low-down trick.'

'You're being petty and childish, Kate.' He scowled. 'The world doesn't revolve around you, you know,' he said stiffly. 'I provided what was needed, as any nephew would.'

'Nephew?'

'I'm Agnes's nephew by marriage,' he reminded her. 'Whether you like it or not. Besides, I admire her, especially the way she's stood up to Luther all these years.'

'Don't interfere in future,' Kate commanded. 'I'll provide for all my aunt's needs.'

His scowl deepened. 'Are you forbidding me to visit her again?'

'Of course not,' Kate said quickly. 'But you're always acting behind my back, keeping me in the dark; like you didn't tell me I was buying Mansel's house, and now this pony and trap.' Kate lifted her chin. 'I felt a complete fool.'

'Oh, so your pride is smarting, is it?' he said nastily. 'Or maybe it's your conscience. Too wrapped up in your little romances with Bertram or that scoundrel Mansel Jenkins to think of anyone else's comfort.'

She was affronted. 'How dare you?'

'Oh, I dare all right, Kate,' he said, taking yet another step towards her. 'I'd dare to do anything where you're concerned.' He paused, suddenly smiling at her in a way that made her scalp prickle. 'I'm surprised you're not afraid to be alone in the same room with me. I might attack you again.'

'Don't you come any closer,' she warned, edging towards the door. 'I'll scream.'

'Scream away, then,' he said, making a darting movement at her.

Kate whirled and fled, wrenching the door open. In the doorway, she turned her head to see if he followed. He'd hardly moved from his original position, and grinned at her in a most insolent way, and she realised she was the butt of his joke again. He was treating her as though she were a simple child, and her anger swelled.

'You're a damnable bounder, Simon Creswell.' She spat out the words. 'Acting the gentleman, but despite your fine clothes and glib tongue, you're just a common, ill-mannered, money-grubbing bounder.'

His face darkened, but he didn't move. 'I take that from no one, not even you, Kate.'

'I hate you,' she said viciously. 'A divorce is worth any shame and ridicule just to be rid of you.'

'You'll never be rid of me, Kate, I promise you,' he barked in fury. 'You'll be *my* wife for the rest of your life.'

23

---•◆•---

Kate was in the gallery above the hall when she heard conspiratorial voices below, and recognised her brother's intense tones and Delphine's breathy responses.

Kate hesitated, feeling guilty at eavesdropping, but as she turned to do the decent thing and retreat, Mansel's name was mentioned, and she held her ground. Curiosity getting the better of her, she leaned carefully over the banister.

'What's that bloody man doing here again?' Evan asked fiercely. 'Kate will be embarrassed.'

'Don't use that sort language before me, Evan,' Delphine snapped back, and he mumbled what sounded like an apology.

'I won't bar my friend from the house,' Delphine went on in a low voice. 'Just because your sister was fool enough to throw herself at him. God! She's pathetic.'

Kate clapped a hand to her mouth to stifle a gasp, feeling hot blood flood her neck and face. Everyone knew! Oh, the shame of it!

'Friend?' Evan's tone changed. 'Are you sure that's all he is, Delphine?'

'Oh, Evan, my dearest, of course! How could you doubt it?'

There was a silence except for the rustle of silk, and Kate ventured to peep down. They were in a passionate embrace, there, openly in the hall, where anyone might appear at any moment.

She was as shocked at their recklessness as at the ferocity and abandon of their kiss, and she drew back, suddenly ashamed that she'd witnessed emotion so primitive between two people. And yet she wouldn't move out of earshot. Her name had been mentioned and she must hear more.

'If ever I find you've been unfaithful to me, Delphine,' Evan said dangerously, 'I warn you, I won't be responsible for what I do.'

'You share me with Luther.' There was amusement in Delphine's whisper.

'That's different. Besides, I despise him,' Evan replied. 'I don't count an ageing man as a rival. But Mansel or any other man would be another matter entirely.' There was a catch in his voice. 'Don't force me to do something desperate, Delphine, for both our sakes.'

'I'm yours alone, Evan, dear, you must know it in your heart,' Delphine murmured, and Kate was astounded at her audacity and duplicity. 'No other man means anything to me.'

There was silence again but Kate was too scandalised to look. She couldn't move from her position until they'd gone.

'I'll come to your room tonight, my darling,' Delphine whispered. 'Just after midnight. Then I'll show you exactly how much you mean to me.'

There were intense and excited whispers from Evan. Kate couldn't distinguish his words, but Delphine gave a throaty laugh in response.

'And more, much more,' she said. 'I'm your slave, Evan, dearest, your bedroom slave. Do with me as you will.'

He sounded mollified by her answer.

'Oh, by the way,' Delphine murmured. 'I've invited Mansel to stay as a guest for a week or two.'

'What?' Evan's voice was razor sharp.

'A smokescreen, my darling,' Delphine cooed. 'Another man in the house will divert suspicion. Think! With Luther away we can enjoy each other every night, all night.' She gave a low laugh. 'And every morning, too.'

'I warn you, Delphine, I won't be betrayed.'

'Oh, come along, Evan, dear,' she said. 'We'll be missed shortly. I'll go in first. You follow in a minute or two.'

Delphine swished away. When Kate ventured a look Evan was leaning against one of the pillars in the hall, taking a cigarette case from his inside pocket. After a moment she gave a little cough and descended the stairs. He glanced up calmly as she came down, his face expressionless. She hardly knew him for the man who had a few minutes before behaved so outrageously with another man's wife.

She longed to tell him of Aunt Agnes's conviction that Delphine and Mansel were lovers, but held her tongue. He'd frightened her by the way he'd spoken earlier; so wildly as though desperate. She began to see him as a man who couldn't control his feelings. Pausing near him, somewhat confused, she struggled for something to say.

'Have you heard from Eirwen recently?' she asked, and then wished she hadn't for his expression became thunderous.

'Don't mention that woman's name again,' he said. 'That part of my life is over.'

'Don't be absurd!' Kate snapped. 'You've a son.'

'I *had* a son,' he said. 'I've disowned him along with his mother.'

'Evan! You can't mean that. It's inhuman, unnatural.' Appalled at his callousness she couldn't keep quiet any longer. 'I saw and heard you a few moments ago,' she said accusingly. 'Standing on this very spot, making love to Delphine. Disgraceful! That vile woman is destroying you, Evan. She's deceiving you. Aunt Agnes says—'

'Mind your own business, Kate,' he interrupted fiercely. 'You're hardly in a position to lecture me, considering the scandalous way you've been carrying on with Mansel Jenkins.'

With that he turned on his heel and headed towards the drawing-room, leaving Kate standing open-mouthed with shock and humiliation.

A few minutes passed before she found the courage to follow him. As she opened the door and went in she felt everyone would be looking at her with ridicule, but to her relief no one paid any attention to her entrance, except Simon, whom she pointedly ignored.

Luther was standing near the fireplace, with Delphine leaning against him in the crook of his arm, her hand on his chest, like a loving and faithful wife, while they both chatted to Mansel.

Kate pulled her glance away quickly, unable to bear the hypocrisy. Feeling suddenly isolated, she moved to stand with Bertram near the window, as he looked out at the darkening September evening.

'Penny for your thoughts,' she murmured softly as she came close to him.

He turned to smile at her, rather sadly. 'I was wondering what Paris would be like this time of year,' he said wistfully.

'It's beautiful at any time, so they say.' When he didn't reply she looked up into his face. 'You still long to leave me, then?'

His beautiful eyes were sorrowful, and the look wrung her heartstrings.

'You were never mine to leave, Kate,' he said softly. 'I need to find someone who does belong to me.'

'Oh, Bertram!'

At that moment, Chivers appeared, and the room was in general movement towards the dining-room. Bertram offered his arm and she gladly walked in with him, aware of Simon's scowling presence hovering nearby, but she kept her gaze firmly averted.

The atmosphere at the table was easy enough to begin with, but when Luther related how his nephew's opposition to his plans had finally and ignominiously collapsed, gloating over it, Simon sprang to his feet, his face clouded with bitterness.

'A rigged vote if ever there was one,' he burst out. He pointed a shaking finger down the table at Luther. 'That was no victory. That was chicanery.'

There were gasps around the table, and Kate thought he must have gone mad to say such a thing to his benefactor.

Luther looked profoundly shocked. 'How dare you?' he blustered. 'And at my own dinner table, too.'

'If I don't dare, no one will,' Simon said loudly. 'Your schemes are faulty and foolish, and your vanity will drive our company to ruin.'

Evan got to his feet, too. 'What's going on, Simon?'

'Sit down, both of you,' Luther bellowed, going red in the face, and Evan immediately sat.

Simon remained standing, his shoulders hunched belligerently. 'I won't sit down,' he shouted. He took long angry strides towards the head of the table, and Luther rose to face him.

'Have you gone completely insane?' Luther asked incredulously. 'Attacking me like this before everyone. You're making a spectacle of yourself, man. I hope our guest excuses you.' He glanced apologetically at Mansel. 'Mansel, my dear boy, you must pardon—'

'Damn any guests!' Simon interrupted in fury. 'I want them to know you're a charlatan.'

'That's defamation of character, I'll not tolerate—'

'I met Bevan Thomas in town earlier.' Simon shouted him down. 'He'd just returned from Cardiff, where you'd sent him on a wild-goose chase. He didn't even know a special meeting was called, so how could he appoint you his proxy?'

'He's my ally,' Luther stormed. 'It's a standing agreement. Thomas and I are in complete accord and we trust each other.'

'He says otherwise.'

'He's a liar!'

'Is he?' Simon nodded his head. 'You've got some explaining to do,' he said. 'For example, how deep is your involvement with Dr Penfold?'

'What?' Luther rocked back on his heels. 'What're you talking about?'

'More dirty, underhand work, perhaps,' Simon said. 'When the police went to Penfold's house to arrest him today on very serious charges, they found he'd absconded, but not before he'd managed to liquidate all his assets. He's known to have boarded a vessel bound for New York.'

'What's this to do with me?'

'Someone warned him,' Simon asserted in an accusing voice. 'Someone who feared what he could tell.' He pointed his finger at Luther again. 'I believe that someone is you. What did he know about you? Something so damning you helped an evil monster escape justice.'

'I've had enough of this outrage,' Luther shouted, throwing down his napkin. He took a step forward and wagged a finger in Simon's face. 'You're an ungrateful wretch. I lifted you from poverty, gave you employment, provided you with a rich wife, and you knife me in the back.'

'I owe you nothing,' Simon roared. 'I swore revenge on you the day my beloved mother was buried.'

'Revenge, eh?' Luther nodded. 'Well, you've overplayed your hand.'

'I demand you explain—'

'Be quiet!' Luther commanded in a thunderous voice. 'I see I've nurtured a viper. Up until this moment you were my sole heir.'

Simon looked surprised and Luther nodded.

'Yes, Simon. You're my flesh and blood so I willed all I possess to you.' He shook his head vehemently. 'But that's finished!'

Luther paused to look around the silent group at the table. His face was pallid, while dull red patches blotched his cheeks.

'As from this night,' he went on, his voice low, 'I disown you, Simon. You're cut from my will completely.'

He came shakily round the table to Delphine's chair and laid his hands on her shoulders.

'Instead, I leave all I possess to my dearest wife, Delphine; my house, my wealth and, yes, even my major share of the business.'

'Oh, Luther, my darling,' Delphine cooed. 'I'm so honoured.'

Kate felt sick at the look of ill-concealed avarice on her stepmother's face.

Luther raised a trembling finger again and pointed at Simon. 'You're finished,' he said, breathing heavily. 'I leave for London tomorrow, after I've seen my lawyer. When I return you'd better be gone from this house, you and your wife.'

With that he reached out a hand to Chivers who'd been standing by silent and inconspicuous throughout the bitter exchange.

'My room,' he said shakily, and Chivers stepped forward quickly to assist, leading him away.

Everyone stared at Simon.

'He's guilty, I tell you,' he said defensively. 'He let that monster, Penfold, get clear away to save himself. I suspect if Penfold had talked Luther would've gone to prison for the things he's done.'

His glance fell on Kate briefly before he strode from the room.

The silence that followed was broken by Delphine's tinkling laugh.

'My dears, what a performance,' she said lightly. 'Simon was never the diplomat, and now he's ruined his expectations.' Her glance turned on Kate. 'How will you like living in Sketty, I wonder, so far from the social whirl?'

Kate stood, fuming. 'Well, you've got all you wanted, Delphine,' she said wrathfully. 'I hope you're satisfied, but I doubt it. Leeches are never satisfied.'

Delphine merely smirked at the insult. 'You're right, Kate,' she said. 'I'm not satisfied, yet.'

'Don't think you've seen the back of me, because you haven't,' Kate went on heatedly, not caring what the others thought. 'Old Grove House will always be my home and no one will put me out. Simon can do as he likes, but I'll defy Luther to the bitter end.'

With that parting shot, she followed in Simon's wake.

The following morning, unwilling to mope, and determined to be about the house as much as possible, Kate was on her way to the library when she saw Luther's lawyer arrive. She paused as Mr Walters acknowledged her and asked her how she was, then he disappeared into Luther's study.

Kate stood in the hall a moment longer, wondering at the silence in the house. Simon hadn't been at the breakfast table, and she was curious. Probably he was still sulking in his room.

Watkins came by carrying a tray of coffee bound for the study.

'Where is Mr Creswell?' she asked him.

He looked surprised that she should ask. 'He left early this morning, Miss Kate, bag and baggage.'

Kate was astonished that he'd given up so easily. Hell would freeze over before she left her home to the likes of Delphine.

She went on to the library and, taking a book from the shelf, settled on the window seat to read. She was annoyed when Delphine strolled in, an impudent grin on her beautiful face.

'Why're you still here, Kate? Your husband left hours ago.'

'I've already told you,' Kate replied waspishly, closing the book with a snap. 'I've no intention of leaving, and you can't put me out.'

'We'll see about that,' Delphine said. 'When Luther's dead and everything's mine, there'll be nothing here for you.'

Kate stared, shocked. Those were terrible sentiments, even for Delphine. 'You anticipate your husband's death, then,' she rapped out. 'How convenient.'

'Luther isn't young,' Delphine said defensively. 'It could happen any time. When it does I'll sell the business and this dreadful old house.' She patted her coiffure. 'I'll marry Mansel Jenkins. He's desperately in love with me, worships me.'

'Huh! He's yet to discover what an evil, conniving bitch you are,' Kate sneered. 'He's a cad, so perhaps you deserve each other after all.'

Delphine was scornful. 'Better to be an evil bitch than a frigid milksop like you.'

Kate shook with suppressed anger. 'So, Luther will die,' she exclaimed. 'With a little help from his wife, perhaps? Maybe I should warn him.'

Kate was satisfied at last to see two pink spots appear on Delphine's otherwise flawless cheeks.

'You'd better watch your loose tongue, and keep your mouth shut,' she rasped. 'Or else something may happen to you, too.'

'Don't threaten me, Delphine,' Kate retorted. 'You think you're riding high now, but what if Luther finds out about your sordid little affairs with Mansel and my brother? Luther's a vengeful man.'

'He won't believe your jealous lies. He has only contempt for your intelligence,' Delphine said with confidence. 'Besides, you don't understand the power I have over him, over all men.' She gave a disdainful laugh. 'How could you possibly know, a virgin like you? I pleasure them in ways you couldn't even imagine.'

'You trollop!' Kate blurted in dismay. 'You disgusting high-class whore!'

'Oh dear! Are your ladylike sensibilities offended?' Delphine said mockingly. 'I'm surprised you even know the meaning of the word. Women like you mustn't own up to animal passions.' She laughed. 'You've no idea what you're missing.'

Kate felt contaminated even talking to her.

'I wouldn't be *you*, Delphine, for all the wealth in the world,' she said. 'You'll come to a bad end. Mark my words.'

Delphine looked amused. 'Perhaps you're right,' she said lightly. 'But at least I'll have lived.' She looked down her nose at Kate. 'While you, you pale pathetic creature, will never know true excitement, the thrill of conquest.' Delphine lifted her head proudly. 'Men have fought over me, even killed themselves because I threw them off.'

'You're despicable!' Kate whispered, shocked. 'I believe you're insane.'

Delphine's lip curled with disdain. 'And I've never liked you, Kate. I've watched your feeble attempts to snare my brother. So laughable! Now I have everything you once had, and no one will take it from me. No one.'

Her lips parted in a feral snarl.

'So, I warn you. If you get in my way I'll crush you, step on you like I would a filthy cockroach.'

24

Three Weeks Later, Early October

'Welcome home, sir,' Watkins said as Luther stepped down from the hansom cab. 'We weren't expecting you, and so late in the evening, too.'

Luther took a florin from his pocket. 'Give that to the cabbie,' he said to the footman. 'Then bring in my bags. Oh! And be very careful with that hatbox. A special gift for my wife.'

'Very good, sir.'

Luther was uplifted by a sense of satisfaction as he stepped through his own front door, to be greeted by Chivers. He was aglow with triumph, a feeling that had lasted throughout the long train journey from London.

'If I may be so bold as to say so, sir,' Chivers said softly as he helped him off with his overcoat, 'you're looking very well. Your stay in the capital has done you good.'

Luther straightened his waistcoat, and adjusted his cuffs. 'I've had a very successful few weeks,' he replied with en-thusiasm.

More successful than he'd imagined. His dream was finally reality. He'd accomplished the almost impossible, despite that rogue Penfold and his backstabbing nephew. He was making his mark on the outside world at last, and he felt magnanimous. He cocked his head to look up into Chivers's face.

'What do you think of a move to the big city, Chivers? Butler in a fine residence in Mayfair, no less.'

Chivers raised his eyebrows. 'A move, sir?'

'I can safely predict, my man, that this household, with a few exceptions, will be moved to London within six months.'

'I look forward to that, sir.'

Luther took out his pocket watch, noting how much time there was before dressing for dinner. A half-hour to spare. He'd promised Bertram a sitting for the portrait immediately on his return, and he intended to keep that promise.

'Where's my wife?'

'I, er . . . I believe Mrs Templar is in the old nursery. I mean, the studio, sir.'

Luther smiled. Delphine and Bertram were discussing his portrait, no doubt. Delphine had already said she couldn't wait to see it hung next to hers in the drawing-room.

After climbing two flights of stairs, Luther felt a little breathless as he finally reached the nursery door. Delphine wasn't expecting him home so soon, and he pictured the pleasure on her lovely face when he walked in and surprised her. He turned the doorknob carefully and, quietly pushing the door open, stepped inside.

One gas mantel only was lit, and in the draught from the open door its flickering light seemed to stir the room into seething movement. Instead of the murmur of quiet conversation he'd expected, there were other sounds, animal, primeval sounds, that made the hairs on the back of his neck stand on end.

Luther stared around, momentarily dumbfounded. Bertram had a woman in here, and they were engaged in some disgusting activity.

Was it Kathryn with him? This was scandalous, outrageous!

Luther lunged forward, intent on bringing the coupling to an end, and then he halted and stared incredulously.

On the couch under the large window was a writhing tangle of bare limbs, and two naked torsos, bucking and jerking with such ferocity he thought they must destroy each other. Mesmerised with shock, he could only stare as they performed the age-old dance of life, feeling his own blood pound in his veins, until moved by disgust, he shouted.

'Bertram! What's the meaning of this? I demand an explanation. Who is this woman?'

The sound of his voice had a startling effect on the pair, for they were suddenly limp and stilled, as though dead, an idea which Luther found equally shocking.

'Oh! God, no!' Bertram murmured, his tone mortified.

As though in slow motion the bodies disentangled themselves. The woman rose from the couch, and glided unhurriedly towards Luther, a swagger in her stride as though revelling in her nakedness.

Delphine! Luther's eyes bulged in disbelief. Delphine! It couldn't be her. It didn't make sense. He was hallucinating.

She stood before him, one hand on her hip, sweat glistening on every contour of her naked body. He stared transfixed at the mocking smile on her face, and thought himself in some terrible nightmare.

'So, Luther, you've caught us out at last. How clever of you.'

He opened his mouth to speak, to ask why, but no coherent sound came. His throat had closed up at the realisation of what he'd seen. He could only stare helplessly.

'What?' Delphine went on at his silence. 'I've been enjoying another man, and you've nothing sensible to say?'

'Delphine, for pity's sake,' Bertram murmured miserably from the couch, where he was trying to cover himself with a shawl. 'Why're you torturing him? It's inhuman.'

Luther managed to release his tongue, which had cleaved to the roof of his mouth, and struggled to speak. 'I . . . I can't believe what I see with my own eyes,' he croaked. 'It's a nightmare. It can't be real.'

'It's real enough,' she said. 'Bertram's been my lover since puberty. My first lover.' She smiled. 'But not my last.'

She stretched her arms high above her head in a languid movement, before bringing her hands down in stroking movements over her breasts, her belly and thighs.

Luther watched each gesture with the intensity of a mesmerised rabbit. His blood was pounding again, and there was a strange buzzing in his ears. He clutched at his collar with shaking fingers, feeling it was choking him.

'My lovemaking skills were taught to me by many lovers,' she said. 'I'll hone them on many more.' She laughed. 'Are you shocked that I'm unfaithful, Luther, or is it that I'm unfaithful with my own brother?'

Luther felt his collar shrink; it seemed to cut into the flesh of his throat, and his eyes were bulging again in their sockets. He wanted to rave and shout, but no words would come. Again he was locked in a terrible silence.

Delphine's amusement increased at his struggles. 'Are you jealous?' she asked. 'Do you want to kill me?'

With a supreme effort Luther took in a great breath. 'Don't speak,' he said gutturally. 'Don't say another word. I can't bear it.'

'Perhaps you want to kill yourself?' suggested Delphine.

'For God's sake, Delphi,' Bertram cried. 'Haven't we had enough of that?'

'Be quiet, Bertie.' Her expression was cold and her tone careless. 'If my husband can't live with our secret, then let him die. I'm tired of him, anyway.'

Luther tried to answer her but only a choking sound came from his throat. His eyes were beginning to blur and the room was spinning.

'I never loved you, Luther,' Delphine went on waspishly. 'I loved only your wealth, so you see, you've nothing to live for now. You might as well be dead.'

Suddenly the room began to revolve even faster, and he tottered to a cupboard nearby and leaned against it. Great tides of pain were rising in his chest, the flow of blood roaring in his ears. He felt at a distance from everything, and didn't know what was happening to him. He stretched out a shaking hand to her.

'Delphine . . . I'm ill . . .' He felt as though he were strangling, and lurched sideways. 'Delphine, please . . . call a doctor.'

'You pathetic little man! Why don't you die?' Her tone was vicious.

Bertram cried out in distress, but she took no notice.

'Kill yourself, Luther,' she ranted. 'Take some sleeping powders as your first wife did – or did she? Perhaps you killed her?'

'For God's sake, Delphi,' Bertram cried. 'Have some pity on the man.'

'Have pity? Why should I?' she said scathingly. 'He means nothing to me. It's time for the whole truth. Let's hope it's the end of him, then I'll be rich . . . we'll be rich.'

Luther clawed at his collar. 'Call Chivers,' he croaked.

'Bertram isn't my only lover, of course,' Delphine went on mercilessly. 'Evan, your own stepson, has made a cuckold of you, too. I've slept with him since I met him.'

357

'Evan?' Luther stared, the buzzing in his ears almost drowning out his own incoherent thoughts. 'Why, Delphine? Why? Didn't I give you everything you asked for?'

'It was never enough,' she said callously. 'It could never be enough. I want, I deserve more, much more. That's why I plan to marry Mansel Jenkins.' She laughed. 'Yes, he's also my lover. Very ardent and exciting a lover, too. I'll have a virile young husband instead of an old man.'

Luther stared at her, hardly recognising her as his wife. What manner of woman was she? A fiend, a devil? He had to get away from her, get out of this room, and find help.

He turned and staggered towards the door, but Delphine moved, suddenly blocking his way, her eyes gleaming with such hatred, Luther felt afraid, as the terrible pain in his chest and head throbbed.

'When you're dead and gone,' she hissed at him, 'I'll have all your wealth. When I marry Mansel I'll have his, too. Of course, my own dear Bertram will always be at my side.' She laughed. 'And in my bed.'

Suddenly finding strength from somewhere, Luther raised an arm as though to strike at her but she moved quickly out of reach.

'Get out!' he said, his voice strangled. 'Get out of my house, you filthy hellcat! You're no longer my wife.'

'You won't get rid of me so easily.' Delphine spat out the words. 'I'll dance on your grave yet.'

Beyond reason now, Luther stumbled towards the door, arms outstretched before him. But even as he moved forward she was right at his shoulder, spitting words of poison into his ear.

'You can't be rid of me, the scandal would ruin you. Do you hear me? I'll make it public. You'll be a laughing-stock. Ditch me and you can forget your dreams of a mercantile empire, you sorry little man. I win, Luther. I win everything!'

Luther reached the door and wrenched it open with what little strength he had left, and staggered along the corridor towards the staircase, Delphine's cruel laughter ringing in his ears.

He wanted to shout for help, but the powerful throb of blood in his head drowned out all thought, everything in the world, except his pain. His heart felt tight in his chest, and his head seemed as though it would explode. Terrified of what was happening to him, he lurched forward, clutching at his throat, and teetered at the top of the staircase. Someone must help him!

Kate was in the drawing-room well before the gong sounded, where she'd been most of the day, feeling a need to stake a claim since Luther's edict that she must leave.

At the piano, she let her fingers run over the keys, playing an old tune that had been her mother's favourite. She was startled when the door suddenly burst open and Luther staggered in, taking uneven steps to the fireplace.

Kate jumped up. 'Luther! What on earth's wrong?'

She was appalled at his appearance. His collar and cravat were awry, his hair wildly disarrayed, and his features were grotesque, blotched red and white.

Kate ran to him and grasped his arm as he reached the fireplace, his hands outstretched to clutch the mantelpiece.

'Luther, you're ill. Sit down. Whatever's the matter?'

She tried to draw him towards a chair, but he flung her off, his eyes wild.

'Take your filthy hands off me, you dirty slut!' he cried out in a terrible voice. 'I've done with you.'

'Luther!'

He reached on to the hearth and lifted up the heavy iron poker, raising it above his head in a threatening manner. Kate recoiled from him, and screamed in terror at the look of hatred on his face. But he turned from her and struck instead at the portrait of Delphine above the mantelpiece. The iron crook at the end smashed into it, slashing a jagged tear in the canvas. He struck again and again.

'There!' He turned on her, brandishing the iron. 'There, you whoring bitch!' he shouted in a high-pitched voice. 'I'll destroy you as I've destroyed this likeness. You'll rot in hell, you and your lovers.'

'Luther!' Kate cried out, cringing at his fury, her fingers clutching at her throat in fright. 'What're you doing?'

He tottered again and the iron dropped from his fingers to clatter into the hearth. His mouth was open and his eyes wide as he stared at her, but instinctively Kate knew he saw nothing but his own private hell. He swayed, and before she could reach him, he crashed down in a heap before the hearth. Kate let out a piercing scream.

'What the hell's going on?' Chivers burst into the room, and seeing his master prostrate on the carpet rushed to kneel beside him.

''Strewth!'

He lifted Luther's head to support it on his thigh, feeling for a pulse in his throat and then looked wide-eyed into Kate's face as she kneeled next to him.

'This is bad,' he said in a shaky voice. 'Very bad. I blame myself.'

'What do you mean?'

'I could've prevented it,' Chivers said quietly. 'But I thought it was time that vicious trollop got what's coming to her. I never dreamed this would happen.'

'Chivers!' Kate cried, feeling near hysteria. 'I don't understand.'

'Never mind that now. The master's had a seizure. Ring that bell,' Chivers ordered. 'We've got to get him to his room and send for a doctor.'

Watkins came and the two men carried Luther up the stairs and to his bedroom. Kate followed in their wake, wringing her hands, not knowing what she should do. Suddenly she wished with all her heart that Simon were here.

Watkins was sent to find a physician, while Kate sat at Luther's bedside waiting. Evan had been out most of the day, and hadn't returned, and even after all the noise and fuss there was no sign of Delphine or Bertram, which Kate found very strange.

She looked at Luther's death-like face, and realised Delphine had done something so terrible, it had shattered her husband's mind completely.

Kate clutched her cold hands together. She had no love for her stepfather, but was appalled at what had happened to him, and was afraid, too. If Luther died this night, Delphine would control everything, and Kate's whole life, her whole past history would be destroyed.

The doctor arrived, a tall, distinguished-looking man, who introduced himself to her as Dr MacNaish.

'You're his daughter, and the next of kin, I take it,' Dr MacNaish said to Kate as he removed his coat, and stepped to the bedside to take the patient's wrist between finger and thumb.

'No, she's not! Mrs Creswell has nothing to do with this household,' Delphine said loudly from the doorway, and sailed in with a rustle of silks. 'I'm Mrs Templar.'

She turned to Kate, her expression hostile.

'Please leave immediately, Kate. The doctor and I wish to be alone.'

Infuriated, Kate retreated, but after a while went to find Chivers, to demand an explanation of his strange remarks earlier.

Mrs Perkins and Daisy were in the kitchen. Chivers, she was told, was in his room, packing.

Kate climbed the back stairs to the servants' quarters under the eaves with dread in her heart. What was happening to her world?

In one of the larger bedrooms she found Chivers, with a battered portmanteau on the narrow iron bedstead, which he was filling from the chest of drawers.

'What're you doing?' she asked, annoyed.

His eyes widened when he saw her, but he didn't stop placing clothes carefully in the case.

'Packing, Miss Kate. Getting out. You ought to do the same. Get off after that husband of yours, and before the master pops off.'

'But why?'

He paused for a moment. 'It's all up here, Miss Kate. The master was all that stood between her and me; something I could hold over her head, like, while he was fit and in his wits. Now he's laid low she'll have me, probably on a trumped-up charge of stealing the silver, or something.' He gave a snarl. 'She's a viper, that one, a blooming viper.'

'But my stepfather isn't dead yet,' Kate said. 'And you're needed here, Chivers. You're deserting him.'

'Believe me, Miss Kate, he's as good as dead,' the butler said seriously. 'I listened at the door, heard what the doctor told her. Can't move, can't speak, and isn't expected to live more than a couple of months, if that.'

Kate put her hand to her mouth, overcome by the news. She'd hated Luther for so long, but never wished him dead, and certainly not a living death as Chivers was describing.

'What can we do?'

'Nothing,' Chivers retorted bitterly. 'That bitch's got hold of everything.' He shut the lid of the portmanteau with a bang, and then looked at her. 'Gather up what valuables you can, Miss Kate, jewellery that belonged to your mother for instance, and get out. Otherwise, she'll claim everything.'

'I'm not running away,' Kate exclaimed defiantly.

'More fool you then,' Chivers muttered as he lifted the portmanteau on to the floor. 'She'll dismantle this family, this household and everything in it.'

He paused and looked solemnly at Kate.

'I've rubbed shoulders with some dangerous people in my time,' he said. 'But never one like her. It's true what they say. The devil is a woman.'

He stepped past her to reach for his coat and bowler hanging on a peg behind the door, and put them on.

'Goodbye, Miss Kate. Think about what I said. Get away from her before she does you a mischief.'

She watched in astonishment as he manoeuvred the heavy portmanteau on to his back, and trundled off down the back stairs.

Kate didn't pause any longer, but hurried to her own rooms. She had no intention of leaving Old Grove House to the mercy of her stepmother. But she needed an ally. Simon must return. He was the only one who could deal effectively with Delphine. But how to get word to him? She was in no doubt Delphine had already taken charge, even of the stables.

Watkins answered her summons.

'What instructions has Mrs Templar given about dinner?' she asked.

'Dinner is cancelled, Miss Kate. Instead there'll be a cold collation laid out in the dining-room. The family . . .' He coughed. 'Or what's left of it, may help themselves as they wish.' He gave another little cough. 'Chivers has bolted, Miss Kate.'

'I know,' she said, taking a thoughtful turn about the room as she spoke. 'A cold collation, eh? Then you won't be missed this evening with no table to wait on.'

A worried frown creased his young face and his gaze was uncertain. Kate took a purse from the bureau drawer and brought out a sovereign.

'Put on your coat and hat, secretly, mind,' she said. 'Go down to the main road and find a hansom cab. Take it to Mr Creswell's house in Sketty.' She handed him a slip of paper. 'I've written the address here.'

Panic spread on his face. 'Oh, I don't know. The mistress watches us servants like a hawk. Lose my position, I could.'

'You'll do it, Watkins,' Kate said in a firm voice. 'For the master's sake. Mr Creswell's needed here very badly.'

'Very good, Miss Kate.'

Kate began pacing again. 'Ask Mr Creswell – no, *tell* him that he must return to Old Grove House tonight. Explain what's happened to Mr Templar. And, Watkins, anything left out of the sovereign you can keep.'

He brightened. 'Oh, thank you, Miss Kate.'

'Now get along quickly,' she urged. 'And remember, no one's to know you've left the house or where you're going. Do you understand?'

Watkins grinned and touched his forelock. 'Leave it to me.' He turned away and then paused to glance back at her over his shoulder. 'The house'll need a new butler,' he said hopefully. 'I'd like to apply for that position.'

Kate lifted a hand and pointed to the door. 'Be gone about your business,' she said sternly, though trying to hide a smile at his impudence. 'There'll be no house or family to butle for if Mr Creswell can't save it.'

Kate gave up waiting and went dispiritedly to bed, leaving a candle burning next to the clock. A small sound woke her suddenly, and she saw the candle had burned very low, although giving enough light to see the time was three in the morning.

The sound came again, closer. With a jolt she realised she wasn't alone and sat bolt upright in bed.

'Who's there? Is that you, Ethel?'

A tall figure appeared out of the shadows and stood at the side of the bed.

'No. It's me.'

'Simon!' Kate said, drawing the bed covers around her. 'What're you doing here?'

'You sent for me, damn it!'

'I didn't expect you to barge into my bedroom at this unearthly hour,' Kate retorted spiritedly. 'Why didn't you come sooner?'

'It wasn't possible. There were things to see to.'

To her annoyance, he sat down on the bed. Kate hastily edged away, moving her legs and feet to the other side of the bed. She didn't like this new familiarity.

'How's Luther?' he asked. 'What's the situation?'

'Well, he's still alive apparently, but only just,' Kate said. 'Delphine won't allow anyone near him, apart from the doctor, and a grim-faced nurse.'

'She can't stop me seeing him,' Simon said firmly. 'He's my uncle.'

'Delphine's ruling with an iron fist,' Kate said. 'Luther must have twenty-four-hour nursing care, apparently, so Daisy tells me.'

'I've already been to his rooms. He's not there. Where is he?'

'On the floor above this room,' Kate explained. 'Within hours Delphine had the nursery converted into a sickroom. It has an adjoining room for the night nurse.'

'Keeping him isolated from the rest of the house,' Simon mused. 'I wonder why.'

He rose from the bed.

'I'll need to call a special meeting of the board. Someone must replace Luther as chairman, and quickly, before Delphine has a chance to act.'

'You should take over,' Kate said quickly.

Simon smiled ruefully. 'There'll be plenty of opposition to that.' He shrugged. 'Still, I can do nothing until a more civilised hour.' He took off his coat, throwing it on the bed. 'Meanwhile, I'll get some sleep.'

'Not in here,' Kate said quickly.

'I've been to my old room,' Simon said. 'The bed's already been stripped down, and Mansel Jenkins is in the guest room.'

'Then share with Evan or Bertram.'

'Don't be absurd, Kate.' His tone was brittle. 'This is as much my apartment as yours. Surely you can spare half the bed.'

'Certainly not!' Kate was fuming. 'Just because I sent for you it doesn't give you leave to take advantage of me. You're here to deal with Delphine, nothing more.'

'Then I'll sleep on the sofa in the sitting-room,' he said bitterly.

*   *   *

Simon was gone from the sofa when Kate glanced into the sitting-room before going downstairs the following morning, and there was no sign of him at the breakfast table. Mansel was the only other person there, tucking into a full breakfast with obvious gusto. Kate's mouth twisted in anger when she saw him totally unconcerned with what was happening in the house.

'You're still here, then,' she said pointedly. 'I thought you'd have had the decency to leave yesterday, immediately after Luther's seizure.'

'Delphine begged me to stay,' he said casually. 'Moral support, you know.'

'Moral support, my foot!' she said with deep disdain while walking stiffly to the chiffonier to fill a dish with porridge. She brought it to the table, and he frowned at her.

'What do you mean by that?' he asked uneasily, raising a coffee cup to his lips.

She glared at him. 'Oh, don't pretend to be the innocent with me, Mansel,' she snapped. 'You're probably the reason why Luther has suffered this stroke. He's discovered you and Delphine are lovers.'

Mansel almost spluttered out a mouthful of coffee. 'Of course he doesn't know!' he cried, then looked confused and shamefaced at his slip. 'I mean . . . this is outrageous, Kate. How dare you accuse me of such dishonourable behaviour.'

Kate uttered a scornful hoot. 'You snobbish bungling hypocrite!' she said scathingly. 'You're beneath contempt.'

He stood up, red-faced, and threw his napkin on the table. 'I won't stay here to be insulted,' he said.

'Then go, and good riddance!' Kate said loudly, as he strode from the table. 'And don't come back. You're not welcome here.'

'That's for Delphine to decide,' he said huffily from the doorway. 'I think you'll find, Kate, your days are numbered in this house.'

Suddenly Kate lost her appetite and pushed away the dish of porridge untouched. As she rose to leave, Watkins appeared with a fresh pot of coffee and some croissants.

'Watkins, have Mr Creswell's room made up right away, please,' she ordered. 'He'll be staying indefinitely.'

'Watkins!' Delphine's ringing voice sounded in the doorway. 'You'll disregard any instructions from Mrs Creswell from now on. She's in no position to give orders in this house.'

The footman hovered, looking in bewilderment from one woman to the other.

'Well! Are you deaf, man?' Delphine cried irritably at him. 'If you want to remain in my service you'll get about your business now.'

'Very good, Mrs Templar,' he said, looking decidedly frightened, and hurried away.

Delphine glowered at Kate. 'How dare you issue orders to *my* servants in *my* house.'

'*Your* house? So, my stepfather's dead, is he?'

Delphine looked discomfited for a moment. 'Of course he isn't dead.'

'Well, you're acting as though he were,' Kate said. 'Obviously, you can't wait for it to happen.'

'As a matter of fact,' Delphine said, 'he appears a little better.'

A spasm passed across her face briefly, and Kate would have sworn it was a spasm of fear.

'He came out of his stupor in the night,' Delphine went on in a low voice. 'He was able to make himself understood to the nurse well enough to ask for water.'

'I insist on seeing him,' Kate said immediately. 'And Simon should see him, too.'

'Out of the question,' Delphine grated defiantly. 'Dr Mac-Naish is with him now. Luther's still a very sick man. I don't want him upset.'

Kate looked at her stepmother with narrowed eyes. 'What're you afraid of, Delphine? Does Luther know about your lovers? Has he threatened to throw you out?'

Delphine's eyes snapped. 'Be quiet!'

'I'm not a servant,' Kate retorted. 'You can't shut me up.'

Delphine's lips tightened, and she looked furious. 'I've warned you once to stay out of my way,' she grated. 'Whatever happens will be your own fault.'

'Your threats don't frighten me,' Kate said resolutely. 'But you're frightened, aren't you, Delphine? Luther will recover and he'll change his will again. You'll be destitute.'

Delphine's answering look was venomous. 'Get out of this house,' she rasped. 'Before you're carried out feet first.'

'Are you actually threatening my life?' asked Kate incredulously.

Delphine remained silent, her eyes filled with hate, and Kate felt a chill race up her spine, and was thankful Simon was at hand.

Delphine really was dangerous, but she was also fearful, and therefore capable of anything. Luther might recover long enough to take his revenge. How much longer would she allow him to live?

25

Mid October

Bertram was about to go down to breakfast when Delphine burst into his room and, rushing at him, grasped the lapels of his coat in panic, looking up into his face, her eyes wide.

'He's spoken,' she said, her voice hushed with dread. 'He said terrible things, promised all kinds of revenge. Bertie, I'm afraid. What're we to do?'

Bertram pulled her clutching hands away from his coat impatiently. 'How can you blame him after what he witnessed?' he asked bitterly. 'How many more men must die for you, Delphi?'

He'd been wondering how much longer he could endure the situation, and was having serious doubts about her sanity.

'Luther mustn't be allowed to consult with his lawyer,' Delphine said feverishly, eyes wide and staring. 'He mustn't meet with Simon Creswell. Simon's already taken steps to prevent me getting control of the firm,' Delphine whimpered. 'Everyone's against me!'

Sickened, Bertram tried to turn away from her, yet he was heartened to know Luther was recovering some of his abilities. It salved his conscience somewhat, although guilt and blame were heavy on him.

'He mustn't talk to anyone,' Delphine clamoured, clutching

at his coat again. 'I won't lose everything now. You must stop him. Do something, Bertie!'

Bertram shook his head. 'I wash my hands of it all,' he said decisively. 'I'm leaving, Delphi, leaving you and all this sorry mess.'

She looked at him, appalled and disbelieving. 'You can't leave,' she burst out furiously. 'You can't exist without me.'

'I don't care, don't you understand?' he cried, waving his arms about to emphasise his feelings of helplessness. 'I don't care whether I live or die. I lead a useless and sordid existence.'

'You have your art.'

'I've nothing,' he shouted. 'You've seen to that.'

She opened her mouth to protest, but he shouted her down.

'You've done this to me, Delphi, can't you see it? You destroy everything and everyone you touch . . . even me.'

With a murmur of deep hurt, she reached forward, trying to touch his face, but he pushed her hand away, filled suddenly with revulsion.

'You've taken my very life,' he said hoarsely. 'And made it into an ugly yoke. I can't bear it any longer. I've had enough.'

'You ungrateful creature,' Delphine retorted in pealing tones. 'I gave you everything.'

Bertram stared at her for a moment, realising he was seeing her for the first time, seeing behind that haunting beauty that had enslaved even him, her own brother.

'You gave me nothing but degradation and guilt,' he said, a catch in his voice. 'You fed off me, Delphi, like a shark feeds off its prey.'

She looked furious and her eyes narrowed as she glared at him. 'Who's turned you against me? Is it that mealy-mouth Kate?'

'It's you, Delphi; you're the one who's turned me,' he

shouted. 'You've never let me be my own man. I've been your puppet, your plaything since we were children. You don't want me to be happy; you don't even love me, not even as a brother.'

'That's not true,' Delphine said. 'All we ever had was each other, but now it's different, don't you see. We have wealth now, or at least we will when Luther's dead.'

Bertram grimaced, filled with disgust. 'Don't talk like that!'

'It's the only way. He's determined to ruin me.' She paused, her face turning pale. 'Every day he gets stronger. He's got a will of iron. I underestimated him.'

Suddenly, despite his revulsion at what they'd done, because she was his sister, he felt pity for her, and grasped both her hands. 'Let's get out, Delphi,' he said impulsively, putting thoughts of freedom out of his mind. He'd sacrifice it to save her. 'Now, this minute, you and me. Leave everything behind and start afresh. I'll . . .' He gulped, quelling a sob. 'I'll stay with you, I promise.'

'No!' She pulled her hands from his grasp. 'I won't let him destroy me,' she said harshly. 'You must help me, Bertie. Go where you will afterwards, but help me to be rid of him first.' She paused. 'For all we've been to each other.'

'What?' He stared in disbelief. 'What're you suggesting?'

'He's only half alive,' she said persuasively. 'He'll never walk again; he'll always be dependent on someone. What kind of a life is that for a man such as he is . . . was?'

He stared at her in horror. 'You're unbelievable, Delphi. Murder? You're insane.' He shook his head. 'It's crazy even to think you can get away with it.'

She reached forward to put a hand on his chest, that certain smile on her face, inviting and suggestive, the smile he'd always given in to, but no more. With an angry exclamation, he recoiled from her, and her expression hardened.

'You'll do it,' she commanded. 'You'll do it for me, because you can't refuse me, Bertie. You never could refuse me anything.'

'I won't commit murder for you,' he said, shaking his head. 'I'm leaving this house before the week's out, and I don't care whether I have a penny to my name or not.'

He half turned away then looked at her with contempt.

'To think I was willing to sacrifice my freedom to give you another chance.' He shook his head sadly. 'I've finished with you, Delphi. It's all over.'

Stepping around her, he left her standing alone in his room.

Arriving home later than usual, Evan paid off the cabman, glad to be back from the shop. The front door stood open, but no servant appeared. He stepped into the hall, cursing the slackness of the household since the onset of his stepfather's illness and the butler's departure.

Then someone came out of the drawing-room. It was the older night nurse carrying a large wine glass full to the brim with port. She didn't see him immediately, and jumped visibly when he spoke.

'How's my stepfather this evening, Nurse?'

Her reddish face flushed even deeper for some reason, and she looked confused for a moment. 'About the same, sir,' she answered at last.

Evan stared at the glass.

'It's for Mr Templar,' she said quickly. 'He asked for it.'

'His speech has improved then?' Evan asked eagerly, anxious about his inheritance. It worried him what would happen should Luther die. In that case he should get his money immediately, but he wasn't sure.

'When will he be well enough for visitors?'

'Most any time during the day, sir,' the nurse said. 'Patients such as Mr Templar need stimuli. He can't move, and speech is difficult for him. Long hours alone make him frustrated and anxious.'

Evan frowned. Delphine had assured him most emphatically that the doctor forbade all visitors. He stared at the nurse, the coarse redness of her cheeks, and the rather shifty look in her eyes. Was she competent? He looked pointedly at the glass again.

'Should he be drinking port in his condition?'

She flushed. 'A sip or two won't do any harm, sir.'

Balancing the glass carefully, she hurried away towards the green baize door at the back of the hall leading to the back staircase. With a shrug, Evan climbed the main stairs, resolving to see Luther as soon as possible. Now was the time to insist he got his money. In his weakened state Luther couldn't refuse.

He was surprised to find Delphine waiting for him in his rooms. It was obvious she'd been crying, and he hurriedly took her in his arms. She leaned her head against his chest, clinging to him, sobbing softly.

'Whatever's wrong, my darling?' Evan asked anxiously. 'Is it Luther? Is he worse? I was just asking his nurse—'

'Evan, dearest,' she wailed. 'I can't go on!' She threw back her head to look up at him. 'My life's unbearable without you, without the comfort of your love.'

'Delphine, my dear.' He was awed by the deep passion in her voice, and the look of misery in her glistening eyes.

'You've treated me coldly these last few days,' she whispered. 'Don't say you've grown tired of me already?' Her tone was piteous. 'Or do you doubt my love because we've not been together since Luther's collapse?'

She looked fearfully into his face. Evan didn't know how to answer. He'd had terrible nights of doubt, tortured by the suspicion she was with Mansel Jenkins.

When he didn't answer a sob escaped her. 'There's nothing between Mansel and myself. What must I do to make you believe me?' Her lips trembled. 'How could you even think it of me, Evan?'

He couldn't meet her gaze.

'You couldn't be more wrong,' she went on quickly. 'He adores me, of course, and it amuses me, but I feel nothing for him.' She shook her head vehemently. 'Nothing at all. I swear it on my life.'

He gripped her shoulders, suddenly overcome by anxiety and anger. 'Your life, Delphine, that's exactly what you risk,' he said raggedly. 'If I find out Jenkins is your lover I'll . . . I'll kill you, I mean it.'

Despite his threat, her smile was tender. 'Only you have my heart, Evan, now and for ever.'

She reached up and kissed him lightly on the lips. He felt the surge of desire that always came with her touch, and gathering her fiercely into his arms, kissed her fervently.

When he released her she lay her head on his chest. 'I've stayed away because it wasn't right for us wantonly to enjoy each other while Luther lay in his sickbed, helpless,' she said quietly. 'I have my principles.'

He couldn't help suspicions invading his mind again. 'Then why are you here now?' he asked, his voice harsh.

'Because I'm only human!' she wailed loudly. 'I can't stand being apart from you any longer.'

She looked up at him with glistening eyes, desperation in her gaze. 'Help me, please, Evan,' she whispered. 'For pity's sake, help me.'

'Darling,' he said, remorseful of his doubts. 'You shan't suffer any longer. What can I do?'

She gripped his coat with an urgency that astonished him.

'We must be together, Evan. I'll go mad otherwise.'

'But how?' Evan asked miserably.

'I'm so unhappy, Evan.'

She pulled away and went to stand before the fireplace, her back turned to him, her shoulders drooping.

'Since Luther came out of his stupor he's a changed man,' she said, her voice quivering. 'He hates me for some unknown reason. Wishes me dead. I think he's gone mad.'

'It's the illness,' Evan suggested uncertainly. 'Perhaps the medicine is affecting him.'

'No.' Delphine turned to him, shaking her head, her expression solemn. 'It goes much deeper than that. He says terrible things to me, and treats me like a leper.' She lifted a handkerchief to dab at her eyes. 'I've begged him to see you, Evan, hoping you could talk some sense into him, but he won't hear of it. He says he hates and despises you as much as he hated . . .'

She paused, staring at him wide-eyed, her trembling fingers pressed to her lips for a moment.

'Oh, Evan! I hardly dare say it,' she breathed. 'Luther hates you as much as he hated your mother, Alice, and wishes you were dead, too.'

The muscles in his face stiffened, and anger swelled in his chest. Delphine ran to him and, reaching up, took his face in her hands.

'Evan, you're a saint; so forgiving of a man who's almost

destroyed your family. Many men would kill him for that.' She
gently pressed her mouth to his for a moment. 'I admire you
for your brave restraint, my dear.'

'I'm no different from any other man, Delphine,' Evan said
in a hard voice. 'I can't forgive or forget. I hate him as much as
he hates me, and I thirst for revenge. I wish the seizure had
killed him. We'd all be happier if Luther were gone.'

She laid her head against his chest. 'I'm beginning to hate
him, too,' she said. 'He keeps us apart. If you grow tired of
waiting for me I'll kill myself, Evan. I mean it!'

'I'll never leave you,' he reassured her and, drawing her
closer, kissed her tenderly.

'If only he *were* dead,' she said softly. 'After all, he's a
helpless cripple with nothing to live for. It would be a kindness
really.'

'I'd gladly kill him, but not for kindness,' Evan said harshly.

'Do you mean it?'

'Yes.'

She snuggled closer to his chest. 'I know how it could be
done,' she said quietly. 'Easily and quickly, without anyone the
wiser.'

Evan tensed, startled, and she pulled away from his arms.

'You're shocked that I'd say such a thing,' she blurted,
looking up anxiously into his face. 'You don't love me enough.'

'I love you beyond all reason, Delphine.'

'Then you think me wicked to wish Luther dead.'

'No,' he said soberly. 'We both wish it, and haven't we
suffered too long?'

She clutched at his hands and brought them to her breasts,
where he could feel the pounding of her heart.

'I'm afraid,' she whispered.

'Don't be,' he said quickly, his mind racing with this new idea. With Luther dead all money worries would be ended. 'You won't be involved. Tell me your plan.'

'Every night,' Delphine said. 'The nurse goes down to the drawing-room and stays there for about an hour or more, drinking port, while the rest of the house sleeps.'

Evan snapped his fingers. 'I caught her red-handed earlier smuggling a glass of port upstairs. She said it was for Luther, but clearly she's the tippler.'

Delphine nodded eagerly. 'While she's gone you could slip into the nursery from the old iron staircase at the back of the house. Luther's weak and couldn't struggle or cry out if a pillow were held over his face.'

'Everyone would think he died quietly in his sleep,' Evan said thoughtfully. 'With the nurse tipsy she might not notice until morning.'

'Oh, Evan, my darling.' Delphine threw her arms around his neck. 'Do it tonight. I'll be a widow by morning, and free!'

He stared at her excited expression and a shadow of doubt crept into his mind again. She'd betrayed Luther. Perhaps she'd betray him, too. By God! If he couldn't have her no one would!

'Yes, I'll do it, Delphine,' he said solemnly. 'But only if Mansel Jenkins leaves this house immediately, only if you promise never to see him again.'

Her smile was strained, and she lifted her hand to her throat. 'Evan, my darling, don't you trust me yet?'

'Those are my terms,' he said gruffly. 'If he means nothing to you why would you object?'

She looked chastened. 'I don't object,' she said quickly. 'In fact, I'll see him straight away, make some excuse . . .'

'No!' Evan said. 'I'll tell him myself. I want him gone before dinner.'

She caught her bottom lip between her teeth, looking at him doubtfully. 'You will do it tonight, won't you, darling? No last-minute pangs of conscience. You'll do it for us, for our love?'

'I promise you,' he said, suppressing the chill that ran up his spine. 'Luther Templar will die this night.'

26

Unable to sleep, Kate got out of bed, slipped into her wrap, and walked across to the French windows. The back lawns and the shrubbery below were bathed in moonlight, so bright it lit up her room. It was a beautiful night, but she couldn't appreciate it, not with her mind in turmoil.

If she hadn't lingered in the small sitting-room at the top of the stairs earlier that evening, she wouldn't have overheard the bitter exchange between Mansel and her brother in the gallery outside, and wouldn't be worried out of her wits now.

Evan had sounded incensed, almost hysterical, as he declared that he and Delphine would marry when Luther died.

Evan couldn't marry while Eirwen still lived yet he'd sounded so adamant, and a chill ran up her spine at the malevolence in his voice, as though he knew the exact moment of Luther's passing.

Mansel must have been alarmed, too, for within the hour he'd gone, bag and baggage.

Kate pulled her wrap closer around herself, feeling the chill again. She wished Simon were still in the next room, asleep on the sofa. She'd wake him, discuss it with him; but he'd moved to the guest room as soon as Mansel vacated it, even before the sheets were changed.

She was about to turn back to the bed when a sound outside made her pause. Her heart jumped into her mouth as she realised someone was on the iron staircase and climbing up. Fearfully, she stepped behind the drapes and waited. A figure appeared cautiously, first head and shoulders, and then stepped on to the landing outside her window.

Kate covered her mouth with her hand to prevent a gasp escaping as, in the brilliant moonlight, she recognised Evan. He paused for a moment, looking towards her window, and then continued climbing the stairs, which led to Luther's sickroom.

When his feet had disappeared from view, Kate carefully opened the French windows and stepped out. The platform creaked under her weight, and seemed to tremble. Grasping the handrail to steady herself, Kate looked up. There was no sign of Evan on the stairs above.

What was he doing in the sickroom at this time of night? She felt that inexplicable chill again and began to climb towards the nursery. Standing at the open doors she looked in.

The room, lit only by the moon, seemed like a stage. Luther's prone figure lay on the bed, looking smaller than he had before. Evan stood beside him, a feather pillow in his hands. As Kate watched he lowered it slowly towards the sick man's face. Galvanised by horror, Kate sprang forward into the room.

'In God's name! What're you doing, Evan?'

With a startled gasp, Evan jumped back from the bed, and spun round to face her, the pillow slipping from his hands to fall on the floor. Kate's cry was louder than she intended, and Luther uttered something incomprehensible, although his eyes remained closed.

'I have to do it, Kate,' Evan bleated defensively. 'For Mother, for the family.'

'Have you gone raving mad?' she hissed, appalled and

outraged. 'Were you about to commit murder? I can't believe it!'

'He deserves it,' he hissed back viciously. 'He stole the company from our family, and almost ruined me. And look what he did to you. I tell you, he deserves it.'

'You're lying to yourself, Evan. You're doing it for Delphine,' Kate said desperately, taking a hesitant step towards him. 'She put you up to this, didn't she? Admit it.'

'All right!' Evan's face twisted in fury. 'I'll divorce Eirwen. Delphine loves me. She does, Kate! She'll be mine when he's gone.'

'You blind fool!' Kate said hoarsely, straining not to shout. 'She'll never marry you. That venal bitch has you tied in knots, just so you'll do her dirty work for her. As soon as Luther's dead she'll toss you aside.'

'It's not true!'

'Of course it's true!' insisted Kate. 'She's laughing behind your back, laughing at us all. She's nothing better than a common whore.'

Evan raised a fist, his eyes blazing in fury. 'I should strike you down for those words, Kate.'

'Go on, then!' Kate hissed defiantly. 'That's the second time you've threatened me with violence. Perhaps you'd murder your own sister, too, for the sake of that evil she-devil?'

Luther cried out briefly, startling them both, and his hand, lying on the counterpane, twitched spasmodically. It made Kate's skin crawl.

'Where's the nurse?' she whispered, looking about her, suddenly more frightened of being caught here than of her brother.

'Tippling in the drawing-room,' he said harshly, although his fury had subsided.

'She could return any minute,' she said urgently. 'We mustn't be found here.' She darted forward and grasped her brother's arm. 'Come on!' she urged, her heart in her mouth.

He resisted, staring down at the sick man. 'I promised Delphine . . .' he began, but his shoulders drooped dispiritedly.

Tugging at him, she drew him towards the French windows, and he allowed himself to be led out on to the iron stairs, and went before her down to her room.

Once inside, Kate closed the windows, and lit a candle. Evan sat on the bed, his face white in the flickering candlelight.

'Delphine's as desperate as I am,' he said plaintively. 'We're at our wits' end.'

'Rubbish!' Kate replied, impatient with him now they were out of danger. 'Delphine's never been desperate in her life. The woman hasn't a nerve in her body.'

She stood in front of him, marvelling how weak he seemed now, hardly like a man capable of murder, yet that schemer had driven him to it.

'Delphine has bad blood, Evan,' she said gravely. 'And the morals of an alleycat. She made no secret of it to me.'

He jumped up, his expression suddenly thunderous again. 'How dare you insult her?' he burst out. 'You don't know her. You've never taken the trouble to be her friend.'

'Delphine can be no woman's friend,' she cried angrily. 'She despises other women. You're no more than a pathetic pawn in her game, but you're too much of a fool to see it.'

'You're jealous of her,' Evan blurted. 'Because of Mansel Jenkins.'

'She and Mansel deserve each other,' Kate retorted furiously. 'She's openly boasted to me that she intends to marry

384

him. He's free and wealthy. He'll inherit his father's business, and that's what she's after.' Kate gave him a piteous glance. 'You don't stand a chance against that.'

'She loves me!'

'She lies though her teeth,' Kate shouted, losing patience again. 'Killing Luther would make her rich, and free to marry any man she chooses, but not you. You'd have served your purpose. She might even have betrayed you to the authorities. You'd make a handy scapegoat if anything goes wrong.'

'I won't listen to this.' He marched towards the door.

'You've failed her, Evan,' Kate warned, desperately. 'She'll toss you aside like an old boot.'

He went out and slammed the door, the sound reverberating through the house. Loud enough to wake the dead, Kate thought, and shivered. She was suddenly exhausted and collapsed on to the bed, pulling the covers over her.

When the sickroom was quiet again except for Luther's hoarse breathing, Delphine left her dark hiding place in the sluice room. Seething with fury, she stood at the bedside, staring down at her husband, inert, but still very much alive, still very much a danger to her future.

Damn Kate! Damn her to hell!

She stooped and picked up the pillow. Bertram had failed her, and so had Evan, thanks to Kate's interference. Now she must do this herself. Lifting the pillow she stood with it poised above Luther's face. But was she strong enough? The nurse might come up at any moment, and if Luther resisted, delayed her, she might be caught. Going quickly to the door, she locked it. Now she'd have time to get away if disturbed.

She picked up a heavy fire-iron from the hearth, and tested the weight in her other hand. One blow from this would silence him immediately, but it might take more than one blow to kill him, and bludgeoning was a messy business. Delphine considered carefully. She'd counted on the killing looking like an accident. There must be no investigation.

She was about to replace the iron in the hearth when the heat of the fire still burning brightly in the grate gave her the answer. Luther would die in a fire. No one would question that.

As quickly as she could she gathered the oil lamps, one from the nurse's bedroom, the sluice room and the bathroom. There was plenty of paraffin still in them. Removing the wicks, Delphine poured the fuel from each into an enamel bowl, and then splashed it on the heavy window drapes on the other side of the bed, the floor around the bed, and the rug. The remainder she threw over the counterpane on the bed. Luther wouldn't escape this fate.

Taking a taper from the glass jar on the mantelpiece, she put it into the fire. When it was well alight she touched it to the drapes. They were old and dusty and caught fire immediately.

Delphine jumped back, astonished at the speed with which the flames were taking hold. As she watched, the velvet-embossed wallpaper near the bed began to burn, the flames racing across the expanse of wall as though in a twinkling of an eye. Fragments of burning drapes fell to the floor and, in moments, a circle of flames enclosed the bed.

'Goodbye, Luther,' she said softly to the sleeping man. 'I hope you know how much I despise and hate you.'

The fire-iron was lying before the fireplace where she'd dropped it. She picked it up as a new idea came to her. Kate, too, must die in the fire. She knew too much.

Flames jumped to a nearby rug, and Delphine flinched with sudden fright. It was time to go or be trapped, too. She darted towards the French windows just as the drapes there burst into flames.

Fire needs air or it dies, so she left the windows open. Quietly she descended the iron stairs, pausing on the landing outside Kate's window. Carefully and quietly, she put the fire iron through the metal handles of the doors. It made a very effective bar.

But Kate could escape through her bedroom door. That too must be barred.

Delphine ran down the remaining stairs easily, her way lighted by the moon. She had the key of every door in Old Grove House on a chain around her waist. The kitchen door was locked, but she soon opened it, and hurried into the main part of the silent house, and towards Kate's apartment.

The corridor that led to Kate's rooms was decorated at intervals with gilt mirrors, under which stood half tables, with a small armless chair each side. Delphine carried the nearest chair to Kate's door, and silently jammed the back under the handle.

Let the snivelling, pious little bitch try escaping from that.

With satisfaction at her night's work, she made her way to her own room to await the alarm.

Nurse Fowler hauled herself up the final stair, but at the last moment caught her foot in the tread and almost fell headlong, spilling some of the contents of a glass she was carrying.

Oops-a-daisy! She straightened her cap and smothered a giggle but couldn't restrain a loud hiccup. Oops! Pardon, Mrs Arden!

'Shush!' she said softly to no one in particular, and walked unsteadily along the passage to the sickroom. She turned the knob of the door carefully and pushed, but to no avail.

'What's up?'

Carefully, she put the wine glass on a nearby table and, grasping the knob firmly, gave another heave, but the door wouldn't budge. Bending, she put her eye to the keyhole, but the key was in the lock. She couldn't see anything, but suddenly was aware of a smell, a terrible smell that made the hairs on the back of her neck stand on end. And then the smoke drifting through the crack under the door entered her nostrils.

Nurse Fowler straightened as though she'd been shot in the rump, opened her mouth and screamed. 'Fire!' Suddenly as sober as a judge, she ran pell-mell back along the passage to the stairs. 'Fire!'

Kate was vaguely aware of a very distant commotion. It was nothing to do with her; she didn't want to wake, didn't want to face the reality of life at Old Grove House. The commotion persisted, so she wove it into a dream. Presently, her dream changed, and now someone was trying to smother her. Fighting furiously, she woke with a start and sat up in bed coughing. Motes of moonlight danced in a strange mist that enveloped the room, and then, coughing and spluttering, she realised the room was filled with smoke.

She almost fell out of bed in panic and terror, feeling she was still in her nightmare. She ran in the direction of the vestibule, to the main door of the apartment, and in the inner darkness fumbled with the key, and despite her trembling fingers, managed to turn it in the lock.

She was caught in a bout of coughing again as smoked billowed out from the bedroom, and now she could hear crackling. Fire! Oh, God! The whole house was on fire!

Kate tugged at the door and when it wouldn't yield, thought she'd turned the key the wrong way. She struggled to release

388

the lock, but still the door wouldn't open. She pulled at it in panic, feeling the smoke fill her lungs. It was jammed! How could it be jammed!

Stop it! Stop it! she commanded herself sternly. Think!

Of course, the French windows and the iron stairs. But first she must cover her nose and mouth. She ran into the bathroom and soaked a towel in cold water, and placing it over her lower face, ran back into the bedroom.

The smoke was thicker now and she was disorientated for a moment, turning and turning on her heel in rising panic. Suddenly she realised the moonlight, although diffuse, was still visible through the thickening smoke, and lunging in that direction she hurried towards the way of escape.

Reaching the French windows she thankfully lifted the brass latch and pulled. The doors rattled but wouldn't open. She pulled furiously, panic-stricken. Something was preventing them opening. Kate paused in her struggle. Both doors barred? It was no coincidence. Someone was trying to kill her.

Kate was filled with horror and disbelief. Surely Evan didn't wish her dead. Not her own brother? Or was Simon showing his true colours at last, trying to profit by her death?

Someone must know she was here. Someone must care. But who was left she could trust?

The smoke bit into her eyes, and despite the wet towel, it was in her throat and lungs. She couldn't last much longer. If someone didn't realise she was trapped and come for her soon, she was finished.

Desperate for air, she threw a heavy candlestick against the windowpanes, but the glass didn't even crack. Panicking as the smoke stifled her every breath, Kate beat frantically at the window but to no avail, and then, knees buckling, she slid senseless to the floor.

27

Evan raced across the front lawns towards a group of people in night attire standing huddled together near the trees, well away from the house, their faces turned to the fire, reflections of scarlet flames flickering on faces and in their frightened eyes. Someone was wailing loudly.

His frantic gaze searched the group as he approached, and he gave a little groan of thankfulness to see Delphine among them, her diaphanous negligee billowing out about her, stirred by the lively night breeze that was rifling through the surrounding trees, the same breeze that was whipping the flames into an inferno.

Tearing his gaze away from the burning house, he joined the group and stood next to Delphine, slipping his silk dressing-gown around her shoulders. She turned her face to him and he was disturbed by her expression of elation.

'Thank God you're all right,' he said. He looked round as there was another piercing wail that echoed beneath the trees. 'How the hell could it have started?'

The nurse, the only person fully dressed, seemed hysterical. Mrs Perkins, the cook, hair in curling rags, had an arm around the woman's shoulders comforting her.

'I lost him,' the nurse shrilled, looking pathetically into the cook's sympathetic face. 'But the door was locked. It was locked.'

Shocked and distracted by what was happening to his home, Evan glanced again at the stricken house. Flames were leaping from the upper windows and under the eaves of the west wing, and running along the edge of the roof with alarming speed. Even from this safe distance he could hear the crackle of burning wood and glass shattering in the heat. They needed help quickly if the rest of the house was to be saved.

'Has the fire brigade been sent for?' Evan called to Watkins, standing nearby in a long nightshirt.

'Mr Creswell's ridden to the police box in the Uplands, sir, to give the alarm,' the footman said, his teeth chattering.

Evan cursed under his breath. The police box was probably two miles away. At the rate the fire was gaining hold, the fire tender, relying on horsepower, would arrive too late.

'The door was locked,' Nurse Fowler shrilled again even more loudly. 'I don't understand.'

Delphine made an impatient sound and, to Evan's astonishment, darted forward. She swung the nurse around and slapped her hard across the face. The woman fell back a step, staring, stunned but still blubbering.

'Be quiet, damn you!' Delphine hissed.

Watkins gave a gasp, and shocked tutting came from Mrs Perkins.

'Bloody cheek!' said Daisy, the maid.

'Steady on, Delphi,' Bertram murmured. 'She's in shock.'

But Delphine was mistress of the household and didn't look at all repentant.

'She needs to be silenced,' she said, moving away. 'She's hysterical. It's her fault, anyway. The drunken fool probably started the fire in the first place.'

She turned to gaze at the blazing house as though mesmerised. Evan was shaken by her action, and glanced towards the snivelling nurse, her words and obvious distress beginning to sink in to his consciousness.

The fire must have started in the sickroom, but he doubted the nurse was responsible. Undoubtedly, Luther was now dead. Delphine was free.

He moved closer to her to speak in her ear so they wouldn't be overheard.

'How could Luther's door be locked?' he asked quietly. 'It was standing ajar when . . . I left him, and I didn't lock it.'

She didn't turn her head before replying. 'Are you certain?'

'Of course I'm certain!' he rasped.

He was about to say more but the sound of a terrific crash from the direction of the house dried the words in his throat. Part of the west wing roof at the front had fallen in and new flames were shooting heavenwards. There was a soft laugh from Delphine as she watched the inferno, and Evan felt a cold hand clutch at his heart.

'You did this,' he accused in a low voice. 'It was you.'

She turned to him, her triumphant smile so brilliant it not only outshone the moonlight, but the flames, too. 'Yes! Yes, I did it,' she told him in a fierce undertone, her eyes gleaming. 'I had to, because you failed miserably, you and that interfering, sanctimonious sister of yours.'

'Oh, my God, Delphine! You've destroyed my family's property for the sake of your freedom.'

Her expression was disdainful. 'I only did what you didn't have the guts to do,' she said. 'By now my husband's dead, and all that was his is mine. I'm free, free to take whom I choose, a man worthy of me. But it won't be you, Evan.'

Those were the very words Kate had spoken only a few hours ago.

'Kate was right,' he uttered in a strangled voice. 'You've lied to me all along.'

He felt as though she'd taken a knife and cut out his heart. Pain ran through his body like hot acid. He stared down at her. It was like looking at a stranger; he didn't know this woman.

'You never loved me,' he said with conviction.

'You're so gullible, Evan.' Her tone was cold and cruel. 'So willing to be deceived. I could never love a weakling like you. At least Luther had some spirit in him.'

'I'll kill you,' he said in impotent rage. 'You've destroyed me along with the house, but it won't do you any good. No other man will have you. I'll kill you first.'

Her lip curled in disdain at his pain. 'Don't be absurd,' she grated. 'You're not man enough.'

Her eyes flashing scorn, she moved away to stand next to her brother, placing an arm around his waist. Evan stood immobile, staring. He felt cold, numb and empty.

Simon rode up the drive full pelt, regardless of his sweating horse. When he got around the bend he reined up sharply as the house came into view, and was filled with consternation to see how much the fire had advanced. The great glass dome over the hall was gone, and only twisted girders remained. The west wing was fully ablaze, and flames were running along the roof over the east wing.

Dismounting, letting the exhausted horse trot away, Simon hurried to join those helplessly watching the conflagration, halting at Evan's side. His brother-in-law was white-faced and hollow-eyed, as though in a trance at seeing his home destroyed.

'The police have informed the fire station. They hope the brigade will be here before it's too late,' Simon said to him breathlessly. 'They asked about a water supply.'

Evan didn't answer but simply stared at the fire. After a moment, Simon gave up and moved towards Watkins.

'Is there an outside water supply?' he asked urgently.

'Tap next to the kitchen door,' Watkins said. 'And a well down by the stables.' He looked bewildered. 'Do you think they can really save it, sir?'

Simon shrugged and looked about him. 'Where's Miss Kate?' he asked. 'I thought I saw her standing near you before I went for the fire brigade.'

Watkins shook his head. 'Haven't seen her, sir. Haven't seen her at all.'

Simon quickly darted to and fro through the small throng, but Kate wasn't there, and suddenly a great terror overtook him.

'My God!' he yelled at Evan. 'Kate's still inside!'

Evan started out of his trance, and for some reason turned slowly to look at Delphine. She was smiling back at him, though in his state of panic, Simon couldn't see what there was to smile about.

'I'm going in to get her,' he shouted, and set off at a run towards the house.

'I'll come with you,' Bertram volunteered, and the next minute he was running at Simon's side.

'Bertie!' Delphine screamed behind them. 'Come back! Don't be a fool. She's not worth it.'

But her brother took no notice.

'We'll never reach Kate's rooms by going in the front entrance. The fire's too fierce throughout the west side,' Bertram panted at his side. 'There's that iron staircase at the back. It might still be intact because the fire seems to be gaining ground mostly in the front.'

'You're right! Come on!'

They reached the bottom of the staircase at the back of the house and looking up Simon could see the top floor above Kate's room was well alight. No flames were visible yet in her apartment, although smoke was seeping out through the closed French windows. He glanced apprehensively at the roof, and even as he watched flames quickly enveloped the ridges. His mouth dried in horror as he realised the roof could collapse at any moment. Kate wouldn't stand a chance in that inferno.

'We must be quick,' Simon said urgently.

'She could be anywhere inside,' Bertram warned. He put his hand on Simon's shoulder in sympathy. 'It may already be too late.'

Simon didn't reply, but stepped on to the stairs. He wouldn't let himself think of that possibility. Kate was alive. She *must* be.

Simon thought the iron handrail felt warm to the touch, but decided it was his imagination. He scrambled up as fast as possible. As he was about to step on to the landing outside Kate's bedroom window, the terrifying sound of metal fracturing erupted beneath him. The stairs shuddered violently, and lurched, almost throwing him off balance. He clutched anxiously at the handrail to save himself, and looked down on Bertram's upturned face.

'Are you all right, Simon?'

'Something's giving way by the feel of it,' Simon panted. 'Stand well back.'

He prayed the staircase would hold until he'd found Kate and got her safely away, and took another tentative step up.

His heart almost stopped beating at the sudden shriek of metal rupturing, and then the main supports of the stairs collapsed completely. There was a warning shout from below as in a sickening split second the tread beneath Simon's feet fell away, leaving him suspended in empty space, then falling.

Instinctively, he made a desperate grab for the edge of the iron platform, and next instant was swinging precariously in mid air. Pain such as he'd never known before stabbed through him at the powerful jolt on his arm and shoulder muscles, but he hung on, fighting it with all his strength.

Frantically hanging by his fingertips like a monkey from a branch, Simon managed to look down between his feet in time to see Bertram, about thirty feet below, scuttling out of the way as the remainder of the stairs, girders and treads smashed down into the shrubbery.

'Simon!' Bertram yelled up at him in panic. 'For God's sake, hang on. Don't try to move. I'll get up to you somehow.'

'Wait!' Simon called breathlessly. 'I've got to find Kate. I'm going to risk climbing up further if I can.' As he spoke his mouth filled with smoke. 'Get some help.'

'I'll go down to the stables,' Bertram called. 'There must be a ladder about somewhere.' After a moment's hesitation he ran off down the slope towards the stables.

Simon swayed helplessly, hanging on to the edge of the platform like grim death, although his fingers and arm muscles were already numbed by the strain of supporting his weight. He couldn't wait for Bertram to come back. At this very moment Kate, his darling wife, could be suffocating to death perhaps within yards of him. Or she'd burn to death if the roof fell in.

The awful thought renewed his strength. With a supreme effort he deliberately accentuated the swinging motion, gritting his teeth at the pain, and praying fervently that the landing would hold. When he thought he'd gained enough momentum, he flung his leg upwards.

His knee banged against the edge of the platform. The extreme pain almost made him bite his tongue in agony. Gasping with effort, he made another attempt and this time his knee found a purchase. With another mighty heave the upper half of his body was on the landing, and thankful, he scrambled forward, gasping for air, but finding only acrid smoke.

Afraid of a further collapse, he got carefully to his feet, and grasped the handles of the French windows. Desperate now, he tried to wrench them open, but the doors wouldn't yield.

Panic and terror almost overwhelmed him, but a small voice in his mind warned him to be calm. Think! Was the door locked? Had debris jammed it?

It was darker at the back of the house and smoke was swirling down from above, getting into his eyes, making them water and burn. He cursed the moon for moving its light away when he needed it most. He ran his hands over the door handles and found a long piece of smooth metal had been rammed between them. He recognised the feel and shape of it. A fire-iron! The door had been deliberately barricaded.

Simon tugged at the iron until it loosened and he was able to free the handles. He jerked the door open and stumbled inside, coughing helplessly as a thick cloud of smoke billowed out.

He opened his mouth to shout Kate's name, but the smoke filled his lungs and he couldn't speak. All he could hear in the room was the crackle of flames as the main body of fire inched nearer with each second.

Blinded, Simon dropped to the floor, hoping to find some breathable air, and crawled forward on his stomach. He'd gone a few feet when his groping hands touched something soft and yielding and he realised without being able to see that it was a human body. He gave an involuntary cry of despair, but all that was emitted from his throat was a dry croak.

He got to his feet and, lifting the inert form into his arms, he turned and stumbled forward, praying he was heading in the right direction for the open windows.

With another prayer of thankfulness, he stepped out on to the iron landing, but the smoke was now so thick he couldn't see what was happening below. He laid his burden down, and ran his hands over the head. It was Kate! Streaming eyes blinding him, he pressed his fingers to the side of her throat, feeling for a pulse. He cried out as a gentle rhythm was just discernible beneath the skin. She was alive, but for how long? She'd already inhaled too much smoke. Was he too late?

'Kate!' he croaked. 'Kate, my darling, don't die. Don't leave me. I love you.'

There was a shout from below and between swirls of smoke Simon glimpsed two figures running, carrying an extending ladder between them. He was relieved to see Bertram had Trott with him.

'I've got her,' Simon croaked, his mouth so dry he could hardly make a sound. 'But for God's sake, hurry. I don't think she's breathing.'

The ladder was placed against the wall next to the landing, and the groom scrambled up. Simon was holding Kate in his arms again, ready to descend, though he could hardly see for the watering of his eyes.

'Give her to me, sir,' Trott said, as he stepped up beside Simon. 'I'll carry her down. You're nearly done for yourself.'

'No!' Simon was reluctant to let Kate go.

'Come along, sir,' Trott said persuasively. 'I've done a bit of fire-fighting in my younger days. I understands the fireman's lift. You go down before me, sir, and trust me.'

When all were safely off the ladder, Trott, with Kate slung over his shoulder, scuttled across the lawn away from the house.

'Let's get away from by here,' he called urgently to the two men. 'That wall's likely to go.'

At a safe distance Kate was laid on the grass, and the men knelt around her. Simon felt a new terror engulf him to see the greyness of her face. She looked dead already.

Trott was feeling for her pulse again.

'She alive, only just,' he said. 'But she isn't breathing.'

Holding her by forehead and chin, the groom bent over her and put his mouth to hers.

'What the hell are you doing, man?' Simon roared, grabbing at his arm, trying to pull him off.

'It's all right, sir,' Trott said calmly, pushing his hand away. 'I've seen this done before. You blows in their mouth and air goes in their lungs, and they snaps out of it, well, most times. Don't always work. We'll have to take it in turns, sir. Like this.'

Taking a huge gulp of air Trott bent and blew forcibly into Kate's mouth. Simon stared, still affronted. He saw her chest rise and fall with Trott's every effort. He did this several times until he was red in the face and gasping.

'Now you, sir,' he panted to Simon. 'And then it's Mr Harrington's turn. We've got to do it, or she'll die.'

It seemed an eternity to Simon but in reality he knew it couldn't have been more than three or four minutes before Kate's body began to convulse, and she was coughing and gasping for air.

Quickly Trott rolled her on to her side, where she continued to cough and splutter, her eyes staring wildly, mindlessly, as she gulped in the fresh night air.

'We must get her to a doctor, Mr Creswell,' Trott said,

getting to his feet. 'I'll go and fetch the carriage and bring it round here.'

Simon sprang to his feet and grasped the groom by the hand.

'Thank you, Trott. You saved her.'

Trott shook his head. 'No, you did it, sir, by going into that inferno after her. I've known her since she was a child. It'd break this old heart to see anything happen to her.'

As Trott ran off towards the stables, Simon lifted Kate into his arms, and feebly she put her arm around his neck, but her head lolled back alarmingly, her skin grey. He began to jog towards the stables, anticipating Trott's return with the carriage.

'I'll come with you, Simon,' Bertram offered, falling into step beside him. 'You may need help, and besides, I'm dashed fond of Kate, you know.'

'I'd be very glad of your company, my old friend,' Simon panted gratefully. 'Kate's not out of danger yet. I pray no great harm has been done.'

He thought about the barricaded window, but decided not to mention it to Bertram. It was all too obvious that the fire wasn't an accident, but had been set deliberately. Simon ground his teeth. The only person in the house capable of such wickedness was Delphine. She had a lot to answer for, and answer she would. Once he knew Kate was safe from harm he'd return and confront Delphine with her crime. She'd almost destroyed this family, and Bertram was his friend, but he'd be damned if he let her get away with murder.

'Do something! Do something!' Delphine shrieked, tugging frantically at Evan's arm as he stood apart from the others beneath the trees. 'I'm afraid for Bertie. Find him, Evan, for God's sake. Bring him to me.'

In the moonlight her face was ashen, and Evan saw she was on the point of hysteria, but he was still angry with her, and pushed her hand away impatiently.

'We must wait,' he said brutally. 'There's nothing I can do.'

Only hours ago he'd been ready to commit murder for her, now he felt only revulsion and a cold disdain.

'If Bertram dies in that house, remember, Delphine, you did it,' he said tersely and without pity.

'Oh! Damn you to hell!' Delphine wailed plaintively. 'Someone must help me.' Clutching her hand to her throat she turned helplessly to look at the blaze. 'My darling Bertie, where are you?' she cried out. 'The only man I ever loved, the only one who means anything to me.'

Evan felt a cold chill run down his spine at the passion in her voice. 'What're you saying, Delphine?'

Delphine turned back to him, her expression defiant even in her hysteria. 'All right! Yes,' she whispered hoarsely, her eyes wild with anguish. 'Bertie's my lifelong lover. No one, husband or otherwise, can mean more to me than he does.'

'Oh, my God!' He stared. 'You can't mean it?'

Disturbing images came into his mind and he recoiled from her. 'It's revolting!'

She lifted her chin. 'I'm not ashamed of it.' She tossed her head angrily. 'Why look so shocked, Evan, after the things you and I did together?'

'That's different,' he said wretchedly. 'I'm not your brother, and I thought you loved me.'

'I love Bertie,' she said with a sob. 'No one else.' Astonishingly, she grabbed at his arm again. 'You *must* save him for me. You must! Bertie's my life. Everything I did, I did for him. I can't go on if he dies.'

His mouth dry with shock and disgust, Evan stared at her,

hardly able to believe her words. She'd killed Luther in cold blood, and she'd probably killed Kate, too. Suddenly his disdain ignited into a boiling rage.

'You murdering incestuous whore,' he rasped out, not caring whether he was overheard. 'Keep away from me.' He pulled his arm free from her grasp, and stepped back from her.

'I worshipped you, Delphine, sacrificed everything just to possess you, but you're nothing better than a common street slut; worse, even they wouldn't do what you've done.'

She stood there trembling, twisting her fingers together incessantly; her eyes were wide, staring at the raging inferno. She wasn't listening to a word he said.

He'd never before seen her without her shield of iron self-possession. Her power and beauty seemed diminished and he marvelled at the change.

Suddenly she seemed aware of him again and moved closer, trying to put her arms around his neck. He couldn't believe her gall in the face of her confession, and her arrogance in believing her power over him was undiminished.

'I'll be yours again, Evan, yours alone, I swear,' she murmured, 'if you'll save Bertie. Don't let him die.' She gulped. 'I love him so much I'd gladly die in his place.'

Her passionate words and self-conceit brought an unbidden notion of revenge into his seething mind; and he steeled himself not to recoil from her touch.

He felt hollow, empty of all hope or feeling. At once he knew, without the shadow of a doubt, that there was no future for him. He didn't want the useless life he'd been leading; didn't want his wife or child. He'd wanted only Delphine, and now she'd taken that from him in the most cruel and despicable way.

He saw for the first time that she was bad to the bone. She'd taken the life of sweet, innocent Kate, and didn't deserve to live herself.

'Do you swear on your life that if I save Bertram you'll forsake all other men for me?' he asked her.

He almost laughed as she placed her hands over her heart, her expression intense as she swore the oath solemnly. It was an empty oath, he realised. She still thought him a fool to be manipulated, and he vowed then that Delphine wouldn't survive this night, either.

'Stay here,' he said. 'I'll look for him.'

He left her standing under the trees and moved quickly towards the house. He didn't feel afraid any more, and the hurt she'd caused was strangely eased, leaving him calm and determined.

Nothing mattered any longer. The fire Delphine had set was their destiny. It would burn away all the guilt in his heart and all the evil in her soul.

As he rounded the corner at the back of the house, he glanced down towards the stables and was in time to see Luther's carriage, Trott whipping at the horses, disappear along the back lane. There was no sign of Creswell or Harrington. Perhaps they'd been in time to save Kate. He prayed that they had been. But even if Kate was alive, Delphine's fate was already sealed.

He stood watching the house burn for a few moments as though in a dream and then, icy resolution numbing his mind, returned to Delphine. He ran across the lawns towards her, as though in a panic. To his consternation Watkins and Daisy began to move towards Delphine, as though they anticipated he was bringing news.

They mustn't be allowed to interfere. Already he thought he

heard the fire tender bell clanging along Sketty Road. He had mere minutes to take his revenge.

'Bertram's in the house!' he shouted to Delphine. 'I saw him at an upstairs window, trapped.'

Delphine gave a piercing scream and, throwing off Evan's dressing-gown, started forward at a run, her negligee floating behind her like wings. Watkins tried to grab at her but she evaded him and rushed on towards the house. The footman was ready to go after her, but Evan stopped him.

'Look after the other women,' he rapped out. 'I'll go after Mrs Templar and bring her back.'

Delphine was running like the wind towards the front entrance, oblivious to all danger. Even though he knew he was rushing towards his death, Evan was right behind her as she burst through the open doors, and hesitated in the smoke-filled hall, the floor covered with smouldering debris.

The house was filled with deafening sound, a continuous roar, like that of a wild animal in a blood frenzy, and he realised it was the terrible voice of the fire, and they were almost at the very heart of it.

The obnoxious smell of charred wood and fabric filled his nostrils. Intense fear gripped him then, and a horror swamped him at what he was about to endure. He couldn't face it, not even for revenge, and, with a cry, he turned back towards the open door.

'Which way, which way?' Delphine screamed, making him pause in his retreat.

She was turning, turning on her heel, frantic. Then, seeing his hesitation, she shrieked at him. 'You cringing coward, Evan, you're deserting me!' she railed. Her face contorted with rage. 'I despise you, you spineless weakling. Do you hear me? I curse you!'

He stared at the naked contempt in her eyes, and knew it was true, and he was angered anew. He'd show her just how spineless he was. He pointed towards the still intact staircase.

'That way,' he said tremulously, although resigned now to his fate. 'We'll reach him soon, but we must hurry.'

She screamed Bertram's name as she rushed up the wide staircase, Evan at her heels. She ran, coughing and stumbling, along the gallery, guided by his pointing finger. It was getting more and more difficult to breathe, and the roar of the fire was growing in volume as it raced nearer. It sounded hungry.

His heart was pounding in fear of what was to come, but she didn't seem afraid as she continued to call her brother's name.

Suddenly, there was a new sound: masonry was crashing down behind them, and Evan realised with renewed terror that an inner wall had collapsed into the hall. They were trapped; there was no retreat now. They'd reached the point of no return.

Despite the deafening roar of falling masonry, she still didn't seem to sense the danger. His heart heavy, he led her further into the house, but away from the midst of the fire. There was no urgency any longer; it was too late. Nothing and no one could save them now. The speed with which it consumed everything, the fire would quickly find them.

Delphine held the hem of her negligee over her nose and mouth against the billowing smoke as they reached the door of his own rooms. They'd made love here countless times. It was fitting they should die here together.

'This is the room,' he said hoarsely, gasping in what little air was left in the passage. 'This is where I last saw your beloved Bertram.'

He flung the door open. The room was filled with smoke, and Delphine hesitated on the threshold.

'Bertie?' she whimpered, her cry lost in the howl of the approaching inferno. 'Bertie?'

Evan pushed her from behind and she staggered forward into the room. He followed, slamming the door shut behind him and locking it. He quickly took the key from the lock and threw it carelessly into a smoke-filled corner. Delphine move forward into the room, arms outstretched before her, still intent on finding her brother.

'Bertram, Bertram, my darling boy, I'm here. I'll protect you like I've always protected you.'

'He can't hear you. He's dead,' Evan said savagely.

'No! No!' She swung round to face him. 'Don't say that. Where is he?'

'I don't know and I don't care,' Evan rasped.

'What? Evan, what stupid game are you playing?'

Smoke billowed around them but he could still see her face clearly. Her hair was dishevelled and grimy streaks marked her cheek. She was staring at him, half haughty, half terrified, but not for herself, he realised – not yet.

'I lied to you, Delphine,' he said, moving forward to grasp her upper arms tightly. 'Tricked you, as you tricked me.'

'Bertie?'

She turned her head away, her gaze straining into the hazy air about her, and then looked at him, her eyes flashing hatred.

'Where is he, Evan? What have you done to him?' she demanded, her tone jarring. 'If you've hurt him I'll kill you.'

'I told you, Delphine, he's not here,' Evan said hollowly. 'He never was. You've been led into a trap.'

'Trap?'

There was another thunderous crash somewhere in the house and he felt the floor shudder beneath his feet. The end was coming sooner than he'd thought.

Frightened, he shook her violently, overwhelming rage rising against her. She'd brought him to this desperate plight. She'd even taken away his will to live.

'Listen to me, Delphine!' he croaked, his mouth dry from the smoke and fumes. 'You're going to die, do you hear me?'

She really looked at him then, her eyes focusing on his face for the first time. For a moment he thought she didn't recognise him, then her eyes gleamed in sudden under-standing, and her lips drew back in a snarl like a wild thing caged.

'You pathetic miserable swine!' She struggled violently in his grasp. 'You can't keep me here. I must find Bertie.'

Again she tried to wrench herself loose from his grip, but he held her fast. Without warning she raised her hand, fingers clawed, and raked her fingernails down his cheek. The pain made him cry out, and without thinking rationally, he struck at her upturned face. She fell backwards on to the floor, but twisted her body like a cat to scramble away out of his reach.

'It's no good, Delphine,' he said, panting. 'You can't get away from me.'

His mouth was ash dry and his eyes were gritty and streaming from the smoke. His lungs hurt each time he took a breath, and he wondered if he'd have enough strength to finish it.

'Neither of us will leave this room alive,' he said.

The smoke was getting thicker, but he saw her white form rise like a ghost near the foot of the bed as she hauled herself to her feet.

'Evan, this is madness,' she said, coughing. He heard the harshness in her throat as she struggled for air. 'You love me; you know you do. Luther's dead. We can be together now, for the rest of our lives.'

'Liar!' Evan tried to bellow the word, but the sound was just a croak. 'Even as you die, you lie. But no more.'

'Don't be a fool!' she uttered hoarsely. 'I'm a rich woman. We can go away, start a new life together. I'll give up Bertie, I promise you.'

'Your promises are as worthless as you are, Delphine,' Evan rasped. 'But you'll cause no more pain. No other man will have you. We'll die together on that bed.'

'You're mad, Evan!'

'Not as insane as you, Delphine.' He moved towards her again. 'Why did you have to kill Kate? What did she ever do to you?'

'She was in my way,' she said, edging away from him towards the fireplace. 'She stopped you killing Luther, and she thought she could take Mansel from me.'

She half turned to the mantelpiece, glancing about as she did so, and he knew she was looking for a weapon to use on him.

'Besides,' she went on, 'I never liked her.'

There was a hint of triumph in her croaking voice, and anticipating her next move, he made a lunge at her, but her arm was already raised, and she struck out at him viciously with a heavy candlestick.

The blow glanced off the side of his head and on to his shoulder. Numbing pain almost stunned him but he stayed on his feet. With a snarl he wrenched the candlestick from her grasp, and throwing it from him, clasped her in a bear hug. He could break her back now if he had a mind to, but that would be too merciful.

'Let me go, you beast!' She struggled like a mad woman. 'I hate you. I loathe you.'

'So you should,' he panted, struggling to drag her towards the bed. 'I'm the one who takes your miserable life.'

Screaming, she fought violently, her terror real at last. But he could feel no pity or remorse, and overwhelmed her. They fell together on to the bed.

'Oh, God! Evan!' Her dry voice shook with dread. 'You can't do this to me. You can't. It's inhuman.'

She struggled again but his weight held her down.

'Let me go, you pig!' she cried. 'You've got no right. I don't deserve to die.'

'Kate didn't deserve to die,' he panted. 'You had no mercy for her. You had no mercy for anyone, not even your brother.'

'I don't want to die!' she whined again. 'Save me! Let me live and I'll give you everything I own. I'll be faithful only to you, I swear.'

'It's too late for all that, Delphine. I couldn't save you even if I wanted to.'

She whimpered in terror, her face inches from his own, and suddenly, despite everything, he wanted to kiss her just one more time.

'How many times have we lain here together, Delphine?' he asked in a hoarse whisper, but she was sobbing in disbelief. 'Did my love really mean nothing to you?'

'We laughed at you, Mansel and I,' she hissed, suddenly defiant. Even through her tears her tone was laced with contempt. 'We joked about you while we made passionate love.'

'Be quiet, you contemptible whore!'

Her laugh was brittle, like dry leaves, the sound as cruel as sandpaper on tender skin. 'Mansel thrilled me as a lover, and satisfied me as you never could.'

Suddenly, the drapes around the window burst into flame.

'Oh, my God!' Delphine open her mouth to scream, but all

that came from her throat was a choking gurgle. 'Save me, Evan! Don't let me die like this.'

'It's here,' Evan said, his face close to hers. She was trembling violently. 'The fire has come for us.'

'No! No! This can't be happening, not to me.'

Abruptly she stopped struggling. 'Listen, Evan,' she panted urgently. 'We can still get away. Help me! For pity's sake, help me.'

'It's too late for us both,' he said, feeling suddenly serene. 'The fire is all around us.' The irony of it struck him. 'The fire that you set to kill your husband and Kate has become your funeral pyre, Delphine.'

There was a great straining groan and a mighty roar above their heads. In the remaining seconds that followed Evan knew that their wait was over, and so did Delphine. She let out one last blood-curdling scream as the roof and floors above collapsed in on them.

28

---◆◆◆---

First Day of March 1901

As the carriage rolled up the twisting drive towards the ruins of
Old Grove House, Trott at the reins, Kate thankfully breathed
in the air, which hinted at an early spring, and was glad to be
alive.

They rounded the bend and the blackened remains of the
house, already overgrown with weeds and rough grasses, came
into view. Kate shuddered, unable to suppress the chill that
ran up her spine. It was the first time she'd been back here
since that awful night.

'Destroyed!' Aunt Agnes rasped, sitting beside her. 'All that
my father and my grandfather built up, destroyed in one night
by that evil woman.'

'We shouldn't speak ill of the dead,' Eirwen murmured.

Kate shuddered violently again, the stark ruins of the house
suddenly bringing home to her the full horror of what had
happened, the terrible fate she'd narrowly missed. The
memory of being trapped would haunt her for the rest of
her life.

'You're not catching cold, are you, Kate, dear?' Eirwen
asked anxiously. 'Was it wise to come here today, and in an
open carriage, too? Keen the wind is, mind, and I don't trust
this early sun.'

Kate smiled reassuringly at her sister-in-law sitting opposite, grateful for Eirwen's attentive and devoted nursing over
the months, as true as any sister. Now Evan was gone, she was
comforted by the deep affection that had grown between
Eirwen and herself; thankful for what little family she had left.

'I'm much better now, Eirwen,' she said. 'And I need to feel
the fresh air on my face.' She smiled again. 'You mustn't
worry so. I'm stronger than I look.'

And it was true, yet it was only recently that she'd realised
just how close to death she'd been.

'Kate's right,' Aunt Agnes said, drawing the rug more
closely around her own legs. 'We Vaughan women are made
of sterner stuff.'

As the carriage rolled closer, Kate steeled herself to glance
towards the ruins again. 'Stop here, Trott, please,' she called
to the groom. 'I'll walk the rest of the way.'

'Oh, no, Kate, dear, don't do that,' Eirwen exclaimed in
alarm. 'You might get your feet wet.'

'I'll be all right,' she replied. 'I need the exercise.'

'I'll come with you,' Eirwen suggested eagerly, pushing the
rug from her legs.

Kate leaned forward and patted her sister-in-law's hand. 'I
want a quiet word with Simon,' she explained, as she accepted
Trott's assistance to step down from the carriage.

'Your walking-stick!' Eirwen called. 'You've forgotten your
stick, Kate.'

'I don't need it now,' Kate replied with conviction.

Still, she found it took some willpower to walk towards the
ruins without flinching. A group of labourers were already at
work among the blackened walls, swinging heavy sledgeham-
mers as they set about demolishing what was left of Old Grove
House.

Simon was talking with a man, obviously the boss of the labouring gang. They parted company as she approached, and Simon turned, a look of surprise on his face.

'Kate! Are you well enough for this visit? You may find it too distressing.'

Kate lifted her chin, a mood of defiance settling on her. 'I think it right I be here to witness my home being razed to the ground.'

A spark of emotion flashed across his face for a brief moment.

'Oh, I forgot,' she went on sharply. 'None of this belongs to my family any longer.' She swept her arm around to indicate the rolling lawns and the surrounding trees. 'All this belongs to you now. You finally got what you wanted.'

'That's unfair, Kate,' he said sharply. 'Perhaps you'd rather it belonged to Bertram Harrington?'

Kate was sobered by the thought. Bertram would have inherited everything according to Delphine's will. But, surprisingly, Luther had never made a new will in Delphine's favour, and Kate was inclined to believe her stepfather, perhaps guided by his astute lawyer had secretly realised the kind of woman he'd married.

'Of course not,' she said, more reasonably. She lowered her gaze. 'I'm glad Bertram was able to go to France to paint after all.' She hesitated. 'It was good of you to help him gain that dream, Simon.'

'About the demolition, Kate,' Simon said. 'I did discuss it with you, and you agreed it was the best thing to do.'

Kate fidgeted. She was more upset than she'd anticipated, seeing her former home levelled, yet knew she was being unreasonable still to be piqued that Simon had inherited everything, not only his uncle's property and considerable fortune, but also Luther's shares in the business.

'You did agree, Kate.'

'Yes, yes,' she answered impatiently, then felt guilty. Had she thanked him properly for saving her life? She looked up into his face, feeling her colour rise. 'You've been fair, Simon, making sure Eirwen received Evan's inheritance. You risked your own life to save me. I can't thank you enough.'

His expression softened as he smiled down at her. 'There's no need for thanks,' he said. 'You're alive. That's all that matters.' He hesitated, looking uncomfortable. 'Kate, there's something I must say to you. If you'd died in that fire—'

'Excuse me, Mr Creswell, sir.' The gang boss appeared suddenly. 'Perhaps you could inspect what the men have done so far. And then there's the question of the cellar, sir. I recommend that it be filled in immediately.'

Simon was staring down at her, a vexed expression on his face at the interruption.

'We'll talk later,' she said quickly. 'I can see you're busy.'

'No, Kate, we must talk now.' He turned to the gang boss. 'You know your own business, Mr Driscoll. Just make the whole area safe. I'll make my inspection tomorrow.'

Simon led her to the edge of the lawns, and the broad trunk of an ancient tree, where they sheltered from the cutting edge of the March wind.

'I can hardly believe this had happened,' Kate said sadly, looking back at the workmen busy on the ruined walls. 'It's all such a tragedy and a terrible waste. If only it could've been avoided.'

'I suppose you're looking to blame someone?' Simon asked testily, his mouth tight. 'And I'm the most likely candidate?'

She was surprised at his sudden change of mood. 'Well,

now you come to mention it,' she answered smartly, 'changes at Old Grove House began when you arrived.'

'Is that so? It's time for some home truths, Kate,' he said brusquely. 'All this would never have happened if you'd let Bertram leave Swansea last summer, when Delphine was in Italy.'

'What? That's absurd,' Kate snapped. 'What's that to do with anything?'

'Everything.' He hesitated, and then went on unwillingly. 'There's something you should know about Delphine and Bertram.' He hesitated again and looked towards the workmen.

'Well, go on,' Kate snapped, impatient at his reluctance.

'Their relationship was . . . unnatural,' Simon said. 'They were lovers, Kate, and had been from childhood.'

'I don't understand. What do you mean.'

'I mean they lived as man and wife, even after Delphine married Luther.'

Kate's mouth dropped open and she was astounded. 'I don't believe it!' She stared up at him in anger. 'What an outrageous thing to invent! You're saying this because you think I'm still in love with Bertram.'

'Don't be a little fool, Kate,' Simon snapped impatiently. 'He's my friend. I promised him never to reveal it, but you need to know the truth.'

Kate was furious. 'Oh, so according to you I'm to blame for this.' She pointed at the ruins. 'All because I asked Bertram to stay, to be my friend.'

'I didn't say that,' he said. 'Last summer was Bertram's one chance of making a clean break from Delphine. She dominated him totally, controlled him, as she did most men she met.'

Suddenly uncertain, Kate put trembling fingers to her mouth.

'Is it really true?' she said tremulously. 'Bertram told me he loved me.' She looked up at him apprehensively. 'Did Evan know?'

'I think he must've at the end.'

'And Luther, too.'

Simon nodded. 'I believe this is what brought on his stroke.'

'Bertram, of all men,' Kate whispered, and then shook her head. 'I can't believe him capable of such behaviour. It's unthinkable.'

'He did love you, Kate,' Simon said soberly. 'But she'd never have let him go free, and he knew it.'

Kate was silent for a moment, thoughtful. 'How long have you known about them, Simon?'

'Years. Bertram confessed to me not long after we became friends,' Simon said. 'I tried so often to help him break free.'

Kate's lips tightened in anger. 'What on earth were you thinking of, inviting the Harringtons into our home, knowing the kind of woman Delphine was?' she said.

'I invited Bertram alone,' Simon snapped. 'I wanted him to escape.'

She stepped back, glaring at him. 'You brought this tragedy down on us,' she said. 'The death of my brother, of Luther, the destruction of Old Grove House is entirely your fault, Simon.'

He sighed deeply, and lowered his head. 'You're right, Kate. It is my fault, but no malice was intended. You must believe me.'

'You can't dismiss it just like that,' Kate said, her voice quivering with emotion. 'I'll never forgive you, Simon, never.'

He started forward, his expression distressed. 'Don't say that, Kate. We have to go on with our lives.'

'What lives?' she asked scornfully. 'What have I got to look forward to?' She saw the years stretching ahead, empty years without love, without children. Her life had been saved, but for what?

'Let's not quarrel, Kate, not now,' Simon shook his head. 'Delphine's dead. Don't let her do any more harm. She's laughing at us from the grave.'

It was a sobering thought. Simon was right. Delphine's evil must die with her. Kate swallowed her anger. 'Then where do we go from here?' she asked in dejection.

'That's up to you, Kate,' he said. 'Let the past be forgotten.'

Kate was silent, turning her head away. She caught sight of the ruined house and the horror burst in on her again. Suddenly without warning, tears flooded out.

'Of course you'll never forget Evan, or your life at Old Grove House,' Simon said quickly, taking her into his arms to comfort her. 'But a new life is beginning for us both. Walk by my side, Kate. We'll face it together.'

Kate released herself reluctantly from his clasp, conscious that his embrace was more than comforting. All at once she wanted that comfort more than anything else. Hope lightened her heart a little. The future, hers and Simon's, need not be a barren waste. She remembered Aunt Agnes's words. Her unhappiness was of her own making.

Self-consciously, Kate dabbed at her wet cheeks with a handkerchief, looking up into Simon's eager face, seeing him in a new light.

'I must pull myself together before I face Aunt Agnes and Eirwen,' she said.

'There's something else, Kate,' Simon said hesitantly. 'It's evident Evan forced Delphine into the fire. He meant her to die with him.'

'No! It was an accident.'

Simon shook his head sadly, and Kate knew she couldn't deny the truth any longer.

'Eirwen must never know,' Simon said. 'For the boy's sake. As far as they are concerned Evan died trying to save life not take it.'

With a nod of agreement, Kate moved towards the waiting carriage.

'You haven't answered me,' he said as he strolled by her side. 'Can you forget the way we were brought together? Will you share my life as my wife?'

He caught at her arm, making her pause in her step and looked down into her face. She suddenly realised how beautiful his brown eyes were, and she wished he would kiss her with all the passion he'd shown that day in her apartment, and couldn't help flushing at her own thoughts.

'I am your wife, Simon, and I'm ready and willing to be a true wife to you.'

He beamed and took her hand and held it against his lips for a moment, and then drew her arm through his, walking her towards the carriage. Kate felt warmth flood though her veins, and her heart beat with a new, exciting rhythm.

'Evan's shares are in my trust for the time being,' he said conversationally. 'But I've a suggestion, Kate, which may interest you.'

She glanced up at him expectantly, and he smiled at her.

'Mrs Creswell,' he began. 'Will you take a seat on the board of directors until Russell comes of age?'

Kate almost stumbled in surprise; her mouth fell open, and she was speechless for a moment. 'Me! On the board?' she said at last, staring up at him. 'A woman conducting business, sitting on the board at Vaughan & Templar?'

He nodded, grinning in delight at her astonishment. The revolutionary idea made her gasp again.

'The other directors won't stand for it,' she said wonderingly.

'I'm chairman now,' Simon said firmly. 'I think I can sway them, make them see sense. Do you accept?'

'Oh, Simon! Do you really believe I'm capable?'

'My wonderful girl! Of course you're capable, as capable as any man I know, probably more so.'

'I accept!' Kate agreed with alacrity, wanting to jump up and down with elation and pride, too. And then she paused, flushing again as a new prospect occurred to her.

'I accept the seat as long as it won't interfere with motherhood.'

'Motherhood?'

Kate put her hand against the lapel of his coat.

'Well, I am a married woman, Simon,' she said shyly. 'And I love children and have always wanted a large family. We will have lots of children, won't we?'

'Oh, my darling Kate!'

She lifted her face to him, and he kissed her eagerly, his arms slipping easily around her waist. Kate felt she could have stayed like that for ever, but was suddenly conscious of a voice calling her name. Leaning into the warmth of her husband's body, Kate looked towards the carriage. Eirwen was waving.

'I suppose I'd better go,' Kate said reluctantly, unwilling to leave Simon's arms. 'Eirwen's anxious to get back to her boy and Mrs Trobert will have the lunch ready.' She looked up into his face. 'Will business keep you here much longer, Simon?'

His embrace tightened around her possessively.

'There's nothing here that'll keep me from you now, Kate, my darling,' he said huskily. 'I'll ride alongside the carriage. We have unfinished business of a tender nature at home, you and me. You'll never escape from me again.'